Judith Ivory

Black Silk

AVON BOOKS

An Imprint of HarperCollins*Publishers*

AVON BOOKS
An Imprint of HarperCollins*Publishers*
10 East 53rd Street
New York, New York 10022-5299

For Barbara, the book's first editor
and for Carrie, the book's last.
Your support from the start
has made the most wonderful difference.
I thank you both from the bottom of my heart.

I

Pandetti's Box

Being heretofore drown'd in security,

You know not how to live, nor how to die;

But I have an object that shall startle you,

And make you know whither you are going.

JOHN WEBSTER

The Devil's Law-case

V, iv, 109–112

— *Chapter 1* —

APRIL 1858

In the billiard room, the mantel clock ticked softly, its sound muted by the room's furnishings. Thick oriental carpeting. Dark paneled walls. The walls were hung with pastoral paintings, which were not terribly good but were terribly English—dogs, horses, the hunt. On one wall, heavy damask drapes all but obliterated tall, narrow windows, the only view to the outside. These draperies were a deep emerald green, fringed and tied and tasseled in gold. The fringe and tassels, repeated at the pockets of a billiard table, were the only froufrou in the room. This room was one of several that made up Freyer's, a gentlemen's club on St. James's Street, and it was intrinsically what the newer clubs could only pretend to be—old, masculine, unrepentantly upper-class.

The gold in the fringe and tassels was the worn, dignified gold that spoke of generations. Just as the movements and mannerisms of the men in the room, their very diction, said each was the scion of a long line of progenitors, all of whom had walked these soft carpets, or carpets just like them, since the beginning of time—or at least since the beginning of taste and decorum. It was the reassuring, upper-class English myth: tradition. The illusion of wealth perpetual, past and present, as a way of warding off worries for the future. Nonetheless, Freyer's *was* the oldest and probably poshest of such gentlemen's clubs in London, and Graham Wessit belonged in this club, at this billiard table, bending over it.

He stood well balanced on one foot, the other in the air. He was stretched out across the green felt, his belly flat, almost horizontal against the table's mahogany rail. His arm was extended more than halfway up the playing surface, in a long white shirtsleeve. (He'd taken his coat off two shots ago when the balls had broken badly and the betting had doubled to above eighty pounds.) His concentration ran down the length of his arm, down the line of his cue stick, past the loose crevice he'd made of his fingertips, to the pristine white of one small ivory ball. This awkward little object, the cue ball, sat smugly at a near-unreachable angle over a clutter of irrelevant, multicolored balls. But it also sat in direct line with a red ball Graham intended to bank and sink.

He was sliding the cue stick back and forth a fraction to feel the balance, taking a last measure against a mother-of-pearl inlay—a sight—on the table edge, when the clock began to strike.

Noon. Graham cocked his elbow. A far-off flurry of commotion distracted him for a moment. Out front in the reading room, someone had come in. Someone who was perhaps not a member. The butler handled such things. His voice could be heard. "Now see here—"

The mantel clock struck the third beat and then the fourth in a regular, dependable rhythm. Graham refocused and hit. The tip of his cue made a neat tap against the cue ball. The cue ball, in turn, hit the red, sending it against the cushion. This bright ball cut through a narrow strait, just missing three other balls, and began down the length of the table toward the pocket at Graham's hip. The clock was striking seven, eight, nine—

And the disturbance in the outer room grew loud enough to make Graham look up, frowning. Several voices were added to the butler's, among them a woman's. "I know 'e's bloody well 'ere!"

This incongruous sound circled in the outer room and rose in volume. It seemed to be going through the reading room, gathering force like a tornado. It clanged into a lamp. It opened and shut the door to the adjacent room. Graham had just registered that this storm was moving in his direction when the door to the billiard room, already ajar, burst back on its hinges, rapping the wall with its force—the force of several people trying to enter at once. A young woman, a very pregnant young woman, clamored out of a confusion of men, all of whom were trying to contain her.

"Now see here, young lady—"

"This is no place—"

She squirmed free, amazingly agile. "You keep yer filthy 'ands—"

Voices overlapped. Where did one grab a pregnant woman? seemed to be the question of the hour. Tilney, the man beside Graham, tried to intervene. "Madam, there must be some misunderstand—"

"Ain't no bleedin' misunderstandin'. If 'e ain't in this room, 'e's in another."

Ah, thought Graham, a lady come to fetch her old man. Or, no. Given her manners and speech, a businesswoman come to collect on a sidestepped fee, for she was no lady. She was barely a woman. Like a kitten sadly fat from her first heat, the little creature looked hardly more than sixteen.

For a moment longer, Graham was still more amused than involved. The girl jostled her way through gripping hands and recriminations. She elbowed one man and grabbed another by the collar. She wanted to be in their midst. She was scanning the men's encroaching, remonstrating faces, looking them over as thoroughly as they were trying to turn her about. After a minute of this tussle—the men would not organize themselves for her inspection—she clambered up over the edge of the billiard table, standing on it to look down on them all.

Graham had one more instant of time to be awed afresh by the way Fate had singled him out: He was taller than anyone else in the room, darker, lanky; he was also, he knew, by far the handsomest man in the room. Not for the first time, this fact made him uneasy.

"You!" the girl screamed, as if accusing him of this singularity. She yanked hold of his cue stick. He let the lunatic have it and took a step back.

All eyes turned toward Graham.

"You!" she cried again. "You bloody nob. Thinkin' you kin do this to me"—her finger poked toward her belly—"and not 'ave a care! Well, I aim to see the 'ole world knows I got me stuck with the earl of Netham's . . ." The familiarity brought him up short, made the moment extend endlessly. She knew his face by title, though Graham himself could swear he had never met, never known the girl in any sense of the word. ". . . the earl of Netham's brats," she continued. She took a breath. "Twins!" she shrieked. "Them doctors at Sheffield's tell me it's twins! Bloody 'ell!"

"Now wait one moment—" He took a step toward her.

Instantly, she hunched down, bringing the stick she'd commandeered forward, like a crazed young soldier armed with a gun and bayonet. She thrust it at him. Graham ducked a second later than he should have. He took a solid rap on his cheekbone—the girl nearly put his eye out with his own cue stick. Infuriated, he caught hold of the shaft and yanked the stick from the girl's hands. She lost her balance, and the men rushed forward. They dragged her off the table by her ankles and an elbow to cart her screaming and kicking from the room. Graham could hear her even as she was put out the front entrance, the heavy doors closed in her face.

For a few seconds, Graham found himself alone. He braced his arms on the billiard table, trying to gather himself together. His palms were wet. Blindly, his mind was trying to give meaning, make sense of the entire absurd event.

Then he noticed the red billiard ball. It was looking up at him from the pocket by his hand, in the exact place where he had intended that it should go. He stood staring at this planned and executed little trick he'd learned to do, while shaking from the horror, the rage he felt that all his life did not obey so well as little balls rolling across a level surface of smooth wool.

The incident would go down in Graham's mind as one of the more embarrassing and unpleasant in any of his recent experience. He had already thought of a dozen ways the girl could know his face and name—he was hardly unknown. But he didn't know *her*, and he couldn't reconcile himself to becoming the object of a stranger's recriminations. The thought *I don't deserve this* kept rolling around in his head. He hated the self-pitying sound of the phrase, but it wouldn't leave him alone. His mind wouldn't clear. "Buck up," his comrades told him. But he couldn't. He sent for a double brandy and collapsed into a chair, the blue of cue chalk still slashed up his cheek. He was still in a frayed state when his cousin, William Channing-Downes, caught up with him that day.

It was William's club as well. William arrived about a half hour after the raving young woman, to circulate among his fellow members in quest of money; he was perpetually short of funds. Happily, Graham hadn't but ten pounds on him, which he gave up just to hear William stop complaining.

It was a strategy that didn't quite work. "Let me tell you what has happened to *me* today," William said as he folded Graham's money into his pocket. He then proceeded to regale everyone within earshot with the insults heaped on him by a dead man. "I am the most wronged son who ever drew breath. . . ."

William prattled for half an hour before getting to anything of interest. Graham barely listened, since it was seldom necessary to respond to William and since Graham had his own dissatisfactions to mull.

Besides, he knew the gist: Three weeks before, the marquess of Motmarche, William's father, Henry Channing-Downes, had died. Here was old news, though Graham had yet to figure out how he felt about it. He himself and Henry had never gotten along. William, however, had figured out very well how he felt: greedy and deprived.

". . . so Henry's will this morning, right there, out loud, in front of everyone, leaves me, his one and only son, a small lump sum, hardly anything, while it leaves her, that *woman*, every square inch of the unentailed properties, every half-penny of income from the rentals and investments, then even goes on to ask the crown"—he made a whinny voice—"please, please to allow my beloved widow, the marchioness, to live out her days at my dear Motmarche." He reverted to a normal voice. "He wants her in my family home, while he leaves me nothing or next to it! Can you imagine?"

Actually, Graham *could* imagine. For William, the true and only son of the marquess, had unfortunately for him, been born out of wedlock. Another member of Freyer's, a barrister, earlier that morning had already made everyone's eyebrows rise quite high with rumors of Henry's widow inheriting a vast fortune, the extent of which William now more or less corroborated by the extent of his outrage.

He ranted and raved, circling Graham's chair, while issuing irrational diatribes against the woman. "I'll contest the will!" he announced finally. On the basis, so far as Graham could understand, of the insanity of not leaving him more.

William, whose loose brand of logic was always diversion, pulled Graham from his gloom. "What's she like?" he asked.

"Who?"

"Henry's widow."

Till now, Graham had never given Henry's wife much thought. Henry, he had always assumed, liked her. For a dozen years, it had been clear that William did not. William drew her as a drab, bony creature with wide protruding eyes the size and color of plums. He called her a letter-writer and smart-mouthed female who was vain of her own cleverness and learning: typical of Henry's tastes. In the past, this had been sufficient to render her thoroughly uninteresting to Graham.

The size of her inheritance, however, would have made anyone curious about her.

"What is a woman doing with that kind of money?" William answered the question with a question.

Graham had nothing against women with money.

"What is a woman doing with that kind of responsibility?" William shook his head in despair.

"How much younger than Henry is she—was she?" Graham knew there had been some age difference.

"Who knows? A lot." William was not one for details that afternoon. His father's wife was and always had been a pernicious enigma, secretly insoluble, meant to confound him to the grave. As for Graham's own episode with the pregnant young lunatic, he had no compassion whatsoever. "You know, Graham," he advised at the end of his harangue, "you should have known better than to have relations with a crazy girl."

"Pardon?" Graham blinked.

William had taken it into his head that the girl had marched in here with cause, that Graham was the procreator of unacknowledged twins.

No, no. Let it go. Graham reminded himself that his cousin was simply holding to the lifelong conviction that, between them, Graham was always getting away with something. Still, Graham's scalp rippled in unease as William went on in presumption.

"After all," he told Graham, "all people have fathers. And fathers ought to be required—indeed, shackled—to their sons in every conceivable manner from the very start. Let not the sins of the father . . . Besides, what could one expect? After all," William smirked and added with a raised finger, "a man must lie in the bed he has made. Retribution, et cetera. Having had the cake, been celebrity to the gossip . . ."

Graham rubbed the bridge of his nose.

The girl on the billiard table was not the first young woman to throw herself at Graham, though she was the first to do so quite so literally and dramatically. Graham had a history of women putting themselves in his path, trying to grab his cue, so to speak. It was a true phenomenon. People commented about it, joked over it. If anything, it puzzled Graham. Handsomeness alone couldn't account for it; there were other handsome men who didn't have nearly the trouble he had with women. He himself, he supposed, would sum it up much as William did. The women weren't really reaching for him, but rather at his shadow, at the aura of his celebrity.

Graham could pinpoint the beginning of his notoriety. It had begun on the night his father shot his mother, then turned the pistol on himself. In this manner, Graham had become the richest, most landed six-year-old in English history—then the most transient one. He had lived in a total of eight households before coming to rest, at age ten, in the home of the marquess of Motmarche. By then, however, Graham had raised a good many eyebrows on his own. Fawned over, felt sorry for, he'd been given more latitude than was good for him. He had become headstrong, a little scoundrel, though nothing much worse.

Until Henry. For reasons that completely eluded Graham then and now, the marquess had suddenly stepped forward to take Graham as his legal ward. Since he and Henry were first cousins, perhaps a sense of family duty moved him to make the gesture; certainly any personal rapport was not a factor. Graham and Henry proved capable only of aggravating each other. And the friction that built up between them turned the young scoundrel into an ingenious, full-scale rebel.

At twelve, Graham destroyed the gardener's shed while hiding there with forbidden firecrackers. These ignited coal oil, and Henry's shed went up in smoke. At fourteen, he was taken to hospital for having imbibed a poisonous quantity of gin—one and a half bottles in two and a half hours. By eighteen, his "attitude" determined his life once and for all: He was thrown out of Cambridge, which was saying something, since Henry had enough pull there to keep Kublai Khan walking the corridors of St. John's. By nineteen, Graham had appeared on the London stage, a brief fling that helped him financially; after the university incident, his guardian cut off all funds. Graham Wessit was crowned irredeemably wild.

Gossip and Scandal moved in. These two ogres hadn't let him alone since. If he took a new mistress, if he fell from a horse, he might see it in the back pages of the newspaper the next day. For the most part, Graham had come to take this abuse philosophically, the way one adjusts to rude relatives who've become permanent house guests. Still, it was a little alarming to see his infamy appear in the flesh, to watch it scramble onto a billiard table and confront him with its awkward, pregnant belly—as if it could not only come to life but could now multiply.

"Would you like to break?" William asked. He had racked the balls. Over the next twenty minutes, he proceeded to lose Graham's ten pounds and another ten in personal notes to Graham and the three other men who picked up their cues.

The men took turns shooting and lamenting, consoling each other over the necessity of dragging hysterical pregnant women from tabletops meant only for games. She had put a scuff on their green wool. They meant well. In their way, they each wanted Graham to know they were on his side.

"Ghastly," one said.

"Unconscionable," said another.

Graham bent over the table. He dropped a yellow-striped ball into the far corner pocket.

"Why Graham?" someone asked sympathetically.

"Because he's ripe."

"Because she thinks he can afford to help."

William dropped the last item of this list on Graham just as Graham was taking his next shot. "Because, all protests aside, she probably expects something, having paid him her due."

The ball went wide of the pocket by six inches. Graham stood up.

"Well, that's irrelevant," the next man defended him. "A girl can't just walk into a gentlemen's club and expect, because of one night . . ."

Graham put his stick down and walked out.

— Chapter 2 —

By a name
I know not how to tell thee who I am.
WILLIAM SHAKESPEARE
Romeo and Juliet
Act II, Scene ii, 53–54

Three weeks later, the matter of the lunatic with the twins had become a bit more difficult to walk away from. Graham stood under the burden of it, waiting in a large, overfurnished office at Inner Temple, one of the Inns of Court.

He stared bleakly out a window. A fire crackled behind him, making the room where he stood warm and dry. Outside people sloshed through mud and puddles, through the dark, quiescent promise of more rain. With two fingers, he wiped a circle in the humidity on a windowpane. He could see people running, trying to reach their destinations before the imminent downpour came. Everyone seemed to be moving, glancing toward the sky; everyone, he noticed, but a single person.

A woman stood at a distance. Framed by the window, she was the only part of the picture that appeared not to be trying to escape something. She was standing in the walk not forty feet away from him, talking to someone above her on the steps.

Graham fixed his eyes on her, oddly disturbed that he should be more aware than she of the coming storm. All was movement around her. Kinetic eddies of people. Billowing cloaks and skirts. Nervous shiftings of horses and carriages. He could feel these tremors in his bones, like an arthritic prescience for weather gone wild.

He tried to stretch this tension out of himself. He reached his arms upward and out onto the wall on either side of the window, but this relieved nothing. He stood there, feeling doomed, while the woman outside—her calm, head-nodding dialogue—began to annoy him. Why couldn't she see, at least, that it was about to rain? he wanted to ask her. But of course there was no way to penetrate glass, to leap the bed of cyclamens, the civilized patch of lawn, the shin-high topiary hedge, to shake her by the shoulders if he must; no way to make her feel his own dread. She never even looked his way.

He wiped the glass again and watched. He could see nothing special in her. Her black dress blew in the gusts, darting, snapping, its hem a foot above the hedge one moment, calm and out of sight the next. Hide and seek. This became the pervading fascination, the whipping skirt with a mind of its own. And the curious woman, unmindful of everything around her, of even the tug of heavy, jerking fabric.

Behind him, down a hall, several men were mumbling. Their voices rose and fell on the tides of legal rhetoric. Graham felt in fact rather at sea: Not three days after the incident of the billiard table, the idiot girl had filed suit. Much to Graham's disbelief, she had brought formal charges against him for paternity.

He had laughed at first. What incredible cheek. How could the girl imagine that she would gain anything by such an insupportable lie? Graham had turned the matter over to his lawyers with all the righteous irritation of a man maligned without cause.

There had been two court hearings since then, the first of which had not been particularly pleasant. Graham's barrister couldn't seem to keep the court from referring to Graham as "the notorious earl"—a label Graham found not only prejudicial but also offensive to his taste. There was certainly more to him than this vapid summation; he was more than some upper-class, mustachioed villain who wickedly seduced innocents. All the same, the next morning he had shaved off his rather fashionable mustache. He now stood barefaced and less *chic*, but more open to inspection.

The offhand bias of the first hearing, however, had only hinted at the disaster of this morning's, the second. Virtually every pleading his side had presented had been denied. The other side's complaints were entertained at length and with grave consideration. The matter had been set for trial. Graham was astounded. He was about to be tried for something he didn't do by a judge who, at every breath and in the tritest terms, pronounced him depraved. An award in the girl's favor loomed as a sudden and real possibility.

Graham had come immediately from this hearing to Inner Temple, feeling that such a desperate situation required a desperate remedy: He stood in the chambers of one Arnold Tate, Queen's Counsel. There, with his own solicitor and barrister at his back, Graham waited. Tate was overdue. Graham wanted the Q.C. brought in as lead on this lawsuit that already looked lost. An hour ago, he had moved heaven and earth, the sullen barrister at his back, and twenty pounds sterling into the pocket lining of a magistrate to obtain a certificate for two counsel, in mid-legal-stream as it were.

Graham had remembered Tate from a matter some years back and had the sort of grudging, ambiguous faith the loser gains for the winning counsel: Having been in court once before, and now looking at two losses for two, Graham was determined to reverse the trend. Nothing seemed more appropriate than to have the man who slew him in the first do battle for him in the second. Still, Graham was nervous. He was impatient. He was intimidated by memory, by finding himself in the midst again of so many bewigged and robed counselors sailing all around, it seemed, like black death ships under full, important sail.

Out his window, he watched the foul weather gather. He and his lawyers had been dodging small showers all morning, but now the elements were summoning something much larger.

His solicitor asked if Graham wouldn't care to sit, then told him he was not to worry.

"No," Graham thanked him. "Your advice and counsel have proven worthless so far, if not outright dangerous. I'll stand."

The solicitor fell silent.

After fifteen minutes of unrelenting gloom, Graham became aware of a little drama taking place outside his window. To his surprise, he recognized Arnold Tate was a part of it. Seeing him, Graham raised a hand to rap on the windowpane. But instead a ring on his finger made an unplanned clink on the glass, which turned both solicitor and barrister toward him abruptly—and Mr. Tate not at all. Tate was on the steps to the building. He seemed of two minds as to whether to descend the stairs. He stood, as if poised for a spry run down them, talking haltingly to the stones in the walkway below.

The woman in black was on the walk, listening.

"You needn't."

"But I want to," she said.

"Against the advice of counsel."

She simply smiled in response.

"Henry never intended things to become so difficult. He would understand."

Still the smile, but she had turned her face away from him. She looked young, with regular features and fair hair.

"I wish you would listen—" Tate tried again. "That part of the will—" he said. "I don't think Henry was thinking quite right."

"Then you agree with William: He was not of sound mind."

"Of course I don't."

"Then one must assume Henry asked with reason."

"Undoubtedly, but I could do it. To request that you deliver it personally—"

"Is a small enough thing to ask."

Tate sighed.

Clouds rumbled distantly. The weather dwarfed the lawyer's stature. Outside his book-lined office, he was an insignificant smear of color—yellows, reds, and browns on the grey steps to a grey building. The woman in black was part of the darkening sky, her strength of purpose as palpable as the smell of rain in the air.

After a moment, he said, "All right, you're going to take the box to him, as the will asked. But remember he's a black sheep, if ever there was one. Don't be misled by a glossy exterior."

"Ah." She lifted her head and gave an ironic little smile. "He is handsome."

Tate made a gust of objection through his lips, the sound of a middle-aged, slightly paunched man trying to minimize such an attribute. "Just don't be misled by that."

"I won't be. Nor put off by it."

"Handsome men don't have to account for themselves as often as they should."

She thought about this. "You're probably right."

"And he's worse than just handsome. He's selfish. Unruly. A breaker of rules, a builder of nothing."

"You don't like him, I take it."

"I didn't say that." Tate paused, frowning. "He's rather likable," he corrected. "But he's also one of the most frustrating, directionless young men I have ever met. Not your sort at all."

"Ah, young, too." She smiled and looked down. "Young and handsome. No, definitely not my sort."

Tate pulled a glum mouth, then contradicted himself. "Actually, he's not so young anymore. He must be approaching forty." After a pause, he added, "He's one of those men one doesn't expect to age very well: perpetually eight years old. He has no vocation, no avocation, no occupation—except drinking and gambling and women. He consorts with a married woman, an American."

She laughed, gently shaking her head. "Arnold. Having impugned the man's character, you are now trying to slander his taste as well. Stop being so smug." She continued to smile, not meanly but with a kind of teasing forbearance. "If the man is shallow or dissolute or immature or whatever you're trying to say, I'm sure I'm not so stupid as to miss it. And in any event, I'm only delivering a harmless little box Henry wanted him to have."

The lawyer clamped his mouth shut.

They stood in silence; Tate, frowning with a tight mouth, she, looking down, trying to minimize her faint, intransigent smile. Then Tate's expression slowly began to change. His mouth too began to turn up at the edges until his expression had quite surprisingly broken into a wide display of artificially even teeth.

"How did Henry ever tolerate you?" he said. "You're pigheaded, do you know that?"

"Thank you." She gave him a sly, sidelong glance.

"And you make me feel foolish."

Though foolish in a good way. She made him feel young; it was written all over his toothsome countenance.

He stood there beaming, the color rising in his cheeks. A distinguished man in late middle age, embarrassed by the pleasure he took in a young woman's smiling and cajoling. He looked at his shoes, at the sky, trying to regain his balance, his superior posture.

In the uncomfortable silence, he asked, "Did you ever meet him?"

"Whom?"

"Netham. Graham Wessit." He made a face. "This handsome young man you are going to meet. On such feeble introduction." He nodded toward a box she was carrying. It was black like her dress, barely definable except where her hand wrapped around its sides.

"No." She let her attention drift. Her smile became vague. "Do you know," she reflected, "the one time in twelve years of marriage that Henry did go to visit this cousin, he refused to take me along. It was the only time we were separated. And the night he left, our roles reversed themselves so peculiarly, as if *he* were the child—with clubhouse secrets he was dying to tell, but didn't dare share. He was so cryptic, apologizing that he couldn't behave 'more admirably.' " She stopped, frowning for a moment, as if something were amiss. Then she shrugged this off, laughing. "*Henry*, more admirably. Can you imagine?"

"He didn't want you to go. He wouldn't now."

"Yet he's *sent* me with the box."

"That *silly* box!" Tate made an imaginary throwing-away with his hands. "Henry left the man nothing else. That should tell you something."

"He slighted more than his cousin. Will it be all right, Arnold—truthfully? William is so angry."

The lawyer became more erect. "In Henry's own words, his high regard for you will be 'declared as tangibly as a husband can make it.' " Tate shook his head. "An incredibly huge bequest—there is no precedent for a woman inheriting so much. But you will have it." He smiled. "The probate court will uphold Henry's true intentions. We will have William's claim dismissed in no time."

She contemplated this for a moment. "In no time," she repeated. She looked at the attorney. "It's all very crass from one angle, isn't it? I wish he weren't dead—I miss him, but here I am arguing over his estate." She gave a short laugh. "At heart, I'm still a butcher's daughter."

The lawyer blinked, then fell clumsily into just-remembered protocol. "I'm so sorry about your father. It must be dreadful to lose both a father and a husband in so short a time."

"It was easier with my father." Her gaze turned to the folds of her skirt. "Henry was there. We talked. He helped so much. I didn't get along with my father, did you know that?" But then with a mock brightness and without waiting for an answer, she continued. "You should have seen the funeral. By far the butcher's grandest social event."

"He wasn't exactly a butcher—"

"But he was. He killed and dressed animals, though on a rather large scale. You see?" She looked up and opened her arms. "He was so clever at it, he married one off to a marquess."

She was suspended for a moment in that balletic position of raised arms. As if music had stopped for a count of three.

It felt like that many heartbeats for the man watching from the window. Graham leaned closer, fascinated, transfixed. The woman's open arms seemed to remove status, station, even in some way her female gender. She seemed to shed everything in those moments, everything and anything limiting or superfluous to simply being human. The hint of a perfect, unself-conscious candor affected Graham, the way great beauty suddenly moves something in one's chest; the way profound horror quakes the soul. He couldn't decide if he was enormously attracted or almost squeamishly repelled.

Then the moment was gone. Shyly, the woman folded her arms back over a solid item she had lifted. Just as she was tucking it back against her, Graham noticed her gesture had put the black box she had been carrying into clear view. It was square, thin, the size of a box of handkerchiefs, and easily held in one hand. Then this too disappeared, lost in the shadows of the woman's arms.

A few minutes later, the rain broke, like a curtain descending. The view beyond the window became no more than a blur of people scrambling for cover. Water was pounding against the glass when Graham heard Arnold Tate's voice in the outer office. He said something to his clerk, then entered the room Graham occupied.

"Who was the widow?" Graham asked.

Tate responded as if Graham were still twenty, his age when they had last spoken. "You should be ashamed to ask."

"What's her name?"

"Channing-Downes. Lady Motmarche. The late marquess's wife. Does that sound familiar?"

Graham's own reflection in the window glass looked back at him, briefly startled. "Of course," he answered.

"Give me a moment," Tate said, as if to cut off all further discussion, "while I put her papers away and have a look at your legal brief."

Five minutes later, Graham sat in the vacant chair between his solicitor and barrister. He wedged himself into it, folding and bending a body never meant for the narrow, curved design. In uncomfortable situations, Graham became particularly conscious of his own height and doubly conscious of it when he saw others fidgeting and standing up straighter.

Tate rose and pushed his chair in, as if he would stand for the whole proceeding. Then he stretched, got books out from a case behind the desk, and laid them out on the desktop, three, four, eight, more; fortification.

Tate was a balding man of perhaps fifty-five, of medium height, with a tendency to carry slightly more than medium weight. He was squarely built and bluntly shaped with small feet and short, spatulate hands. He had to strain at the high shelves, the heavy law. Graham could have spanned several volumes at once with his long fingers.

"Shall we begin?" The Q.C., in a valley of books, aligned papers on the desk.

Graham had a sense of the past repeating itself. The barrister still seemed the adversary. The sound of his voice— mellifluous, Olympian, full of sincerity—worked undoubtedly to his professional advantage, but it was not reassuring. It implied that truth could afford to be questioned.

Graham claimed one last trivial digression, a curiosity he couldn't quite dismiss. "Her complete name," he said, "I should know—" He could vaguely recall old letters, bits of remembered conversation, and these memories made him want to smile for some reason. "You didn't tell me her first name. I'm sure Henry told me once, yet I can't recall—"

Tate looked up, his cheeks puffed as if he might blow Graham away.

"It is a sound, virtuous, old name," he said. Then his cheeks sagged, as did his head. "Her first name is Submit."

— Chapter 3 —

Submit Wharton Channing-Downes. The name sang like a musical crescendo of English social mobility at its most fluid. Submit herself, however, would have been the last person to call her given name "sound and virtuous," albeit old. It was Puritan, and thus it was suspect. Faith, Charity, and Prudence might occasionally work in the kitchens of large houses, but they did not sit at the dining room tables with Elizabeth and Anne.

The name in the middle, however, picked up purpose and direction. Submit's maiden name was not beautiful, but practical and easy to say, like a song to which everyone knew the words. Wharton, via John Wharton, was repeated and known; it had worked to be where it was. John Wharton had built himself the largest abattoir in southeast England. In his hands, it had run at a huge profit that allowed him many luxuries, not the least of which was to attach his name to that last: Channing-Downes. Not one but two thin, blue refinements of melody, harmoniously—and in hyphenated hyperbole—ending the name on one rich, protracted note of triumph. The marquess. A name as old as the title itself. For Henry Channing-Downes was not just a marquess but the primogenitary descendent of *the* marquess, the very first. Four and a half centuries ago, Robert Channing, earl of Sherborne, had married a king's younger, untitled granddaughter, Sophia Downes. The king had been so pleased with Robert's choice that he had extended the earl's district to the frontier, to the mark or march—and then extended the earl's title to reflect this elevation. He designated Robert a marquess, an honor specified to be above all other earls. The Channing-Downes patent predated all others, the very title itself being invented to honor the name.

All of this did the woman attached to the name little good as she bolted for cover. The widow of an august peer could get just as wet as anyone else in a rainstorm.

Submit Channing-Downes let down the veils of her bonnet. Meager as they were, they were the only protection to which she currently had access. Thunder clapped. Then she spied across Middle Temple Lane a carriage, a double salvation, offering both cover and transportation.

Submit grabbed up two handfuls of black skirts and broke from a trot into a dead run. She got to the vehicle just as the clouds opened up. As the first large drops splattered her shoulders, she hesitated. The carriage was empty, which was good; but it was driverless, which was not.

A voice called out, "Ho, ma'am!" She looked around to see a man, the driver, waiting for his next fare from under the overhang. He signaled for her to get in, then disappeared inside the building—it was a pub. He had gone in presumably to pay his bill. The wind gave a strong gust, lifting her crinoline to the point of almost carrying her away. She grabbed hold of the coach door handle, using it like an anchor, then yanked on it and heaved herself up.

Inside, she lifted her veil and wiped at her face with dry gloves she retrieved from her pocket. The gloves did small good. The wind had penetrated the hat's veil, sifting rain into a mist that left her face wet. Her shoulders were wet as well. Her right sleeve, the last part of her to gain shelter, was soaked. God help the hems of her skirts.

She could hear the rain beating from all angles, pounding against the leather and wood of the carriage. The rain echoed within her little hollow of dry air in a continuous cacophony. The vehicle itself rocked slightly from the barrage. Submit began to spread herself out into the little space. She took off her soaked and sagging hat, shrugged out of her shoulder cape, and found a carriage blanket. Then damp, wrinkled, and breathless from her mad dash, she leaned back into the cushions and let out a sigh of satisfaction. Another calamity averted. As the time stretched out, she even began to feel content, listening to the storm raging around her on all sides. She liked a good storm, so long as she was sheltered, dry and secure inside.

Indeed, she could have conceivably felt less than dry and secure. She had spent the morning with a barrister, discussing how to put a roof back over her head: William Channing-Downes had not only contested Henry's will, he had also put Henry's properties, including her home in East Anglia, into the custody of a probate court. Distribution was withheld indefinitely. His case had been so forceful—a force Submit didn't quite understand yet—that she had been evicted from her home. This put at her feet three very considerable losses in a very short time. The roof over her head. Access to a sizable wealth. And the worst by far, Henry Channing-Downes, her slightly cantankerous husband, forty-three years her senior, with whom—though few would understand or believe it—she had been very much in love.

It was in isolated moments such as this, in the midst of a rainstorm, that she could grow not precisely despondent or grief-stricken, but very, very quiet. It occurred to her that without Henry, without his silly goads and puns and clever pomposities, without his infinitely loving, spurring encouragements, she might never live life as richly again.

Submit was interrupted from this thought by a banging somehow different from all the other outside noise. Not all the knocking and pounding on one side of her carriage, it seemed, was coming from nature's hand. Someone was yelling and hammering on her carriage door.

Another fare, she thought; someone who had seen her get in and wanted to share. Carriages would be scarce in this kind of storm—it was quite possible that her driver, along with a great many others in London, had decided to weather the worst of it from inside a pub. There was plenty of room, and she was in no hurry, she supposed. She cracked a window—a woman didn't "share" with just anyone who asked; thieves could play on compassion. She shielded her face with one hand while holding the leather closure with the other. Lightning lit up the street for a moment, and thunder boomed in response. This sound cut through the air with the same sort of jarring surprise with which Submit recognized the person standing out in the rain.

"William?" she called.

The man outside raised his hands to his mouth. "I want to talk to you," he shouted.

She did not particularly want to talk to him. She was astonished even to see him here. But she leaned forward and released the latch. The door opened, and the upper portion of William Channing-Downes was suddenly framed by the opened panel. He stood squinting at her, trying to peer into the dim carriage, while water ran off the brim of his hat.

"Submit? Is that you?" He seemed unsure suddenly as he hunted for a sign of her in the dark interior.

"What do you want? How did you find me?"

His face was dripping with rain, his eyes narrowed—he couldn't seem to believe in his own good luck, or else perfect connivance. His mouth hung open, as unlatched as the wet, gaping carriage door. He said nothing more for a few moments. Then his lips quickly reshaped themselves into a smile, an expression that could only be termed bizarre in view of the plastering he was taking from the rain. He took his hat into his hands and drew himself up.

"Why, it is you, my dear! I thought so when I glimpsed you from Fleet Street. How are you?"

Submit always found something mildly entertaining

about William. Having never cultivated any orientation but expediency, he had all but obliterated any sense of what was natural. As in this case: his willingness to stand not merely in rain but in sheets and torrents so that he might exchange pleasantries with a woman he was cheerfully planning to divest of virtually everything she possessed.

For years, Submit had tried to find something, anything, that she could like about William. She had conducted this search for the sake of Henry, who had tried all his life to find something likable in his son and failed. Submit had discovered, however, that whether she liked William or not was of little consequence, even to William: He himself would have been much happier to inspire jealousy or fear. The crux, in recent years, had become not how to like him but rather how to keep rein on her own rampant sense of superiority and contempt.

The best that could be said for him was that he possessed a kind of unblenching charm—disasterproof, humiliation-proof, and, as today, waterproof. He could run it out onto his face when he wanted it and tuck it back into the pockets of his sagging jowls when he did not. After forty years of training, this odd pleasantness served well enough for him to have a moderate standing as a gentleman. His father had seen to a gentleman's education and, when he was alive, a comfortable trickle of money, which William managed like a gentleman—that is to say, not at all, since gentlemen did not dirty their hands with such matters. His chief occupation was spending; his secondary, gambling; his third, inveigling new creditors. He had little affection for anything other than money and what it would buy. And upon Henry Channing-Downes's demise, that was what the father had left the son: a secure principal on which to draw income; a small—yet what could already be termed dwindling—fortune. The only thing he possibly valued above money was something Henry couldn't leave him: status as a gentleman of title.

For Henry's only son was Henry's bastard; so far as Submit understood, William had no claim on any title. She attributed his various legal moves as merely device, meant to cause her maximum aggravation. William had been raised among people of power. He knew the system and how to use it to leverage his way into a larger settlement—which she was probably going to give him, though she wasn't sure how much would satisfy him right now. Exactly what was enough, she wondered, to make a misbegotten son stop wishing for legitimacy?

"Do come in out of the rain, William."

She moved to the far side of the carriage, tucking her feet and skirts up into the darkness on the seat beside her. As he entered, she watched him trying to locate her by her voice. The brief, muted light showed nothing but her damp shoes abandoned on the carriage floor. As he closed the door, the carriage became cavelike, rank with humidity, the smell of wet leather, damp satin.

"I thought you might not ask."

"I was getting wet."

"I shouldn't think that would bother you, having felt the warm flow of love in the form of piss in the bedsheets."

Submit made a sound of disgust, then let the remark go. The concept of dignity meant as much to William as it did to a stone boulder—and he would roll right over anyone who allowed his incredible insults to give offense.

He removed his coat and hat, then blotted his face with a handkerchief. "Is there a blanket?"

There was an extra one folded on the seat beside her. She couldn't resist throwing it at him from the dark.

He made a startled noise as it hit him in the face. Then he began arranging it over himself. He took perhaps a minute with this before he asked, as if he were making small talk,

"How are you getting on? Word filters to me that you are at a hostel."

"A woman's boardinghouse. Griffin's on Chaney Circle."

"I know. I went there first. That's how I knew to look for you here."

"Then why do you ask?"

"Are you comfortable there?"

"I would rather be home."

He snorted. "In *my* home." He settled back into his corner of the carriage. "So, you find that gauche, insensible William is not without friends?"

"I find you are not without confederates."

"The same."

"Then you are pitiable as well."

The beat of rain dominated briefly. Outside, there was a distant series of thunderclaps.

"What do you want, William?"

"Are you pregnant? You should know by now—"

She laughed.

"I would be more delicate—" William was mildly put off course by the laughter. He collected himself and continued. "But then, you are not a stranger to the particulars of breeding, your family having made a science of cows. Well?" he asked. "Are you?"

She didn't answer his rude question. "You have petitioned for a title?"

Through a circuitous route of petitions and politics, William might gain himself a courtesy title or perhaps, by the longest stretch of the imagination, one of Henry's lesser honors. The marquess had an earldom or two, a viscountcy all trivialized by the marquessate. All this was of course contingent upon there being no legitimate issue.

"I've found I can petition if you will sign an affidavit. If you will only be gracious about all this—I have an offer for you."

"Someone's given you hope?"

"Perhaps, though the Home Secretary won't allow anyone to even speak on my behalf, so long as there's a chance Henry might have left an heir."

"Let's hear your offer."

He cleared his throat. "You withdraw any claim on that old stone castle in East Anglia, that hasn't even so much as running water at a pump valve. That, and all the property connected to it. Then I will leave the way clear to the cozy little London house with all its conveniences—Margaret is virtually sobbing that I want to move her from it; you would be much happier there. Then we split the rest."

It took several seconds for her to digest the meaning of this. "You want Motmarche?" she asked incredulously.

"What else?"

She relaxed, again laughing. "You are petitioning for the title of marquess of Motmarche?"

"I am petitioning for them all."

It took several seconds more to take this in. She said finally, "I don't know what to say in the face of such bald, blind—and unrealistic—ambition. For goodness' sake, William, you want more money than Henry left you. Eventually, you want to put the word 'lord' before your name. I will do what I can for you on both; I'm more than willing. But I—"

"I want Motmarche."

She laughed again. It was involuntary. It was making her almost giddy to hear this said out loud. Of course he wanted Motmarche. He would just as soon have everything. "Well, I don't see how you'll get it," she said. "You haven't a claim in the world."

"Unless I had the title."

"Which no sane man in the world would promise you."

He made a smug sound, down his nose. "True. Henry promised it to me."

"Oh, for the love of God—"

"He did! All my life I lived as his son, as he wanted. I lived my life as his legal heir, and he knew it! He never once stopped me or told me otherwise—"

"Because he didn't need to. The world will stop you. Henry didn't need to tell you the obvious." She leaned toward him in the dark. "But I am going to tell you something obvious, just for the record. See if you can understand this, William: Motmarche is my home. I lived there with your father, not unhappily, for almost half my life. His books are in the study. My piano is in the music room. Everything familiar to me is there, the games, the teacups, the silly rug by the fire with the holes. Everything I have done or acquired as an adult is in that house. And I am entitled by law to live out my days there, with or without children. Apply for the baronage in Devonshire. I'll help you there. It's grand. Its rental properties are lucrative—"

"It's not enough."

"You'd be happy there."

"You'd be happy on Charlotte Street."

She frowned. To pretend they were plotting each other's happiness was, at the very least, dishonest. She spoke plainly to him: "*You* have lived in the house in Bayswater for as long as I have known you. I don't want to exchange dwellings with you. I don't want to exchange anything with you. Not with you, nor Margaret. And the will left *all* the properties to me. I have told you, you may stay in the London house, and I will stick by that if you will drop the stupid abeyance eviction. But I must tell you, my lawyers are filing similar papers this week to have you out of Charlotte Street. I am going to fight you on this, William. If you don't stop this nonsense, I shall turn every bolt I can reach. That castle, which happens to be in the middle of your coveted marquessdom, is all I have left, and I won't give it up just so you can paint a coat of arms on your carriage." She punctuated this with a brisk churning movement of wool and silk and crinoline and sat back into the dark.

There were two or three minutes of stuffy silence.

William sat like a baffled hound, as if he were sure he'd been on the right track, but now his prey seemed to have doubled back on him. "Of course," he started, "if it's that you mind your change in status to the Dowager Marchioness, there might be some sort of accommodation—" He stopped, apparently able to see that this wasn't the way, either. He was suddenly alert. Even in the dark William's nose for a person's financial fix was excited by the subtlest discrepancies. "Your maid didn't answer at your rooms." The girl was obviously not in the carriage.

"I let her go."

"Money?"

"You know it is. Everything is tied up for both of us. This is so stupid—"

"I have enough."

"Well, I don't." She said it forcefully.

"Sign the affidavit, and I'll settle all but the inalienable lands."

"You'll give the rest to me?"

"I'll split it with you."

She made another breath of a laugh. "How good of you. You'll take half of all the assets you have least chance of getting in return for my helping you along to the remainder. I'm not signing anything."

"You are a greedy woman who doesn't know her place."

"That's possible."

"And you will starve."

She hesitated. "There is a small trust, an income."

He was puzzled. "Henry? But I was sure—"

"Don't worry, William. It is very small."

"Can you live on it?"

"I hope to avoid knowing."

"You can't keep a maid on it." He was satisfied. "And your brothers won't help you. They got no more than you did of your father's business. They would hardly welcome their marchioness sister's imposing on their already strained means." He cackled over her estrangement from what remained of her family. In fact, her brothers, seven of them, to a one had deeply resented her marriage.

"One of your cousins may help me." She more or less threw the idea at him like the blanket—it was a bluff, but she was sick to death of his telling her what she already knew. "A Graham Wessit. Henry suggested I pay him a call."

This produced a moment of grim astonishment, then a snort. "I don't believe you."

"It's true. Henry very specifically asked that I make a point of seeing the man."

Her charade seemed suddenly plausible. She drew the box on the seat beside her a little closer in the dark. There were any number of ways Henry could have had this little bequest delivered. Submit felt a twinge of insight. Henry never did anything without purpose. She was not just delivering the case for Henry; perhaps he might be doing something for her. It was possible, very likely in fact, that he had anticipated William's reaction to the will. Perhaps this cousin really would be of help.

"Well, this is a bizarre development," William said. "Gray is going to be amazed, I daresay."

"You know him?"

"Everyone knows Gray, my dear. You don't?" He seemed to lord this knowledge over her for a moment, as if it gave him a particularly savory upper hand. Then he added, "Oh, I forget, you have never been much for coming to London."

"I didn't think he lived in London." The earldom was synonymous with land in Devon and Dorset. She had been expecting to make a day trip by train.

"Oh, but he does. He is here now. The season in London.

Summer in the country. The usual tours of Bath. He travels with the ton, my dear." He clicked his tongue. "He has titles, you know."

"An earl—"

"Oh, no. I was thinking of all the other ones. Let's see. He was once called the Father of London Theater."

"He is a dilettante?"

It took several seconds to realize that William was not answering but indulging in a smug, punishing little silence meant to put a young woman—who never listened to him properly anyway, the silence said—in her place.

"An amateur thespian in his university days," he said at length. Another pause, then, "But the name comes less from that, I imagine, than from his propensity to conceive children with actresses." He chuckled. "I do like it, though: You reach for every shilling and stature Father ever possessed, then, when it looks as though there may be a battle, you speak of blithely sidling up to the man he hated most in the world— don't believe for one minute, my dear, that Father intended you ever ally yourself with Graham Wessit. The mere thought, I promise you, would make my father not roll but spin in his grave."

"Oh, William—"

"No, no. You must get the full picture. When Netham's parents died—they killed each other, you know—and no one knew what to do with the brutish little earl, Father took him in. Henry, as Graham's cousin, was his closest family, so Henry became his legal guardian. Gray and I were raised together. He is my contemporary, not Father's. Did you realize that?" William seemed to delight in the possibility that she hadn't. "No, I suppose not; Father would cover his bets."

This surprised a laugh from her. "And what is that supposed to mean?"

William left the question dangling. "Father never spoke to him, of him, or gave another thought to the monster once he had him out of the house. Kicked him out, you know. Without a penny, before his majority. Father—"

"Oh, hush." She leaned across the shadows and, with a sharp tug, yanked the blanket from his knees. "Leave."

He didn't understand.

"Dorset—even London—and East Anglia are a bit too distant from each other for convenient visiting, William, though Henry did visit this cousin once. He went to him when he was ill—not precisely a declaration of hate, I would say. Now, get out."

William sputtered, then became brittle with indignity as the door between them swung outward, opening into the street. Daylight blared through the open doorway.

For several seconds there was nothing but the sharp noise of rain, made louder and more immediate by this sudden access. Rain spattered the step. Below the step, it ran in whooshes, parted into wedged currents by the wheels of the carriage. Incensed, William rose, hovered. He poised in the aperture and looked back, as if he were threatening to throw himself into a river and do himself in.

"Well. Well, you will see," he said. It was an old, familiar frustration for him, she knew. He saw himself as older, more experienced; he was sure he knew more than she. And yet she paid no obeisance to these facts. William's bitterness was the lament of a man cheated. "Let me just tell you, young lady, it was no simple matter of the prodigal son. There was *no* fatted calf. You never saw Graham at Motmarche Castle, I would wager; neither by invitation nor by his own accord. Henry severed him. Like a gangrene. Graham Wessit is a selfish, self-indulgent, self-willed"—he looked for the right word—"sybarite." William seemed suddenly and immensely pleased with the euphony of his own judgment. He drew his chin up. "And he is a frenetic lunatic: He will incinerate you."

With this satisfying prediction, William Channing-

Downes reached back for his wet bundle, his coat and his hat, then hopped off his perch into the stream of a rainy London day. He walked and rotated, picking his way through the shallower puddles, arranging his overclothes with all the preening delicacy of a fowl at its bath.

— Chapter 4 —

Submit, Submit, Submit. All the rest of that morning and into the afternoon, Graham found himself absently playing with the word, the way one twiddles a tune that won't leave one's head. It annoyed him. The woman's name was irritating, echoing as it did all his courtroom difficulties. That morning, the pregnant girl's attorney had been allowed to use the word and all its cognates on Graham in a way that had had him visibly flinching toward the end. Poor submissive miss, having submitted with all submittable submission. . . . But at the same time, the name distracted him, engrossed him. He wondered how the woman outside Tate's office had managed to stand so calmly, while wearing such a preposterous name. Did the woman speak to herself as such—*Now, see here, Submit.* Graham couldn't imagine ever using that first name aloud.

By evening, however, Graham discovered himself still trying to. As he was lifting his chin before the mirror to button a collar, he caught himself mouthing the word. *Submit.* Strange, he thought, as he knotted his bow tie. Why should he be preoccupied with it? He knew nothing about the woman, except that from a distance he liked the look of her—wisps of black voile and silk blowing in the wind. Was that all that he liked? No, he'd seen a dozen widows, in and out of the wind. It was something else, he reasoned. Certainly, it was not her connection with Henry. That appalled him; he'd liked her better before he'd known.

Perhaps that was what he liked: He knew almost nothing about her. He laughed at himself, for he suspected, from the experience of waking up frequently beside strangers, that he was especially attracted to women he didn't know. It was the mystery, he supposed. There was something essentially female in what was hidden, unknown. Yes, that must be it. And Henry only added to this. It seemed incredible to him that so . . . so what? . . . so sultry a woman could be—

Graham stopped, one white satin butterfly dangling at his neck, his hand holding the other in place. Could a woman he could barely see be sultry across forty feet of grass, as she spoke to a lawyer on the walk at an Inn of Court? He picked up the end of the tie and pulled it through. Yes, she could. And that was the really mysterious part. How had bookish, prudish old Henry come up with a sultry bride?

He lost track of his own question as he slipped his arms into the armholes of a favorite vest. His valet came up behind him to tie the waist ribbons in back so the garment would fit snugly. Then Graham slid into the offered arms of a tailcoat of evening black, fine French worsted wool with a silk collar and revers. The coat matched his pants, which bore silk braid up the outside of each leg.

His white shirt, white tie, and black evening suit were elegant but standard fare. They might add up simply to a Frenchified Englishman, and, if they did, that would put him in good but unremarkable company with a number of men who would be carousing in London that night. Certified *chic*. But there were the calculated notes of idiosyncrasy. For example, the watches: Graham picked up one, two, three, four, each lovely, each different; he collected them. He looped their chains, one at a time, through the buttonholes and watch pockets of his vest.

Graham's chest became garlanded with a variety of slender gold chains. The vest itself, a floral brocade of rose, green, and indigo, was a virtual trellis of watch pockets; it might carry a dozen timepieces. Some pockets received watches, others did not. The total effect became something difficult to classify and very hard to ignore.

And this was the intent. There was a kind of aggression to the way Graham dressed. Once, when he was first being passed from family to family, his hair still in curls, he had had an encounter with some older boys. They chased him, toppling him over in a field, and rubbed alum into his mouth to make him pucker, they said. They did nothing more than hold him down and move their bodies on him, but he had been left with the sharp taste, like residual alum, of self-disgust. *Pretty, pretty*, they had taunted. He had hated being pretty. Then he had found a way to embrace it.

Graham drew a fifth watch chain through the glorious embroidered vest, then tapped his feet into black kid shoes with top caps so shiny he could have seen his face in them. He knew he dressed well and that tonight this would count for something. He was going to a party of more than three hundred people, all in the upper social strata. He was dressed for confrontation. He looked rich with a hint of the mutinous, which spelled money, leisure, and the power of class distinction. Graham had put distance between himself and those boys in the field, two of whom would actually be sitting somewhere down the dinner table from him tonight, and the distance was on display.

Graham grabbed up his cape and gloves and gibus. The top hat was collapsed. With a flex of his wrists, he popped it to its full height and set it, at the slightest angle, on his head. At the front door, he remembered his scarf. He called back for it. His valet dropped it from the first floor, over the banister. It sailed, flitting downward in long, erratic spirals, obeying gravity leisurely like the white silk tail of a kite.

Graham was able to pull on one glove as he watched, slide each finger carefully, then snatch the scarf out of the air with his bare hand. He wrapped the scarf twice around his neck, though it was still long enough for both ends to wave delicately over his abdomen and groin. Then he put on the other glove as he shouldered past his butler and went out the door. He was eager for the familiar routine of a party; eager to put this horrible day behind him.

It was twilight by the time Submit arrived back at Griffin's Boardinghouse for Women. The rain had let up, but the wind had not. As she went up the front walk, her hooped skirts swayed restlessly, their undulant sides bobbing and bowing in the wind. Then in a sudden gust, the weather pressed her skirts all the way against her legs; the steel hoops lifted in back. Cool air shot up the backs of her calves.

As she came in the front door, the wind gave her dress a last ferocious snap. The top layer, black voiled silk, separated from the body of the garment. It snagged on the corner of the brass letter drop. For a moment Submit was caught, but once she saw the source of her problem, she unhooked herself with hardly more than a glance, then moved easily into the foyer, while simultaneously removing her gloves. She closed the door, and the room grew still. In the quiet of the semidark foyer, the dress, its filmy overlayer, settled like a spirit come to rest onto the domed heaps and drapes of watered silk.

Dressed in this concoction of pure upper-class fashion, she walked down the narrow foyer of a tidy middle-class hall.

"Mrs. Griffin?" she called.

Mrs. Griffin's daughter appeared from the doorway. "Yes, madam."

"Mary." Submit smiled at her. The young woman was perhaps twenty and had two small boys. She lived with her parents, her husband having been killed at Balaklava. "Your mother was going to prepare my bill."

"Yes, it's right here." The young woman disappeared into the room.

Submit followed. The Griffins' apartments were like all the rest in the small building. Neat, convenient, and straining to be more. In their brochure, the Griffins called their dozen small flats "elegant," a description that was more wishful thinking than fact.

Mary handed her a piece of paper, along with several letters that had come in the day's post. "Your mail, m'lady." She paused and then added, "We're sorry to be losing you."

Submit smiled tightly. She set her gloves and parcel down. The nicer London boardinghouses had no trouble staying full or getting a good price. With the lawsuit now in its third week, Submit could no longer afford the Griffins' "elegance."

Early this morning, she had put a deposit on a single room at an inn on the outskirts of town. The room at the inn was spacious, but also—the kindest word was "rustic." And neither inn nor boardinghouse was much like home. After the cavernous halls of Motmarche, neither city flat nor country inn seemed a very suitable life. Submit tried not to think of home. Giant, regal old Motmarche. Quiet. August. Surrounded by fields and farmland. Within walking distance of the cosmopolitan joys of a university town. Motmarche and Cambridge with Henry, she thought sadly, had been perfect, the best of all possible worlds.

As she handed over the payment, Submit outlined for the girl what she had already worked out with her mother. "I'll be leaving tonight after dinner. I'll send someone in the next day or two for my larger bags. My mail can be forwarded to the old posting house at Morrow Fields. Unless—" Once more, Submit toyed with the idea of asking this cousin, Graham Wessit, for some sort of help. It occurred to her that the notion with which she had tormented William today might be more than half true: Perhaps Henry, by asking her to deliver the box, was sending her to this man as a kind of potential ally. As to the man's reputation, Henry could be wonderfully open-minded and independent in his judgment. And so could she. "Unless I notify you otherwise," she concluded.

Mary nodded. "Would you like tea now? Or would you prefer to wait for dinner? It will be another hour."

"Tea now would be nice. Thank you."

"Why don't I bring it to you in the parlor?"

"That would be fine."

As she passed by the stairs, Submit noticed that her trunks and bags had already been brought down and tucked under the stairwell. She separated the portmanteau she would be taking with her tonight from the rest, placing it by the front door.

The parlor was a neat, homey room that overlooked the front street. It was a room everyone shared, though thankfully there was no one else around. It was too late for the teatime gathering, too early for the predinner group that usually congregated here.

Submit set down her gloves and the box she was to deliver on the tea table, then went over to a mirror that hung above a small writing desk. She shrugged out of her short cape, throwing it over a wing chair, then, in front of the mirror, began to remove her hat.

The evening light coming only from the fireplace and street's gaslights outside cast a glow across the chair, the writing desk, across Submit herself. Yet she found the dark atmosphere of the room comforting, almost cheerful. She could hear Mary downstairs in the basement kitchen setting out a cup and saucer, starting her tea. Mrs. Griffin was somewhere overhead, humming, turning down the beds. Mr. Griffin was making his rounds, stoking the fires for the night. The orderly English life. Submit let go of her worries. This sort of routine reassured her. She didn't doubt that she could find something like it, even at an old inn on the edge of the city.

From a drawer of the writing table, she took out a tinderbox. She meant to light the kerosene lamp on the table but paused. The fire burned brightly in the hearth. Beyond the window at her elbow a streetlamp glowed; it stood not five feet away. The room was bathed in soft shadows and light. She put the tinderbox down. A sudden patter on the window glass announced that the rain had resumed again.

The patter broke into a light din, the rain blurring the gaslight as it came through the window. Submit turned, watching the room wash in ghostly patterns that quivered over the walls and objects around her, light that moved as if half-alive. It was beautiful; it was eerie. No, it was too fine a sight to disturb with the bright light of a lamp. So she went over, gathered up her mail, brought it back to the wing chair by the window, and sat to read the day's post by the window light, embraced by the shadows of weather as they rippled across the dry, quiet room.

There was a bill from a doctor. She would have to check her records in the morning; she had thought she had paid them all. Other than this, there were the usual: two cards from people who had known Henry—Submit knew almost no one in London—who had called. A handful of letters, notes of sympathy. Then she happened to catch sight of a name on one of these, a letter delayed and forwarded from Motmarche.

Graham Wessit, the earl of Netham. Submit glanced at the broad, flat case on the tea table. She wondered what was inside it—and wondered if she should perhaps open it, to have a look. No, it wasn't hers, she told herself.

She opened the note from this Lord Netham, but found no clue inside as to his real significance, if any, in Henry's life. There was merely a string of formal, conventional sentiments written out in a round, perfect hand on the neat linen page. Even the signature was sterile—and vaguely hypocritical, for underneath the earl's name was the phrase "Signed in the Earl's absence by" and another name. The work of a personal amanuensis. The earl had presumably dictated his sympathy, the way a man orders a box of new shirts, but had had actually nothing to do with the sending of it—any more, the perfunctory nature of the note said, than he ever honestly expected to wear the feelings he had sent along.

A moment later, Mary knocked. "Your tea, madam."

"Come in."

Mary entered the parlor, looking around. "Would you like me to light the lamp?"

"No, thank you." Submit could tell by her hesitation that she did not approve of a young widow sitting alone in the dark. It would be interpreted as morose. "Dinner at eight?" Submit asked by way of signaling the young woman she would be more sociable later.

"Yes, ma'am."

"Thank you again."

Mary frowned at the outside light playing on the walls, at the leaping shadows from the fire. Submit got up to escort her out, closing the door after her. On her way back to her chair, she picked up the black papier-mâché case from the tea table.

She brought it over to the window. It had once been pretty perhaps, but that was years ago. A white orchid with a deep pink throat had been painted onto the black surface of its top, but the glossy lacquer over this had cracked and yellowed the image. The box had no lock. For a moment, Submit fingered the latch. It was loose. The contents weren't protected from her curiosity, and Henry of all people knew she was inquisitive.

She lifted the lid and leaned a little closer to the window, toward its diffuse, watery light. Rain pattered. The warmth of the room had fogged little crescents into the corners of the windowpanes. At first, in this dim, reduced light, the exact nature of the contents was obscured.

Just sheets of paper. The paper was a soft thick rag. The inside of the box, above, around, and underneath these sheets, was softer still. The box's lining was truly a pleasure to touch—folds of soft, black satin. The satin was unusually fine, extravagantly tactile. Submit liked it, yet somehow, when combined with the box's black lacquer exterior, its pink and white orchid, the total effect wasn't exactly to her taste. It was *de trop*. The costly, overluxurious lining was much more than was required simply to protect the sheets of paper from shifting around in the box. They were drawings, she realized. It was a small art case.

In the watery light, she could just make out the delicate tracings of ink sketches, thin, graceful lines intertwining with more graceful lines. Slowly Submit recognized in these the features of faces, or parts of faces. The closed eyes of an ecstatic expression. An open mouth, as if in song. The drawings had an ethereal nature, the strangely passionate quality of a Pre-Raphaelite hand, like the work of Mr. Rossetti and his friends. Submit thought that, perhaps like this unconventional brotherhood of artists, the creator of these sketches had sought to represent faces in religious epiphany or ecstatic concentration. She lifted one drawing from its case and braced it in the open lid to take a better look. Then she nearly lost the entire lot of them, jerking with such a start that the little drawings ruffled briefly into the air before they settled back down into their black-lined case.

"For the love of God!" she whispered, leaping to get the lamp. As she fumbled with the tinderbox, her hands shook. The surface of the writing desk blazed into light. She spread the pictures—there were an even dozen of them—as best she could under the bright kerosene lamp. She could not believe what she saw.

They were illicit pictures, sketches of naked men and women doing God knew what to each other.

Submit's heart began to pound. She looked up suddenly, as if someone were about to find her with these. Ridiculous. Dinner was an hour away. No one would be down. She could hear activity in the kitchen below, the Griffins talking and preparing the food. Bending over the writing desk, Submit quickly tried to shuffle the pictures back into their box. But the paper was soft and limp. The sketches bowed when she tried to tap them into order. In the end, she had to pick them up and align them one at a time. When she at last got the mess together, latched it into its case, she brought it up to her chest, crossing her arms over it, and turned to lean against the desk. She once again looked around.

No one. Of course. Her heart thumped against the papier-mâché lid. There was no one to see what she held, and no one would intrude. Yet this was an oddly comfortless thought.

For the first time since Henry's death, Submit felt alone.

The only person she might have confided in, Henry, was gone. In fact, it was his doing that she even had this vile, stupid box. What on God's earth had Henry had in mind?

And who, pray tell, was this nasty cousin?

Submit reached and turned out the lamp. The room fell back into darkness, though it wasn't the same. Rain pelted the window, matching the rhythm of her heart. The mullioned pattern of the outside light wavered over chair and desk and carpet, casting itself like a net over Submit herself. She wished she could throw away the wretched art case, pretend it didn't exist, but she couldn't. Even if she took it back to Arnold, let him take over, she couldn't ask him to take over all the questions this impossible little box had opened up.

What had cultured, refined Henry been doing with a box of crudely explicit art?

Submit was not so naive as to think there weren't certain perverse souls who actually fancied such things. But Henry, surely Henry wasn't one of these people. And this cousin . . .

Submit jerked around, turning to grab up her mail from the windowsill, where she'd left it. She tapped through it until she found what she wanted. An envelope with a London address. Yes.

A moment later, as she half-ran down the hall, she called, "Mary! I won't be staying for dinner after all!"

— Chapter 5 —

Across London, Graham sat at a dinner party. All around him, people were talking. They were seated at long tables covered in white linen and set with gleaming silver and goblets of wine that sparkled, burgundy red, through the cuts of crystal. Silver candelabras, set somehow into heaping clusters of orchids, graced all this at intervals. The candlelight made the tables shimmer. The room itself glowed. A steady lambency came from its periphery, from gas piped into wall fixtures. But this modern innovation had yet to reach the ceiling, where thousand-candled chandeliers scattered chips of light—diamonds and prisms—over the room's ceiling and walls. The effect was stunning. The soft light from the tinkling, shifting tiers of candles overhead made everything look warm and pleasant, perfectly beautiful. It should have been a perfect night. But, just as the servants were bringing on the first course, Graham heard the billiard table incident introduced as a topic for conversation, like an added delectable hors d'oeuvre.

"Graham has certainly gotten himself into a little fix," someone said with a laugh.

Graham had been relaxed, one elbow resting on the back of his neighbor's chair as he flirted with her, but upon hearing his name he grew silent and cast his eyes down. Someone responded to the comment, and someone else responded to that. Graham felt the muscles along his shoulder and arm tighten. He put his arm down.

As he listened, the story took on a different tone. Absent the clublike camaraderie of men, it became, "Oh, Graham, you've driven another one mad."

He fidgeted and tried to take this in good humor, but

the underlying assumption of the teasing—that he was somehow involved with the girl—became harder and harder to bear. He spoke up once—"Honestly, I've never met the girl"—which was a mistake; it only seemed to shift the focus.

"Of course you're innocent, love. All gentlemen are innocent when a laundress"—the girl's occupation, it turned out—"wants to rattle their money bags or squeeze their nuptial hand."

The torment continued through French asparagus and roast beef to English pudding and cheese—with Graham growing silently, morosely furious with everyone around him. He told himself he really shouldn't be angry. Only idiots could leap to such wholly false conclusions. But he kept looking at everyone enjoying the joke. There were so many of them, and he couldn't believe they were *all* stupid. He was caught feeling furious and foolish at the same time, without defense.

The whole experience left him with a rolling stomach and a grim mouth. And the keenest desire to be somewhere else.

After the ladies left, he somehow managed to gag down a glass of port. When the gentlemen at last rose to go to the ballroom, Graham nodded and smiled, then slipped out. He headed outside for a terrace he knew would be unpeopled and unlit.

The terrace offered little respite. It was still raining, and the night was pitch black. Graham could barely see his own hands planted before him on a wet marble rail. Over the railing somewhere he knew there was a garden, but seeing it was hopeless. Perfect, he thought. What a perfectly dismal day, right to the end. The night was too terrible to stand out in it. He was too ragged to repair his own self-respect. A seducer of laundresses and, someone had added, housemaids. What could he say in response? It was true that at one time he had found irresistible the charms of a woman on his own upperhouse staff.

Perhaps William was right, Graham thought. He himself was afraid to face up to facts. For a moment, the very thought of listening to William unnerved him. His cousin was certainly not very astute. But perhaps even an idiot could happen upon a little truth. There were so damned many clever people here tonight who seemed to agree with his blasted cousin. Perhaps they were all right. He was nothing more than an overpretty, shallow man inclined to take advantage of women, a raffish stereotype. He certainly knew how to play that role well enough to win applause for it.

Graham had been on the real stage some two hundred times, which was to say he had earned a living as an actor for part of his twentieth and twenty-first years. His had been a brief career and one certainly not long enough to tell if he had an aptitude for acting, but he had never had trouble finding work, which was a kind of praise in itself. He had had an immediate presence for his height, his good looks, his name—all provided a kind of underground notoriety. He never played a large repertoire but rather limited stock parts: foolish lovers, villainous lovers, handsome villains. His looks fit perfectly into the popular concept of the brooding romantic. His background carried the rest. The parts were always upper-class men, and he lent aristocratic characters an unusual credibility. Unlike any other actor on the stage, he *was* a gentleman, so he had no trouble being convincing in that part.

Convincing was all he strove to be tonight. He hoped to convince anyone who looked at him that he was calm and happy, in control of himself. He walked the length of the terrace until he stood in a penumbra of light. This came through high terrace doors that opened into a ballroom beyond. He smoothed his vest, straightened his cuff, and com-

posed as best he could a presentable self with which to step
forth.

With two hands, he thrust open the terrace doors. The
ballroom was brighter than the dining room, a blur of colors and lights that swayed in three-quarter time. Music.
Laughter. Masses of people. The room swirled with waltz-
ing prosperity, with champagned well-being and conspicuous success. It announced in every swoop of the music the
certainty of—everyone would say tomorrow—a brilliant
party. So brilliant, in fact, that after the dark terrace, Graham was left squinting and blinking.

As he stepped forward, the crowd opened up for him. He
broke into it, counterpointing the waltz of the ballroom
with his own military march. Faces turned, spectators of his
one-man parade. Some queued up to stare. Others wanted
to be part of his procession.

"Your lordship."

"Good evening." He talked and smiled congenially with
anyone who addressed him, socializing, bald-faced, with a
grace acquired over years of experience, the confidence of a
man playing an acclaimed role.

As he passed a member of Parliament, the man said,
"Mrs. Schild is looking for you." Two steps later, another fellow repeated the exact sentence, adding, "She has outdone
herself tonight." It was her party; she rented this house in
London.

"Thank you. She will be so pleased that you are enjoying
yourself."

From behind him, someone called, "Happy birthday."

Graham tried to hide his dismay. He had turned
thirty-eight today, but did not wish the fact known. *Age
without wisdom*, he had complained to himself. He had
been so sure, in some distant time ago, that the two were
inseparable. Only after much protesting had he been able

to persuade Rosalyn Schild to make nothing of his birthday, though it had been the original impetus for the
party.

The person behind him, a young man, caught up and
nudged him. "The sign of Gemini."

Graham blinked. He didn't understand.

"The end of May. The sign of the twin stars."

It hit him. The billiard table girl. It was common knowledge she claimed to be carrying twins. He shoved his way
past, nearly flattening a young woman in his path.

Rosalyn Schild came up beside him.

He leaned toward her. "I think all England is here," he
complained.

"I know, isn't it wonderful?" She spoke brightly. "It's going well, don't you think?"

"Beautifully."

Her attention darted over her shoulder. "Don't ruin it.
Where have you been?"

"I'm not ruining anything."

"Please, Gray. I feel so English tonight. Play the English
lord, not the wet blanket." Rosalyn was not English at all.
She was from Philadelphia.

He made a face at her back.

And she swung on him. She put a finger in his chest. A
servant with a tray of glasses stopped into his shoulder
blades. He was pinned against her finger.

"You were completely ungracious at your end of the
table," she said. "Taciturn, glum. You hardly ate. I couldn't
catch your eye. People will think you're quite unhappy."

"I am unhappy."

"They'll think with me."

"It has nothing to do with you. Let's leave together. That
should suit them."

"You know I can't."

He made a mock smile. "Then just a carriage out front."

"God." She rolled her eyes and reached up. She patted his cheek, returning a much more ingenuous smile than his.

He caught her hand, turning his mouth into it, and bit the ball of flesh at the base of her thumb.

Her smile went slack. Her arm relaxed in his. Her fingers curled against his cheek. "Lord," she murmured. He licked the center of her palm—it tasted acrid, the taste of perfume. When he let the hand go, she put it to her breast, staring at him. She wet her lips and smiled again, though a little less certainly. "We'd better dance."

She began to lead him toward the music. Over her shoulder she said, "There's a woman in the reception room. She's been waiting for nearly half an hour. She says she must see you."

"Then why are we going this way?"

"I've been waiting longer." He watched her bare shoulders give a shrug. "I've never seen her before. Her name is Motmarche. Lady Motmarche. Should I have invited her in? She's dressed as a widow."

Graham stopped, puzzled a moment, then redirected himself toward the reception room. Rosalyn Schild managed to scramble back around him, grabbing a handful of watch chains. She stood on tiptoe, her face frowning into his.

"Do you know her?"

He spoke over her head, trying to move her out of the way. "Not really."

"Why is she here?"

"I don't know. She shouldn't be."

He managed to rotate their two positions. They seemed to be inventing their own dance, the back-and-forth movement between them every bit as complex as the turns at the center of the room. The orchestra suddenly stopped. People clapped. He thought he was about to leave Rosalyn behind once more when he was forced to look down. She did not clap. She would not relinquish the watches. He had to take her hands in his and bend each of her fingers individually out of the chains and buttonholes at the bottom of his vest. Then he let out a harried breath. She had clutched two of his fingers into her fist. The orchestra began again.

"It's a Viennese. Listen." It was indeed a fast Viennese waltz. Ever buoyant, she said, "Come dance and spin me round and round till I can't stand. Then just at the end, kiss me. Let's be happy and gay. And romantic."

"I think that wouldn't go over very well."

"It would with me."

"Remember whom you're entertaining."

"Certainly not you."

He sighed. "Rosalyn, I'd just as soon not remind anyone tonight of—anything romantic. Dinner was a bit much for me."

"What? That twit with the twins again? Come now, you can't let people—"

"But I do, apparently. I don't like being the butt of these jokes. Not after suffering the reality of it all day. Be a good girl and understand."

She wrinkled her nose and mouth. "I'm not anyone's good girl."

"No. Thank goodness." He freed his fingers, enveloping her hand in both of his. "Now let me see what this woman wants. Then I'm retiring early. You can wake me when you come to bed." He manufactured something more like a smile, which usually pleased her, but not this time.

"You can't leave. I was counting on you—"

"You are doing wonderfully well on your own. I'm very proud of you. Proud *for* you. It has nothing to do with me, you must believe that. It's your own doing in spite of me, in fact. I'll come back before I retire, for an hour or so to say my good-nights." When she didn't immediately respond to that, he added, "And spin you once around the dance floor, if you'll put up with my clumsiness."

"You're never clumsy."

He touched two fingers, first to his mouth, then to hers.

"But you're a third-rate romantic," she said, then with hardly a pause, "I love you."

He disappointed her again, somewhat perversely this time. "What a lucky man I am."

"Cad."

"A third-rate slander. You should have been in court this morning."

She lifted her skirts, turned, and dropped her eyes over one shoulder. "Well, if you can find me when you return—"

"I'll find you."

"If I'm not in the ballroom, you can check the carriages."

"Now who's the cad?"

"Women can't be."

"Of course they can." He forced her retreating chin around. "I love you, Rosalyn; happy?"

She stuck out her tongue, didn't look happy at all, turned and began to negotiate the masses. Half a dozen people away, she was talking animatedly again. Then she laughed so hard that she had to cover her mouth with her hand, and the laughter still came out noisily. He watched her, but she never looked back. The laughter was not for his benefit, he knew, but for her own. She had a facility for dredging up happiness from her bottommost moments, as though she tapped some hidden spring and up came artesian joy, an unending supply. Without props or prompts—this was a trick he would like to learn.

Rosalyn Schild could have had a foul disposition and still been sought after. She was stunning. Large-boned, buxom, beautiful in an exuberant, unwithholding manner, she was as radiant and full-blown as a blood red rose with every petal bent back. People held their breath when they first saw her. She was wealthy and stylish. Tonight she wore a ma-

genta gown for which there was not a match in the room
(but then she had special access to the new aniline dyes, her
husband reputedly being in textiles). She was as genuinely,
wonderfully, certifiably fresh as anything Graham could
imagine ever coming into his dismally homogeneous life.

Rosalyn was as un-English as a Thanksgiving dinner—
an American feast provided at the expense of an American
husband and sampled somewhat warily by an English elite
interested in such esoterica. She was the novelty of the season, a curiosity with the good fortune of not disappointing
the curious. She proved to be just what the complacent
English mind wanted to believe about Americans. She was a
great Anglophile, impressed into speechlessness by title and
royalty, and—though a bright woman—with no head for
keeping any of it straight. She was naturally polite and
could be deferential to a fault. Thus protocol and English
culture, as she turned them upside down, were generally
kind to her, for she provided amusement without expense
to ego and with such gracious and ingenuous charm that
there was a minimal loss of face to herself. It was tacitly assumed that, had she been born English, she would have
been queen; but being born American she was through no
fault of her own a dunderhead—a gross underassessment
of her abilities, but suitably and soothingly ethnocentric.

To her credit, the dunderhead had produced a shimmering affair much attended by the people she most wanted to
impress. It was the final seal on her English acceptance.

The first of her acceptance had begun with the earl of
Netham, Graham Wessit. He had stumbled onto Rosalyn
nearly five months before; truly stumbled, for he'd been
quite drunk. Sober morning had revealed good instinct—
or else one of those bolts of good luck that occasionally
strikes on behalf of the helpless and innocent, categories to
which Graham could only lay claim when dead drunk. But
instinct or good accident, he was, overnight, paired with

her, and it was not a disagreeable match. Rosalyn had gone on to exceed the most optimistic of expectations. Besides her fine attributes, both social and physical, she was an unfaultably good companion. She was considerate, bright, and affectionate; her sexual attitude, straightforward and satisfying. He liked her. He might, he considered, even love her. In any regard, he enjoyed her company, not only publicly, but privately.

As for Submit Channing-Downes, her mere presence and the fact that Graham was about to meet her gave him the queerest sensation. He remembered William's assessment of her, the opinion he himself had held for so long by default. Plain and drab, William called her. Yes, Graham recalled from that morning, he could see how someone might think that; whatever there was about her that attracted, it was subtle. Dry, William said. Yes, Graham had even gone further. In his own mind, he realized, he had relegated her to a composite of the two or three other women he had met in Henry's house. He had made of her either a woman who spoke offhand in sage, witty remarks or else a silent soul who stared out over the tops of eyeglasses from behind large, exophthalmic eyes as she wrote letter upon letter to all manner of people. She would be the daughter of some don or beadle. Or poet. Wrong, all wrong, Graham thought now. None of these women would have come here to find him tonight. He was delighted that reality had proved imagination to be just that—pure, groundless, self-indulgent fantasy. Having had a glimpse of the real woman this morning, he anticipated liking her tonight.

This and a great many other pettinesses rushed about through Graham's thoughts, like so many disturbed moths and spiders; dust on old notions being brought out to air. Henry was dead. Nothing drove this home so tangibly as the fact of receiving his wife.

Graham was madly revising the marchioness of Motmarche to make her young, attractive, plausible, when, as he rounded the archway, he was confronted with the quarter profile of a woman he only marginally recognized. It had to be Henry's wife, for she was alone in the reception room and covered—buried—from head to foot in black. He hesitated, found himself wary, looking for a sign, even a small corroboration that this was the woman he had seen outside Tate's. She seemed different. The very way she was standing gave him pause. Far from open, her arms were clutching something to her chest, a seeming prop of this new mood. It looked to be a flat box, perhaps the flat box from that morning. She hugged it in front of her, in the posture of someone terribly cold. Or else straitjacketed.

It was this stiff, constrained back he came up on. Black taffeta stretched taut over moiré shoulder blades. She was staring at a huge painting that hung in the reception hall. The picture ran many feet above her head. It was a full-length portrait; Graham did not know of whom, only that it was kept for its ornateness. Rich colors, gilt-framed, and draped with heavy aging fabric. At the sound of Graham's steps, she tried to drag her eyes away, but clearly this was difficult. Her eyes slid down the drapery and along the room, pulling reluctantly over the items that lined its walls. Picture, chair, picture, settee, picture, small table, vitrine. Until her objectivity rested on Graham.

He was brought up short. She was so unexplainably different from anything he had imagined.

She was small and thin, though not what he would have called bony, and her eyes were not the color of plums. They were merely blue. Her thick, curly hair was pale, a kind of colorless blond. It was also damp—she wore no bonnet. A fine mist of droplets had sifted into the wayward bits of hair that were trying to escape a tight chignon. Her skin looked blanched beneath a speckling of faint freckles that were more numerous across her nose. The most outstanding thing about her was that she looked very, very young, not in her thirties but in her twenties. Graham was surprised. He had assumed she would be closer to his own age.

"Lady Motmarche? Netham," he introduced himself with a nod. Then his familiar name, "Graham Wessit," as an act of cordiality to a cousin, an interesting cousin. "May I be of service to you?"

The little marchioness responded to his politeness with some inanity of her own. They nodded through introductions. Her voice was soft, controlled, strangely sweet. The sound of it was the nicest thing about her.

Graham dropped his eyes down the woman, as if there were something he might have missed. There wasn't very much to her. She was all dress, yards and yards of prim, proper widowhood.

It was then that he recognized what she was holding.

Graham blinked. The room shifted. Air seemed to push up against him rapidly all at once, as if a railway train had come out of a tunnel with him standing squarely in the middle of its tracks. Like an idiot, he could do nothing but stare.

There, cradled in a pair of narrow black arms, was something he hadn't seen in twenty years. And something he could have happily gone another twenty without. Henry's widow was holding an art case known sometimes by the underground name of Pandetti's Orchids and sometimes by the more bluntly crude double entendre: The little widow held Pandetti's Box.

— Chapter 6 —

Submit found the earl of Netham to be almost a walking corollary to the box: entirely too good-looking, suspiciously decorated; a glossy exterior.

He was tall, loose-limbed, broad-shouldered. His clothes were fussy and pretentious, his coloring dark. He had black hair and black eyes that spoke of Moorish blood from the century when English titles were earned in Aquitaine. His eyes were set deep beneath a sharply defined brow, the sort of facial architecture that invited dark, dramatic circles under stress—there were traces of these now. The eyes themselves were large and heavy-lidded. They turned down at the outside edges at a melancholy angle: beautiful, romantic eyes.

They were the sort of eyes—he was the sort of man—over which women could make asses of themselves.

Submit spoke her apologies and explanations with a kind of aloofness from this fact. "So sorry to disturb you at this hour ... difficult to find you ... on my way out of town. ... My husband, Lord Motmarche, left you a small bequest, which I have brought and would like to discuss ..."

When she produced the box, the man smiled politely and stepped back from it. "What is this?" he asked.

"I've just explained. The marquess of Motmarche left the case and its contents to you in his will." She watched for some further reaction.

He was stoic. "No, thank you."

"No, thank you?"

"I don't want it."

Submit let the box sink into her skirts. In the room beyond, music swelled for a moment above the sociable noise of a crowd talking, drinking, laughing. In the empty entrance room, Submit had to speak quietly so her voice wouldn't echo. "I don't understand," she said.

He made a brief, perfunctory smile. "I can't take it, though I appreciate that you've gone out of your way to bring it to me. I'm sorry."

Now what? Submit had known it would be difficult to ask a stranger what he knew about Henry and the contents of this box. She had never imagined she could not get the stranger—ostensibly the owner of the box—even to look at it.

Submit glanced down at the burden she still held in her hand. "I have been told," she said, "that you and Henry were not on the best of terms, but surely—"

"Henry and I were on no terms at all. I haven't seen him since I was nineteen. Exactly half a lifetime ago."

More puzzling. She said, "But when you were ill three years ago, he visited—"

The man made a snort of disbelief. "If he did, I was unconscious at the time."

Submit felt completely turned around. She reached for the only explanation she could think of: "You know what's in it," she said flatly.

He shrugged. "Poison. Something vile. If Henry left me anything, it would be something despicable, insulting." He looked at her fully and heaved a huge sigh. "I'm sorry. I have no idea how you came to be named for this errand, madam, but let me assure you, you have been used for something Henry never had the nerve to do when he was alive."

Submit's back straightened. "Whatever my husband left you, I'm sure he had a perfectly justified reason—"

"Malice." The shadowed eyes fixed on her, looking sadly,

meanly convinced. "Lady Motmarche, I hope you will not consider me too rude when I tell you I simply cannot accept that box or anything else from Henry Channing-Downes. I prefer to remain after his death just as I was during his life: forgotten. I'm sorry your late-night trip here was for nothing. Now, may I get you a carriage, or would you prefer to come in for a while?"

"Perhaps I haven't explained well," she began again. "I don't know what to do with it if you don't take it. This is part of the legal settlement—"

"Keep it. I make you a legal gift of it."

"But you have to take it—"

"Why? I can't be compelled to take a gift."

"Why would you refuse it?" When he didn't answer, she asked, "Do you know what's in it?"

There was a long pause before he finally committed himself to a direct response. "No." He looked at her levelly. "Lady Motmarche, I am trying to spare us both embarrassing explanations. I could never predict what Henry might do or want to do to me from one moment to the next. All I know is that, for my own peace of mind, I have steadfastly refused to have anything to do with Henry's designs on me since I was nineteen years old. I apologize if that is offensive to you. My refusal honestly has nothing to do with you."

"Except that I can't understand it. Why would anyone be so impossible as to refuse Henry's attempt to make a last contact, especially after so many years? If you don't even know what's in it—"

"I don't care what's in it." His voice rose slightly. The riveting eyes narrowed. "It could be filled with thousand-pound notes on the Bank of England. It doesn't matter." He left a measured pause, then lowered his voice, a trick that made his height and sharp good looks a little menacing for a moment. "Knowing Henry, however, and how we felt about each other, it is more likely a box full of adders. I should be very careful, if I were you, about opening it."

His eyes shifted away from her. Submit found herself speaking to the side of his face. He watched the dancers through the archway in the ballroom. "Henry never did anything to anyone," she insisted, "that wasn't based on the best of motives—"

He answered this with a perfect, blatant non sequitur. "How lucky you are to be leaving London." He didn't even look at her. "It's been an ugly May."

"Pardon me?"

"London. You said you were leaving. Where are you going from here?"

Submit blinked. She wanted to smile at the bluntness—the rudeness—with which he had dropped the topic of concern to her. "I, ah—there's an inn at Morrow Fields. I've hired a driver, who's waiting outside."

"Ah. How nice. Just far enough to be rural." His thumb absently stroked his vest over the outline of a watch—he was wearing about ten of them—as if he could tell time in this manner. "And close enough to make by midnight. Too bad the weather isn't better for travel."

The traditional English conversational refuge: the weather. The rain outside on the stoop whipped up to a light patter suddenly, as if to give his absurd digression some validity. Submit would have none of it. "Well, yes," she said, "and I had rather a devil of a time getting here. Lord Netham—"

"Please. You may call me Graham, if you like. We're cousins."

Again, she fought an urge to smile in disbelief. She was taken aback by his familiarity, then completely undone. "Look here—" she said, and he did.

He turned to her, smiling warmly and directly into her eyes. Briefly, he touched her shoulder. For one quick second, there were all the vibrations of sincerity, friendliness, an incredible personal charm. Where he touched her, chills— surprising, involuntary—ran down her arm. She drew the case to her chest again. Then his coffee-black eyes lifted away, above her head. She realized he was scanning the entrance room, looking for someone, anyone he might honestly want to talk to.

"Excuse me," he said. "I'll send someone to fetch your coat."

Submit was staggered, amused, confounded. To keep him from going, she had to lay a hand on his arm. "No," she said. "And I think you should take this. Henry would want you to."

"Henry?" He glanced down. At the mention of the name again, his expression soured. He frowned.

"Henry Channing-Downes. Your guardian. My husband."

"Yes, of course. You have my condolences, madam." There was a pause before he added, "For losing him, that is."

She wasn't very inclined to thank him. Submit could not remember when she had had a more difficult or perplexing conversation. She blundered along for a few phrases more, speaking of Henry briefly, formally, holding the man's arm. Then she happened to catch a look at the box, still in her hand. It occurred to her suddenly that anyone this evasive, this desperate to get free, knew what the box contained. Her smile from a moment ago broke fully onto her face.

Submit didn't move, made no further offer of the case, asked no further questions. She let a silence grow between them, standing on the knowledge that Graham Wessit was acquainted with—had perhaps even enjoyed—a boxful of embarrassing pictures.

Oddly, it was her silence that Graham finally heard. He

was quietly stewing over Henry, looking for a way to dismiss the mention of him. In fact, he was looking about the room, looking for an excuse to dismiss this disappointing woman altogether, when out the corner of his eye he saw her smile. His inattention had cost him any hint as to why.

But he could not have missed the effect. She had small teeth and, he noticed, a smaller jaw—two top front teeth overlapped in order to make room for the rest. Oddly, this parting and showing of teeth was so strongly feminine that he was brought up short. A knowing smile peered through a diffident complexion. Nothing totaled. The sum of her parts should have been unremarkable, vulnerable, almost childlike. Yet she demonstrated an elemental duplicity, the way street children can seem canny. Then another wrong adjective came to mind in describing her. Nubile. And Henry, old Henry, was not dismissed. Graham found himself trying to tally her approximate age twelve years ago. Fourteen? Fifteen? Sixteen at the outside. Henry would have been fifty-nine. Graham's skin prickled.

The widow let go of his arm as she picked up the conversation again with some stiff, conventional nonsense. But he was just as glad to let her talk; he didn't know what to say, what to think.

The dead guardian seemed to be lurking. Graham started to feel old sensations. His childhood and adolescence clung to the widow in wisps, as if she'd just climbed through an old trunk of his youth. Cobwebs seemed to dangle from her, more vital than the memory of specific events. She triggered the reliving with just a word, an intonation, of inchoate emotions he knew were familiar but couldn't identify. He began to realize Henry Channing-Downes was in every sentence she uttered. Out of context. Out of time. Out of the grave. She had his vocabulary, his inflection, his favorite idioms. Only the peculiar femininity was hers, unshadowed. The shy, imbricate smile—no more than a social mechanism, but ticklishly pleasing, as if it ran lightly over his skin. Then gone.

It dawned on him suddenly that he was staring. He quickly looked away. There was a sense of nothing being where he'd put it. He was lost in the conversation. It would have been difficult to explain that he was bored with it on one level and incapacitated by it on another.

There was an intrusion of noise and rain and wind. Half a dozen people came in the front door, shaking, stomping, dripping. A nervous laugh echoed from their midst, more chatter of weather, exclamations of relief to be out of it. Servants came. The routine of arrival broke into the private conversation. The little catch of tension was allowed to dissipate into the noise of the others. With merry murmurs the newcomers shed their wet clothes and warmed to the atmosphere of the dry, bright house.

Graham lowered his voice and came inches closer to her. "William and I speak regularly," he said. "One hardly knows what to believe of all he says these days, but I know his suit was intended to put you out of a house." He was so puzzled by this woman. He meant to make amends. "If you're in need of a place to stay, I have a flat on Haymoore Street."

Her shoulders, face, and eyes all raised together a fraction, suggesting mild surprise.

He pressed the matter. "If you're in dire straits—"

"Thank you, but I couldn't even consider such an offer."

"I hope you are not refusing for fear of imposing—" It occurred to Graham to add, "I assure you I am not making a suggestive proposition."

He got a faint smile from her. A member of the other party had begun to sing a pub song. "The mucking rain, We may as well drink." Trying to be serious in the midst of this was beginning to take on a furtive quality, becoming a collusion between himself and the widow.

"I'd never think that." Her voice was hushed.

Except that was exactly what she was thinking, he was sure; that he wouldn't offer a woman help honestly. He brushed the palm of his hand down his ornate vest. "You shouldn't believe everything William tells you," he said.

Her smile broadened, as if she were easily smart enough to know this, and to know why he would suggest it. "He has a great deal of specific criticism for you, doesn't he?"

"You should hear what he calls you."

She paused to put the tip of her tongue against the compacted teeth. She eyed him for a moment, then looked away to watch the other group in the room. A laugh from that quarter punctuated their own silence.

Graham spoke to the side of her face, the clean, juvenescent profile. "Stay in the flat. It's staffed anyway. It's nothing in the way of trouble to me."

"Why?"

"Mud in William's eye, if nothing else."

"I haven't the time or patience to be vindictive," she said, implying he shouldn't, either.

The implication, even the syntax, were Henry Channing-Downes's. One of Henry's little maxims—or a good imitation, since Graham had long forgotten the specifics—on Guarding Good Character. Again the hair on the back of his neck stood up. "There are many things," he said, "I wish I could have done for your husband. But we were on such bad terms. Let this—"

She interrupted. "If you really want to do something for me—or Henry—explain what you know about this box."

He stared at her, muzzled by his own sharp resentment that she had circled back in this direction. He couldn't decide if he liked or hated this woman.

Then he didn't get a chance to decide. Rosalyn Schild glided into the room. She immediately became its center.

She must have been summoned on behalf of the late guests, for she greeted them directly. Smiles. Good-evenings. Bussed cheeks. Squeezed hands. A beguiling enthusiasm that jumped social barriers.

Between Graham and the widow, a tangible barrier materialized. The black lacquered box. "Here. Take it, or I'm leaving it." She nodded her head to indicate a little table beside them as she held the box out. "It's yours. You can burn it, toss it, whatever you'd like."

She went to set the box down. Instinctively he grabbed it, taking a firm hold.

Wide, shallow, shiny. Raised brush strokes of white, pink, and rose on black. He nearly gagged at the concrete feel of this apparition. He pulled at the box. But oddly it stayed in the air. He felt the paper walls of it giving between his thumb and palm, collapsing. He realized two other hands had an untentative hold. The widow had not let go. And Rosalyn's hand had a delicate but firm grasp of the other side—she was adjusting the box down an inch to see the other woman's face.

"Hello." Rosalyn surveyed the widow a moment, then smiled. She began to provide introductions. Her hand fell away, then the widow's. Graham put the box behind his back, into both his hands.

The just-arrived group congregated around Rosalyn and himself. She introduced him to a Member of Parliament he already knew, saying every word of his own full title as if printing it on a formal announcement card. "And you know, of course, the Right Honorable the Earl of Netham."

Graham shifted his weight to his other foot as he fidgeted with the box behind his back. He was barely following the conversation when he saw Rosalyn duck around and between them, like a game of London Bridge. There was a tugging on the box at his back. His grip tightened.

He whispered beneath the conversation to her, "What are you doing?"

Though the M.P. was expounding on something, the whispering and Rosalyn began to draw interest.

She made a face and laughed. People turned. "What are you hiding?"

Even the M.P. was willing to concede to her change of topic.

"What is this?" Rosalyn had decided to make a show of it. "A present? Let me see."

She pulled at the case while Graham attempted to maintain it without appearing too interested in doing so. A minor tug-of-war ensued. The more he defended, the more certainly she would have it.

"Rosalyn—" He tried to get a warning off to her as he gave up the box.

But she only answered by glancing first at him, then—making sure he saw—at the widow. She connected them with a mischievous look of mock jealousy. Graham was silently appalled. He stared steadfastly back at Rosalyn Schild, admonishing her in all seriousness not to open the box. He threw a look to the widow; it was her fault, so she might at least help. Then worse. When he looked back at Rosalyn, her smile had become silly—half cross, half baffled, pasted onto her face as if she had suddenly taken her own teasing too seriously.

She drew her lips together, not very attractively, and began to fiddle with the case's latch.

He turned away and put his hands behind him again. He swallowed, took a breath, then took another. Breathing seemed to be something he had to do consciously or he was going to pass out. He became unsteady. Then he lost track of every idea, notion, and person around him: of all but the mortifying notion of being associated with this box, the disaster that was about to open in his face again.

"Are you all right, Graham?" Rosalyn touched his arm.

He turned partly around, like a man coming out of a stupor or coma. In the space of what seemed like seconds, something important had changed.

Rosalyn was talking to the widow. ". . . you mustn't," she was saying, "muck out into the rain all the way to that godforsaken posting house. I have plenty of room." She turned back to Graham. "Are you all right? You're absolutely green." In a softer voice, she added, "Lady Motmarche explained. I didn't realize your guardian had died. I'm so sorry, dear." She leaned closer to whisper, "I didn't know it was his."

Graham was at a complete loss. He looked at Submit Channing-Downes. She was unmoving, expressionless, and inexplicably in possession of the papier-mâché case again. It was closed, safely latched tight.

Rosalyn, he realized, had given up her pursuit of his hidden feelings, having settled on some others: shock and grief. She treaded lightly with him now, making herself a buffer again between him and everyone else. He could hear her, in hushed tones, quietly staking him out, hers to understand. ". . . since the loss of his cousin . . . has come so obviously close to the bone. . . ."

She was trundling everyone out of the room, while moving the widow into the house. "Fipps, see that Lady Motmarche's things are unloaded from the carriage."

To this purpose, the double doors to the outside were swung open. A crisp gale swirled rain in, lifting all the ladies' skirts about. Chaos. Submit Channing-Downes stood motionless in this, one hand held against her skirt, the other arm loosely wrapped around the retrieved box. She was faced away from Graham in profile, steady against the wind, the only fixed point in the commotion besides himself. It was at this moment that the night air suddenly braced him with clarity. He understood something, a small reason for the peculiar affinity he felt for the widow. She, as only himself, had no curiosity for the contents of the box: As sure as there were plagues and troubles in the world, she had already opened it.

— Chapter 7 —

Submit awoke to the sound of laughter. Somewhere beyond her bed, a woman with a lovely voice was laughing uncontrollably. The sound was sweet and musical, like distant, pealing bells. She rolled over. The sheets felt coarse, stiff. They smelled like sun, the outdoors, flowers—lavender. She frowned and rose up on one elbow. She didn't recognize the room.

The laughter came again. "Oh, Graham," someone said outside.

Submit realized why her surroundings were unfamiliar. She had only seen this room by lamplight, when Mrs. Schild's housekeeper had escorted her here. And she'd been so tired, she hadn't seen the bed at all. Last night she had just shrugged out of her dress into her nightclothes, then climbed in.

She tried to climb out now, but the bed was very high. She missed the stepstool as she slid down. Her nightgown rode all the way up the backs of her thighs. Her bare feet plunked onto a rough wood floor that hadn't seen wax in an age. She padded across to her bag.

The portmanteau she had grabbed in haste as she had raced from the boardinghouse last night was now under a bench by the window. She'd dragged it across London to the earl of Netham's house, only to find his house—an ancient monster of a building—locked and dark. It was by chance that a servant had happened to come from around the side to tell her that if it was important she could find the earl at a party another cab ride away. She had lugged the bag back into the cab, then left the driver waiting with it for more than an hour while she'd waited to speak with a man who, it would eventually become clear, was not going to say anything of substance at all.

So much for immediate remedy, for satisfying concern and horror and incredulous curiosity all at once. This cousin of Henry's raised more questions than he answered, leaving her rainy, nocturnal sojourn to yield only two certainties: Graham Wessit knew unquestionably what was in the box, and what was there bothered him as much, or more, than it did her. Submit remained baffled by the box, the man it was intended for, and Henry's connection to any of this.

She had never witnessed a house so bright and full of people as this house last night. It was a planet away from the sedate gatherings in Cambridgeshire. People had carried on till well past two in the morning, the real diehards taking over then. Party Charlies. Ineffectual young upper-class men who distinguished themselves chiefly by being fashionably extroverted, exceedingly foolish, and generally loud. Several such young men had thrown two young women—equally enthusiastic, it seemed—into the fountain out back at about two-thirty this morning; she had heard them outside. Such high-toned friends Graham Wessit had.

Submit shoved the black lacquered case aside as she slid her bag out. She opened it and rummaged through, retrieving her hairbrush. After unweaving her hair from its haphazard braid, she rose and began walking around the room again, vigorously brushing thick hair that ran a foot past her waist.

The room, though small, was quite satisfactory. Submit knew from her climb up the stairs last night that it was near the attic, the last guest room before a ladder of stairs that led to the servants' quarters. She looked around. There was a single bed, a narrow wardrobe, and a small table barely large enough to accommodate a chipped pitcher and basin.

Save the bench under the window, these were the room's only furnishings. It didn't surprise or disappoint her, however, that her accommodations were a little less than what she was used to. What surprised her was that she should have accommodations at all.

Submit bent over at the waist to brush her hair from the back. Its ends touched her toes. Each day it took half an hour to get a brush through this hair, to make it smooth enough to fix into a chignon. Her hair was not unattractive; it was thick and curly. But it had too much thickness and the wrong kind of curl for her tastes—she unleashed every morning an avalanche of wild springs. Relatively satisfied with her brushing, Submit threw her head back. She was standing, trying to tame her hair into a mass she could grasp with both hands, when another sound, one she couldn't identify, came from outside.

The room had a single window over the bench. It was small and round and open a crack. Through this opening, she heard a crisp, irregular click. She listened for a moment, her hands in the air.

She wandered toward the window, then leaned on the bench with one knee as she looked out, nudging the window sash out with her elbow while she twisted her hair. The window let in bright sun, about nine inches in diameter of it, and a clear view. On a terrace, about forty feet below, Graham Wessit was having his hair cut.

She could only see the back of his head, but there was no mistaking who it was. The earl's barber was trimming around the earl's ears, trimming dark hair as glossy as lutestring silk—she owned ribbons that shiny. Submit managed to fix her own hair into a wad at the nape of her neck, then realized she had no pins.

She found new ones in her bag. The light, feminine laughter came through the window again. It belonged to Rosalyn Schild, who was also on the terrace below. Submit rose, sticking pins in her hair, and looked out the window. Mrs. Schild was eating at a table set with what looked like cakes, sausage, and fruit. Another man sat with her, someone Submit didn't know. He watched the lovely Mrs. Schild, while the woman didn't give him so much as a glance.

Submit watched the stranger steal a piece of muffin; Mrs. Schild didn't notice. This man, like the hostess and earl, was very well dressed. He was fair, a perfect example of Anglo-Saxon good looks. There these three beautiful people sat, a huge tree overhead waving spots of sunlight over them, the terrace, and the lawn. It was hard to have eyes and not enjoy them from a distance. Though judging by the glances and postures and stolen looks, not to mention the stolen bits of food—Rosalyn Schild poked the man's hand with her fork when he went after another piece of cake—Submit was just as glad not to enjoy them up close. London society, with its pecking and pinching, just wasn't her sort.

Submit bent to put her brush back, then a sound drew her up again. Graham Wessit was laughing. He had a deep, genuine laugh, the sort that made a person stand still and look at him. He lifted a plate she hadn't seen and braced it on his knee. The other two smiled. Even the barber laughed at whatever Netham was saying, his scissors in the air, while the earl leaned forward to take a bite of something. Toast and jam. Uck. Submit made a face. How did he keep the cut bits of hair off the jam? She shook her head, smiling.

Submit scrubbed her face and put on a fresh dress, her only vanity being a great many buttons. Her black dress buttoned from her waist, up her throat, to her chin with small buttons made of cut jet. She looked in the mirror. Neat, clean, no foolishness; substantive. She felt perfectly prepared to go down and ask the earl if she might talk to him briefly alone. For one second more, she stared into the mirror.

What was it she wanted? There was a small, distressed

voice in her head now, growing stronger. It said Henry had hidden things from her. Yet she still could not believe he'd hidden a secret, salacious life, a life of onanism or worse. Some men were the sort to relish private vice. Others simply were not. What she wanted, she supposed, was to hear Graham Wessit say, yes, he himself had a small collection of boudoir art. (He would be a little embarrassed, a little uneasy about admitting this.) He was something of an erotologist, a very interesting area of study, this. (He wouldn't admit to actually drooling over the pictures.) Henry, the earl would say, left these as a kindness to his former ward, knowing the earl had an interest in such things. These were especially good examples of the more graceful erotica, aimed at an audience with artistic sensibilities. . . .

She longed to hear an intelligent reason for Henry's keeping then bequeathing this box. It was more than mere convenience that had made her stay here last night; it was more than mere duty: She very much needed a good answer to the mystery of Henry's—no, Netham's—black box.

Down a corridor then around, Submit worked her way toward the center of the house. Mrs. Schild's London residence was built for entertaining. The ballroom downstairs had such a high ceiling that for three floors nothing but corridors wrapped around it. Tiny guest rooms were tucked along these, so that Submit walked along the outside of the building looking out on neat, tended gardens, the terrace and fountain in back. The master living quarters lay over the dining room, entry room, and front parlor. This complicated the maze and slowly distracted Submit. As she wove her way through hallways and stairwells, she became more or less pleasantly involved in the process of trying to map the house.

On the last set of stairs, the sight of Graham Wessit coming into the central entry room below stopped her. He was walking backward, laughing, speaking to the people outside, while his hands reached behind him for the knobs of the double terrace doors. For a moment, he stood in a wedge of sunlight, a kind of halo outlining him, casting his shadow backward into the room along the floor. Then he closed the doors, turned around, and stopped dead. Submit stood on the last step of the staircase. Over the banister she faced the same man as last night, ridiculously handsome, conspicuously decorated to emphasize the fact. Something about him set her teeth on edge. There was an aggression to the way he dressed, as if he wanted not merely to bowl a person over but knock her down with his good looks.

"Well," he said. Conversation chattered on the other side of lace curtains and glass doors. Inside, the room had grown shady and still. "Aren't you the quiet one."

"May I speak to you for a moment?"

He came toward her, his watch chains jangling against buttons and fobs, his heels marking this sound off like measures of music, a little symphony of rococo taste. Without breaking rhythm, he said, "I have to get something. They're waiting for me outside." He made a kind of graceful pivot as he went past her, walking backward again. "I'm sorry."

His contrition lasted for less than a second, the space of a quick, brilliant smile. He turned around and kept going.

"Wait."

He glanced over his shoulder.

"I want to talk to you about the box."

"Ah, the box." He nodded soberly but didn't break stride.

"It will only take a second."

The smile over his shoulder this time seemed wry. "All right. You have a second." He hesitated for exactly that much time, then headed into the dining room.

Submit followed, trying to hold the distance he was putting between them. Her hooped skirt had begun to swing and wobble. She grabbed up the sides of her dress in handfuls.

The dinner tables from the night before had been stripped and pushed into the center of the room, while chairs had been stacked along the walls. "I—ah—" She frowned. With a push of his arm, he leaped a table, while she was having to thread and steer her way through them. He headed toward a passageway that would lead to the servants' hall downstairs.

At the doorway, he paused. "Sorry." He held out his hands, a man helpless against demanding, impatient friends. "They really are waiting for me." For an instant more, he looked at her. Again she faced his smile, aware of how charming, social, and practiced it was. Then, surprisingly, she faced something else. There seemed a nuance to this smile, a faint irony, as if there were a subtext to this whole silly chase. Submit felt a warm fluster rise into her face as she watched him disappear from sight.

What in the world? she thought. She was left standing among the tables, feeling blank and stupid and, as she looked around, trapped. Her skirts were pressed into a contorted shape. From all sides, she was at least three tables away from any straight path back. With a deep sigh, she began to work her way out of the dining room's network of furniture. She would wait with the others outside.

On the terrace, two men and another woman had joined Mrs. Schild and the gentleman. A great many people from the evening before had spent the night. Submit became a quiet part of the group as they congregated at one end of the terrace. She gravitated to their periphery, looking down over a railing to a lawn and fountain, the fountain graced by a few too many cherubs. Otherwise, the back garden was pleasantly simple, green grass partitioned by borders of flowers, colorfully geometric. Submit was enjoying this view, the warmth of sun filtering through sparse branches overhead, and the generally undemanding company, when she heard Graham

Wessit come out again. He had a distinctive way of moving, she realized, a quick, athletic gait that seemed at odds with a man so tall.

A half dozen more people followed him. He had brought with him a small chunk of silvery metal and a file. As he squatted in the middle of the terrace, Submit too was drawn. Everyone clustered around.

Graham Wessit was filing powdery shavings onto the terrace's marble floor. Submit bent over, observing, pressing her hands onto her knees.

"What is it?" she asked.

Others murmured answers, but nothing very specific. Rosalyn was giggly. "It's stuff, he says, that explodes if you make it powdery and set a match to it."

Submit was a little alarmed, though everyone else seemed enthralled. The rasp of metal on metal held each person's attention.

"Where did you get it?" someone asked.

"A chemist." The earl teased the American woman. "A 'pharmacist' if you speak Philadelphia English."

Submit straightened up. "It's magnesium."

Fireworks. The publication of Mortimer's *Manual of Pyrotechny* had been greeted with great interest a year and a half ago. It was a study of the ancient Chinese secrets of exploding light displays, which London society—the queen herself—considered high entertainment.

The earl looked at her a moment, putting a brief pause in the rhythm of his task.

She frowned. "You'll hardly see it in the sunlight. And it's dangerous. It pops."

He tilted his head at her again, seeming more amused than forewarned by her pertinent information. He reached into his pocket and pulled out a box of matches.

Submit stepped back. "That's not very smart," she warned.

"Ah, is that what you're doing?" He smiled up at her. "Trying to be smart?"

"No—" She changed her mind. "Yes. Is there something wrong with that?"

"It can be a terrible hindrance to simply having a good time."

He struck a match and threw it onto the pile of silvery powder. It made more light than she'd imagined, a rather nice *whfft* and a white burst accompanied by several sharp snaps.

"Ahh!" The earl jumped back, quickly brushing off cinders.

As Submit watched him examine a neat hole in his trousers, a little jolt of satisfaction ran through her. It was surprisingly sharp. The fancy-pants know-it-all, she thought. A novice had no business fooling with fireworks, and they remained dangerous even if one knew very well the chemistry and mechanics involved. Netham should have stuck to the properties of gold, how gravity draped it from watch pocket to watch pocket on a glittering vest.

Feeling as though she'd won something, she repeated, "I'd like to speak with you. Could I do so now?"

He threw her a look of exasperation, though for a moment there seemed a hint of humor in his expression. "No," he said emphatically and smiled, as truculent and rational as a two-year-old. He was on the move again, heading toward the far terrace steps at the end of the house.

"Where are you going?" Submit had to walk quickly, or she was going to lose him again.

"To get more magnesium." Between statuary and stone urns, he began down the steps, taking them in leaps, two at a time.

"More? Aren't you finished ruining your clothes?"

At the bottom of the steps, he glanced down. He picked

at something on his pant leg, inspecting the damage now with what seemed like fastidious concern. "You think I've ruined my trousers?"

"Without doubt."

But when he turned, he had a smile that was thoroughly unabashed. "And such a dandy as myself," he said, "should be aghast at that."

The humor, creased deeply into a wide smile, took her by surprise—as did something else. There was an astuteness in his face, an awareness that said he might not be quite so easily summed up as she'd first thought.

She was left standing halfway down the stairs, perplexed, trying to puzzle him out. "I'm sorry," she said.

This held him there a moment, interested in her apology, though not impressed.

She added, "I'm sorry if I've treated you like some sort of dandiprat."

"I am a dandiprat." He cocked his head and leaned his arm on the plinth beneath a stone urn. "Why do you think you're so damned smart?"

She blinked. "I don't."

"Why do you think I'm not?"

She laughed a little nervously. She was beginning to feel giddy, like someone turned upside down. "All right. You're a *clever* dandiprat." He liked that better; so much so, in fact, she couldn't resist adding, "Still, you don't know much about magnesium."

"Mag-what? Those big words confuse me."

"Mag-NEEZ—" She realized he'd said it a few moments before and stopped.

He laughed, shaking his head at her. "I make my own fireworks. From copper and niter." He shrugged. "I've used other things, lately magnesium, depending on what color I want. I know a great deal about magnesium. I'd just prefer to brush off the sparks rather than miss them close up." His smile broadened into something strangely uninhibited. "I rather like it, in fact, when they explode all over me."

"How very dangerous."

"It's thrilling actually. It doesn't hurt."

All she could say was, "I'd bet it takes a toll on your clothes, though."

He began walking, backward again, along the path that ran against the house. He was still looking at her when he said, "Nothing, I'd bet, compared to the toll your caution takes on your sparks." He turned out of sight.

Submit felt confused for a moment, then turned around and felt an unreasonable embarrassment.

Rosalyn Schild was standing at the top of the stairs. She did not look happy, and beyond her stood a curiously quiet little crowd.

— Chapter 8 —

Submit found Graham Wessit to be paradoxically elusive in this house. He was either everywhere, marching right into the center of things, or nowhere in sight. By early afternoon, she had still not spoken to him about the box; she could not even find him. Finally, in a front corridor, she stopped a servant to ask if he knew where the man was.

"Why, he's gone home, madam."

"Home?" This possibility hadn't occurred to her. She sank onto a little stuffed bench in the hall. Which home? she wondered. Home to the house in Belgravia or home to the flat on Haymoore Street or, she wondered, was the family house in Netham itself "home"? She was right back where she had started last night.

"He'll return, I assure you, madam," the servant told her.

Yes, she thought, he probably would. All the same, she felt a little irritated and just plain tired of the whole game. If he had been *trying*, Henry's cousin could not have made asking about the box more difficult.

Of course, Graham *was* trying.

In the aftermath of last night, he had developed a kind of resentful gratitude toward Submit Channing-Downes. The excuses she'd made for him over the box, her repossession of it without so much as a word, were favors he both appreciated very much and minded in the extreme—unsought favors badly needed, which he wouldn't, on a bet, repay in kind. If Henry's widow expected any sort of discussion to ensue over that stupid box, she had another think coming.

Cheerful in this knowledge, Graham bounded through the side carriage entrance of his London house, past fluted alabaster columns and up spiral marble stairs. His shoes tapped and echoed throughout the round, wide staircham- ber, a tattoo that rose up, around, and above him, spiraling with the stairs toward his private rooms.

"John," he called, his voice preceding him up three wind- ing flights. High above him, he saw the man's head pop over the railing. "Draw me a bath! I want to be gone again in an hour!"

Graham was in fine spirits. He looked forward to a change of clothes, then a day of pure fun. He had come home to pick up more magnesium by the bagful. He might even bring back some of the other components of his fire- works. In his shed behind his London house, he had bags of gunpowder, niter, copper sulfide, magnesium, barium ni- trate, sulfur, and more. He knew how to build green stars and skyrockets and tourbillions; there was hardly a known fire display he couldn't make, and he could extemporize new ones offhand. He always laughed when he talked about this. "One of my many useful accomplishments." The gen- eral uselessness of this knowledge, however, didn't stop him from enjoying it—particularly when other people became enthusiastic and wanted to see more, as they had at Ros- alyn's today.

At the top of the staircase, John handed him his mail.

"Thank you. Is there hot water?"

"I lit the coal half an hour ago."

"Good fellow."

His man already had hold of the top of Graham's coat, lifting it off his shoulders. Graham shrugged out of the arms as he walked, alternating his hold on the mail. He un- did his own neckcloth and top shirt buttons, discarding be- hind him his tie and shirt collar. His manservant followed along, gathering items in his arms.

Graham handed back an empty envelope. His mail con- sisted of a bill for twenty-five teapots, two quid each, silver-plate, a bill from the plumber who'd converted his dressing room to a bath, and a letter from Claire, Graham's daughter.

Graham had two children, Charles and Claire. Both lived in boarding schools abroad. He tore open Claire's letter and began to decode her tiny, elaborate handwriting. The letter's contents were not particularly newsworthy. She needed "a small advance on next month's allowance."

"When you go down for fresh towels," he told his manservant, "tell Sheffield to come up." Sheffield was Graham's secretary.

"Sheffield, sir," the man replied, "has been conscripted into tallying accounts and writing receipts. There has been a bit of a crush on today."

By a "crush" the man meant a larger than usual crowd roaming the grounds and downstairs interior of the house.

Graham had a slightly unusual living arrangement. On a Sunday at this time of year, his house and back gardens were always swarming with people. This was due to an interplay of economics and family history.

All the earls of Netham had been wealthy, but not monumentally so, yet Graham lived in a house fit for a king. His London property took up a square English block. This was a lot of land to own in the best part of the city; the only person who owned more was his neighbor, the queen. He could see Buckingham Palace from his northwest windows. His house was older than the palace and almost as ornate. Graham lived in only the upper rear portion, however. The house was much more than any one family, let alone one person, could ever inhabit. It was also too large to afford and too valuable to give up.

Historically, much of the building and grounds had been closed until Graham's great-grandfather had opened up the back gardens to "friends." This had been a magnanimous, and probably exhibitionistic, gesture. Tea had been served three afternoons a week to whoever wished to come and admire. This had become somewhat popular. Then the next earl, Graham's grandfather, had opened up the front portion of the house itself, and it had gone from being merely popular to being public. He had instituted a brass dish for donations to help defray costs. Eventually guides and caterers had been allowed to come in. By contract, they answered questions and served tea five days a week for a percentage of the profits. By the end of the last century, the house had been given over to the phenomenon of domestic tourism.

Graham's own father had added his bit when he so famously shot his wife, then himself. People flocked. For a shilling in the dish, most of London and its visitors had walked through Graham's house at one time or another. It had acquired a strong sense of public ownership. Graham simply had never had the strength, or money for that matter, to turn this around. He had learned to live companionably with tourism, residing in the upstairs rear of the house in the private quarters entered through the carriage foyer. It was ample. No one disturbed him. He had become comfortable with the fact that his steps were heard overhead, explained and interpreted by some historian below. "Now, that is the present earl. . . ."

The present earl yanked off his trousers and stepped into a tubful of hot water, blissfully lauding to himself the miracles of modern plumbing. His secretary managed to slip upstairs with paper and pen a few minutes after that. Submerged in three feet of water and with a fat cigar between his teeth, Graham puffed out a severe letter on profligate spending to his daughter, then instructed that a ten-pound note be included with the letter. He knew that lecturing Claire, then giving her money, was contradictory, but he didn't know how else to handle the girl or, for that matter, her brother.

He knew he was not the model father. He was hardly a father at all, in fact. He had a tendency to forget the children—a thought that gave him pause. Frowning and watching smoke rings drift over the tub and wisp to nothing, he tried to remember if he'd mentioned them yet to Rosalyn.

He'd better do so soon. Such large things began to seem like secrets when they went too long unspoken. Rosalyn was already up in arms that he had a widowed cousin who could track him down at a party. Why hadn't he told her he had such a cousin? she had wanted to know this morning.

"I didn't know myself."

"What were you talking to her about at the end of the terrace?"

He'd rolled his eyes, amazed that she would pay attention to this. "Are you jealous?"

"Should I be?"

He expelled a quick breath, having to feign exasperation. "For God's sake, Rosalyn, she's a pale little thing with frizzy hair and crooked teeth."

Luckily, lightning didn't strike a man down for lying with fragments of reassembled truth.

The pale, frizzy, little crooked-toothed woman aroused a mild but persistent curiosity in Graham. She interested him—an interest he was in no hurry to share with Rosalyn. He couldn't have explained to her or anyone else why he was intrigued by the widow. She wasn't very pretty. She wasn't even very nice. Perhaps it was having the secret of dirty pictures between them. Or all those mounds of swaying, slithering black silk. The steel hoops under that silk had to be so thin, an expensive undergarment bought by Henry, he reminded himself. Her skirts jiggled and shuddered at the slightest movement she made. Graham dropped her into a category, hoping this would sum her up and sort her out—she was what the French would call *une beauté mystique*. A woman with no obvious beauty who managed by some quirk of personality to be mysteriously appealing all the same. Take away that smug air, those fancy hoops and full skirts, and what would you have?

Graham was laughing at himself as he stepped out of the tub and picked up a large towel. He found his clothes laid out on the bed. He was fastening the bottom buttons of his vest when his valet came in carrying a handful of watches. As the man bent to thread a watch chain, Graham took the whole lot from him. "Thank you, John. I'll take care of the rest myself. Go down and tell Royce to open up the shed, will you? Oh, and tell him to stay and mind it till I come down. You know how people are."

Graham moved to stand before a wide, lead-mullioned window twice as tall as himself. In this light, he set a watch that had stopped, then stood there winding it, absently looking out the window. His eyes fixed on a curious little scene taking place outside, three stories below him. A large family was posing among the statuary on his back lawn before a man with a gadget that was becoming more and more common. The man had his head bent down under a black cloth as he looked through a box on stick legs. A portable camera. There were men who took these around, traveling in wagons full of chemicals, making pictures inside these cameras with a smear of glop on a sheet of glass.

Beyond the photographer and his subjects, Graham could see his own gardener's shed where he kept his fireworks, much as he had kept firecrackers in Henry's years ago—happily, he had not yet burned down his own shed. Royce, the gardener, and John, his manservant, waited dutifully outside, guarding a shack full of explosives, including a box of magnesium chunks. Graham quickly tucked in the rest of his watches. The group who'd witnessed the display at Rosalyn's house had told a few other people who'd missed it. A larger group was waiting at Rosalyn's to see whatever he might choose to take back with him. This positively delighted Graham.

He picked up his coat, slipping it on while trotting down the rear stairs. On his way to the shed, he decided to have a good look at that camera-thing first.

When Graham Wessit returned, Submit was dismayed to discover he'd brought two more people with him, as if the house weren't busy enough. Another two dozen human beings had arrived by mid-afternoon. Carriages kept rolling up. Vehicles pulled into Mrs. Schild's drive with the frequency of bees to a hive. The place had begun to swarm with activity. Tea, an opera, then a late-night supper were planned, invitations to which Submit politely declined. People were actually arriving with two and three changes of clothes. To this assembly, Graham Wessit added one photographer and his helper. It seemed the earl was about to take pictures of everything. He was full of enthusiasm and fascination for a newfangled camera. She couldn't get his attention, try as she might.

She followed him and the photographer out onto the front lawn. The only way to get his attention there, however, would have been to stand in front of the camera lens. The earl, directing the photographer, wanted pictures of the house. Pictures of Rosalyn. Pictures of Tilney, the blond man, from this morning, who, after the first photo, wanted his image to appear on every photographic plate. Pictures of the cats: Rosalyn traveled with eight. Pictures of the earl himself. Graham Wessit, always agreeable, took pictures of virtually anything that would stay in one place. Submit found herself always moving to stay at his back. She wanted to talk, not be in his photographs.

A growing group moved with the earl to the back terrace. Two neighbors came over to watch. Submit followed, thinking he would soon give up. But he kept inventing more pictures, while discoursing with a vagabond photographer on the subject of light. More people, the postman, two maids, the cook, and the scullery, were drawn to follow the sight.

And he *was* a sight. In the late afternoon sunlight, Graham Wessit removed his coat. He rolled up his shirtsleeves and bent over the camera, taking instruction. He sported a bright red vest that made the sleeves of his shirt look even whiter, his coloring all the more dark. His face and forearms, Submit realized, were deeply colored by the sun. His wrists and flexors were corded with veins and solid with muscle. He had a broader, stronger physique than she had imagined. He was a dandiprat with the height of a Titan and the build of a rugby fullback.

And the face of a Byron: Submit was caught short as he straightened up, his eyes lifting over the heads of a group sitting in front of him on the grass. Submit, on the terrace behind them, felt an odd rush. She was the center of his attention for a moment. He smiled and mimed an offer. Would she be willing to pose? His open palm indicated a raised flower bed that had gone to poppies. Submit was caught off guard, embarrassed at being caught staring. She frowned and shook her head no. Flustered, she gave up. She went inside bewildered, wondering why he would want a picture of an unphotogenic woman standing in a patch of floppy, wild weeds.

More than an hour later, as the sun was finally setting, she heard people in the front parlor. At last. He would have to stop taking pictures; he was losing daylight. She went toward the sound of voices. When she opened the parlor door, he was on the other side of it—and so was the idiotic camera. The earl was moving people into position for a group photograph. He moved a man by the arm, then took Mrs. Schild by the waist, picking her up and setting her on the back of a sofa. She had to grab the mantel of the fireplace to keep from falling backward. Everyone shrieked in delight. Submit walked into this only to find herself taken by the shoulder.

He sat her into a chair, then did a double take. "Lady Motmarche." He was surprised to find her sitting suddenly in the midst of his picture. He recovered smoothly. "How nice. You have to sit *very* still."

She got up immediately. "I would like to talk to you."

"Talk," he said.

She followed him over to the camera, which stood on stilts. By now he had the photographer posing in the picture. He was operating the camera himself. He ducked under its black cloth. Submit was left talking to a hooded head and left hand. As the hand offered her a box of matches, she noticed it had three rings on it.

"Here. You know what you're doing. Step back when you light that stuff on the tray."

His right hand moved a tray toward her. This hand wore two more rings, one an arabesque of rubies that wrapped around like a red snake.

Submit's eyes dropped down to the red vest hanging out so brilliantly from beneath the camera's black cloth. His vest, like the one last night, was dripping with gold watch chains.

"I would like," she said, "to look into your face when I speak to you."

He laughed. "Fine. Come under here."

Everyone in the room laughed.

Submit drew back. She spoke more softly. "I'm sorry," she said. "Can you see me later?"

Graham Wessit lowered his voice as well. "Where would you like to meet?"

Her skin prickled. "I—um—" For a moment, she couldn't speak.

Behind her, the photographer's helper took the matches

from her hand and whistled loudly. "Ay! She's after your cockles, ya' know. Ain't she a funny one to flock after yooo—"

The room exploded in light. Submit saw spots. She breathed in a smell of burnt chemicals—magnesium. It was foul. The air was thick with smoke. When she focused on Graham Wessit again, he had pulled his head out from under the cloth. He threw her a brief, puzzled frown.

Submit's patience left. "Maybe I should go—"

"Don't be sensitive. He was just having fun."

"Don't patronize me."

His frown darkened. "Then maybe you should."

"Should what?"

"Go." He added, "And take everything you brought with you."

The box. She'd wanted to ask about the box. But she said instead, "Fine. Maybe I should. Since I truly don't know how to talk to a man who, on ten fingers, can wear five rings. You are absurd, do you know that?"

She didn't even wait for his reaction. She walked out.

— Chapter 9 —

Graham was more wary of Submit Channing-Downes after that. Though she didn't bother him anymore, neither did she leave as he'd suggested. Henry's wife became Rosalyn's houseguest, and not just for the night. The day after the incident over the camera, a load of trunks arrived—all Submit's worldly, or at least undisputed, goods. It looked as though the widow were here to stay, and Graham could make neither heads nor tails of how this had come about.

Henry's abrasive, enigmatic, strangely appealing little wife took up residence under the same roof as his own mistress. This seemed incredible to Graham, a situation too prickly, too strangely interesting, for him to do anything but circle. Then, as the real and bland events of day-to-day life made their inroads, the widow's presence became almost theoretical. Only once, after the day of the camera, did Graham actually see her in the house, and then only from the back. He didn't even realize who it was until she was quite well past—he recognized her by a distinctively brisk churning of taffeta. This characteristic sound was apparently something others noticed as well. The Black Fairy, Rosalyn called her. "An eerie one, that one," she would say as Submit fluttered overhead on a staircase, disappearing with all the rustle and flurry of great, substantial dragonfly wings.

Henry's widow was not just odd, Graham decided, she was otherworldly. Everyone in the house agreed. He was glad he had a more fun-loving and down-to-earth woman for his own.

A few days later, he was buttoning his pants, watching his fun-loving, down-to-earth woman fight her way through a huge tangle of striped Indian muslin. Rosalyn had put the bottom of her dress over her head a moment ago. Now, from the inside, she was trying to find her way to the top. An arm poked through one sleeve. Still no head. Beyond the parlor door, Graham could hear an annoying racket. Carpenters were dismantling the façade in the ballroom that had been erected for Rosalyn's gala party last week. Decorators were coming in today to paint over the walls. Her house was in a state. It had taken an act of premeditation for Graham to enter it this morning.

All for naught, so far as Graham was concerned. He was going to be late for an appointment with his lawyers. He had come here with the express intention of making himself and Rosalyn blissfully content for a few minutes. Instead, he and Rosalyn had fallen into what had amounted to little more than animal copulation. The rhythm and aesthetics of the whole thing had been roughly as pleasant as the saws and hammers grinding away in the background. Graham couldn't imagine what had gone wrong.

Rosalyn's head popped through her dress. Muslin dropped as far as her crinoline. It sat awkwardly in a bunch around her waist for a moment, then she shook the skirt down. Her dress was rumpled, but muslin was supposed to look that way. Graham glanced down at himself. The knees of his trousers were covered in red lint—bits of wool from her new carpet.

"My man is in the kitchen," he said. "When you are presentable, I'll call him. My trousers are a mess."

She shrugged. "Whatever you wish."

He looked at her, annoyed that she took a distant tone with him. The ungrateful creature. When he had just braved an army of servants and carpenters to make love—

No, he had just *nailed* Rosalyn, twice for good measure, in her front parlor. Conceivably, neither of them felt very satisfied. Not only had the outside world been a rattling nuisance, the room inside had been no great help. Among tiny tables, stiff-backed chairs, and a skirted piano, there had been no place to do the deed properly. They had ended up on the floor. He'd taken his coat off to be comfortable, then Rosalyn had wanted his vest and shirt off as well. Her hands had a generally wonderful and unholy interest in the muscles of his belly. But now his elbows and forearms itched from rubbing on the thick, cut wool of the rug. Rosalyn couldn't be much better off. He would not have traded the irritating itch on his arms for the same feel on his bare ass.

Graham fastened his collar with one hand, while digging down a chair cushion with the other for his bow tie. "I shouldn't have come," he said.

"You should have come yesterday."

"With your servants getting into every room, cleaning every damned possession?"

"They weren't cleaning every damned possession."

Graham frowned at her, then asked, "Do all American women curse?"

"I was under the impression English gentlemen did not."

"They restrain themselves. In front of ladies."

"Damn your English snot!" She threw a cushion at him. "The only time I'm not a lady is in here, and you love it!"

That wasn't quite true—at the moment he hated it. But she had made her point. He grew sullen.

Her voice broke. "You could have come the day before."

"I was here, but I ended up playing croquet with Tilney. You were indisposed, as I recall. Feeding the cats, all ten million of them—you and the Black Fairy." Graham was a little shocked to hear this mean name come out his own mouth.

"You *wanted* to play—beat—Tilney."

"I didn't." He did. It was always hard not to clobber Tilney when he made some foolish challenge. Graham had been trouncing Tilney at nearly everything since he was ten years old.

"You did!"

"Maybe I did." Some of Graham's anger abated. "Why does Lady Motmarche feed your cats?"

Rosalyn was taken aback at this change of subject. "Out of gratitude, I suppose."

"For what?"

"Well for—I don't know. She needed a place to stay. I convinced her I didn't mind her being here. It seemed the right thing to do."

Graham was taken aback himself for several seconds. Then he gave a short laugh. "Yes." He was humbled once more by Rosalyn's directness. She was both mean and kind without worry for subtlety, unlike the widow who was so subtle and aloof that she was entirely undecipherable. "Well, I'm glad she's finally let someone get in close enough to help."

"I thought if I didn't, you might." Rosalyn paused. "Did you offer her the flat?"

Graham turned his back. He began to tie his tie as he faced a wall mirror. "Why would you even ask?"

"She inquired about it yesterday, asking Tilney if it were a proper flat, one you actually rented."

It was, though Graham had occasionally been generous with the flat on Haymoore Street. He had allowed "close friends" to stay in it if they needed to. Several of those close friends, women, had stayed for extended periods of time.

"I mentioned it to her," he said, after what was becoming an awkward pause. He gave the tie a sharp twist and pulled it through. "I don't have a tenant for it right now, you know."

In the mirror, she raised one eyebrow at him. "I know. Just see that you don't."

He glanced over his shoulder. "What? I'm not allowed to sleep with anyone else?" A little more harshly than he'd intended, he said, "And what about your damned husband? It seems to me you might just crawl into bed with him every fortnight or so."

Rosalyn's look softened, as did her tone. "Do you want me to stop sleeping with my husband, Gray? I can, you know."

Graham could think of only one way she might put her husband off. Only one legal way—and it was extremely legal. He had a quick, horrible presentiment of himself in court again, this time as co-respondent, the adulterous earl. He sighed and let the whole thing drop.

What hypocrisy, he thought. He wasn't even sure he minded that she slept with her husband. He only minded that she should try to dictate to him how he use his own flat. Lord, they were both frazzled. Too busy. Too deprived. Both his life and hers had conspired against the physical side of their relationship for more than ten days—Graham had counted backward in surprise just this morning. This was why he had roared into the house, found Rosalyn, then dragged her into the first free room he could find. But now that they were finished, he was feeling more unsettled than before.

He picked up his vest and walked over to the cord by the wall. "Can I summon my manservant now?"

"You are always in a rush."

"I'm going to be late to Temple Inn."

Without a trace of a smile, she folded her arms. "You should have summoned your man half an hour ago," she said. "Just think of the time you'd have saved."

It occurred to Graham, as his carriage pulled away that day, that he and Rosalyn were not getting on as well as they should.

In fact, his remaining week in London seemed to be characterized by all that didn't happen, didn't work, that didn't go as well as he'd planned. For one, Rosalyn wasn't staying in London. After cleaning up, there was the great, wonderful dither of closing up. The season was over. Rosalyn was to spend a fortnight with her husband in Kent before retiring for the summer to Graham and Nethamshire. Cleaning quickly gave way to the process of storing and throwing covers over everything. More and more Graham began to avoid Rosalyn's house. It too closely paralleled the uproar in his own.

Graham was closing the living quarters of his London house as well. Like most with financial wherewithal to do so, he intended to spend the summer in the country. He was opening his house southwest of London in the rather amorphous region known as Nethamshire or Netham. There he would be entertaining a number of friends.

Once, as recently as eighty years ago, Netham had been a real place, a county in the southwest of England; the earldom had had its geographic corollary. During some political redivisioning, however, the land had lost its official designation. It now sat astride two counties, the name retaining meaning only for locals and certain Londoners who associated it with the earl. It was his territory, his domain, relegated to a kind of fictitious standing as a place to live, though he did in earnest own most of what had made up the county.

Somehow, all the places where Graham lived seemed to have this "other" dimension: "I live in a museum," he told Rosalyn once, referring to his house in London. But he got no sympathy there. Rosalyn, in fact, loved to ride over at dusk, when all the tourists and guides had left, so she could step over the velvet cords. Her favorite naughtiness was to step up onto the platforms and invite him to make love on the exhibited beds. Daring romance, she called it; delusion, Graham complained to himself. He resented that she should be so thrilled with something about him that had nothing to do with him himself.

"On these stupid, musty platforms," he accused her once, "you are making love to a myth, the English upper-class rake, as if I were a kind of obscene tourist attraction."

At such comparisons, Rosalyn's eyes only widened. "Oh, yes!" She stepped happily over the boundary line into the areas of his house he didn't live in, into a public pretense he didn't inhabit, leaving him on the other side of the ropes, feeling damned if he refused—alone—and damned if he did not. When he stepped over and made love to her, it was always with the growing unease that his whole life was somehow becoming roped off.

Or roped in. By the end of the month, it was clear that Graham was stuck in London, at least through June. The mess with the billiard table girl dragged on. Not only would he not be able to break for Netham early, as was his custom, but he was going to arrive late. All his guests would be there before him, which sent him into a sulk.

Normally he left before the end of the season to prepare for his summer guests. This was a trick he had learned. He'd found he could gracefully bow out of the last exhausting weeks of London social life by being fastidiously gracious himself. For the last three or four years, he'd been leaving early for Netham. This year, he had to make all the arrangements by messenger—which he found truly annoying—and which led to another grievance for his growing list: He couldn't keep a full staff in London. It had always been convenient and more economical to keep a skeleton staff at Netham or in London and have the full retinue attached to himself and whichever house he was using at the moment. In this case, his regular household staff had to be broken down a little at a time and transferred ahead of him to Netham to prepare for his guests.

His cooks were the first to go, needing time for the planning and procuring of food in large quantities. The guests who would be joining him would initially number about thirty, plus families. It was a gathering of a wholly different nature than anyone would find in London. Children, dogs, nannies. The thirty or so adults who brought these families with them were hand selected. Over the years, the group had been culled down to about two dozen friends Graham genuinely enjoyed and who seemed to enjoy his company in return. Besides these people, there were also a few who, whether they liked him or not, openly and unctuously courted his good graces. Graham's summers were as blatantly weighted in his favor as his good conscience and self-respect would allow. He structured them purposely as a kind of antidote to the rigors and protocol of the London season. No testy dinner parties. No operas that put him to sleep. No dancing and talking in circles of etiquette. His summers were informal, he enjoyed them, he was himself—and he sent anyone packing who gave him a hard time over any of this.

The business with Tate and the paternity suit was at the top of Graham's list of problems during those last weeks in London, though the words "top" and "list" were misleading. They implied an order, something the lawyer and his tactics defied. It was this that held Graham in the city and this that ultimately made him wild to leave. While he tried to organize the Netham house from eighty miles away, tried to close and yet live in an only marginally functioning household, and tried to see the bounding, romping Rosalyn off on not such a bad note that they couldn't manage a better footing later, Mr. Tate, Esquire, shot through his every day with either worry for or the actuality of one of his legal machinations.

Though a trial had yet to commence, Tate had everyone marching into court for what seemed like endless technicalities. Each day seemed to bring a new hearing. Tate made a motion to dismiss, a motion for summary judgment, then various motions to strike for redundant then immaterial then impertinent matter. In short, he convinced both sides, Graham included, that on a sheer procedural basis alone going to trial with him would be ghastly. Graham's pugnacious new barrister intended to fight every inch of the way and on every level, it seemed—from procedure to rules of evidence to the merits, if they ever got to them. As if this weren't enough, Tate had begun to interview Graham privately for details. "Why would she accuse you?" "How does she know you?" "Have you ever slept with any very young girls?" Graham hoped fervently that the other side was as intimidated and appalled by all this as he was.

The carriage jostled heavily as Rosalyn Schild got into it. It was loaded with boxes and trunks. From the outside, Graham closed the door. He watched Rosalyn arrange her skirts, then lean back toward him. Through the open window, she looked down at him.

"I will be much better company," he said, "in Netham."

He had intended this remark to be the end of a conversation, not the beginning of one. But Rosalyn raised her hand, fiddling with the pleats of her bonnet. "I'm jealous." She delivered this non sequitur deadpan. "She's had your quiet, attentive company every day for a week."

She was speaking, he knew, of the courtroom girl, the woman who was taking up most of his time. "You could always come with me to court," he said.

Rosalyn rested an arm, then her chin, on the open window's edge. "No, thank you." She left an irresolute pause, then seemed to make a decision: "I don't like you much lately."

Graham stared at her. "I don't know what to say to that. I don't either, I suppose." He waited. "I shall miss you. I feel quite friendless at the thought of your going. To continue alone—"

"You're hardly ever alone." She pursed her lips. "Too many people."

"With all the 'good-natured' elbows in the ribs? There is nothing like that sensation for feeling alone."

"You're too sensitive."

"You keep saying."

"Will you miss me really?"

"A solemn oath."

"I could stay, tell Gerald I'll be a day or two later."

"I don't think that would help."

"In fact, you're anxious to get rid of me."

He made a sniff of protest. "Only when you make such shrewish statements."

She hesitated. He could feel her looking for his face, which he patently avoided giving her. "I'm being honest," she said, "despite how tasteless and colonial that is." She left another pause, then said, "You are relieved to have me going."

He made a louder protest, *pff*, and rolled his eyes at her. His American mistress was accusing him of being too English, too smooth and sophisticated to appreciate honesty. He mugged a face, wanting to show her this wasn't true.

He got a weary laugh. "Perhaps not this minute," she amended, "but in general."

The carriage leaned abruptly away from him. Her driver had mounted from the other side. Springs and leather squeaked, then rocked back into place. The horses took on an awareness, an agitation.

He heard Rosalyn take a breath. "I'm going to leave Gerald. I'm going to tell him. I have already, haven't I? Left him, I mean."

He turned his head sharply. The expression on her face told him she had been waiting, poised to calculate his immediate reaction. He stared at her, not certain what she saw, then shrugged. "Do what pleases you."

"And what pleases *you*?"

"You do. Just as you are."

"Married."

"It doesn't matter."

"I see."

The carriage rocked once more. Graham stepped toward the driver, yelling at him—a guttural sound, less than a word, but expressive of his exasperation. As he turned back to Rosalyn, he had not quite calmed his voice. "You picked a fine time to tell me this. Can't you wait to put me on trial till you come back? I had no idea—"

"A blind man could see—"

"Don't make me justify myself. I've had enough of doing that lately."

"Well, I've had too little explanation, justification, whatever you want to call it. I don't know where I stand with you."

"I love you." He said this so aggressively that she started.

Then her eyes narrowed, and she said nothing. She only stared at him.

"Rosalyn, this is hardly the moment—" Hearing how peremptory he sounded, he reached for her, trying to give her a quick kiss good-bye.

But she pulled back. "On your dresser. I left you something. A little gift. Because it amused me, though I hardly think you will enjoy it now." There was a crisp break, the back-and-forth movement of wheels and prancing horses. "I want you to read it anyway. Out of meanness now, I think."

"All right." He tried again for the kiss.

She jerked away into the shadows of the carriage. "You bloody hypocrite." She was more put out than he could account for.

Her English expletive registered as odd. He had a second to wonder where an upper-class American woman had heard it. "Bloody" was not a word he himself used very much; he used milder ones or stronger ones. Then the carriage wheel at his elbow churned in the stones. He backed up quickly. The vehicle seemed to wobble under her anger all the way out of sight.

Graham was left frowning in the dust of Rosalyn's clean exit. The whole conversation seemed to have gone too perfectly her way. It had probably been rehearsed. Women did that. It had probably taken her a dozen practices to get that exit just right. Then he recognized that *he* was the actor. This affair was about to surpass any involvement he had had in recent years. It was becoming significant, and something in him shuddered at the prospect. A part of him had begun to reenact the familiar, unoriginal play: *How to Part Company.* Excuses had begun to occur to him. *I can't. I'm sorry. Good-bye. Good luck. Break a leg.* Was it only the male of the species, Graham wondered, who was anxious about permanence, responsibility, growing up? Surely not. Then another good reason not to marry Rosalyn Schild occurred to him, though by this time he hardly knew whether to trust his own motives, since it was such an overly suspicious thought: Perhaps Rosalyn wanted to marry him so she could sleep with someone else. (He recalled that Tilney used the word "bloody" all the time.) Part of Rosalyn was happy and didn't want to be anything but an unfaithful wife.

At home, Graham found three consecutive issues of *Porridge*, a popular weekly, on his dresser. He thumbed through them, unable to understand what more he was supposed to do with them.

It was more by accident that later in the evening, before going to bed, he came across a serialized novel in the magazine—episodes two, three, and four in these issues, by one Yves DuJauc. The French name implied the fiction would be a little racy. Graham began reading. The story was romantic, the sort of thing Rosalyn would like. Then he became slowly, lividly pale. With explicit, obvious allusion, someone had decided to caricature the worst and most lurid aspects of his life. This was being done in public again, in fiction, in black and white. The hero of the episodes was Wesley Grey, the title, *The Rake of Ronmoor*, the subtitle, "The Villainous Exploits of an Earl's Depraved Heir."

— Chapter 10 —

*I am so sorry to have put upon you so selfishly at my leaving.
You must forget what I said and only remember that I love
you. I shall be with you soon, your bare Rosey with flowers in
her hair, flowers up her bum! When you see the bustle I have
bought! There is a Frenchwoman here, a couturière, who says
by next year all the ladies' dresses will be pulling to the back—
no more hoops like big bells with our legs gonging around inside! And this little bustle will be the trick! Wait till you see.
You must imagine your entire London garden tucked into my
fanny (what a wicked thought!), draped over with satin. A
deep rose gown, I have bought for you. It is so chic, so naked.
So little corsetry! I think of you where it touches me. Oh, the
bounce of this soft little bustle! Silk pillow-petals stuffed with
bits of fine cork, patting my bottom as I walk! Exquisite! I am
so à l'anglaise to look at, so yours to the touch. I flush continually when I wear it, from vanity, from memory of you, and anticipation. I have never missed you as now. Gerald is horrid.
But he says, and it is true, that my excessive bottom comple-
ments my outrageous dress and vice versa. He hates it, and you
will love it. I feel as though I have left him years behind me. He
stares at me as though in a daze. Oh, and I have bought a pair
of drawers. You will laugh when you see. They are black silk!
Such fun. I love you, love you, make love with you each night,
though he paws me incessantly. He is a bear! A walrus! I feel
like a fish next to him, sleek and clean and shimmering, and
all he wants to do is devour me like a huge meal in a bite, then*

*pick his teeth. I have not made love with him once, and I won't.
I shall leave him no matter what. But you mustn't worry.*

Your Rose

June 7
Dearest—

*I cannot stand that you will not write to me here. Truly, Ger-
ald would never notice. It is not even a matter of pulling the
wool—his eyes, his head, are so full of nothing else. Besides, I
have many friends who write, even a gentleman friend. The
Member of Parliament you met at the party wrote to thank
me for the evening three weeks ago. He thanks me also (I
have to giggle at this) for introductions to you. He hints he
would like to join us in Netham. Actually, his wife, I think,
prays and pressures to meet you. But I do not answer, knowing how you like the invitations to come from yourself. Still,
wouldn't a Member of Parliament be nice, so official and
sanctioning?*

*The MP and wife are wild for the serial. (Have you read it?
Were you able to laugh?) They, of course, noted the watches
and house and height of the villainous hero, not to mention the
other similarities. Was the twit ever your laundry maid? Who
is Yves DuJauc? Do you know him? He certainly knows you,
doesn't he, dear? Don't be angry that I am enjoying it. I keep
looking for myself, but not yet. Perhaps in future episodes . . .*

In all events, write! I love you and miss you.

*Yours,
Rose*

*P.S. If it will ease your mind, send a note to my London ad-
dress. I will send someone to check now and then.*

June 11
Graham,

*Gerald has asked that I stay another week. I don't know
whether it is my vanity or venality (he says I am good for business and buys me a new dress for every luncheon, for every
tea), but I have agreed to stay. Or perhaps it is because I don't
hear from you. It is odd how I can settle into the dullness of this
place. So like home. Sweet Savage Security. I believe my pulse
races when I am with you, my cool English darling, but I must
trust my memory for that. You refuse to remind me. Couldn't
you dash off a few understatements for me, darling? I rather
miss you, Rosalyn. That would be an understatement,
wouldn't it? It's so hard to tell with you English. I must go. I
am exhausted from doing nothing.*

Love,
Rosalyn

June 15

*Shall I come at all, you beast? We traveled to Bath, where I ran
into Peter Tilney. He implicates me as the writer of your "slow
murder," saying you as much as said so. You idiot. How could
you imagine me so treacherous as that? I shall not bother to
come unless I hear from you. We are guests of the Adamsferrys
in Camden Place.*

R

P.S. Enclosed is episode six. I hope you choke on it.

— Chapter 11 —

Use every man after his desert,
and who should 'scape a whipping?
WILLIAM SHAKESPEARE
Hamlet
Act II, Scene ii, 555–6

A few nights later, Graham and some of his friends gathered at his club. It was a kind of last hurrah before they all, save Graham, left the city for the pleasures of the countryside. Over brandy, several of the men discussed a list.

As the idea unfolded, Graham was expected to be full of gratitude and smug camaraderie. They half joked, half offered to get up six signatures—the legal number required on an affidavit to declare a woman a prostitute and thus unentitled to paternity compensation. There was something of the battle cry bursting through the men's calm, though it was unclear whether they were plotting strategy in the sexual or class war. But in either case, even wishing he could be part of their solid front, even liking the brandy-sipping, hushed-voiced comfort of any solidarity, Graham refused to make the girl a whore. If she was so, she would be one in fact, not by fabrication. Such was the clarity of his vision, he told himself. He was not that sort of fellow; these jolly friends were drunk. He could smile it off.

"But it's a capital idea," one of them persisted. "Just in case."

"I appreciate what you are trying to do. But I am defendable." "Defendable" was the word Tate had used that morning when the judge had set the trial date, June fifteenth.

"A laundress, of all people. Why, if she's allowed to make

hay of this, there is no telling for any of us. Whether you rogered her or not—"

"I didn't," Graham said tightly. "I am going to get a vindication. I deserve it."

"Ah." The others chuckled. One of them paraphrased *Hamlet*, "If we all got what we deserved . . ." He left this unfinished except for a knowing smile and a wiggle of his eyebrows.

Graham's own smile left his face. He felt highly ethical in ignoring the advice of the list. He was right, and he was coming to understand that he *wanted* the trial. It was his chance to make everyone admit publicly that the seducing, irresponsible side of him had been overdrawn far too much, for far too long.

He wanted a larger vindication than he'd first realized, and he wanted it worse than he'd imagined. *I am an innocent man*, he told himself. It seemed imperative that someone recognize this, so imperative that he braced himself and marched into what he knew would be a harrowing process.

He could almost feel the gears of the legal system engage and begin to grind forward—that one evening's brave optimism with his friends was the first thing to be ground to bits.

Tate became Graham's main human contact. The counselor, it seemed, was going to prepare for trial with the same vigor with which he'd tried to prevent it. The next week, he called Graham into his office to coach him through "potentially dangerous questions," beginning with, "What are the most horrible things you can imagine anyone asking you?"

Tate knew the answer to this one, to Graham's breathless amazement. How often do you copulate? Do you use any means of "protection"? Have you even been tempted, just once, not to? For the first fifteen minutes of this, Graham could barely see in front of him. His vision kept shifting and blurring. If Graham protested, the barrister pounded the desk and made fearsome predictions.

"I'm not asking this for my own titillation! The other side is going to be much less delicate. Answer the questions directly, yes or no. Leave me to do the objecting!"

Eventually, Graham was giving up information he'd never dreamed he'd be discussing. Whom he was sleeping with a year ago, their names, and their ages. Whether they would deny it or come forward as hostile, whether they might speak up for him, whether any had been or could be pregnant.

Graham had no idea what his attorney would do with these facts in an open courtroom, but he handed himself over to the mercy of Tate. Or Fate. Or Whim. Or Life or God. Whatever lay beyond Understanding. Graham was confounded to remember Henry that week and his damned philosophical approach to life as he made what Henry would have called "Kierkegaard's leap of faith." To survive, all mortals had to trust in someone, something, Henry claimed. Though, unlike his friend Kierkegaard, Henry was not a God-trusting man; he made the leap of faith in himself—as if *he* were God. In any event, for Graham it was an unsettling leap. He didn't truly trust Tate, or Fate or Life, or even Henry or himself, for that matter.

The day the trial began, he was relieved to be getting on with it. Reality could only be easier to face than all the worst-case practice for it.

"Be upstanding," a clerk called as he pounded a long staff on the bare wood floor of the courtroom. The judge entered. He was a tall, gaunt man, his copious robe seeming all but empty as it swirled around him. His entrance silenced a noisy gallery of spectators and a bevy of lawyers. The courtroom was packed.

The morning paper had carried the details. It would be an open bench trial, meaning no jury. The presiding magistrate would make all determinations. This magistrate, looking like God Himself from over the top of the high dais, banged his gavel, and everyone sat.

Graham spotted the girl as people shuffled into their seats. She was awkward, having to reach behind herself to find her chair then balance her way down into it. Any less caution and her belly would have sent her keeling over. Lord God, she was pregnant. Her belly was two or three times the size it had been the day she had climbed onto the billiard table at Freyer's; she could not have gotten onto a billiard table now. Graham could only stare at her enormous proportions and wonder that mortals could accomplish—and be encumbered by—such monumental feats.

Happily, when the girl began to speak from the witness box, she no longer seemed so much a monument as a naughty, apprehended child. She was nervous. As she spoke, she began to suck on a strand of her hair, pulling this in and out of her mouth between words as she shifted her eyes from the judge to her lawyer. She was measuring her credibility as she went along, engaged in what appeared increasingly to be a poor job of lying. Graham sighed in relief. Her lawyer began to more or less testify for her, sprinkling his questions with such phrases as "a wicked man of superior age, wealth, privilege, and position . . ." His tone implied that these were other than laudable conditions. "A man who used the power of his class—"

Tate objected. "Did an entire class have its way with this young woman?"

"Oh, no, sir," the girl volunteered. "It were just one man."

The courtroom tittered.

"Counselor," the magistrate told the opposing lawyer, "we mustn't forget these serious charges are leveled against an individual man."

"No, sir. And a blackguard of a man he is, if ever there was one."

"Point taken." The judge picked up a pen and made a note, as if jotting this down. Point one—earl of Netham, blackguard. This was the same judge, Graham realized, who had referred to him throughout the early hearings as the "Black Earl."

Tate took exception. "The earl's *reputation* is bad," he said, as if the judge hadn't heard quite right.

"The earl of Netham's reputation is worlds beyond 'bad,' counselor."

"But a reputation alone cannot make a woman pregnant."

Spectators crowding at the back of the room laughed.

The judge pounded his gavel. "There will be no provocative tittling here," he said without a trace of humor. He leaned forward across the dais and spoke to Tate. "A bad reputation, counselor, is usually earned by deeds accomplished by the man himself. Now, are you going to argue with me or with learned opposing counsel?"

Both, Graham thought, *since the two of you seem to be in such bloody harmony.* But Tate only stood back and tented his fingertips, as if weighing the question like a serious interrogative.

"The point I wish to make," he said finally, "is that even the worst, most licentious of men cannot produce every baby in town."

The judge responded with surprise and benevolence. "Ah. Point taken." He made another note. *Blackguard and villain might not make all babies*, Graham imagined and glared. *Thank you very much, Arnold Tate.*

The situation did not improve from there. The girl claimed her current state was the result of a single evening. "Which a man who has had many such evenings," her counselor was allowed to expand, "might easily forget."

"But you, my dear," Tate said on cross-examination, "would remember very specifically. Can you tell us when and where?"

"All Saints' Day, backstage at the theater. The Royal Surrey."

From depositions, Graham had known the date. His own memory—and witnesses—put him in the theater district that evening, but at the Prince Regent two blocks away.

"Two blocks." Tate raised a finger, smiling. "That's a very long way for a man to impregnate a woman, even for the very virile earl of Netham."

The back of the courtroom erupted in sniggers. The judge himself seemed to be fighting a thin smile.

Graham began to realize he was not going to celebrate the vindication he'd planned.

A theater doorman was produced who swore he'd seen Graham offer the girl a lift home. " 'e says, 'Eh, girlie, ya' wants to 'ave a ride in me mighty fine carrich . . . ' " And so it continued. What wasn't ludicrous was either ugly or personal or scurrilous.

Graham jumped up once to utter an indignant protest. "Of all the stupid—"

The judge's gavel clamored. "Sit down."

"If you possibly can," said opposing counsel.

"Please do," Tate added wearily.

Someone in the gallery yelled, "Shove the bugger down!"

Graham spun around, ready to leap over benches, ready to take them all on. Two sergeants at arms grabbed him by the shoulders. He would have swung on them, too, if he hadn't heard an echo in the gallery. "Styoopid." This word, the pronunciation he'd given it, passed around the back benches like something wonderful to touch, as if he'd thrown them a shred of his clothing or tossed them a piece of his arm. Wonder, fear, and fury blurred into red before Graham's eyes.

The opposition continued to argue, chiefly from the basis of a character smear. The magistrate listened to the slurs without disallowing so much as one. Graham sat there seething with anger and self-pity. After a while even Tate stopped objecting, and this seemed to be the worst treachery of all. Graham's own counsel began to phrase all his arguments in predefined terms, making no attempt to recast Graham as anything but the spoiled, aging lord of money, peerage, privilege, good fortune, and selfish temperament— someone essentially wicked. Neither Tate nor the court saw any irony in this. In fact, Tate's version of Graham seemed, if anything, more extreme—an uncomfortable, unsympathetic parody of the scenario Graham had never been able to accommodate with any grace. A mockery. Graham was least discomfited when allowed to sit, criminally silent, and watch what he could only take less and less seriously.

By the end of the day, Graham had wrapped himself in what little dignity remained to him and had drawn back from the whole thing. He refused to see himself as the man they were painting, even when they occasionally did so with events and circumstances that were true and familiar to him as part of his own life.

The next morning, it seemed that nature herself was conspiring against him. In the intervening night, the girl had gone into early labor. By ten that morning, she still hadn't given birth. The other side asked for and was granted a week's recess.

Graham had ridden to the Royal Courts of Justice in a state of bristling rebellion. Now he rode home enveloped in gloom. He thought of the girl struggling, trying to give birth, then these thoughts turned selfishly, peevishly back toward himself. As he walked in his own side door, he was overtaken by a sense of exhaustion.

Waiting for him in the morning's post was the last of Rosalyn's letters. He shoved it aside, holding a vague grudge against her for simply not being here. In her absence, something seemed to be going wrong.

He didn't want his mail, didn't want to eat, didn't want to deal with servants. He wanted to go somewhere and just lie still. As the morning wore on into afternoon, this mood bore down on him until he sat in a dark corner of his study feeling heavy and sluggish, as if something inside him couldn't get air—as if his spirit itself were suffocating. He realized Rosalyn had somehow been carrying him, sharing with him her blasts of oxygenated energy and good temper.

And without her or the structure of the trial, the feeling only got worse: Moving through the next few days was like moving underwater.

Just getting up in the morning took incredible effort. Graham found himself dragging from bed to breakfast to teatime to dinner, trudging around chairs with sheets thrown over them, around cabinets being emptied of their finery. The last of the belongings he'd need at Netham were being crated and trunked and taken away. His servants were doing their level best to pack around him. His house was strewn with boxes.

"What's in that?" On the third afternoon, Graham stopped a servant carrying a pasteboard box from his bedroom.

He made the man put the carton down and open it. It was full of shoes. Beige ankle boots with dark toe caps. Evening shoes of black patent leather. Graham picked up a pair of grey felt spats, handling them, trying to remember when he'd last worn them. Frowning, he threw them back in.

"No, go ahead. Take them." But he prowled back into the bedroom, looking for more boxes.

In his dressing room, his valet was carefully going through his drawers.

On seeing Graham, he stopped. "May I do something for you, sir?"

"Yes, let me." He pushed the man aside.

"This, these, and these," Graham said as he handed him an unopened box of handkerchiefs, a pair of cuff buttons someone had given him, and a set of silver studs he'd never worn. "These shirts just came from the tailor. They may as well go, too."

With a puzzled look, the man dumped the lot into a large empty trunk in the center of the floor.

"And these." Graham handed him a fistful of neckcloths. "And these can go." A handful of collar stays. Graham felt a surge of initiative.

He opened a second drawer. "I don't like this shirt. I like this one." He set it aside. He was digging through the drawer, looking for something; he didn't know what.

But the touching and handling of his things felt good. Immeasurably good. He tossed the book from his bedstand into a trunk. He was only halfway through reading it, yet seeing the book at the bottom of the trunk gave him the oddest sense of dispatch. He picked up his humidor full of cigars and tossed it in, too.

"Your Lordship, you use those," his valet protested.

"Right. So I'll need them at Netham."

Graham yanked open the doors of his jewel keep and began unloading all its tiny shallow drawers. He tossed watches toward the trunk, his valet catching, sometimes missing, watches that flew too wide of the mark.

"Sir—"

Graham moved to the wardrobe. Like a madman, he hefted out an indiscriminate load of clothes. He piled them into the trunk too, feeling as he did a wild sense of elation. "God—" He emptied the wardrobe into the trunk until it was too full to close. He threw some things out, slammed the lid, wasn't satisfied, then stuffed the things back in. He really stuffed it, climbing into the trunk to mash everything down. Then he shut the lid and climbed on top of the trunk. He felt a rush.

He stood on the trunk, panting. It still wouldn't close. "Where's another?" he asked his valet.

The man was standing back against the wall. "Another trunk, sir?"

"Right."

"Ned is packing the linens from the linen press in one."

Graham was off. Down the hall, he packed that trunk too and every trunk in the house he could lay his hands on. And there were still drawers and shelves and cupboards of things he hadn't even begun to empty.

"More trunks," he called to Ned, his under butler.

"We don't have any, sir."

"Buy some."

"I would have to send to Abercrombie's to make some up, sir. With everybody leaving, sir, there are none left in town, sir."

Sir, sir, sir. He would not be soothed with deference. "Oh, shut up. Just *unpack* all these," he told the man. "We'll start again. I'll have to be more selective."

And this selection he attacked with more enthusiasm than he had had for anything else lately.

His toiletries and writing paper and every pen and inkwell went. His summer clothes, his best soaps, his sharpest razor. All that was significant was packed off to Netham. The game was laid. He screened each possession for its importance to his daily routine. Though he gave frightened servants the mumbled explanation, "for my later convenience," there was never any doubt that he was stripping the house of everything intimately familiar to him.

Then he went to work on the staff, creating total upheaval. Those vital few who remained for some modicum of comfort Graham dismissed summarily to the country, including his own manservant and barber. The last livery, butler, footman, and groom went. Word had it that a housekeeper and gardener, with possibly a maid here or there, remained but avoided him for fear of being sacked. That was all well with him.

The removal of these things and people filled him with a sense of accomplishment. And it resulted in another gratification: Inside of twenty-four hours, he was as literally isolated in his vacant, comfortless house as he felt emotionally.

For a day or two, he languished in aloneness like some palliative drug he had taken to excess. He slept long irregular hours and ate more irregularly still. One night, when the rest of the city was asleep, he found himself suddenly awake with no watch in the house and the four clocks downstairs stopped. He tried to doze until dawn, but it seemed hours and hours in coming, with him waking countless times. He rose, found some stale bread and cheese in the kitchen, then, tired after his night's vigil for morning, he slept again. When he awoke this time, it was dark. He had slept an entire day and into the night, having eaten only one meal.

On the sixth day of the trial's recess, Graham, along with his solicitor and junior barrister, was called to a meeting in Tate's chambers. Graham arrived red-eyed, unshaven, and forty-five minutes late.

Tate greeted him with, "Are you sober?"

Graham gave him a surly look. "No. Have you got a drink? I haven't had breakfast."

The lawyer's mouth pulled into a line. "You look terrible."

"I *feel* terrible. Can we get on with this?"

"Sit down." Tate tapped his finger onto a sheaf of papers. "We have the first fruits of our labors. The other side has made an offer to settle out of court. Mind you, I'm not recommending it, but I'm obliged to show you."

He passed the papers across the desk to Graham. After the first two pages, Graham began to skim the rest. He looked up. "Lord God, where is the pen? Where do I sign?" The offer included no matrimony, no claim to title or land. By omission, the papers were disclaimers if ever he'd seen any.

When Tate didn't immediately respond, Graham leaned forward and said very distinctly, "I want to sign them."

"You understand what they say?"

"I give her an annual sum. She drops all charges."

Tate stood, ostensibly to get together the ink and pen and blotting paper required. Everything seemed to be in a different drawer. "These are still punishing terms. They involve large amounts of money, a limited legal responsibility." He was shaking his head. He couldn't seem to find an acceptable nib for his pen. He rejected several into a basket on his desk. "I can't understand why an innocent man would sign these."

"To escape the beating he is taking in the name of innocence. Can it all be done through you? Set up as a kind of trust so I never have to see the business again?"

"Yes, and through your solicitors. But it makes you look guilty."

Graham threw him a sarcastic look. "So you shouldn't mind."

Tate frowned up at him from the shuffle of papers and pens. "Being right is seldom enough. You must also be persistent."

"How can you possibly say such a thing after the way you've defended me?"

"I know you've objected—"

"You *agreed* with them."

"I didn't argue on any but the vital issues. There is no point—"

Graham had to look away. He sat back in his chair as the offense of the total proceeding reintroduced itself in his mind. "There is great point—" he began.

"Well, I don't see it. If it is slander and defamation you are worried about, I would have to get you someone else."

"Because you don't believe me."

"Your 'believability' is up to the court, not me." Tate returned to the pen-nib business, finally picking one up and pushing it onto the stem of his pen. He began to hunt through the papers on his desk as if looking for something more. "It is because I don't do slander. For your future reference, I do domestic and probate; I could get you someone else from my chambers if that is what you want. But I recommend continuing the paternity for a more clear vindication."

"No."

Tate looked up crossly. "No, what?"

Graham was taken aback. For an instant he wanted to answer, "No, sir," or "No, thank you," whatever he was being coached to say. Then he realized Tate was only asking for clarification. "No, I am satisfied. May I have it?"

Tate handed him the pen.

There was the formality of witnesses. Clerks were called in. Graham affixed his signature and seal, then there was more signing.

Tate tapped all the collected papers together. Over the top of them it was difficult to tell his mood, though it seemed to have shifted from any sincere remonstrance. "These can still be destroyed," he offered.

"I can think of nothing better my money could buy."

Tate *tsk*ed. "A poor man could not afford to throw away his innocence."

"A poor man wouldn't have been sued."

Tate's eyes squinted, performing a little smile, then he shrugged and began to put things neatly into a folder. "Your solicitor will prepare the final papers, but you may sign them here if you wish. We are still officially in trial until both you and the young lady have put your names on the final documents. Can you come in next week? We should have the matter arranged for your approval by then. A trust, correct?"

"If that is the best thing."

"I should think."

"Can you send for me from Netham?"

"I'd prefer to have you remain here until everything is tied down. There might be further discussion on small points. I don't expect any problems, but you should be here. You will have to meet with the girl and her lawyers once more." Nodding to the other men in the room, he added, "And yours."

"Very well." Graham stood to go.

"Shall we say then, unless there's some emergency, two o'clock Wednesday? At which time we shall make you the limited guardian and generous benefactor to this woman's children." Tate paused. Again he made a perfunctory smile. He tilted his head. "It is a shame to see someone your age so cynical. Especially someone who has as much as you."

Gathering his things, Graham said, "I am up to here"— he made a chop at the underside of his chin—"with how much I have."

"I was not referring to money or class. You are an intelligent young man, with the benefits of a good education. A poor man might not have been sued, but neither would have a more innocent man—and I don't mean innocent in this particular case: You are guilty of a much greater waste, and you know it. You are too old to have nothing to show."

"A moment ago I was young and had so much."

"You know what I mean."

"I'm afraid I don't. Is this all included in your fee?"

"You are the same boy, aren't you?"

Graham didn't know precisely what the lawyer meant, but he felt the need to turn away again. He hid a mild, involuntary flush. "I am old enough to resent this continuing attitude of yours—"

Tate waved his hand. "My apologies." He was rising to walk the group of men to the door. "It is only that—habit, I suppose. Henry, I mean. He talked of you. . . . I tend to think of you . . . protectively, in a sense. I mustn't. I'm sorry. You are perfectly right in being angry."

— Chapter 12 —

Submit carried her coat out to the landing and laid it over the banister so she wouldn't forget it. For a change, the coat wasn't damp. The weather had dried out, the rainy days giving way to a series of bright, hot ones. It looked as though London and its environs might finally enjoy what so much of the rest of the world did, a truly warm summer.

In her room, Submit put the last of her bags by the door. A manservant, Mr. Schild's valet it turned out, had offered to take these down. He had arrived this morning to pick up the last of Mr. Schild's clothes. For the past week, except for the coming and going of servants, Submit had had the house to herself. Rosalyn Schild had graciously allowed her to stay the extra days remaining on the lease. The house, however, was about to revert to its English owners; the Schilds' rent had covered the London season, and the season was over. After tomorrow, it was no longer their prerogative to allow her to stay.

It didn't matter. Submit was ready to move on. She even looked forward to the very humble arrangements she had once more made for herself at the inn. In the last few weeks, she had begun to relish even the smallest things as she accomplished them on her own. She would have liked having a more luxurious life, but the fact that she could manage with less, and be happy, gave her satisfaction.

She latched the bag, one of seven, plus a trunk. For a near penniless woman, she laughed to herself, she certainly had a lot of baggage to move around. William had let her take all her personal possessions from Motmarche. If he or his wife, Margaret, had any inclination to use any of their clothes or toiletries from Charlotte Street, she had told him, he had

better let her have hers from East Anglia. Thus, their first
accommodation—they had each come away with the things
from their personal drawers and clothes cupboards.

Or closets, as Rosalyn said. The American woman called
her clothes wardrobe a closet, which made Submit do a
smiling sort of double take. All she associated with the word
"closet" was the W.C., the water closet. The American was
amazing and amusing. Rosalyn herself laughed over these
sorts of discovered differences; she seemed to love them.
But they must have affected her beyond this, for she also
promptly adopted the English way as soon as she realized
any discrepancy between the two cultures. She was becoming a strange kind of ersatz Brit; it was false, but somehow
not unappealing. Rosalyn Schild was reshaping herself, joyously following her own tastes down a path that puzzled the
English and might, Submit speculated, offend the woman's
own stauncher countrymen.

Still, Submit could not help but like her. Rosalyn loved
everything she did, every moment. The people. The dressing. The entertaining. The gossip. The games. Even the
mean competitiveness of her own circle—even when this
was directed pointedly at her. "Aren't people *awful*," she
said with a laugh, as one of the more proper women, paying a call, suddenly left. "She had the nerve to tell me,
'Why, the earl of Netham isn't here, my dear. I didn't know
he *ever* went home.' So I told her back, 'He goes home if
the kitties climb all over him too much. Or when he sees
you coming, darling. You see, he doesn't like anything that
hisses.' " Rosalyn had followed this with a peal of laughter.
"How awful of me, don't you think, Submit?" Rosalyn was,
by her own authority, on a first-name basis with everyone.
"Because, of course, Graham loves me, and I am the catti-
est thing in skirts!"

She was. Rosalyn Schild was incorrigibly vindictive and
self-centered. She was also generous to a fault. She truly

liked other people, so long as they didn't get in her way. She
had even wanted to pay the summer rent on this house—it
would be considerably less than it had been for the season,
Rosalyn insisted; she wanted Submit to stay. But Submit felt
uncomfortable with such indebtedness to a woman who
was so frank with her passions, good and bad. One could
trust Rosalyn Schild to be honest, Submit thought, but Submit preferred to trust herself to be consistent and kind. She
had refused politely.

Outside, a carriage stopped in the street. Submit went to
see if this was Arnold Tate. He had offered to take her to her
next "home." He had also, in fact, offered to pay her way.
Again she had refused. "That would be a fine thing," she
had teased him, "for everyone to whisper how the widowed
Lady Motmarche was being kept by her attorney." He
couldn't argue. She looked out the window, but the driveway was empty. The carriage she'd heard had stopped
across the street.

Submit came back to her bags and was about to ring for
the manservant when she caught sight of the little black box.

She was going to leave it, of course. She had tried to deliver it. Besides, she didn't want it with her anymore. She
had opened it three more times, and the contents simply
upset her too much. It was bad enough the outside was
gaudy; the contents were vulgar enough that every time she
looked at them, they stopped her heart. Let the servants or
the next tenants figure out what to do with the box. It would
serve Graham Wessit right if people came to associate it
with him. Submit frowned at this thought, then lost track of
it. The front bell downstairs rang. Before she could think,
Arnold Tate had come up the stairs, picked up her bags, and
was breathing hard under the strain of trying to carry too
many of them down again.

"Arnold, please. At least let me take one."

But he wouldn't. And he wouldn't let the servants help,

except with the trunk. He put her bags in the front carriage boot himself, instructed that the trunk be tied onto the rear, then raced around to give her his hand. He lifted her, helping her in not only by her hand but also with a light pressure at her waist. She looked at him a moment. She felt nothing. No, of course she felt something. It felt wonderful to have Arnold here. She could count on him to be decent, civil, a true gentleman—even if his idea of suavity included exhausting himself over her bags. She smiled at Arnold.

"Thank you."

He smiled back. "My pleasure."

But a vague unease wouldn't let her return his warmth. She touched his hand. "Arnold." She frowned slightly. "The box I picked up at your office a few weeks ago. The box I was supposed to give Graham Wessit—"

"He didn't take it." It was a statement, not a question.

"I didn't give it to him," she corrected. "I don't know what happened, but I just didn't manage to hand it over as I should have. And now I've left it upstairs—"

"Fine." He drew his brows together. "Don't worry about it." He pushed her skirt in.

She had to stop his hand from closing the door. "Arnold, do you know what it is? What's inside? What it means?"

He paused, the carriage door still in his hand. He looked at the door's edge, at its latch, pressing his lips together in much the way he seemed to want to seal up the vehicle— tight. When he looked back at her, there was an uncomfortable determination in his eye. "No," he said.

Submit leaned back into the carriage. He was lying. "Then be a dear and go get it for me, would you?" Hang him anyway, she thought. She would hoist him on his own closed mouth. "It's on the nightstand."

The attorney hesitated, started to say something, then shut the door gently. When he joined her in the carriage a few minutes later, he handed the black box over to her, then sat silently back into the far corner. Submit offered him no reprieve. She said nothing, and for the forty-five-minute trip he also remained silent. If he had offered one bit of truth about the box, she would have listened. If he had tried to change the subject, she was sufficiently baffled and angry at him, at Henry, that she would have cut him off. As it was, she let him sit there in his dark corner, allowing him to be a victim of his own unspoken thoughts.

Graham was humming as he climbed the carriage-entry steps. The day was beautiful, he thought. Life was rich. Then he opened his own door and remembered: His household was a mess.

The small private entrance area had its few furnishings draped over, its usual knickknacks either hidden or sent off. The door closed and echoed behind him. No one met him to receive his hat.

In his room, the bed was made, a pitcher of fresh water set out by a clean basin—testaments to a living presence, the housekeeper or maid. He realized there was actually nothing that needed his attention, except perhaps Rosalyn's last letter. It lay on his dresser folded over the accompanying ripped-out pages of the magazine. He opened the top drawer and swept the whole lot into it, then rang for a bath.

He found he had a staff of exactly three: one housekeeper, one gardener, and one footman—minus any vehicle to foot. Between himself and the apologetic footman, he managed a shave with only a minor injury—a small gash at his throat, which ruined the first collar he put on. In finding the second, he also found a watch at the back of the drawer. He wound and set it according to the footman's. Then, too efficient, he found himself with a warm and uncommitted afternoon.

Graham told himself he was thinking of Rosalyn until he was actually at her door, ringing the bell. By then, he was having to concoct a more credible excuse to himself: Rosalyn was of course gone from her London house. This left the widow, he expected, once more with nowhere to go; he was there to inquire after her.

But as the door to Rosalyn's house swung open, in the face of a familiar servant, Graham was halted. He mumbled something about a mislaid cloak.

He was admitted into the shuttered house with the comment that he was lucky. The last of the Schilds' staff were leaving tonight, new tenants coming tomorrow or the day after. He could ring if he needed help in finding the cloak. There was some awkwardness, apparently Graham's alone. A butler, then an upper housemaid, nodded to him as they passed him in the hallway; the rest ignored him. He was given much the run of the place, though he didn't move comfortably about. He couldn't shake the feeling of red-handedness as he touched Rosalyn's possessions, her habitat.

He was half an hour at this wandering and rummaging, this guilty search for the nonexistent cloak, when he finally had to admit that his other reason for being here was absent as well. Ironically, wistfully, he found an inexpensive outer coat, a nubby black wool he was sure was Submit's, draped over the banister at the top landing. He had a vague longing to purloin the garment—a hostage. But in the end he put it down. It might, should Rosalyn discover it, become traitor, not hostage, to his secret inclinations. Standing there at the top of the stairs, he pondered the extent of these inclinations. He wanted to see the woman again. That much was clear, but he didn't know what came after that. He only recognized that he wanted something from her by the size and substance of his guilt. Friendship? he thought. With an odd stroke of insight he realized, perhaps more than anything, Rosalyn would not be pleased with that.

The coat was the only trace of the widow. No carefully

phrased questions yielded a hint. There was no forwarding address. And, no, the mistress hadn't taken the lady with her. He hardly knew what to think. He had considered the widow more or less obligated to be on hand, at least until Henry's papier-mâché case had been delivered to him.

Graham sat down in an empty bay window and surveyed one particularly empty room—the front parlor, where he had last spoken to Submit Channing-Downes. He felt lost, deprived, foolish, as if some trick had been played on him. He wanted to blame someone, but candidates were scarce. Therefore, because it was so convenient and easy to blame a dead man, he put Henry at fault. The miserable old man. How could he marry such a nothing of a woman? Such a young woman? A woman who could slip behind a screen of day-to-day trivia, behind the flamboyant Rosalyn, behind Graham's own smug reliance that he had her safely shelved for future reference, and simply disappear, leaving behind only her crumpled coat?

Three days later, Graham was again at odds with Tate, only this time it was to his advantage to say nothing. He was not the object: Tate preached to the courtroom-mother on the subjects of conscience and sin.

"You should be less ashamed," he told her, "of the babies born out of wedlock than to be involving an innocent third party." Graham's advocate to the end, he pressed her to tears to release Graham from the "reprehensible responsibilities" that she, as an "unjust opportunist of his past difficulties," was thrusting on his shoulders.

Graham watched her. Her lip-biting brevity. Her determination. Little was known of this young laundress, but Graham saw enough on her face to doubt she knew the meaning of the word "reprehensible." Her teary silences said she knew only that she was wrong, and that she knew—

lived—circumstances that made her determined to stay wrong. Anyone could have told Tate to save his breath.

But he didn't. He picked at her, deliberately and over a protracted stretch of time, until her solicitor finally put a halt to it. Graham wished then that he had said something. He sympathized with her mortification at being lectured on what had become a moot point. The matter was settled. Still, Tate went on and on in that closed room, trying to make an "honest" woman of her by making her feel guilty.

Listening to all this, so reminiscent of Tate's lectures to him, Graham began to feel a kinship with the girl. In their disparate silences, he recognized himself a week ago—the sliding sense, the deep, unnameable discontent, the signs of heavy burden and the incapacity to communicate to anyone its particular weight. If Graham had been struggling to keep his head above water a week ago, he was staring now at a face that looked half-drowned. She was deathly white and as thin as a cadaver. He remembered someone saying she had hemorrhaged during the delivery of her babies, and she looked it: She was less the feisty, table-climbing girl at the beginning of all this, and by many more pounds than just the weight of twin boys—she had borne two sons.

Sitting in that office, Graham began to feel a peculiar ambivalence toward her that had to do with pity, though not necessarily the generous sort. He felt instead the kind of pity that celebrates a little: There but for the grace of God. . . . At one point, she looked at him directly. Or so he thought. Her eyes became flat and vacant, even as they were flooding over with tears—as if she cried for something far off, far removed from either herself or her present situation. It was an eerie look. In that instant, she seemed as mad as a hatter. And Graham's animosity toward her all but disappeared. He felt a sadness, a sorrow that was for her alone.

At last. He rather weltered in this feeling for her. He sat

there, flexing it, turning it over and over in his mind, like the rediscovery of sensation in a numb limb. He wasn't going to analyze it for its quality or, God knew, try and use it. He was only glad it was there, that he might feel something for someone besides himself.

With the signing of the last legal documents, her humiliation seemed complete. She had gone from starring role to backstage haggling, and she clearly wasn't happy about it. But she signed. She wrote a small, round signature. At one point, Graham's solicitor tried to hurry her, but she snapped that she would write at her own speed and convenience. It occurred to Graham that, though he knew little of her, she had known a great deal about him. His club, his history, his life. Not that any of this was too difficult to find out. But it made him wonder if she *did* know the word "reprehensible" after all. Surely not. Yet she could put pen to paper, and he wouldn't have expected that of a laundress. Perhaps she could write more than her signature. Perhaps she could string together enough words, for instance, to write a half-baked parody of his life, filled with accusations and overreactive emotions. Could a laundress put together a magazine serial? he wondered. Could she be behind *The Rake of Ronmoor*?

She passed the papers to Graham. He signed, then passed them to the witnesses to validate. It was over.

Almost. As she rose, Graham touched her arm. "Why?" he asked. "How do you know me?"

She wasn't going to answer, he thought. Then she looked him in the eye. "Me father. 'E was yer dresser when you was on the stage." After a pause, she added, as if this should explain everything, "Name o' 'Arry. 'E didn't mind so much when I told 'im they was yours."

Graham had no memory of a costume dresser named Harry, but he understood the suit had had something to do with a lie to a possibly irate father. He said, "Well then, I expect he'll be happy now."

She shook her head. "Dead. Died las' week. Been sick a long time." She shrugged. "Doesn't matter."

Still out of his depth, he said, "I'm sorry."

"Just as well. 'E wun't a been 'appy 'bout the money anyway. 'E thought you should marry me." Her gaze drifted a moment. " 'E was a good man. Sacrificin', ya' know?"

"Well, I'm—ah—sorry you lost him."

Again he had the sense that she was slightly deranged. Her look hardened, then focused in a way that made no sense. "You kin do better ' an be sorry. Just remember that." These words had no meaning for him, except that they sounded like an obscure threat.

Graham frowned after her, speaking to Tate behind him. "Is there anything more she can do to me legally?"

"No," Tate replied. "She has the first payment of her annuity. We'll set the police on her if she causes any more trouble. The worst she can do to you is live a very long time."

A day later Graham wrote:

26 June 1858
Dear Rosalyn,

I think I have blamed everyone, including you. My humble apologies. Of the episodes, number six was not so bad. Or perhaps I can at last view it in a less moody, selfish light. The twit is settled; no more laundress, no more twins. I am a free man and can afford to be less piqued. I spoke to the publisher, incidentally, a William Task Pease, trying to glean a hint about the author of his fiction. He was as uncooperative as possible in discussing the pseudonymous (at least that was confirmed) M. DuJauc. But he willingly discussed the serial. He plans, of all things, to bring it out in about a year's time as a novel. I told him I would sue him. Unfortunately, I think he is not as averse to a legal tangle as he maintains, though perhaps I am suspicious of him because I am so hypocritical myself—I am not nearly as willing to embark on another lawsuit as I would have him believe. He says, "Please no," but his eyes twinkle at the publicity. He has won for the moment.

Another idea consoles me, though. I keep thinking of the twit as YDJ. The idea had something to do with watching her sign yesterday. I keep considering the bold and conscienceless imagination it took to get us to that point. Granted, it would be a stretch for her hand to actually write the episodes, but I don't doubt she could do it. (It's not all that well done anyway, is it?) Looking at her, one has the eerie impression of all things possible, of a clear and focused insanity—she has already proved herself capable, the way Bedlam inmates are reported to lift breakfronts and sideboards to heave at people. At any rate, I shall not be the least surprised if a laundrymaid in Ronmoor gives birth to twins. I am rather counting on it, in fact.

So at present I am planning on a wonderful policy of inaction. How much damage, after all, can a girl and a pen do to me? I can't ignore a courtroom and the legitimate power it has, but I damn well can ignore a self-appointed chronicler hiding behind a mask of fiction, especially fiction of such a transitory type: a fiction that replaces itself weekly and promises, by its very existence, to be replaced by another of its own kind in the near future.

I am lagging on a bit here in London, since you cannot be in Netham until the twenty-eighth or so, but also to break the feeling of being rushed and pushed everywhere. I was invited carousing tonight (with Tilney, as a matter of fact, no doubt wanting some new horror to report to you), but have declined. If I'm going to get smashed, I intend to do it thoroughly and quietly on my own.

Today I went riding, after some trouble over finding a horse—I seem to have sent all mine to Nethamshire. I'll explain later. I find myself, by my own doing, in London without a speck of convenience. Not a horse, not a carriage, not a manservant, not even a spare watch. Henry's widow was right. I am a little absurd. But I am content. I wandered outside the city today, much on my own. Tomorrow I shall start for Netham by horseback, having enjoyed that solitary—salutary—means of transportation. The weather is quite nice.

I look forward to seeing you.

G

— Chapter 13 —

Graham's ride outside the city that next day was not quite as uneventful as it sounded in his letter to Rosalyn. He had ridden out to the posting house at Morrow Fields.

By horseback, the inn was just a bit more than an hour's ride from London. The countryside opened up rapidly to the north of the city, and with this, as he rode into it, a sense of anticipation opened in Graham. The signed papers behind him, he took the day for himself. He was going to cast about for the widow once more, he told himself, though this was more an excuse; it gave him a destination. Mostly he liked the ideas of riding, eating a pleasant packed lunch, and enjoying a new landscape. He had never gone in this particular direction from London, and there was something discoverable—like childhood exploring—about a lone ride into unfamiliar terrain.

The sky was cloudless, a dazzling parrot blue. The land, as he left the city behind, began to roll, shifting back and forth between sparse woods and pasturelands. As he traveled through this, somehow the muddle of his life dissolved. He began to feel almost transparent; as if, from the dome of the sky to the roots of the trees, the countryside were traveling through him, not he through it. His thoughts only flickered through him, no more seizable than the shadow and sun that filtered through leaves overhead. He moved along in the diffuse exhilaration of having a perfect, untold, unaccountable day—and of being about his own mildly obsessive project, only for the private fancy of it.

Of course, today's first and final obsession was not the countryside but Submit Channing-Downes—or rather the pursuit of her. Graham didn't actually suppose he'd find her, but he wanted the play of pretending he might. He had recalled the general whereabouts of the inn from his conversation with the widow at Rosalyn's party. This memory was enough to make him ride joyously along now, imagining one moment he would find her there, then consoling himself the next over his long ride for nothing.

As the only posting house at Morrow Fields came into view, it didn't look too promising. It was an old structure, built of arched stones and wood beams. Like most stopovers that catered to a coaching trade, it was more coach house than inn. Graham dismounted and entered a dilapidated door. He expected anything but the proprietor's immediate answer.

"Yea, but she's no' in."

"The lady is staying here?"

This was almost an alarming consideration. Inside, the posting house was a dull, spare place. Bare walls. Worn wood floors. It had the sad aura of something that had once looked nice but was now abandoned. A century ago, when north was still not such a gauche direction in which to travel, it had probably seen its share of wealthy visitors. But now, being in the wrong direction from town and thus prosperity, it was decidedly run-down, though in a clean, make-do sort of fashion.

From the entry room, Graham looked in on a common room filled with tables. An otherwise bare side counter displayed a vase of wildflowers at one end. Some directives on the wall caught his attention, as they were meant to. They were handlettered signs reading off warnings and admonitions: "Meals and bath will be added to the final bill." "Carriages are not to be left at the front entrance for any other purpose than loading and unloading." "Meals will not be served in the common room after ten p.m." Graham wondered if the management wasn't a little responsible for the lack of business. The entire place was empty of people, save the man who, with an air of ownership, swept the floor.

Still not quite believing it, Graham asked again, "She's here?"

"Tha' been told onct and tha' askt again? Don't tha' huv ears?"

"Where is she?"

The proprietor continued his distracted maneuvers with the broom, raising only an elbow to indicate a set of doors. French doors with one cracked lower pane stood at the far end of the eating common. "Oot," he replied, like a reticent owl.

"Thank you."

Graham walked between the tables, around the leftover fashionableness of their linen tops. Each table was set lovingly with silver, as if someone were expected. He touched a chair back here and there just to feel its solidness. There was a feeling of anticipation in the room that felt strange, more than simply impractical—a sense of a great banquet about to begin with no guests, all indefinitely delayed. He moved quickly through the maze of furniture, exiting through the French doors, then found himself squinting into the sun.

What he saw was breathtaking. It diminished the afternoon's ride to the most ordinary of sights. Graham stood under a partial overhang on something of a terrace: stones set together to make a flooring with a few stones missing, grass growing between. A few more weathered tables sat on this, the whole bounded by a low wall. But beyond the dirt terrace was more beauty than any run-down inn had a right to possess. All grass and sky for as far as the eye could see. Deep, vivid green. The blue of the sky was made brilliant in contrast. A breeze combed the field in waves, parting it into deeper shades like a nap. Occasional trees cast shade. Hardwoods, varieties of beech, he would guess. These dotted the green as if casually landscaped into it. Far off, perhaps miles away, poplars towered into the air. Thicker, in running clusters, they put a line between sky and land; a serrate finish as perfect and definitive as a scalloped edge. Graham took in the view. It was a terrific amount of land in any direction, miles and miles. There was, however, no woman in any of it, not a human, an animal, or a house in sight.

Graham went back to question the proprietor further. Inside, the man had begun to get out a service of tea. It was silver, like one that a more southerly posting house might sport. The owner fondled the set unhurriedly.

"She's not out there."

As if in direct contradiction, the man answered, "I be gettin' her tea now."

"But she's not outside."

The proprietor looked up. He had a thin, browned face. His lower jaw folded over his upper in a downcast line, giving the impression of inveterate scorn. "Walking," he said with particular distinction. "I put th' tea oot a' two precise. For th' guests."

"She comes back for tea?" Graham asked.

"Or it gets cool'd."

"Could I take it and wait for her on the terrace?"

"Gentlemen guests set a' ther own tables unless married to or invited by th' lady guests."

"Where will you put her tea?"

"On the terrace."

"Then may I have my own, at my own table, beside hers?"

"Tha's not a guest." The man didn't look up but wrapped the silver teapot, now full, in several turns of muslin towel.

"How much is it to become a guest?"

The man stopped, turned, and considered Graham from his boots to his face. "No bags, twelve shillin's. Thu's a decent place."

Graham was about to protest this customized price, then thought better of it. He produced the required money.

"Wait a' the table. I'll bring it."

The owner brought a wrapped teapot, a cup and saucer, sugar and cream, and a few small biscuits to each of the two tables. These had come and been left standing, with the man serving the empty table with all the aplomb and appurtenances as his own, before Graham caught sight of her.

Punctual. Punctuational, he was reminded. Today, a small dot, the final period at the end of his ride; conclusive, definite. She grew from the poplars, a speck, a black motion separating itself from its surroundings. He waited. Surprisingly, she became not quite the same widow he had last seen. She was wearing a straw hat the color of the day, the color of her hair. And he could see, as she got closer, that the hat was banded by a deep, more striking anomaly: a ruby ribbon that fluttered and shone in the sun.

As she was coming across the field, Submit saw she had company. Another guest sat at a table near her own. It was only when she stood in the opening of the low terrace wall, however, that she realized who the man was. She halted, resting her fingers lightly on the walltop. Her hands had been in her pockets. The stones felt suddenly, keenly cold. Her fingers clenched.

For ten or twenty seconds, Submit couldn't move. Her palms grew clammy. It was one thing to see Graham Wessit at Rosalyn Schild's house; it was quite another to see him turn up in her own private domain. From beneath her broad-brimmed hat, she stared at him. Then she put her hands back into the pockets of her dress.

"What do you want?" she asked.

The question caught Graham half risen from his chair. There was an awkward, too-long pause as he stared at a face overhung with shadows. He glanced at the lifted, folded layers of her skirt. He had forgotten how oddly attractive she could be in a black dress. She was all shadow and shade, all but the glorious hat. Its ribbon fluttered, beautiful, brilliant ruby red.

"The case," he said finally. "You still have it?" He could think of nothing else to say, and he instantly regretted this entry. But perhaps she no longer had the case or would give it up without a word. That was what he counted on, her polite lack of comment.

"Wait," she said bluntly.

Graham watched her move off, the black Druid in a straw hat. He saw the hat come off in her hand as she went through the doors. When she returned, she was carrying the case against her chest, the way schoolchildren carry their books. Graham was dismayed to note that the frivolous hat was now nowhere to be seen.

Submit tapped the box as she set it down on the table in front of Graham. Her discomposure was working its way toward anger. If he truly wanted this thing, after all this time, he could explain now from the beginning.

"Why in God's name would Henry give this to you?" she asked. "I never knew him to have any such interest." She sat down opposite Graham, preparing for a long chat with the box between them.

He took it immediately into his lap, out of sight. "I liked your hat," he said. "Shall we have tea?"

"That"—Submit pointed a finger onto a grey plank of the table—"is not like him."

"The little case?"

She gave him a censuring look. "What is *in* the little case."

"You told me it was his; it must be 'like' him."

"Do you know what is in there?" Without waiting for an answer, she added, "I suspect you do."

He gave an uncertain smile and reached for the teapot. "If you don't mind. Since you don't care to—" He would pretend he didn't know, if she would let him.

"Open it," she said. "Please."

This left Graham frowning and pouring.

The tea smelled strong to him and was much too hot for the day. But he went through the motions, giving himself an opportunity to understand her attitude. She seemed to have a very different interpretation from his as to the contents of what he held in his lap. Why would she possibly want to discuss what was in there? Then it occurred to him that time and Henry's peculiar sense of—what? humor?—might have worked to his advantage. He glanced over the rim of his cup. She really didn't know the significance of this box, he realized. At least a partial ignorance sat, unaware of itself, on her face. Dear, incomprehensible Henry. Graham put his cup down and slid his chair back. He opened the case below her level of vision.

He started slightly and felt his face warm. He couldn't decide how he should react. He began to shuffle through the heavy pages of paper. They were, all twelve of them, there. Finely detailed ink drawings, each with its naked man and woman bonded together in some contortion. Breasts, bellies, half-open mouths. Defiant penises raised like fisted arms over the terrain and shrubbery of testes and open thighs. Somehow, reviewing these pictures with the woman across from him was not something he was prepared to do. Graham closed the box and went back to the tea.

Submit leaned on her elbows, putting her chin in her hands, and stared. She waited for this disconcerting man to explain as Henry might have; she waited for profound insight.

When he just sat there, saying nothing, filling his cup a second time, she asked, "Why? Why would Henry think that was a good thing to leave you? You knew the other night, you *knew* what was there. And you must know too that he wasn't like that." She wanted very badly to hear this confirmed.

Meanwhile Graham took pleasure in the indicting silence. Dirty old man, he thought, marrying such a young— and trusting—girl. He wiped his lip, then touched his forehead with his napkin. The tea, the afternoon, not to mention this particular lapful of drawings, were a warm combination.

"He was," Submit continued on her own, "such a straightforward man. Why would I not know he kept this sort of thing?" Graham watched her face rise up out of her hands. "Or at least suspect? I can't, even knowing it now, put it together with him." She waited again for Graham to offer some logical understanding. "Can you?" she asked.

He played with the cup and saucer. "We never completely know people, I suppose."

"But not like this. Henry was a *gentle* man."

"Henry?" The table wobbled as Graham moved his long legs under it.

"I—Of course, Henry."

Graham stated what he had always considered a simple fact. "Henry was a pompous, belligerent, domineering son of a bitch."

She sat back. She was finally shocked. Where lewd pictures had failed, Graham realized, he had had enormous success.

His language, he thought. Why had he been so emphatic? "Forgive me—" But he could see it was not that. Some whole mood had changed. She had expected a shared experience, a shared viewpoint, where one simply didn't exist.

He gave his full attention to the teacup. Its footed base, unglazed where it had been cut from the wheel, ground in the saucer against spilled sugar. Finally, for something to do, he pinched the cup by its handle and drank it dry.

"He could be harsh," Submit offered, "give you a piece of his mind when he wanted to."

"Or the back of his hand."

There was another break. "I suppose you knew him differently from how I did. Under different circumstances."

"I suppose."

Nothing connected them. They did not seem to have even a piece of Henry in common.

"The pictures. You didn't expect them?" she asked.

"Hardly."

"Why you?"

The subject exhausted him. He told her as much by a look.

She looked away. "I'm sorry. I don't mean to make your receiving them as reprehensible as Henry's hiding them then giving them to you."

"I wouldn't be too angry with him."

"Well, I am. I feel so—deceived." Her eyes fixed on him. He was overwhelmed for a moment by a brave, disconcerting intelligence, an unflinching, unshrinking scrutiny. Then she bowed her head. "And you know things you're not saying. You know all about this in some way. Were there more? Was Henry—peculiar?"

"Henry was decidedly peculiar."

"*That* way."

"What way?"

She made a little reprimanding snort.

"Not that I know of," he answered.

"Are you?"

He frowned sharply. "Perhaps you'd better be more definite."

"You know. Do you go in for that sort of thing? Like it a lot?"

"What sort of thing?"

She turned away. "Looking. Pictures. It excites men sometimes, doesn't it? Does it you?"

He didn't know what to say. A woman he had considered a prude was outmaneuvering him on the subject of dirty pictures. "That is quite the most private question I have been asked in the last few hours."

"But does it?" she insisted.

Graham couldn't understand why she would force herself through this. "It can," he said, "and I'm not sure that's peculiar."

That proved something. The young widow stood and walked to the wall. She leaned back on it. Then his frank response drew an unforeseen, reciprocal candidness. "They stir me a little," she admitted. Self-consciously, she laughed.

It was the nicest, strangest sound. Her laughter, unvocalized, had a soft, shudderlike quality. She laughed with her mouth closed, her smile slightly crooked, this appealingly lopsided expression faintly narrowing one eye. He didn't think she was aware of it—it was not artifice, but when she smiled, her wise young face took on a wisdom that was worldly and strictly female: beguilingly sly.

"You have no idea what a surprise these were," she said. The smile faded, leaving behind the narrow, thoughtful look.

"I can imagine."

She shook her head—no, he couldn't—then raised a hip slightly and pulled back her hoops. She sat on the walltop, leaving one foot to dangle above the dirt floor.

"Perhaps it's normal," Graham Wessit offered. "A husband doesn't tell his wife everything."

Submit sniffed at that. "My husband was my friend." Then she objected violently to her own statement, shaking her head. She came off her perch in one movement and strode to the far side of the patio. She put her back to him.

She bent her head so low that Graham wasn't sure if she had given up the head-shaking or not. He watched her for a while, until his own silence began to feel contemptible.

"I was sent down from university for these," he said finally. "Henry must have wanted me to know—oh, I don't know what. But I'm sure it wasn't for prurience he saved them. Quite the opposite, I imagine. One last sermon from the grave. It must have been irresistible."

Submit looked around. "You passed them at university?"

"Like a bag of crumpets."

"And got caught?"

"And expelled. And jailed and—more. I read humility that year and took a First."

He watched her face. It remained blank—perhaps the politest expression possible under the circumstances. At least the head-shaking had stopped, the self-reproaching questions, the hypothesizing. Her comment that the pictures "stirred" her was curious to him—it was curious that she would have such stirrings, more curious still that she would mention them. There was something about her. . . . He speculated to himself that Henry might have secretly fancied the pictures. Looking at his wife made unusual things possible for Henry. Young love. If not a penchant, at least an interest in the angles and curves of firm, green coitus.

She had turned her back again. Her chignon was thick, the tied volume of baled hay. It made her fragile body seem to need a ballast to counter the weight. The heaviness rested against the nape of her neck. It seemed to press at her spine. Then he thought perhaps it was not the outline of spine he saw, but French hooks beneath a placket. He stared at the dress's closure.

She turned suddenly. Again he was confronted with her smile, its faintly crooked and intriguing friendliness, her direct eyes. And he realized that by telling his reluctant little partial truth, he had made her indebted to him: He had given the husband an upright and plausible motive for passing pornography.

"I can't put you with him," he said. "You are totally unlike any woman I ever knew growing up. Of Henry's, I mean. He liked ones who could talk you into the ground. On politics or books or finance or something. He liked ones who carried banners, in their eyes if not in their hands."

She laughed, a breathy sound. It was their first agreement.

He smiled. "He was so—old," he continued, "even when he was young, if that makes any sense."

"I'm old." But she was more amused.

"Are you?"

Her eyes—bannerless—teased, a feminine refusal to discuss age. Or else she was saying it was unimportant. "I couldn't comprehend it myself for a while. To like Henry so well, I mean. He was my father's choice. But I did come to like him. Exceptionally well." Then, as if she had bungled, she added, "I am sorry you didn't. He was full of wit and intelligence—he was a sensitive man in many ways."

Graham restrained the awkwardness he felt. Her evaluations—elevations—of his former guardian at every turn seemed so wrong. There was no right way to respond: He couldn't be honest, and he couldn't bring himself to be polite. The impasse again widened, leaving a gap in the conversation. At length, he stood to go.

As he did, the case slid from his lap. It crashed on the flooring, splitting its hinge and spilling its contents. Pictures scattered out across the stones like someone's burdened, babbling conscience confessing up in graphic detail.

Graham bent immediately, trying to gather it all up. "The stupid perversity of it," he mumbled. "Swooning and groaning over these stupid things for all these years."

"I seriously doubt that he swooned and groaned."

"He hated the whole episode. How could he own them? Will them? Be so preposterously godlike to keep them then dump them on me—on you—with no explanation? I wonder if he looked them over periodically. *That* must have been goddamn sweet torment. The stupidity of it!"

"Mr. Tate kept them for him."

"Oh, splendid!" Graham looked up long enough to shake a fistful of erotica at her. "Are you going to stand there and defend this—this prank, this stupid, posthumous game ... this ... this. ..." The latch wouldn't close. He bent over it, fumbling on one knee. The thick paper stuck out in corners and folds. "There was no reason for him to involve you in this. Although you certainly take it in your stride: Nothing surprises you. Well, it surprises me! *You* surprise me. These weren't the only surprising pleasures Henry obtained for his old age, were they?"

He meant her, Submit realized. She took a step back. She felt the blood in her face rise.

While Graham felt nothing but exasperation. He couldn't get the case closed. He knelt there, silently cursing it, wanting with all his might to heave the thing into the sky and watch it sail beyond sight. But Submit churned by him instead, as if he'd lit a firecracker at her back. She went by him with such force, she knocked him off balance.

He sat with a *plonk*. "Wonderful," he said to her marching back.

She left him there, sitting in his own pique on a pothole in the floor, holding the black box in his hands. He looked down at it, feeling stuck with it—stuck with its misaligned corners, its broken back, its legs and arms hanging out in wrinkles and folds. Always stuck, it seemed, with having to organize unwelcome pieces of his life that never should have been in the first place. He stood up, finally succeeding in closing the box: Henry's generous gift.

He set it down, only to realize a drawing remained on the ground. "Thank you very much, Henry," he murmured as he picked it up. "You miserable old pisspot."

When he looked back toward the person he wanted to speak to most, she was already a third of the way to the poplars, a black, shifting dot on the vivid greensward. He cursed Henry again, then started after her.

— Chapter 14 —

In the open field, her own dress was the only movement—so it was easy enough to tell he was behind her, half walking, half running, trying to catch up. Submit walked as fast as she could, hoping he would drop back once he saw there was no point in pursuing her.

The poplars and their shade waited in the distance. She longed to be there again, yet she didn't dare move any faster. The late afternoon sun dazzled, saturated. Her black dress churned about her. Beneath it, at the pace she was going, her legs already felt blanketed and hot. She heard the man behind her, closing the distance.

"Lady Motmarche," he called out. "Wait—"

The sound of his voice only galled her. Graham Wessit was not only brutishly crude but relentlessly stupid as well.

The top of her head began to feel warm—she wished she had her hat. She wished he'd go away. Why had he come here anyway? He was a foul-mouthed, silk-vested popinjay who hadn't the first bit of taste, not for people or clothes. His disdain for Henry mingled for a moment with his garish sartorial affectations. The vest today, she remembered vividly, was green. A dark green velvet with the substance and texture of cut silk. She could have lived a fortnight on the vest's buttons alone—they were *bain d'or*. She heard him come up behind her within a few yards. His pace slowed—a little healthy prudence at last. Then he fell in step just a few feet behind, as if they were out for a stroll.

Submit turned on him. He drew up, startled by this preemptive stop, as she asked him with a sharp, wordless tilt of her head, What exactly did his following her out here prove?

"I'm sorry," Graham answered. "I didn't mean to offend

you." Then, with a grimace of closed eyes, he actually took this back. "Well, perhaps I did. But I—I regret doing so now." He paused. "I'm sorry. I was out of place. Everything else aside, Henry was a highly principled man. His interest in you would hardly have been—"

Submit angled her head up at him. "Henry married me," she pointed out. "He didn't adopt me. His interest in me, for your future reference, was completely that of a husband."

He blinked. He had no more apologies, no more words.

Good, she thought, she'd stunned him a little herself. He grimaced again, then ran his hand back over his head, as if to say it was hot standing out in the middle of the sun. He did look hot. A velvet vest was heavy for summer. His coat was dark. Then she noticed something in his other hand, at the end of one dark sleeve. "Let me see that." She held out her hand.

Graham stared at her palm, held expectantly open. He looked at her face and dropped his eyes to where hers fell. He saw he'd carried the sketch with him from the terrace. It was creased between his fingers, readily available to keep him blundering along. His wrist and arm made an involuntary movement away from her extended hand. Then, with a long, noisy sigh, he turned his contraband over to her.

He waited, cursing himself, the sun, his heavy clothes. He had sent all his more appropriate things to Netham. Why wasn't he there now? he wondered. Instead, here he was, standing in a hot, open field, with a full bladder. He cursed the tea. He had drunk too much. Henry's widow hadn't bothered with it. He shouldn't have; he cursed himself. While the widow, it seemed to him, remained unreasonably comfortable, cool in fact, as she studied the drawing. He was beginning to wonder about a young woman who gave such things so much careful attention. Her intrepid march into truth was beginning to hint at salacious curiosity. Then he saw, to his further disgust, that she noticed what she had missed before.

Submit looked up at Graham Wessit's face, then back to the face of the man in the drawing. She did this again; up again, down. The face of the man on the page was not exactly the first thing that drew one's attention, and it was younger of course, but there was no doubt whose face the artist had drawn onto the limned, naked satyr.

She raised a brow. "Lovely," she said. "You should have sued him, you know."

Graham only laughed, a short, self-disparaging sound, then exhaled a long sigh. He slipped off his coat and began to unbutton his vest. A breeze flapped his shirt against his body, flipped his vest open to the lining. He flung his coat over a shoulder and looked around. They had come out a long way. The first of the poplars was within a dozen yards.

Submit offered the drawing back. "You look cool enough here. Who is the woman? She looks familiar."

Graham didn't take the picture but stared steadfastly to-ward the shade of the trees.

"An actress," he replied finally.

"Elizabeth Barrow?"

He nodded.

"She's pretty."

"She's actually rather nice, too."

"Yes. It looks as though you liked her quite well."

"Like. Present tense."

"Is that a fact? I don't think Mrs. Schild is aware of this."

"Mrs. Schild is unconcerned."

Meaning, Submit took it, that it was none of Mrs. Schild's business. She gave him a doubtful look.

He sent her a tired look back. "She knows," he clarified. "She doesn't worry about it." He raised a brow. "She worries a little about you, in fact."

Submit frowned and looked down. "I know. That's very

strange, isn't it?" Mrs. Schild suddenly became a subject neither one of them wanted to discuss.

She followed Graham Wessit as he walked toward the
stand of poplars.

When he spoke, he startled her by asking a question in
her own mind. "How did Henry get these?"

"I haven't the slightest idea."

"I never knew he'd even seen them, let alone owned
them. I assumed they'd been destroyed. Or gravitated into
the private collection of some fondler of such things."

The slight wind lifted again. She looked at him. Beneath
the unbuttoned vest the wind showed one white trouser
brace. It came down the front of his chest, thin and taut, a
seeming contradiction to the loose shirt, the frivolous velvet. He was a confusion to her for a moment. Stiff tension,
soft cambric, velvet and starch.

Submit glanced down. "Who did them?" she asked.

"What?"

"The pictures. Were they blackmail?"

She watched him sit down in the shade. He leaned his
head against a tree trunk, resting his arms on his knees. He
made a dry laugh. "No." He closed his eyes. "It was no blackmail. A number of us did it together. Elizabeth. The artist.
Some of her friends. Some of mine."

"Why, for heaven's sake?"

"It's complicated. And stupid." He shrugged. "It seemed
like a good idea at the time."

Submit could not grasp this. She sat down. "You didn't
actually pose?"

He sighed. "We did. On numerous occasions." He made a
sound, disgust or simple lassitude, down his nose. "I won't
pretend to make it into anything very acceptable. All I can
tell you is that we found it exciting. The actress in Elizabeth,
I suppose; she loved an audience. And, at the time, I was in
love with the profane, the idea of setting everyone, espe-

cially Henry, on their ears. Elizabeth and I used to get hot just knowing Pandetti was about to arrive."

Submit felt her skin prickle. "Not Alfred Pandetti," she said.

"The same."

She felt warmed, alarmed, and curious in a way that made her stare at Graham Wessit, study him unreservedly while his eyes were closed. "That's impossible," she suggested. "He's part of the Royal Academy, a leader of the group trying to put fig leaves on Greek statues—"

Graham Wessit opened his eyes to look at her. His eyes were more startlingly handsome than she'd been aware. For a second, they took her breath away. Beneath their deep brow, they were the color of India ink. Large, shadowed, downturned, these extraordinarily dramatic eyes fixed on her for several seconds, making her finally look away.

"My dear marchioness," the man beside her said quietly, "Alfred Pandetti, like all of us, has inclinations that are private and inclinations that are public. Publicly, he's simply what his ambition has made him, Victoria's artist, a servant of Her Majesty the Queen."

She shook her head. "You're wrong. People would know. The Academy wouldn't have let him in—"

He laughed softly. "My dear young woman, people don't always tell." He paused. "For instance, Henry didn't. Henry knew perfectly well that Alfred had penned the drawings, but Henry had become somewhat Alfred's patron. Henry had already made a huge to-do among his friends within the Academy over this bright new artist. Alfred Pandetti had a future. I, so far as Henry was concerned, did not. So Henry spared Pandetti—and himself—and threw me to the wolves."

"If Henry did this"—Submit wasn't certain she believed it—"*you* should have told."

"Why? Henry and I both knew I would protect my friends—that's one of the reasons why I had no future."

"I still can't understand why, if you knew this, you didn't say." Then a very good reason suddenly occurred to her. She could hardly believe it, even as she pronounced the possibility: "You protected Henry."

The shadowed eyes clouded further. "I most definitely did not. I would have given Henry over to the Academy, St. John's, Cambridge, every blessed temple he worshiped at, if only I could have. I just had no desire to ruin the career of so talented a man as Alfred Pandetti."

"Then you shouldn't have done the pictures. Someone could still speak up. People become jealous, gain enemies. Anyone who knows might suddenly tell."

"And I'd defend him."

She gave him a dubious look. "By lying?" she asked.

"By focusing on a broader truth."

"Which is?"

"His art: It's beautiful."

Submit was a little uncomfortable with this. She frowned and leaned back onto her hands. A feeling had come over her, a feeling related to the one she'd had when he'd blurted out his involvement with the pictures in order to spare her memory of Henry—the contradictory sensations of disapproval, admiration, and gratitude. She felt confused again now. Graham Wessit flirted with the dark side of human nature and, in an upside-down way, this seemed honest and brave.

After perhaps a minute, Graham glanced again at her to confirm what seemed very unlikely to him—after all these revelations, Henry's widow remained beside him. Mountains of skirts and crinolines were folded and spread, her copious dress encroaching upon his buttocks and shoe. He looked at her black-stockinged ankles peeking out of all this propriety. Irreverently, his mind suddenly called up other images. In all the pictures, Elizabeth had worn black stockings. Black stockings and garters and nothing else. "Aren't you frightened to be out here alone with me?" he asked.

"Should I be?"

"I don't know. Do you pose for sketches?"

Submit made a nervous laugh and rolled her eyes. "My gracious." She addressed the inn on the horizon.

He smiled at the expletive and its underlining remove from such things as dirty pictures. It dawned on him that this woman knew how to keep him at bay—leaving him no sexual opening—while she probed him from one end of his privacy to the other. Like a doctor—*this will only be mildly uncomfortable. . . .*

She glanced at him and asked, "Miss Barrow. What has become of her?"

"Still in London. I don't really see her much anymore. And I am ever so private about it now if I do. If that redeems anything."

"Have you more elsewhere?"

"More what?"

"Oh, I don't know. Sketches, actresses." She paused. "Twins."

He glanced at her sideways, muzzling a meaner response. "Oh, dozens," he replied. "I thought you might be more skeptical than that, might not be taken in by everything you hear." He snorted: "Rumor."

Submit floated the paper between his feet. "Fact."

Graham didn't answer, though neither did he see the picture. He stared blankly into it.

"I could start a new rumor," she said after a time.

He made a sarcastic pull of his mouth as he picked up the picture, rolling it. He used it to dig absently in the grass between his legs.

"In a way, the earl of Netham is very like the marquess of Motmarche." He looked over his shoulder at her. "Henry," she continued, "was susceptible to moodiness, melancholia— almost as if he had an aesthetic preference for discontent. Whenever he would discover himself to be accidentally

happy for even a moment, he grew suddenly disgusted, re-
volted by the ugly simplicity of it. Angst, unhappiness
seemed somehow to him more worthy, more complex. I
would tease him. 'Don't *try* to be morose,' I'd say." She
paused. " 'You can smile if you'd like.' "

Graham stared at Henry's widow. She was still looking
off, wearing a smile *he* liked very much. It was faintly crooked
and richly feminine, the unique little line her mouth could
draw. He wanted to be angry at her for her mildly gleeful and
wholly unsympathetic speech, but he couldn't. She cocked
her head a few degrees, looking straight ahead as she leaned
back on her narrow little arms. Her posture made her breasts
pull taut against the front of her dress. They were plump little mounds. Sitting there smiling, she was naturally, horribly
seductive, it occurred to him. Dressed in her widowhood,
from her throat to her knuckles to the tips of her toes, she was
a little piece of black silk erotica sitting beside him.

He watched her, her weight resting back on her arms, her
legs stretched out before her on the ground. He noticed her
black shoes tapping together, making a little squeak of soft
leather as they stuck momentarily with each tap. When she
caught sight of her own movement, her smile broadened. As
if to counteract this betrayal of seriousness, she tilted her
head down until he could see only her smooth, pale crown.
Then she made a quick, unself-monitored gesture. She
pressed her dress between her breasts—the black dress
looked finally hot. Perspiration showed wet under her arms,
ran a path down the bodice. Graham felt sexual interest rip-
ple over him warmly to settle in his groin. He felt the first
mild lift.

He stretched his own legs out and rolled to an elbow,
noticing her retraction from him. She changed to a more
upright position, contriving to put another inch or two between them. But his hand caught her chin. He stopped the
retreat and forced her to look him in the face.

"I'm not like Henry," he said. "I am not so attached to words and theories that I can't give way to something that feels stronger."

Her mouth pursed. She was glaring at him. Her eyes looked dark and bright against their peculiar little feathering of short lashes. For a moment, these eyes stared over his hand, in open rebellion against attempted mastery, even this small one over a jawbone. She abruptly made a high arch, a display of long, white throat; she took her chin away.

"You are so—" He was going to say "pretty" or "beautiful" or—what?—"winsome"? Did a man tell a woman she was winsome? This woman was, but it didn't matter. He suspected that if he told her there were some universally pleasing quality to her looks, she would only deny it outright. And not without grounds. He stared at her, as if to anatomize his own attraction to her. Her eyes were too large for her face. Her nose was narrow, her chin pointed. Her skin was washed out except for its smattering of pale freckles. He found himself staring at her mouth, her lips as plump and pink and soft as a baby's. She wet them and looked down.

He watched the color rise in her cheeks. Her skin was ivory, he decided, not washed out. And her eyes, behind their canopy of thick lashes, were a changeable, mysterious blue. She was plain one moment, pretty the next. He couldn't figure her out.

"You are devastating," he said honestly. Her skin, he realized, was flawlessly smooth, something a man wanted to touch. What she was was tactile. She had a fine, gold down along her cheek. He watched her mouth, waiting for it to open, thinking of the teeth that overlapped in front. He ran his tongue along the back of his own.

"Don't do this," she said.

"Do what?"

"Don't pretend I'm your sort." Her eyes slid to him rather meanly. "Or you mine."

"I don't have a sort."

"Of course you do."

"Which is?"

"Laughing, pretty women." A pause. "Mrs. Schild."

He made a disgusted sound. "So I am a dark, morose fellow with a penchant for trivial women."

"Mrs. Schild is not trivial."

He made a glum twist to his mouth. "You were meant to deny the *whole* description."

He rolled out flat on his back.

There he sank into wounded silence. Why do this? he thought. Why march in where there were already any number of clues that his forwardness was not welcome? He was rebuking himself silently, indulging in a particularly male groan—sexual overture gone awry—when he felt a touch at his hand. He started and caught her light, cool fingers in his own. It was her turn to look surprised.

"Graham—" she said softly. She tried to politely retrieve her hand.

With her use of his first name, Graham's mouth went dry. He held onto her fingers as he opened his mouth, thinking to respond gently, seductively, *Submit*. But mysteriously he couldn't. The stupid given name, so much a crude command for exactly what he wanted of her suddenly, could not be coaxed beyond the tip of his tongue. The name sat there in his mouth, unspoken. He found himself suddenly with no handle, nothing by which to take hold of even the smallest intimacy, whatever the touch or the name was meant to imply.

He took hold of what advantage he had: He pulled firmly on her hand.

There was a small battle for possession. She leaned away, pulling equally hard. They were immediately at cross-purposes again. His mind was snagged on French hooks, naked sketches, the perspired dampness of the slopes and crooks of her body. His wanting her was all of a sudden much stronger. He dragged on her fingers until she was pulled over, catching herself with a hand on his chest. She righted herself to her knees, looking much like an animal trying to back out of a hole.

This awkward moment held, balanced delicately between his concerns for how far to push it and how very much he wanted to push it further and further. He wanted to pull her down onto him then roll her over and cover her with his body.

He tried to tease her out of her reluctant mood. "If only he were in a pillory now," he said. He offered a quizzical smile.

She looked baffled, then solicitous for an instant. "You were actually pilloried for them?"

When he didn't answer, or only answered by pulling on her all the harder, her sympathetic interest waned. A small, uncertain fear crept into her expression.

For several seconds more, the palm of her hand held the distance. Its pressure seemed to give his heart something to thump against. He could feel every beat traveling into her arm. He could sense her warmth, smell the perfume of the soap she used on her hair. He couldn't recall any recent longing stronger than this. He wanted to penetrate Submit Channing-Downes—physically, but also metaphorically. At that moment, he wanted all of her female mysteries to open up to him, her complexities to unravel right there in his hands, her privacy to yield to raised skirts, parted thighs, deep, wet acquiescence.

While he hadn't so much as kissed the woman.

And neither did it look as though he were going to. She took a worried breath, a frisson. She remained on alert. He could feel her reluctance digging, finger by finger, into the muscles of his chest. There was nothing else for it. He let her go—with a show of upheld, innocent hands.

He was sure he had shaken her confidence, that she was preparing to fly, for she was getting to her feet and brushing herself off. But she didn't leave immediately. She picked up the picture and looked at its grass-stained edges, studied its center of historic bad taste. Then she tore it, neatly at first, in half. Then she tore those halves, then those and more, until the entire picture rested in uneven bits in her cupped palm. She looked at him as she let her hand flatten, her fingers spread. The slight breeze spun and separated the confetti over a wide area.

He watched her walk all the way back to the inn, wondering what in the world it was that she had just said to him.

— Chapter 15 —

Old boy! Sentiment and passion at your time of life,
hey! A pretty how to do, upon my word! You're a man
of the world, I should think. Because you met a pair of
pretty eyes and a bright smile, and a peachy cheek,
you thought they were for you, hey?

Mrs. Steven's New Monthly
"The Shady Side," page 33
Philadelphia, July 1856

The innkeeper brought slices of cold jellied chicken and a bowl of hot peas. It was a meal to which Submit would normally have sat down with appetite. As the daughter of an abattoir owner, she had developed an aversion to red meat. In her house there had always been an obscenely large supply, every muscle and organ sliced and gravied and stewed in cooked blood. Since she was twelve or thirteen, much to her father's consternation, Submit had lived off chicken and cheese, with the occasional variation of fish with chips and vinegar. Above all, she preferred fruit.

She pushed the dinner away now, only half eaten. She felt oddly lonely tonight. It was the sort of feeling that simply knowing Henry was reading in another room would have relieved, she thought. Or inviting Graham Wessit to dinner. It surprised her to think this, but then the whole afternoon had been rather unpredicted, except the advance out on the grass; she should have expected that.

Submit tried to decide what she thought of a man who made advances toward women he hardly knew, toward gentlewomen, widows, widows of cousins—a man who involved himself with actresses and public orgy and pornographic art. She knew what she was supposed to think, of course, fully as much as she knew that on some honest and inquisitive level she was not nearly so appalled as she ought to be. Just as there was something rather horribly fascinating about the pictures he'd taken away with him, there was something perversely interesting about Graham Wessit himself. Submit frowned. This was the trapfall of a handsome man, she supposed. His beauty and charm obscured objectivity. Here was a man, she told herself, nearing middle age, who, it would seem, had yet to have had a meaningful, marriageable relationship with a woman—and a man who had had what sounded like a truly horrible, wrongheaded relationship with perhaps the wisest, kindest man who had ever walked the earth.

Henry. Submit's frown deepened. Why *had* Henry left his cousin those awful pictures? He could at least have put them in a sealed box, so she wouldn't have been confronted with them and the embarrassment. "Full knowledge," Henry had always said. "No expurgated truth, Submit." But—blast him—those things, even out of sight, out of hand, still churned her up. . . .

A good thing, she decided, that she was done with Henry's questionable cousin, that the bequeathed case was in the earl of Netham's possession at last.

She got up from her table and went to the small bookshelf behind the counter, where she'd been invited to browse for a book. Instead, she ended up staring at the register, at her own hand, her own name. Submit Channing-Downes, marchioness of Motmarche.

The marquess and she had had a healthy bedroom relationship. Quiet, normal, reassuring. From the very first, Henry had come to her with a gentle reverence that disarmed even the first thrill of fright. She was married the day she was sixteen, and from that day forward, Henry had come to bed, approximately one night a week, treating her

considerately, hesitantly, as if he had little right. No sala-
ciousness, no unwholesome requests. He seemed almost
guilty in this, the most ordinary of human acts. Submit had
had no qualms. She had accepted the fact that once a week
they would indulge in the ritual of attempting to make an
heir. Like the cows in her father's herds, that was what she
had been bred to do.

A child by the name of Submit was not one to misunderstand her position in life. Her father had given her the name
so that, from the moment of birth, she would know what
was expected of her. He wanted no protests as he shoved
and shouldered his only female offspring up the ladder of
social success: Submit understood, very early on, that she
was her father's bid into the upper class.

She was hardly six when she was sent away to the first
boarding school. She went through a series of girls' schools,
all expensive, all distant from home, and all terribly middle
class—geared to take middle-class girls (and their fathers'
middle-class money) and make them snobbishly self-
conscious. She didn't like these schools at all, nor did she do
particularly well in any of them. She knew her father expected her to become an aristocrat—and she knew this was
not happening by learning to skate in unison with three
other girls or by having the Countess M come watch as a
herd of them leaped around in ballet slippers and Grecian
dress. Here was something of a misunderstanding on her
part, she discovered much later. Her father had been perfectly satisfied with the young lady she was becoming; it was
she who did not want to be a fake aristocrat. Submit did not
want to be a fake anything.

Thanks to one particularly astute teacher, Submit managed to communicate her grief over the predicament in
which she found herself. The teacher put forth the idea of
sending her to Le Couvent du Sacre Coeur, a genuinely
upper-class convent school for girls in Geneva, where Sub-

mit ultimately spent three years. There she became what she could live with and what would ultimately astound, puzzle, as well as make her father deeply proud. She studied etiquette, deportment, Latin, and French. She learned to paint, play the piano, and crochet delicate, perfectly insubstantial webs of lace, a gossamer complexity at which she became particularly adept. But more important than her formal subjects at the Swiss school were her "classes" after hours. From over the top of her crocheting, she watched the daughters of Europe's upper class eat their breakfast, wash their faces, and hold their breaths so their corsets could be tightened. She learned from them the basic engineering of whalebone and wire, so as to make either soft silk or heavy damask stand up and out equally well—while she listened and followed these girls' trains of thought into the basic engineering of the upper-class mind. She learned how to do what she already had some inkling for, how to be both herself and her father's daughter with polish and aplomb.

In Switzerland, Submit also learned the one fallacy in the whole operation. It would still be very difficult, nigh impossible, for her to do what her father ultimately wanted of her: to marry well. No matter how polished she became as an individual, the upper-class married family to family, not person to person. She knew herself to be, if not exactly unattractive, neither so striking as to make a noble scion immediately consider a mésalliance. She realized she had neither the pedigree nor the barrier-breaking beauty for the kind of marriage her father sought.

She found herself living within a paradox. She wanted to be real, she wanted to please her father, and she wanted to be happy—three things she could never do all at once. Meanwhile, her father was busy trying to accomplish the impossible. He searched for the perfect upper-class mate for his daughter. Her fifteenth year was spent in a confusion of "vapors," a condition doctors liked to bestow on females, especially upper-class females who found themselves falling short of their very limited uses—decoration and marriage. To Submit's father, her "delicate constitution" seemed only greater proof that he had created the genuine article, a genuine made-to-be-queen young lady.

It was this year, however, that Submit met Henry Channing-Downes. Nearly overcome by the conundrum she was living—losing weight, losing energy, crying inexplicably to herself a great deal when she was alone, Submit that winter was given what seemed an impossible reprieve. Knowing the "perfect" mate her father was looking for did not exist, knowing that any upper-class husband would necessarily not be able to make a better match, she feared the worst: a stupid man, a man that her father could dupe.

Henry Channing-Downes was anything but that. Clever, sophisticated, erudite, Henry knew, she realized, from the very first moment what her father was up to. John Wharton connived their introductions. Henry, with cool, brisk charm, evaded the sought-after end for several months. But he turned up periodically nonetheless—much to Wharton's continual pleasure. And somehow, somewhere, Submit did something that made her feel wonderful, something that couldn't be taught: She enchanted a man. It was so much easier than she'd thought! With Henry, she talked of what she loved most, books, poetry, science, art. He never minded if she became animated or "unladylike" in her discussions to the point of argument. He encouraged it, in fact, while somehow in the process he became thoroughly and hopelessly enamored. And, best, Henry's defect—the one that made all the other girls and fathers pass him by—was one that didn't matter to Submit at all. He was only old. Her marriage to him had been the most healing, salutary event in her life.

"Submit?"

She looked up. "Arnold, what are you doing here?"

Arnold Tate stood by a table in the eating common, his hat in his hand. "I finished late and thought I should bring these to you." He held two papers out. "They're bank drafts on two different London banks. One's for fifteen pounds, payment for Henry's Kierkegaard biography in *Men of the Age* this month. The other is for a monograph to appear in *Metaphysics Journal* next. Henry licensed all his work, it seems, in your name."

"Thank you. I know." She took the drafts. They were part of the "trust" she had mentioned to William, her only current means of support. "He always had the drafts cut to me. My 'pin money' he used to call it. It was supposed to make up for all the time he spent at his desk writing the things." The unsettling fact, of course, was that the payments would end. A dead man did not produce dependable income. "Thank you," she said again to Arnold. She didn't know why he lingered, turning the brim of his hat in his fingers. He seemed to be at loose ends.

"Have you eaten?" he asked.

"Yes."

"Ah." He was disappointed. "I haven't. Do you suppose the innkeeper would get me something? And that you could sit and talk to me while I ate?" He made an apologetic gesture. "If it isn't too late, of course."

The innkeeper brought more sliced chicken. Arnold had a good appetite. He ate and smiled and smiled some more. He hardly talked at all.

"How is Eunice?" Submit asked about his wife.

He shook his head. "Not well. But you know her." He paused, looking at Submit. "You seem a little subdued tonight. Are you all right?"

She gave him a faint smile. "I suppose I'm a little lonely. Missing Henry."

He looked at his plate. "Yes."

"But not so bad as all that." She laughed. "Cheer up, Arnold. I'll be fine."

He looked at her, really looked for a moment at her hair and face and shoulders, the black dress. "Are all your dresses black?" The question took her by surprise.

"No, of course not."

"How long do you intend to mourn?"

She hadn't thought about it. "I don't know."

"Somehow a year seems so long." This was the conventional length of time, though the upper class observed such conventions less rigidly than the middle class.

Convention. It occurred to her that she was steeped in convention for the moment. She didn't dare step outside of it for fear of horrifying everyone, including herself. Aside from a few days, actually more as Henry was dying than after his death, she wasn't even sure she was mourning at all. She didn't feel dark and black inside. She had hardly cried for Henry. She had accepted his going, once the shock was past, with grace.

"I really don't know," she repeated, "but I'm sure I'll know when I'm done."

"Will you?"

She laughed. "Of course I will. What's got into you, Arnold?"

He shrugged and cut off a bite of chicken. He squeezed some lemon over it. "Feeling old, I suppose. Passed by." He looked up. "You're young, Submit. You belong in pretty dresses." Submit was very surprised to hear this. "I worry when I come upon you like this. Alone. Aloof from any of the usual society even a widow might indulge in." He paused. "Don't you have any fun?"

"Of course I do."

Arnold hesitated with his fork, as if he might say something more, then he seemed to think better of it.

Just as he was leaving, he added, "William is trying to paint you as cold and calculating. Never mind the legal implications of that; I can handle the court. But he plays on behavior that disturbs me a little. You have always been quiet, but since Henry's death you seem almost unnaturally composed. Call it what you like. Reserve. Hauteur. You have a lovely, quiet dignity, Submit. But total control can be a dangerous thing. I would like to see you respond with stronger interest to—to life."

Submit looked down. What was he advising? she wondered. That she go on a spree of "fun"? Or that she indulge in fruitless tears? She felt things, sadness, joy; they just weren't sharp. And, if they were, there'd be no point to giving in. . . .

That night, as she lay half awake, half asleep, her mind seemed to find strong interest in all the wrong things. Pornographic images. Dark green velvet vests, a deep, rich green, the color of moss from the most sunless parts of a forest: The same color, her semiconscious mind recalled, as that of a collar on a favorite dress. A frivolous dress bought for her by a man who was dead. . . .

Henry bought her the dress the year she turned twenty. They'd been married four years. It was white wool, folds and folds of it, enough to slide over a huge, domed crinoline wider in diameter than Submit was tall; a white dress with a dark velvet collar, the color of Graham Wessit's vest. How she had loved that dress. Loved it, then ruined it in one fell swoop. She had only owned it a month.

The destruction of the white dress happened on the very first day that she and Henry arrived on the North Sea coast. Typical of the whole adventure, the trip began with crossed wires, missed communications. She and her husband had rushed to Yorkshire, having received the message that her father was dying. They missed the next message, that he would recover, by mere hours (and missed his actual death entirely seven years later, since it came, as death so often does, without warning or fanfare; it hit Submit's father in the form of an omnibus as he was crossing a London street). When the brighter message of recovery arrived at their home in Cambridge, Submit and Henry were already on a train, hurtling toward Yorkshire and what they thought was tragedy, a man cut down in his prime. When they arrived, they were nonplussed to discover that not only was John Wharton very much alive but that they neither one liked him any better for his brush with mortality.

Submit and Henry were stuck, required to stay at least a few days as a matter of form. John Wharton was gleeful. In the four years they'd been married, he had had little enough opportunity to appreciate in the flesh the splendid, if slightly aged, husband he had found for his daughter. Now, up and on the mend, all he wanted to do was thump his elderly son-in-law on the back and take him hunting and fishing. He wanted to show Henry "his" Yorkshire—and no doubt show the marquess of Motmarche off to his neighbors. A marquess was not something very many of them had seen at close hand. Henry politely declined, using Wharton's illness as an excuse; such activity would be too exhausting. Instead, Henry suggested that Submit give him a tour of what she liked best about Yorkshire—this would at least get them out of the house.

A tour for Submit, however, was a little difficult, since she hardly knew Yorkshire. For that matter, she hardly knew her father. He had paid and coached and pressured her into an upper-class frame of reference, in the end succeeding so completely as to make himself and his daughter incomprehensible to each other. Submit did remember one place in Yorkshire, however, one place in her childhood that she knew and wanted to show Henry. She took him to her cove on the North Sea.

The cove was a peaceful place made up mostly of birds and water, rocks and sand. Nothing was expected of her there. When she was younger, home from school for a month at Christmas and a month in summer, Submit had survived her visits with her family by going, at every opportunity, to this private, sheltered bay.

It was surrounded by steep drops. As one came across the moor then looked over the cliff's edge, it seemed impossible to get down to the inlet—until one found the worn old path that fishermen must have used in years gone by. The path wound down to sea level to a beach. Part of the beach was always above water, a rocky marooned dry patch. But the wider expanse was washed by high tide, only open by low. This meant swimming to the path at high tide. Or waiting. When Submit was younger, she had loved the idea of swimming to her secret place. But she was more cautious at twenty. The day she and Henry went, they timed it to low tide, late in the afternoon.

Submit was wearing the dress. Summer wool. It was so light, the weight and feel of feathers—the feathers from a white swan with peacock green trim. The air was crisp and mild with a bit of wind. The sea was frothy. The day was bright and blue, as if the sun lit the sky from beneath the water, an expansive glow. There was salt in the air. Submit could taste it, if she faced the wind, and feel it on her eyelashes.

She turned to Henry. "Do you like it?" she asked.

He said nothing, but she could tell by his eyes. They took in the sparkle of the place; the water's vastness, the cove's closure. It was impossible not to be impressed. The only land and water he had ever known were the banks that met the Thames or the river Cam. She felt she had given him something; she had shown him the ocean. Smiling, she took their picnic basket from his hand.

A bottle of old port had been bestowed on them by one of the neighboring squires. Like fealty, Henry had observed wryly. In town, they had found some Stilton and walnuts and pears. They had packed these things together into a picnic meal, a kind of celebration that life continued, even for her father. As Submit spread their little banquet out over a flat dry area, she began to hum. The little cove was charged for her, with memory, excitement, anticipation, joy. She was glad to be here, glad to be able to share this with an astute and interesting man.

On her knees, as Submit pinned the final corner of their picnic cloth down with a rock, what could only be described as a sense of place compelled her to her feet. She kicked off her shoes and peeled off her stockings, then yanked up her skirts and untied her crinoline from about her waist. It collapsed into a twist of horsehair and wired hoops. Then she grabbed up her formless skirts in an armload and burst toward the water.

She screeched at the temperature. It was a painful, achy cold that instantly numbed. She shrieked and yelled this information back to Henry, enjoying doing so. Henry sat back at their picnic cloth, waving her on. She started to come toward him.

"No, go back." He flapped his arms and laughed.

"But you," she complained.

"For goodness' sake, I'm not going anywhere. Go on."

She did, holding the lovely skirts high. Then as a wave receded, she lost her balance and fell. She was taken out a foot or two, into a shallow pit of the rocky bottom. When she got up, the water was about her hips, floating her dress, weightless. The dress swam in the salt water, ruined, but Submit was nearly giddy. It seemed a perfect way to ruin it. On the ebb, however, she stopped laughing. As the water receded, she was leaden. She couldn't move in all the wet weight of drenched wool. She was stuck in her pit just feet from the shore.

"Oh, Henry. Help me," she wailed.

"Take it off, you ninny. You can't get out like that." He seemed angry in a way she didn't understand.

After a few minutes of fruitless struggle, she slipped the dress off and returned, under her own power, to the beach and Henry. In just her wet corsetry and pantaloons, she came up to the picnic cloth, dragging the dress in the rocks and sand. She laid the poor thing out to dry, then with Henry's help wrapped the rock-warmed table linen about her shoulders. Her teeth chattered for a short time, but quickly she grew warm.

Henry would not speak through any of this. Not through the rubbing of her feet and her hands. Not through the pears and port. Finally, she did.

"It was *my* dress. And if I don't mind—" She waited. "I can still put it back on for the trip to the house."

But it wasn't the dress or her modesty. Something else had been ruined in the fine day.

"Well, I'm sorry to have had such a good time." She said it tartly as she began picking up.

"You're young," he answered. He stood.

She was uncertain whether his statement was an excuse, a simple fact, or an accusation. "I'm getting older."

"You don't like your father very much, do you?"

"No."

"Mm," he commented. "And me?"

"You'd make a bad father."

"I've been very unfair to you, Submit—"

"Honestly, Henry. Please—"

"No. You can stay here if you wish."

"Where?"

"In Yorkshire. You needn't feel dutybound to stay with me any longer. This marriage was your father's idea. I would still see to you most comfortably."

"This is insulting." As if she'd been pretending to be happy for four years. She turned away from him, reaching for the dress to pull it on.

But he caught her wrists and forced her to face him. Though sixty-three at the time, he was a strong man. He had gout in one leg and recurrent insomnia. He grew slightly breathless going up and down cliffs. But otherwise Henry was a man with good health to his credit. A disciplining parent could not have gripped her more firmly.

He seemed on the verge of saying something drastic, but then, in the quietest voice, he said, "You would be years younger without me. You have jumped directly from infancy to middle age. When I was twenty—"

He broke off and let go, turning to look out over the water.

Submit was just getting ready to draw on the dress again when he called over his shoulder, "Leave it." He barked the directive at her, his vehemence so pronounced she was stopped in midmotion.

Then, in an uncharacteristic gesture, Henry wheeled halfway around, jerked the dress from her and rushed toward the ocean. He threw it in. Submit stood on the rocks and watched his energy, as if the dress were some grey, limp monster he was hurling into the sea.

"Miserable dress," he explained as he came back. "You could have drowned."

They climbed the path, Submit wearing the picnic cloth. (This would give her father something more to think about. He didn't seem to know what to make of the obvious affection between them. It had never been particularly part of the plan.)

At the top of the cliffs, on the excuse that Henry had become winded, they sat to take in the view. From this vantage point, they could see the dress drifting below, a solitary billow floating out on the waves.

Chapter 16

People never do evil so thoroughly and happily
as when they do it from moral conviction.
BLAISE PASCAL
Pensees, number 895

Graham had arrived home from Morrow Fields and had an early supper brought up to his rooms. The night was warmer than usual, almost balmy. The house was quiet. After dinner, he'd felt compelled somehow to dig out Rosalyn's recent letters from his drawer. Presently, in bed, his dinner tray turned over to use as a desk, the ink on the paper still wet, he glanced over what he hoped was the final version of his own long, rather deceptive response to her correspondence. There were a dozen rejected versions on the floor—his written communication to her had become a masterwork of omission.

Putting his state of mind on paper to her was not easy from any standpoint. For one thing, even now, his concentration kept drifting off. Between frank, breezy remarks about the trial, the magazine episodes, and his unsatisfactory interview with the magazine's publisher, his thoughts kept circling back to sunny meadows at Morrow Fields. Ultimately, he could write to Rosalyn of everything but what occupied his mind most. On the page before him, his trip outside the city today had become but a single sentence, a reference revised down to something vague enough to pass for truth without mentioning to Rosalyn what she would not want to hear.

Much he could not have explained anyway. Like trying to explain in a matter-of-fact tone the presence of a ghost: The underbreath of Henry Channing-Downes had been evoked. The box on Graham's dresser seemed almost to breathe in and out from its ugly, broken mouth. Henry's keeping the box, not to mention his method of giving it to Graham, was an ambiguous gesture at best. At worst, much of Graham's discomfort over the whole last few weeks felt as if Henry's hand were in it somewhere. Graham distrusted his own unease. He couldn't tell if he were jumping at shadows, at phantasms created from his own bad feelings for Henry; he couldn't dismiss the unnerving sense that some of his suspicions had substance. The will, the wife, the box—and Henry's motives—did not sum up so easily as he'd glibly pretended to Submit.

If Henry had only wanted to lecture him again over the pictures, there were more direct means available. Tate, for instance, would have conducted a private meeting in a more sober, reprobating tone than Submit had. Or a summons to a formal, well-populated reading of the will would have been a more public shock and humiliation. In either case, however, Graham would have been more likely, and more justified, to give way to victimized anger. Perhaps that was the point. Submit Channing-Downes checked his anger at Henry in ways that Graham could not identify or counter. He wondered to what degree Henry might have known or relied on this, for he surely had involved her with purpose.

This purpose divided itself into three possibilities. The first was the simplest. The wife was a predictable, reliable agent. Her reasonable, off-putting nature couched in femininity would—did—act on Graham in a disarming manner; it let his mind run, uncoagulated by the rage that so frequently saved him from trying to understand Henry Channing-Downes. She gave him the box, then left him to think.

Or, the second possibility, the wife herself might be the object of censure, adding another layer to make two concurrent little games being run by a dead man. Graham rather preferred this more complicated theory: the two of them, the wife and the ward, each serving the dual function of witness and butt, each feeding the other their prescribed shocks and revelations. Certainly, unless she was a wonderful actress—a liar not only in word but also in facial expression and tone—the widow had not been forewarned about the box. Graham wondered what she could possibly have done to deserve this. It seemed so unlikely that this woman, this wife, could have come into a husband's immortal bad graces. Still, the second was Graham's favorite explanation. The idea of a mutual sentencing put him and Submit together. And there was, he knew, nothing like a common cell for breeding fellowship.

The last possibility he liked least and suspected most. The vulgar little box, besides being his own reproof, was the wife's warning. Admittedly harsh (Henry was never one to spare anyone if it was for their "ultimate good"), it would also be unforgettable: Graham Wessit, the cousin who will surely offer condolences if nothing else—who in fact did offer an entire flat—is profane; have nothing to do with him. Henry had withheld introductions for a lifetime, then assured them at his death and on his own terms. He had presented Graham to Submit in a manner that immediately trumped any perceptions of kindness, good intention, or charm by a strong, visual show of baser dispositions. Exhibitionism. Crudeness. Stupidity. A fear of being ignored that eclipsed shame. Graham felt stripped naked in more than just the literal sense of the pictures. He felt he had been peeled back and exhibited down to his most fatuous, juvenile thought. "For his own good." And for hers.

For his own good. This final, parting contact with Henry had that old familiar flavor—no mercy, no remorse. A corrective meted out with a benevolent smile. His guardian had always had a singular taste and aptitude for bringing down a salutary hell onto the heads of those most dependent on his good will. That a young wife could escape this leaning or overlook it seemed impossible.

Graham remembered the most outstanding example of it in his own life. As he shifted in bed, his mind leaped to a single moment, a single emotion. Shock. It had flattened a magistrate's sallow, soft face. It had silenced a courtroom. Graham felt again his own openmouthed chill as Henry's voice uttered one single word at the end of the initial hearing for Graham's part in the pictures.

"No," Henry had said.

In disbelief, the magistrate had leaned forward. The lappets of his wig dangled as he repeated the question. "Do you wish to speak for your ward?"

"No."

At eighteen, Graham had had to organize his own defense against charges of public indecency, moral corruption, and conspiracy to corrupt others. He was able to enlist the help of his tutor at St. John's, his advisor, the sponsor of his boat club, and several classmates. But not a word, not a hand, not a shilling could be entreated from Henry. Henry, in fact, sat with opposing counsel, as if his own sensibilities were plaintiff to the case.

The arraignment was subdivided. Charges of passing illicit materials were answered in Cambridgeshire. In the Greater London courts, Graham and Elizabeth were held accountable for obscenity and for conspiracy to corrupt public morality. Once the civil courts were through with them, a special ecclesiastical court charged them with immoral acts against the laws of God and procreation. There were endless smaller charges, requiring more than half a dozen appearances before five different justices in the two jurisdictions. The opposing counsel, one Arnold Tate, was a friend of Henry's and was inclined to give the young peer and his friends something to remember, which he did: It was a full routing.

The official sentence was six months in an English prison, the Church of England claiming his first day of freedom for the pillory.

Graham could remember his own fright when he had heard the latter. A surprising clarity of detail came to him as he sat there staring at the papier-mâché box on his dresser.

He could hear the sound of bells again, a distant choir rehearsing somewhere, the faint, pure notes of young boys' voices. The ecclesiastical judgment had taken place in the contradicting ambience of pre-Christmas. The church buildings and grounds were delicately laid with a fine, powdery snow, enveloped in a seasonal sense of well-being. Inside, in the closed courtroom, there was the comforting aura, the peculiarly English brand of cozy chill. Then he heard the word "pillory," and Graham became preternaturally warm. He felt his knees melt, his stomach grow hot. He grasped the dock rail.

"No!" He looked about him for some confirmation that he was heard and understood. He looked into the faces of those who judged him and was alarmed by the blankness, the stone wonder that stared back at him. They had no idea of him as anything but a miscreant. He called out, "This is not right," as a rising panic began to supersede pride or good judgment. He twisted his head toward Henry, toward Arnold Tate, the two of them sitting unofficially on back benches, like guests, *amicus curiae* to God's justice. Graham pleaded toward them silently, then with words.

"Henry— They killed a man last year. They throw garbage and rocks—" Garbage and rocks unnerved him equally. He trembled on the hope of Henry's saving him. Surely now. . . . The distant choir sang in a repetitive chorus, something in Latin. The discrepancy between those serene little voices contrasted to the cacophony of complaint and anxiety in Graham's mind: while, as he watched, Henry Channing-Downes neatly packed up his coat and scarves and the carriage blanket he had had over his legs. He excused his way past the knees of a balding, freckled-headed man. He pulled his coat collar up at his back. Other people followed him, obscuring him with their bobbing heads and murmuring feet. The doors opened onto an ordinary winter view—thick falling snow, an overcast monochrome. The room emptied into this, ghosts walking into a wall of snow. And that was that. Graham was left alone, except for the company of his new warders.

He was taken to Holidame, a provincial monastery-cum-prison near Epping. There he waited and fretted, ever mindful of the other impending punishment, which eventually came; no amount of plotting or worry could forestall it. On May 23, 1839, three days after he had turned nineteen, Graham was taken to Cornhill, where he was trammeled hand and foot to the posts that stood outside the Royal Exchange.

It was not as if Henry had raised his own hand against him. Graham was not, then or now, unmindful that his guardian had only let consequences catch up with him. But Henry reveled in every snag, every gnatty detail, every blow. Nothing was too much, nothing was enough. And nothing seemed to gratify Henry more than when, on the third day after bearing his charge home, just as it was looking as though Graham had made it through, he fell into a state of collapse. Scurvy was the name they gave his disease that summer, a half-truth, since this went hand in hand with the ascetic life of Holidame. But it took neither genius nor wisdom to know that this did not begin to explain the young man's sickness.

Submit Channing-Downes might be able to imitate Henry's sounds, his vowels and accents, but she could never duplicate the satisfaction in his voice. To see a charmed child unacquainted with the long odds escape over the years disaster after disaster by no more than fickle good luck was to frustrate a reasoning moralist into near hysteria. When Fate finally changed her mind, nothing was too severe. Graham could forgive Henry some things, but he could not forgive Henry for wanting, needing, Graham's own complete downfall as a kind of rightness that justified his own view of life.

Graham picked up his pen, then surprised himself by the sincerity with which he closed his letter to Rosalyn. "I look forward to seeing you," he wrote, and it was true. He longed for her buoyant, cheerful company.

He signed the letter, then threw sand on the wet ink to blot it, like dirt into a grave; everything about his life in London felt dead. He packed a bag for his trip the next day thinking, *The final arrangements.* Nethamshire called like a paradise.

He was shaving the next morning when he heard the commotion downstairs.

"Now see here, we have been all the way to Netham looking for him, and they *told* us he was here. There is no use his hiding any longer."

Graham came to the banister and looked down. "What is it?" Several men were on the wide spiral stairs. They were trying to make their way up through the housekeeper and footman.

"They say they have come to take you into custody, sir."

Graham recognized a constable. For a moment he imagined that Henry's widow had notified someone, that he was to answer for the pictures all over again. Then more reasonably, and more repellently, he thought of Tate and the girl.

"What is it?" he asked again. He addressed a large, purple-faced man below.

Not that man nor any of the others answered immediately. They only stared up, surprised to find that he was indeed here. Or perhaps they were a bit taken aback. In his right hand, fresh from his shave, Graham held an open razor. This and the altitude of a full floor of stairs seemed to give him an advantage. Slowly, he toweled the sides of his face, keeping his eyes fixed on them. "What do you want?" he reasserted.

They watched for several more seconds before they broke the silence of his house once again. They all talked at once, then a heavy man with a doughy face came forward. He was holding, alas, more papers. "We have a warrant." He shook the document.

"May I see it?" Graham held out his hand.

The man hesitated. In the end, the housekeeper hurried it up the stairs. She looked fearful, as if the paper had her name on it, which, in the economic sense, of course, it did; no employer would mean no position.

They all waited while Graham glanced over it. Being intimately acquainted with the law's veins and variegations of jurisdiction, he smiled. "I am afraid, gentlemen, that this is a Hampshire warrant." Hampshire was one of the counties that his Netham property straddled. "It is not good in London." It was also not initiated by the young girl's attorney and not affiliated in any way with Arnold Tate. It was a general warrant having to do with a criminal inquiry. "What *is* this about?" Graham could afford a generous smile.

The men were puzzled; then they bumped into each other as they all tried to take the warrant back at once. One of them snatched it finally. They examined it noisily among themselves, exchanging recriminations. One man suggested, "Well, you may as well come." With some malice, "We don't really need one, no one would blame us—"

"What does this concern?"

"The woman—"

"What woman?"

"She's dead."

His heart stopped for a split second, the beginning of anguish. She had seemed so sturdy, immortal, in Morrow Fields.

"Arabella Stratford."

The name didn't register.

With a snide look, the man on the stairs explained, "The girl you bred twins on."

"I did not—" Was her name Arabella? "Dead? She is dead?" He could not even picture her. "How?" he asked. "How did she die?"

"That is the question of the hour—of the last twenty-four hours. Damned opportune for you though, isn't it?" After a pause, someone else from the little band added, "She fell from St. Mary's bell tower."

Chapter 17

The facts seemed fairly obvious to Graham. A distraught, none-too-sane young woman had thrown herself from the top of a very high place. Unfortunately, he benefitted financially from her death—his first bank draft, uncashed, was still in her pocket when she was found. In trying to find him, the police had had to trace him through movements that seemed on the surface exceedingly suspicious. And most muddling of all, the girl had left behind a note. A suicide note, Graham was quick to call it. But the note had an ugly twist: It was a suicide note that claimed murder.

They are the earl of Netham's sons now. He has killed me.

"Of course," Graham responded. "I took her up to the church bell tower to shove her off it, but first I let her write a little note—I always carry pen and ink when I'm about to do murder. Then I left the note lying around for the likes of you to find."

The truth was, no one could make much sense of it, though a superintendent of police tried. He questioned Graham politely, ever so carefully, never complaining about the somewhat sarcastic tone of Graham's responses. The superintendent in charge raised only an eyebrow here and there as Graham tried to explain his last few days in London: an unstaffed house; disjointed, unappointed days; while owning a dozen, no horse to ride. Graham tried to manifest an attitude of—mildly insulted, but totally cooperative—candidness. It seemed unnecessary and indiscreet to involve Submit Channing-Downes. So for her sake (and possibly for his own, since Rosalyn was likely to look a bit huffily on a meeting at a remote country inn), he said nothing of that part of his day.

The soft-spoken and suspiciously amicable law officer, however, brought on a change of heart. After half an hour, he rose from his desk and rested his hands on his stout middle. He shook his head, as with genuine regret.

"I am afraid, Your Lordship," he said, "that unless you can give a better account, we shall have to detain you further. The note is written in the girl's hand—a victim's testimony is usually considered very reliable. It definitely points to you. And it was found on her person, prewritten, as though she might have been insuring against foul play. If nothing else, certainly, there is too much left unexplained: I am bound, at least preliminarily, to consider the possibility of murder."

The London Metropolitan Police was housed at number 4, Whitehall Place. It was an ancient building, only a skeleton of its past glory when it had greeted Scottish ambassadors and kings. Submit made her way toward the main building, across the grounds known commonly as Greater Scotland Yard. She was flanked by a chief constable and a policeman in a round bucket hat. The chief constable kept up a respectful conversation, trying to ease her distress. The "bobby," called thus after Sir Robert Peel who had put together the controversial police force, was a ruffian, out of his element when asked to escort a lady.

Inside, the atmosphere was equally daunting. It was institutional in a way Submit had never experienced. There was clutter everywhere. Records hung out of cupboards. Files were stacked on the landings of stairs. Likewise, the offices and corridors were bustling with people. Submit was taken through a maze of inspectors and clerks, uniformed constables and subconstables, to the front offices, which were only a bit more gracious. With her police escort, she entered a small office with a view out onto the yard. Like the outer offices, this one was packed with papers and files stacked on and around nondescript furniture. The impersonal, cramped feel of the place was only relieved in one spot. On a wall, between a cupboard and vertical file drawers, was a small lithograph, done rather surprisingly in the bright, experimental style of Delacroix. In this office, Submit was introduced first to the police commissioner, then to his assistant commissioner in charge of the Criminal Investigation Division, then to a soft-spoken man who looked her directly in the eye. The office was his. He was the designated superintendent for "delicate matters such as these."

Submit was given to understand that a marchioness being questioned in a murder inquiry, involving also an earl of the realm, would be treated with deference. At least for the time being.

"If you please." The superintendent cleared some books from the seat of a spindle-backed chair and invited Submit to sit down. He wore a rumpled suit rather than a uniform, his badge on display on the lapel of his brown coat. In a quiet, unassuming manner, he apologized, "I'm terribly sorry to put you to this trouble, Lady Motmarche. But we felt it was important to bring you into London. Certain questions are best addressed here."

Submit had not questioned the authority of the police from the moment she had first confronted it at her door at Morrow Fields. The methods and sovereignty of the policing process were new to her. For that matter, being called upon in such a manner was new. She had never had even the remotest contact with authority of this sort. Submit sat, not sure what would come of—or how she would handle—any of it.

"You saw the earl of Netham yesterday?"

"Yes."

"When?"

"In the afternoon."

"For how long?"

"I—ah—" She couldn't remember at first, then for a second longer she hesitated, knowing the answer. "For an hour perhaps." This seemed suddenly inordinately long.

The questions continued. The superintendent asked; she answered. Another man, a subordinate, took notes. The questions were few and straightforward. Submit tried to keep her answers equally to the point. Yet she realized she was becoming watchful and defensive, despite the fact that virtually nothing she had to say either obscured the facts or contradicted what she knew as the truth. Then, just when she thought she would be allowed to go, the ordeal began in earnest.

"Would you have any objections, Lady Motmarche," the policeman asked as he leaned toward her, "to answering a few more questions in the presence of the earl of Netham?"

She was taken to a larger office. It belonged to the man she'd met earlier, Richard Mayne, the police commissioner at the head of Scotland Yard. Submit would have preferred the less august accommodations of the other office, but she understood as soon as she entered the reason for the change: Graham Wessit had been made "comfortable" in this room for who knew how long. At the sight of him, something in her chest gave her a little fillip of alarm. He took his feet off a tea table, clicking the front legs of his chair to the floor, coming fairly quickly to his feet. He was obviously not prepared to see her. His coat was on the back of the chair, his necktie having slipped to the floor. His vest was open. His collar lay in a dish on the table. They had given him no warning that she'd arrived. Submit looked down.

"Lady Motmarche," he murmured. He offered no apology and displayed no unease, as if murder and alibis were to be taken in stride.

The superintendent pulled a chair out for Submit and

waved his hand. "No notes, Dixon." His subordinate put down his pad. "Tea?"

Submit only shook her head.

"Well, then. Let's begin." The policeman smiled and sat on the edge of a large desk. "What I don't understand, Lord Netham," he began, "is that you seem to have removed all evidence of your living in London. Why were you hiding?"

"I wasn't."

"But you must admit it would seem so. To a poor, uncomprehending fellow as myself."

Submit frowned. The policeman with a taste for French lithographs had the air of a man who was overqualified for his job; a man with a taste for success. She felt the first wave of sharp concern, of being boxed back into a corner.

"I told you already," Graham Wessit answered, "that I was not hiding. I merely thought that my staff might be of better use to me in Netham. I have guests there, with more to arrive in the next week." He went over to the window, putting one hand on the frame as he looked out.

A white shoulder brace was revealed by his raised arm. It split at his trousers into white satin tabs. Submit stared a moment. The beautiful, disheveled earl of Netham. Consummately undone. It took an act of will not to offer him something, a drink of water or a murmur of encouragement, a kiss on the brow.

"How long has he been here?" she interrupted. And why, she wondered, was he here alone with no one coming to his defense?

As if she had addressed him, the earl took out his watch. He was only wearing one of them, she noticed, a nice one of etched gold. He took it out from the pocket of his forest green vest. "For exactly eight and three-quarter hours," he answered. His eyes shifted to the superintendent. His tone became flat. "I want a lawyer. Either charge me or let me go."

The superintendent said nothing but sat there looking at

both of them. Submit felt an unpleasant realization bring a flush into her cheeks. They had kept Graham Wessit here all day, unwound him, then brought her in before he could put himself back together. They had put him at a disadvantage to see if she had any feminine inclinations to help or protect him. She was nonplussed for a moment to realize she did.

"A lawyer isn't necessary, I assure you," the superintendent continued. "Not at this point. Just think and tell me, Your Lordship. Why did you send even your manservant away?"

Graham stared at him truculently, then looked out the window again. "I wanted to be alone for a time. Is there anything wrong with that?"

"You wished to be without your carriage, not even a horse?"

"There was a mix-up. An inadvertent misunderstanding of my instructions." The man by the window paused, as if to test in his own mind how plausible this sounded. He murmured again the same words, "A misunderstanding."

The superintendent shifted his attention back to Submit. "And he arrived at your temporary residence at—when?"

"It was late in the afternoon when I saw him. He had already been there for a time."

"Then you deny an arranged meeting."

"Of course I deny it. It isn't true."

"Why did he visit you then?"

"To collect a bequeathal. My husband, Henry—" Her voice broke. She sat up straighter. "My husband left his cousin, the earl, a small remembrance."

"What?"

Out the corner of her eye, she saw Graham Wessit put his hands behind his back. His thumb rubbed the edge of his palm.

"I don't believe that is pertinent." She entered fully into collusion.

The superintendent looked at her a moment, then chose a more direct attack. "You contacted Lord Netham?"

"Yes."

"And arranged the meeting?"

"Not a specific time or place."

"Lady Motmarche." The superintendent paused for what could only be dramatic effect. "It seems to me that such an attractive man as the earl of Netham could have all the alibis he wants. You are not under the mistaken impression, are you, that he is somehow worth—what shall we call it?—an evasion of the truth?"

Submit frowned and looked down. "No."

Unabashed, the policeman leaned toward her. "Are you," he asked with another of his prolonged pauses, "somehow *affiliated* with the earl?"

Submit felt a rush of embarrassment. "No." She scowled. "And if this is how you intend to question me, I want to speak to the Home Secretary. I want my lawyer notified." Despite her bravado, she felt her palms growing warm and sticky.

"Please. I'm so sorry, Lady Motmarche." The superintendent was neither dismayed nor alarmed. He merely held out his hands. "You surely must see how truth and delicacy are not always compatible. I meant merely to find out your mettle; I did not intend to offend." He turned back to the earl.

"So, Lord Netham," he continued, "you sent everyone, all your personal and considerable conveniences away, then thought better of it. You rented a horse at, let me see—" The man made a show of consulting his notes. Submit had seen them. They were mostly doodles. The man kept nearly everything in his head, with a frightening capacity for keeping it in particular detail. "Ah, yes, John Feller's Stables. At the rate of three shillings four." The man laughed and stretched his knuckles in front of him. "He clipped you a bit, that."

"He may have. I have never rented a horse before."

"And a stablekeeper would certainly remember a man who paid him so handsomely."

"Lord." At the window, Graham Wessit rubbed the back of his neck. The loose vest drew up along his chest. "Honestly, if I had thought I was constructing an alibi, I would not have been so obvious. Nor made one with so many holes."

"Well, yes. But this is not so bad a one as we can dismiss it, is it?"

"And both—that it is not bad enough and that it is not good enough—are to be held against me." The earl laughed, looking over his shoulder with an impotent shrug. Then a knock came at the door and saved them all another round of questioning.

Arnold Tate came in, unsummoned and unannounced. He was in full courtroom attire: grey, curling wig and silk bombasine robes. He nodded at the man at the desk, murmuring something about hearing of "the present situation" at Temple Inn and only now being able to get free. He pulled up a chair and put it between Submit and the man accused of murder.

Arnold waved a hand. "I am not here. Officially, that is. I am a close friend of the marchioness. I am only here to hold the lady's hand, so to speak." His eyes, filled with reproof, shifted to the earl, who promptly gave the room his full back.

When Arnold looked again at Submit, she thought for a moment he might actually reach over and cover her hand with his. He didn't. Instead, just an exchange of nods. Relief rushed in. Submit was glad he'd come. She realized she'd been holding her hands in her lap to keep them from shaking.

From there, the interview changed in tone. Almost surely this was because Tate sat there in full regalia. The pace accelerated. The superintendent's questions became briefer, less suggestive, and he concentrated more on the scribbled pages of notes than on the faces of his suspects. The barrister's presence made him behave—and it made him less effective.

Graham folded his arms and leaned back on the window ledge as he listened and watched the turnabout. Submit Channing-Downes was intimidated by all this, and even that worked to her advantage. The remainder of her answers were direct, almost fierce. Sometimes she would allow a pause, taking time to consider before she spoke. Or, when the occasional inquiries came to Graham, she would stare out the window as if she could put herself on the outside of the room, the entire matter. Graham frequently found himself staring at her profile, her graceful neck, her soft shoulders. He realized that with very little difficulty he could let loose of all the wrong reflexes. His every instinct was there, alert, ready to behave like the woman's lover. And this was precisely what he must not do—the man would hang them both on the innocent friendship they had hardly begun.

The questioning continued for twenty minutes. Graham became more and more unhappy, wallowing in a mixed sense of déjà vu and deprivation. Submit was not only removed from him by the physical barrier of Tate, she became a stranger—or, worse, familiar in that terrible sense of being so much like Henry. The questions were directed mostly to her. She answered in clipped monosyllables. Yes. No. He was. No. No, never before. Tea. Outside. Certainly not.

She had, like Henry, the ability to rise above such situations. Hers, like Henry's, was the watchful reticence of someone unwillingly involved in something ugly—though she did what Henry would not do. She wrapped herself in the mantle of her irrefutable integrity and saved him.

The only amusing incident concerned Arnold Tate. During the questioning, he became vaguely agitated. He tried to break in once, but the superintendent drew the line. He would give up his marginal prerogatives of insinuation and intimidation, but he would not give up his absolute authority to chair the meeting itself. He declared that Mr. Tate was being allowed to lend moral support strictly at the discretion of the London Metropolitan Police. His eloquent speeches and arguments were not welcome here; if he persisted in trying to interrupt, he would be asked to leave. For the rest of the interview, the barrister sat on the edge of his seat, like a schoolchild bursting to be called upon to add his brilliance to the discussion. But he remained mutely censored, gazing into the side of Submit's face as if he might brace her with his vision alone.

She didn't really need all this heroic gazing. She acquitted herself, and Graham, very well in fact. How very believable she could make it, Graham thought, that he and she were not close friends.

Graham and Submit left at the same time, though in a manner that could hardly be called together. They rose, made their way down the hall, bumping against curious strangers then each other, like two random marbles in a confined play of obstacles. Once outside, Graham saw she was beside him. He touched her arm, wanting to express his gratitude to her. Then he realized, looking into her face, into wide, glassy eyes that didn't see him, that there was nothing to be grateful for. There had been no charity, no kindness, no friendly turn done him. Only an obligation to the truth. Instead he murmured, "I'm sorry."

She didn't even turn.

Though Arnold Tate did. He buttonholed Graham on the front steps as Submit slipped away.

"You should know," he said, "if that stupid little official causes you any more difficulty, that you have a very different and very good defense." Graham did not have much doubt whom Tate might want to save any further difficulties. "I happened to speak to the girl's solicitor yesterday. He mentioned that she had come by a day ago asking what was meant by a 'limited guardian,' which is what you are named in the documents. She wanted to know if you would get the children if something happened to her."

"What did he tell her?"

"That he wasn't sure."

"He wasn't sure!"

"Don't worry, all you have to do is register with the court that taking her children in the event of her death was not part of your understanding of the settlement. Guardianship is always a matter of consent. But this explains the girl's note in a different light, doesn't it? She meant by your 'killing' her that she thought her death would obligate you finally to do what she had wanted all along. It makes it a sure suicide." Tate seemed very satisfied.

"Pardon me?" Graham took him by the arm. "Are we talking about my having to go to court again? Or else be obligated to care for this woman's children?"

"Only briefly." Tate was becoming irritable. At the street, Submit was attempting to hail a carriage. One slender arm was raised in the air.

"Briefly? I don't want to go to court again! I thought I could just pay the money—"

"To whom? Look." The barrister turned toward Graham. "Your solicitors very wisely arranged the money as a settlement on the mother. It was not attached to the children in any way—a device to remove you further from accusations of fatherhood, which you seemed to favor at the time. No one imagined the girl would do herself in, for heaven's sake. We were all busy trying to keep her hands out of your pocket." He added brusquely, "Nor, I might add, did anyone foresee you might argue for the privilege of paying two hundred pounds a year for the rest of your natural life."

"Well, I certainly might—"

"Then speak to your solicitors. I had no hand in drawing up any of the documents, nor did I advise you to sign, as I recall." Tate wrenched himself away.

Graham took the stairs quickly, but Tate was not above a dead run. It was he who won the right to hand Submit into the carriage. Then, just before the door closed, she leaned once more into view. She bent her head toward the counselor as if to consult with him in lowered tones. It was then that Graham saw that she was crying. She was racked with a kind of mourning for which he had no understanding. It engulfed her, as securely and completely as the carriage swallowed her up into its hollow center. In one bounding leap, Tate followed her inside.

Graham was left at the bottom of the steps, no more able to move his feet than his eyes. The door hung open on her darkness. One could hear the hysterical breaks of air across the lawn. Then she leaned forward, her veils drawn over her—she was swathed in layers of filmy black. She closed the door, and the carriage pulled away.

The vehicle jerked and halted and pulled forward again. The street was congested with conveyances, horses, mules, and people on foot. At the juncture behind Whitehall, the leisurely open carriages on parade around St. James's Park mixed with pedestrians and carts and wagons in a barrage of noise. Submit's carriage could barely move. It lurched along with the same uneven rhythm of her breath. "A-Arnold," she said as she tried to control her sobs, "I have to get back to Mo-Motmarche."

Her counselor opened the windows wide on either side. The street noise rushed in, but so did a mild breeze. Through grenadine silk, this breeze touched her hot eyes and cooled her face. Her veil clung to her wet cheeks.

Arnold's shoulder fell into her as the vehicle gave a sudden surge. He righted himself, then drew one short arm around her. "There, there, my dear." He patted her shoulder. "It's all right." His musty, woolly wig pressed against the side of her head.

She turned, repeating into his silk robe, "I ha-have to get back to Mo-Motmarche."

Arnold's voice was quietly bewildered, solicitous. "I am doing everything I can. William simply thinks he can hold out—"

"Give him everything else, all the money he wants—"

"That would not be astute. Motmarche requires a fortune to exist. You can't separate it from its finances, or it will fall beyond use." He paused. "I want to ask you something."

Submit wiped at her face through her veil with the back of her gloved hand. Everything felt scratchy, itchy, irritating against her skin and wet mouth.

"Did he do something?" Arnold asked.

"Wh-Who?"

He leaned away a moment. She was presented with a handkerchief. "Netham," Arnold continued. "Whether you realize it or not, Submit, you are very vulnerable right now." He paused. "You mustn't fault yourself . . . if Netham has done something untoward."

"Arnold, I was dragged all the way to London to say he did *nothing*, which is what he did. Why do you accuse him—"

"Perhaps because he has such a history of being guilty."

"He is an innocent gentleman who is—"

"Extremely good-looking, who looks as innocent as a lamb." He snorted. "As if innocence would stand there with its vest hanging open and its shirtcollar missing. No gentleman would have been seen in that room like that—"

"They questioned him for nine hours!"

"I'm sure they didn't question him the entire time. Some of it was spent waiting while they fetched you."

"During which time they could have let him go home!

There was no reason to hold him like a prisoner in that room! It was pure harassment—"

"Oh, Submit. What *did* go on out at the inn at Morrow Fields?"

She moaned, still crying. "He came for the box. Just exactly as I said."

"Of course. Now, listen to what I'm about to say if you can. You must remember, a peacock doesn't take a sparrow too much to heart. Graham Wessit is thirty-eight years old, without having made a commitment to any woman that lasted longer than a year. Whatever commitments he does make tend to run concurrently at best. His finances are so disordered that his house must be open to the public in order for him to stay afloat. He spends inordinate amounts on clothing, more still on entertainment, has a weakness for flashy jewelry and a greater weakness still for flashy women. No one can make any sense of his life, least of all him. He has never had a profitable interest in anything, only a tyro's interest in a hundred shots in the dark. His only long-standing fascination is, so far as I can tell, for blowing things up. He has burned down two flats, caused a major fire in his back gardens, not to mention half a dozen incidents when he was growing up. Graham Wessit is as scattered and dangerous as loose sparks."

"Arnold." She looked up at him through watery eyes. "You don't need to tell me any of this. I am perfectly capable of sorting out Graham Wessit for myself."

"I am just afraid not—"

"Oh, Arnold— Please just get me back to Motmarche."

He bowed his small, round head. "I don't know how to get you there any faster than I am."

Submit drew in a sob. "I want my life and my husband back!"

"You can't have that, my dear."

"I know," she sobbed, a hiccough of half a dozen breaths.

"I know. Nothing can ever be put back. Oh, Arnold—" Submit stopped trying to control anything. Crying let loose inside her, like vital parts, organs, threatening to sob and hiccough their way up.

The carriage jerked to a steady, even pace, as Submit finally mourned. For Henry. For her lost home, her lost life. And ultimately for her lost illusion: She mourned what every human being mourns in the first moments of full adulthood—that even inside a friend's arms one can be totally, absolutely alone.

Graham watched Submit's carriage as it turned down the Mall. He would have given anything to have been allowed Tate's place just then. He would love to have known, could almost feel, the closed privacy of Submit Channing-Downes's intimate sadness. God help him, but he wanted to know that woman—

A voice interrupted. "Where, Your Lordship, would you like the babies taken?" A short young man in a neat suit of clothes stood beside him.

"The what?"

"I'm sorry," he explained further. "I'm from the district court. The twin boys—" He raised both elbows. "Where shall I have them sent? Can you take them now?" The packages he carried kicked against him, then one of them let out a howl.

Graham could think of no grounds for protest as the man handed them over. They were small, warm, heavier than expected, and faintly, disconcertingly wet. Graham furrowed his brow. As if in response to this, the second baby began to cry as well. Graham found himself holding a duet of screaming, squalling discontent. He stared down.

More bewildering gifts from the dead.

II

The Rake of Ronmoor

He eats nothing but doves, love, and that breeds hot

blood, and hot blood begets hot thoughts, and hot

thoughts beget hot deeds, and hot deeds is love.

WILLIAM SHAKESPEARE

Troilus and Cressida

Act III, Scene i, 140–143

— Chapter 18 —

Graham would tell the whole story to Submit that summer: Shortly after his recovery from "scurvy," he left the sponsorship of Henry Channing-Downes. One night, at the peak of one of his and Henry's more impassioned, circular arguments, Graham simply packed two light bags and left.

Henry, in retribution, shut off all funds: *until you are back where you belong*. At nineteen, Graham became an earl in title alone; he had no legal access to his earldom or any of its income without his guardian's consent. Graham went to Elizabeth Barrow, who took him in, then abetted him further by finding him a livelihood in the only milieu she knew. For almost two years, Graham supported himself by appearing on the London stage. He ate, much to Henry's red-faced confoundment.

The year Graham turned twenty, Henry pronounced his ward dead; a fatal disappointment. For four years, they didn't speak or correspond. Only reluctantly, as Graham began his forceful march back into society in his own style of paradoxically scintillating and sullied ascent, did Henry eventually reestablish a strained adult relationship. A note at Christmas. An invitation to an elaborate wedding to which Graham never went.

On his way to Netham, Graham bent his route around the posting house once more. Actually, it was not on his way, since Netham was southwest and Morrow Fields was northwest of London. He could never say, "I just stopped by . . ." or "I happened to be. . . ." It would always be a planned digression, a decision. This time, the widow was not at home.

She still lived there, he was assured, but was on an errand in town.

He could not wait that day and did not see her. But it set a precedent. He would go out of his way in future trips. "I go there to check on my cousin's welfare," he would respond if anyone were so nosy as to ask. But even he realized these detours had more to do with checking on his own.

Graham rode by horseback to his house in Netham, arriving in the dark. It was just after three in the morning. He was unshaven, unfed, and damp. It had rained the last hour of the way, but it had seemed foolish to try to stop and find shelter at that point.

There was no one to greet him, which suited him. He was an unannounced eight hours—exactly one night's sleep—early. As he stepped into the house, the rightness of pushing on struck him in the face. The house was dry and warm. In a structure that was slow to heat, slow to cool, the atmosphere of late day still lingered in the dark. And there was the familiar odor, as each house has, conspicuous to its owner only in the first moments of return from a long absence. At the beginning of every summer, he met anew the strong smell of lemon oil, mahogany, of age mixed with tallow, burned coal oil, and burned wood. In a house with seventeen fireplaces, the air of Graham's Nethamshire home was always faintly redolent of warm fires and charred stones. This blended with a rich, contradictory coolness and the smell of the earth-bed quarries that had delivered up the walls of the building itself.

Graham dropped his saddlebag where he entered and began to take off a glove with his teeth. A chandelier overhead tinkled lightly from the falling air currents of early morning. The back gardens were in bloom already—as he moved by the east window, the scent of rainy roses wafted toward him. He stopped, felt through a drawer, found matches, then left his second glove forgotten on the candle-stand as he brought a candelabra forward. He lit the wicks, one, two, three. For a moment, his own reflection wavered in the mirror over the table. He saw the dim reflection of a man wrapped to the chin, eyes bloodshot even in the faint light, a stubble of whiskers noticeably flecked with grey on his upper cheeks (causing his side whiskers to creep unfashionably higher and higher). Graham recognized the face, marginally. Then he deposited boots, wet leather, blankets, and damp wraps in a path that led up the stairs. A trail of possessions would eventually mark his exact way to bed.

In his private apartments, he lit a lamp from the wick of one candle. And there, on his bed, the sight of ordinary things gave him very unordinary pleasure. Recovered blessings. Clean sheets, a down coverlet, a fresh nightshirt pressed soft and smooth with an iron, and the book he'd been reading several weeks before.

He frowned. Why had he been in such revolt against these things? If there were something cluttered, something unsorted, about his life, it was not in these inanimate items. He could safely resume a material comfort and sort through the rest later. He got undressed, slipped on his nightshirt, and climbed into bed.

On the following day, Graham discovered that Rosalyn was not in the house. She had been, but she had gone again with her husband, this time to Weymouth. She had not stayed long in Netham, though long enough to make herself at home: Most of her trunks were in a bright, spacious room down the corridor from Graham's—not a very convenient distance for assignations, but it was a room with a sunny, eastern exposure. He could well imagine her in it and was not unhappy she had selected it. Several of her brushes were out on the dresser. Dresses were airing by a window. Her perfume, particularly under the canopy of her bed, clung to the air. Overall, Graham found a harmony of order, both in her room and outside it, that bespoke Rosalyn's presence, her energy and attention.

A number of guests had arrived. Rosalyn had seen to their arrangements. The Carmichaels: father, mother, three older daughters, a toddler boy and a nanny. Lord Peter Tilney with his mother. The Honorable Jerome Moffet with his wife and nephew. Sir Gilbert and Lady Stone. And, surprisingly, Charles Wessit, the viscount Blanver, with his sister, the Lady Claire; Graham's son and daughter. All were settled in. Graham was faintly curious—and amused—that Charles and Claire had shown up early. He had yet to mention to Rosalyn that he had two adolescent offspring, children by a long dead, all but forgotten wife. He wondered how this little omission had gone down with Rosalyn.

He would take the very next opportunity, he assured himself, to put his children in the larger context for her. "I have a rather unfatherly propensity to forget them, to forget my marriage, the whole notion of family life. I have no talent for these things, Rosalyn, no experience as a member of a family. Not even as a child, except of course for the experience of gunfire ending loud arguments." He wondered if she would believe he couldn't marry her because he was afraid he might shoot her. He tried this argument out. "I have a deep, emotional childhood scar." It might have played fairly well on stage—it was being used pretty broadly in the most recent serial episode. In fact, Graham had hardly known his parents. He had hurt worse when his pet rabbit had died. The deaths of his own parents had been more in line with, say, the death of King George. Sad, momentous, but mostly stimulating a desire to jockey for comfort and position under the next reign.

Rosalyn at least was perfectly civil in the note she left behind. She had met both Charles and Claire, she said, then diplomatically said no more. She seemed to have accepted with her customary grace that country life with

Graham would include two spoiled, neglected, rather nasty near-adults.

The staff at Netham had structured the usual upper-class accommodation to the entertainment of whole families. The children were separated off by age. The house was staffed to see to them. The children were regulated either away from adult activities or, as in the case of the older ones, organized to be occasional, silent, secondary participants.

Graham quickly found himself enmeshed in the last days of July, enjoying himself and finding that summer and Netham—and age thirty-eight—were not such bad places to be.

He laughed out loud at dinner. He played cards for pennies and took—with deep, infectious pleasure—seven shillings two off William (who had arrived the day after Graham) and a pound sterling off Tilney. Tilney squawked with satisfying indignation.

On the third day, with the Wexfords, the Smithsons, and the Meadowingtons now among the company, Graham was up at dawn. He stood out front, in pinks for the fox. There, with the others, he drank his breakfast of whiskey and coffee. After the hunt, there would be a huge meal set up on the front lawn for all who came. Graham drank in the liquored coffee, the fresh morning air, and the pleasant spectacle of his own well-received hospitality as he berated the dogs and traded jokes with his guests and the neighboring squires.

The horns sounded, and he galloped off but ended up with the group that lost the fox entirely, wandering about in circles until he fell into—and took—an improvised steeple-chase. Winning it was not a matter of much pride. Some of the best riders were still more successfully hounding the fox, and with or without skill, he had by far the best mount. His horse took to the air like a bird. Graham hadn't jumped since the previous summer, and at the first gate he proved it by taking a solid fall. But by the third hedge, the exhilaration, the anticipation, the experienced leap in emotion that went hand in hand with the physical one had brought back past summers and shed years and concerns. His win seemed to please everyone else, as if he had been returned to them, the prodigal son.

He was cheerfully exhausted as he rode up the cobbles of his own front drive. It was almost ten in the morning, the sun not quite having had a chance to steam up the day. In front of the house, where the sun had to work its way over a copse of trees, the front garden was still in shade. Dew glistened on blades of grass, on foliage, like fine glass beadwork.

A long table covered with a white cloth was set under the trees. On it stood a dozen bottles of brandy, a host of small glasses, cheese and breads and jams and cakes, steaming coffee and tea. It was enough to feed the entire district, which was just as well, since most of the district had either participated or come to watch the earl's first summer hunt. Grooms stood by to take the horses, as did kennelmen to grab the dogs, while miscellaneous servants kept flies and bees from the comestibles.

After Graham, others began to come in. The houseguests and the locals who had joined in the hunt gathered, some in make-do plaids and wraps, the more affluent dotting the cool morning with the hot scarlet of their coats. There were no chairs, the host not wanting to encourage indefinite stays—noblesse oblige had its limits. Guests and locals alike would arrive over the course of the next few hours, imbibe some of the manor house hospitality, duly greet and rub shoulders like the egalitarians they weren't, then depart for home or lodging, returning to their positions in the hierarchy and status quo.

Graham wandered off to the side, nursing his second cup of coffee and his third shot of brandy, thrown together in one cup. He sipped and viewed the scene, thinking of genteel paintings with their posed and perfectly dressed gentry. "For the Hunt." This crowd was more diverse, more rumpled than anyone would dare paint. Perhaps it was more charming as well. He watched and thought that he liked people, speaking as an observer and not a participant.

But he was eventually drawn in again. There were wagers: who would come in next, who would come in before whom, who would get credit for the fox. Several people had already claimed credit—the fox was in (though half a dozen bemused guests, still out, would be hours more in discovering this). Graham was invited to participate in the bets, but ended up being named judge to a different wager concerning a riderless horse—who would come in on foot? The more people pressed him, the more aware he was that he wanted to break for a bath and a change of clothes. But he remained, the roaming host to this affair, chatting and waving people in. A stiffness in his muscles forecast a stiffness in his bones by evening; another dim pain foretold a healthy bruise up his right flank, the result of his fall. Then he saw Rosalyn's carriage roll up, and with it rolled up such a surge of relief and affection that he began toward it at a half-run, despite his aches and complaints.

As the carriage pulled away from the front door, a pair emerged. They saw the activity on the lawn and started toward Graham. Rosalyn and a man. Graham had never seen him before, yet he knew immediately who he was. He stood nearly as tall as Graham himself. He was beefy and full, thick-necked with shoulders that were not easily—or else not very skillfully—tailored into a coat. Graham stopped dead in the middle of his front lawn.

The two people came forward, Rosalyn a few paces behind like a reluctant, errant schoolgirl. The man came forward with a kind of enthusiasm—an unwilling curiosity perhaps. They came close enough that someone should have spoken, though no one did. Rosalyn's face said a thou-

sand things. Apologies, regrets, above all an unprecedented
awkwardness. Finally, the man stuck out his hand in an offer of the bizarre custom shared by Americans and trades-
men, the grasping of strangers by the palm.

"I'm Gerald Schild," he said.

Chapter 19

Grief, Submit discovered, could be a very selfish thing. Though she was sure she had felt grief for the loss of Henry whom *she* had loved, on the day of the tears at Whitehall, she knew that her sorrow was for the Henry who had loved *her*. Henry would have known immediately that she could not "affiliate" herself with a man like Graham Wessit, as attractive as he might be. More importantly, Henry would have understood and agreed that she must go and tell the truth, no matter what others thought. Yet no one, not the police nor even Arnold, seemed to grasp her actions or her motives without reservation. Henry, Henry, she had thought, and cried off and on all the rest of that day. Henry had seen her in a way no one else ever had, and he had loved unquestioningly what he saw. Without him, it seemed a part of her grew dark, as if a light had been turned out, an aspect of her never to be fully known and loved again. Submit felt a part of herself quietly receding from the world's awareness, unknown, and that part hung its head and grieved in deep sorrowful tears, as if with Henry it had suffered a demise.

This was how she explained her tears to herself. Submit hedged away from the notion that her tears were for something else: that she felt bereft of something living, something possible that she would not, could not, have.

On the day Graham missed her at the posting house Submit had gone into London. Practicality had rallied her from her doldrums. She had to get on with the matter-of-fact consideration of next week's rent: She went to London to cash the drafts on Henry's bank.

Henry's writing, through back payment, was keeping her

going. She thanked goodness for what had annoyed Henry no end—for publishers' delayed and dallying accounts. So far, eight drafts had come to her in the first month after Henry's death. In the first three weeks of the second month, however, she had received only three (rather surprisingly from august, though not particularly scholarly, collections the likes of *Bentley's* and *Eclectic Review* and *Punch*). She had tried to put aside some of every payment, but her savings were small. If her future continued in the present train, she would have to go into debt, which frightened her slightly. She didn't know how she would ever repay such a debt if William's lawsuit did not settle quickly and in her favor.

She talked to Arnold briefly to find out how soon she might see something from the estate. He could report only that he was bogged down in the other side's delays. William meant to keep her from all monies for as long as he could, and the English legal system was only too happy to oblige. There was no precedent for her inheritance, nothing by which to make short, clean work of a very rich and titled old man leaving virtually everything of value to his very young, middle-class wife, while his only and illegitimate son claimed foul play.

William was suggesting design on Submit's part, painting her as a greedy, self-seeking young woman who had befuddled the mind of a rich, all but senile old man. Two things gave William's argument some credibility. First, Henry's will, completed just the month before he died, had been written by Henry himself—a surprisingly careless thing to do in view of the intricacies and convolutions of his estate. The document, it seemed, stood to lawyers as a hallmark of obsession, written with loving detail on minuscule point after minuscule point. Henry, so far as Submit and Arnold were concerned, had simply known his son very well. He had tried to seal and secure every avenue on which

William might attack. But the will's careful language back-fired on the chivalrous husband. The document was puzzled over as "obsessive," "uxorious," and "preoccupied," not only by the other side but also by the court magistrates. Whether such judgments made Henry legally mad was another matter. But as William sought to show that his father's mental state was other than perfectly sound at the time he wrote his will, Henry's own overcautious words, left behind in his own hand, lent support to that premise.

In conjunction with this, William's use of the Channing-Downes name and his upbringing in Henry's house were becoming an issue. William was Henry's only son, his only offspring for that matter, and had been raised by Henry. Henry had paid for his education, arranged for his marriage—a marriage in which William had given, with Henry's full knowledge, the Channing-Downes name, like a son, an heir. William had begun to sign himself "William Channing-Downes" at university. Henry knew of the use of the name from the beginning and could have said nay at any of several crucial points, yet he said nothing. Henry never disputed William's claim to his own last name; full honors, William said, by default. Pride and bloodline were added to this. It seemed reasonable, William's lawyers argued, that without William, the marquessate and a great English family would be made extinct. Henry was perhaps alienated from his son, a situation exacerbated by Henry's marriage to "a grasping, much younger wife," but the marquess always intended his son to carry his name, like a flag unfurled in full colors and right.

These arguments had the court's attention, for their newness, their audacity perhaps, though so far no further encouragement was coming William's way. All those concerned were aware that ultimately the disposition of Henry's honors would be in the hands of the Home Secretary, not to mention the Queen, both of whom could be very particular about birthright. Out of wedlock was out of wedlock. The chances of William getting Motmarche remained slim. But the chance of his getting something looked better by the day.

While in London to cash the drafts, Submit offered again to settle hers and William's dispute privately. She tried to entice William with as much as he might, in his most optimistic hour, hope to gain—all properties outside the entailment of the marquessate per se. But William would have none of it. He still wanted Motmarche or nothing at all.

"Fine. Nothing at all."

They were coming out of Gray's Inn, where William's solicitors had offices. Submit was once again trying to get him to understand. She would not give up Motmarche. He couldn't expect it. And she intended to hold on to enough income from everything else to run the very large estate.

"You can't do this indefinitely," she added. "I'm not without resources myself."

"Have another old man lined up, do you?"

Submit gave him a sharp look, suppressing the anger that rushed more and more easily these days to the surface whenever she spoke to William. She picked up her pace as she headed toward the main street. "You should watch your accusations. Neither am I defenseless."

He laughed. "And don't we all know it." Following William's example and her attorneys' advice, she had had him thrown out of the house on Charlotte Street. Neither one of them had a place to call home for the moment.

The crush of carts and horse traffic as they came onto High Holborn made it difficult to see, let alone hail, a hansom cab. William used his umbrella, none too subtly, to keep the struggling mass of humanity around them at bay.

"Perhaps you would be a little more feminine," William said, "more attractive to someone other than doddering old fools, if you were a little more helpless."

"What a bill of goods—"

"It's not. Men like—"

"*You* like to have your own way. Don't generalize beyond that." She caught the attention of the driver of an omnibus behind two horsecarts. "Just don't imagine you can get what you want by bullying me, nor by reminding me that my brand of femininity does not appeal to you. I don't need you to admire me; I just need you to leave me alone."

"You *are* alone, Submit. You just don't know it yet."

Submit reached into her reticule to get change for the omnibus. The vehicle inched its way toward her through the congested traffic.

"Lord," William said with a sniff, "you don't mean to get on that thing?"

She began to weave her way toward it rather than wait.

Behind her, William followed, chattering. "Lord God, Submit, but you've come a long way down."

She glanced over her shoulder as the omnibus conductor took her hand. "I'm getting by." She stepped onto the platform. "You can't be doing any better, and I probably mind less—"

William elected to follow along. When she looked over the gate, he was right there, smiling his smug, irritating smile. She wished he'd go away. She wished traffic would pick up so he couldn't follow so easily. Over the street's, and her own, commotion the hour began to toll from the tower of a nearby church.

"I'm doing quite well, actually," William called. "Margaret and I are staying on Haymoore Street, as guests." When this didn't immediately register, he explained, "As guests of my cousin, my dear."

She looked at him blankly.

"Graham," he expounded. "He says he has no use for his London flat, that we can stay as long as we like."

"Where to, madam?" It was the conductor.

"What?" Submit stared at the man in uniform beside her. "Where to?"

She couldn't think for a moment. "Ah—oh, Victoria Station."

When she saw that William remained, walking gleefully along, she called loudly, "There's dung"—the word *dung* made him start, though not so much as her next words: "There's dung all over the street, and you're walking in it. Look." She pointed down.

Small satisfaction. Truly, it was childish of her. Still, though, Submit enjoyed watching William look down; she enjoyed deeply the sight of his face draining of blood as he once more discovered she was on very good terms with the truth.

Submit all but missed the train station. The omnibus conductor had to remind her to get off. Then, lost in the anonymous clatter of her train, she missed the Balkfield stop entirely, the closest station to the inn at Morrow Fields. She had to take a coach from Sleeveshead all the way back. As she climbed the front steps of the inn hours after she had planned to be home, Submit was lecturing herself. She had no right to be upset or angry, no right to be alarmed. But no matter how she looked at it, giving William the apartments, rent-free, seemed like treason on Graham Wessit's part.

She came into the eating common, taking off her hat. And there, the teary feeling from yesterday at Whitehall all but overwhelmed her again. She sat down at one of the tables and looked around. Her whole life seemed like this room. Neat, ready, empty. She was neither where she belonged nor set firmly on any new path. She felt suddenly lost. The past seven weeks lay like the common room itself, unlived-in, unoccupied. If she was to weather this period, she needed more than just money. She needed something to absorb her, something besides hating and harrowing William. She needed something interesting, something positive and stimulating to do.

That night in her room, she tried to read a volume of Robert Browning's poetry she had found downstairs. But when she came to the lines "the unlit lamp and the ungirt loin," she felt something inside her fold in on itself. She ended the day, quite without meaning to, by staying up until two, fiddling with paper and pen, making poetry of her own as she once used to do. But in the end, her words did not seem poetical to her. She agreed, as she once had agreed with Henry, that her own words were rough and overwrought when they edged anywhere near passion; or were slick and facile when they skirted it rhythmically within the lines.

She went to her bed through a sea of crumpled rubbish on the floor, then lay there in the dark. Her wakeful mind remained alive with inexpressible concerns.

Chapter 20

Graham stood by the window, looking out on a dozen people playing croquet on the back lawn.

Rosalyn came in, closed the door, then sank back against it as if to shut out the fact that her husband was somewhere about.

"Thank you very much," Graham said. He swirled around the last of a brandy he was holding in his hand. "What a delightful surprise."

"I couldn't help it, Gray." As if this were something to count on, she offered, "He's having a ship built in Lyme. They expect him there. He's already late. He has to go soon."

Outside, a lady's skirt dropped over her ball. She walked. Magically, when she lifted her dress again, her ball was in line with the wicket.

Graham glanced at Rosalyn. "Where is he now?"

"Upstairs. He's tired. I think he might take a nap."

He made a snort. "Alone?"

"Yes, alone. I told you, he's tired." She paused. "I'm dying to see you, Gray, dying to be with you. Don't be angry. He's nothing, you'll see. Let him stay a day, then I'll accompany him to Lyme, make him stay there."

Graham looked at her sidelong. "Does he know?" he asked.

"About us?" When Graham nodded, she sighed. "He must at least suspect. Why else would he come?"

Graham stared fixedly at her. "Well. When your duties permit—" He drained his glass, then left to join the group outside.

Mr. and Mrs. Schild left the next morning. Graham had barely seen Rosalyn, had barely known she was there.

A day later, Tilney, who continued to lose nightly at cards, usually to Graham, tried to go for revenge. Bored with croquet, the group decided to improvise something new—a kind of tennis on the lawn. Tilney got very organized about the venture. He took it upon himself to assign men's opponents for a tournament. Graham "drew" Giles, the Moffets' nephew, a naval lieutenant-captain on leave— and fourteen years Graham's junior. Graham decided immediately to lose gracefully rather than make a hot, sweaty fool of himself.

Green grass. Players in white linen. Ladies on the sidelines under a battalion of assorted, colorful parasols. Here was the very picture of genteel summer idleness. At midgame, however, Graham had still not managed to bring himself to lose. The young Lieutenant-captain Moffet was about to serve in his usual manner, an insouciant, effortless swing. The young man looked rested and confident. Graham was not precisely lathered. On the other hand, his shirt clung lightly to his back; very slowly, he'd been wooed into exerting himself.

Tilney sat happily on the sidelines. "Bravo," he yelled now and then to no particular player, for no particular reason.

The serve came. It was within Graham's reach, as were so many of the young man's serves. Graham slammed it. It just barely landed in bounds. The serve reverted, and at the end of a long volley the scorekeeper called, "A deux de jeu." A tied score, the closest Graham had come yet to a win.

Moffet braced his feet, the stance of a man about to play more seriously now that losing had become a possibility, remote as it was.

From the beginning, Graham's game had not been so

poor as to be embarrassing. He'd been playing tennis all spring at his club, was in decent condition, and had a good awareness of the position of racket and ball. But without the customary walls of the indoor court, he could ridiculously overdrive the ball. The game was interesting only insofar as Moffet would not press his superior endurance and placement control; which, with the next return to Graham's inside left corner, it appeared he finally would do. Graham netted the ball.

Moffet served, again right to him. Graham cocked his entire body for the kill. But it was only an attempted murder. The damned thing proved unkillable, continually resurrected, just as lively and back in his court a sixth, a seventh, an eighth time. He ran after the volleys, asking himself, Why was he doing this? What would it prove? That he was twenty-four, which he was not? That he could triumph over Tilney, who was not even on the court? Then, *swack*, he returned the ball, just as hell-bent on the game as he'd been the moment before.

Competitive son of a bitch, he thought, knowing perfectly well he did not mean Tilney or Moffet. *Opposition thrives on opposition*, he remembered suddenly. The words came to Graham, as if from a page, an entire paragraph to quote. Henry Channing-Downes. "You are so competitive," Henry had said not so long ago. They spoke by that time perhaps twice a year; Graham had been over thirty, and Henry still couldn't pass up the opportunity to give him advice. "Don't play the game," he'd said, "and all your enemies, like chimeras, will disperse."

With unmincing success, Graham finished off the other man's serve. He could contemplate losing, to save himself sweat, embarrassment, bruises, exhaustion; but he couldn't actually submit to this simple expedient in practice.

It was just as Graham lost the serve again that Rosalyn

made her reentrance, like a grand actress able to recover from a bad false start. She came across the lawn alone, in a blue hooded wrap that set off her hair like stamen in the throat of some exotic flower. Beyond her, her carriage was pulling into the carriage house. She called, "Graham!" and waved. Graham raised his racket in response. He was glad to see her returned to her old self—dependably, wholesomely gorgeous and free of a husband's restraint.

The lieutenant-captain stared openly.

"Deuce," was the call again.

Graham stepped into a shot traveling toward him so fast it could have been fired from a gun.

It was a short volley, ending when Graham returned a ball that the younger Moffet had simply been unprepared to see come back over his side of the net. The young man sputtered, for he had already begun to walk to the edge of the serve line, ready to secure his victory. When he returned to position, he was red in the face. He lost the next shot by embracing precisely his opponent's worst flaw: He drove at the ball with too much force, sending it well over Graham's head to land twenty feet outside the court.

"Advantage Netham."

Then came a stroke of luck. When Graham served, he tried putting a little spin on the ball, as he would in billiards, and the damned notion worked in an erratic sort of way. The ball jumped almost backward when it hit, beyond returning.

"Game point to the earl of Netham."

Graham glanced at Tilney. Rosalyn let her wrap fall to the ground, revealing an equally sumptuous display of color, the bright orange-pink of a sunset. She walked onto the playing area. "Can the ladies have a try?"

Graham shook his head, meeting her halfway to the sidelines. "Not with me." He tossed his racket down.

Tilney sputtered something about this being only the

first game of a set. Rosalyn never took her eyes off Graham, smiling, beaming. As she linked her arm in his, she said very quietly, as if their first reunion several days before had never taken place, "Hello." Then quieter still, "You look smashing."

"Better than smashed, I suppose."

She kissed his cheek. "You're wet," she said with surprise.

"I'm exhausted. I have been the most incredible fool—"

A voice broke in. "He's bloody well won at everything. Someone ought to teach him that it isn't very hospitable for the host to always win." It was not Tilney but, good-naturedly, John Carmichael who spoke. Tilney, however, seconded this with a hostile and sincere grunt.

Together Rosalyn and Graham settled back onto the sidelines, where people took turns recounting Graham's "foolishness" during the past few days. Rosalyn proved the perfect audience. The steeplechase, instead of the act of bruising bravado that it was, became a main event, a heroic victory. At cards, Graham became sly and commanding, the winner of untold fortune. At tennis, he was already deemed the champion. The stories were meant to flatter. They had flattered once, he thought; they must have. But now they seemed embarrassing, transparent. Yet no one seemed to suspect Graham's discomfort with any of it.

Then, worse, Rosalyn brought something out for all to see: "Look," she said, holding up a little blue book. "Number twelve of *The Rake of Ronmoor!*"

Graham inwardly cringed as most of the ladies crowded around. They teased and cooed, every last one of them speaking with knowledge and enthusiasm for the stupid little serial. Even some of the men made arch, winking remarks, drawing parallels that were unfortunately there to make. The Rake was an energetic Thackeray-like antihero who loved to woo and win.

Graham grew quiet. In the shadow of Rosalyn's parasol,

he tried to imagine a way to fail, a way people couldn't rewrite. He planned how to lose. Though surely he had lost at one time or another. And weren't his losses just as eagerly transformed into melodrama?

He changed his mind. He planned nothing, not winning, not losing, not doing anything the least bit noteworthy. He planned how to be unwritten, how to be seen—and liked?— as an ordinary man. Yet the most ordinary things about him, he worried, sometimes took on significance in other people's minds. He gave up. He couldn't imagine how he could control any of this. The important thing was, he told himself, there were at least a few individuals who knew and liked him for himself, in his human, unfictionalized form. At this comforting notion, he looked to Rosalyn, then like a traitor his mind suddenly yielded up a different name. Submit. And he abandoned his pointless, unfollowable train of thought.

Two ladies took to the court, though they kept score not of points against each other but of the number of volleys they could keep the ball in the air. Eleven, twelve, thirteen; then squeals of disappointment.

People milled about. Many came to greet Rosalyn. She knew a surprising number of his friends by name—some from London, some from a quick study from the first days when she had been quasihostess at Netham before he'd arrived. The young Moffet came to sit near. He hovered. ("The neckbreather," Rosalyn would dub him later, for he would become a fixture of the summer, working his way to stand near her or sit beside her, until she became claustrophobic in the shadow of his unwanted attentions.) So that day, another first, Graham put a protective—possessive— arm over the back of Rosalyn's chair as they watched the games, stroking her shoulder with his thumb now and then.

Rosalyn's bosom rose and fell through all this. The stories and his friends somehow primed her. With nary a complaint, he would be allowed later, he was sure, to mess up her careful hair, her perfect dress. He counted on doing so, in fact, as an appetizer, before dinner. Dinner itself would be a feast. A hot, rich meal of lamb and mint and puddings topped off with a bottle of old, crusty port. He called himself lucky and planned a geometric multiplication of his blessings and winnings. He became bold and lingered with her after the others went in to change. He kissed her on the open mouth, and she let him, in plain view of anyone who might turn. Like an adolescent.

No one did. His life felt charmed. All was well with the world, everything in its place.

The only discordant note was when Rosalyn, lying in bed that night, asked about the orphaned twins. He had left them in a London hospital in the care of doctors; they were weak, fragile little things, it turned out. Nature, it seemed, might finally accomplish what the English legal system had done nothing but ball up; the babies' poor health might soon make irrelevant all arguments over guardianship. Rosalyn responded sympathetically. She already knew of the ordeal of their mother's death, the accusations against him, and of the rescue at the hands of Submit Channing-Downes. As he spoke in the dark, Rosalyn accepted everything as he laid it out. Oh, dear. Oh, dear. How awful for you. Poor darling. The only thing he omitted was the last sight he'd had of Submit and how the memory of it continued to disturb him: those unexplained tears. He could speak almost guiltlessly of the visit to her, "to get the box she'd walked off with." But a sensation stayed with him. It was not precisely guilt—though he knew he intended to visit Submit again and that Rosalyn would look askance at repeated rendezvous at a country inn. All the same, he felt these visits were innocent, even in some way very healthy, though he could not have explained why to her or even to himself.

— Chapter 21 —

The first two or three times, Submit managed to dispatch Graham Wessit without much fuss. He came to thank her for her help at Whitehall. "It was only my duty; no thanks required." He came on his way home from London to see how she was getting along. "Fine. I am managing quite well." He behaved, was polite, and almost lulled her into believing he was what he seemed, a slightly fancified gentleman with ideas respectfully different from her own, who was sorely put-upon by a history of very wild oats, rumor, and jealous gossip.

She came home one morning from the little village nearby, however, to find him at the inn much earlier than he had ever arrived before. She walked into the common room, removing her hat, and found him sitting at a far table with Mr. Hanlon, the innkeeper, drinking coffee and Irish whiskey.

The innkeeper had the good grace to scramble away, trying to minimize their early morning tippling by taking the bottle with him. But Graham Wessit wasn't the least apologetic. He rose and began as if he could give whiskey, at ten in the morning, an historical perspective. "Mr. Hanlon has been explaining that this inn was first a tavern built in 1698." He smiled. His words were clear. He seemed steady enough.

Submit looked at him across several tables, as she played with the pleats where her veil was tacked to her hat. "What are you doing here?" she asked.

He registered her abrupt tone and looked down at his cup, then back. "I needed to talk to you."

"What about?"

He smiled quickly, the reflex of a man used to getting by on his looks. The smile dazzled. It was annoying to see this little trick performed so well. His perfect white teeth set off his dark, sharply planed face. "I was hoping we might go for a walk," he said.

"I'm tired. I've just walked to the village and back."

His expression was one of genuine disappointment, making her feel somehow needlessly mean. What was he doing here, without the flimsiest excuse? Despite herself, she noticed the dark shadows around his eyes, deeper than usual. Another trick, she supposed. This man, who led the most undemanding and restful of lives, had eyes that always looked as if he'd been up all night.

"Is something wrong?" she asked.

"No." The smile pulled tightly back. Inch-long slashes— extravagant dimples—cut into his cheeks. "I suppose not."

"Fine. I'm sorry, I have things to do today." She began toward the stairs.

"It wouldn't take long."

She paused to see him take out a watch, one of six or seven, from the pocket of a dark, nacreous-bronze vest. She frowned. He looked up from the open watch. "Ten-fifteen. You can kick me out at ten-thirty."

She really had to discourage this. "I'm sorry—"

He suddenly unthreaded the watch from the buttonhole of his vest. Glancing up, he asked, "Which ones offend you most?"

"I'm not offended by your watches." But he continued unlooping the chains, making her feel petty.

One at a time, he set each of his watches on the table. Submit scowled at this performance but didn't look away. Then he began on his rings. All five came off, to lie in a heap like a pirate's treasure in the middle of the linen tablecloth, a small, sparkling pile implying that she didn't know how to see him beyond it.

He held out his bare hands. She couldn't tell if he was being sincere or faintly ironic. "What else am I doing wrong?" He looked down at himself, then back up. "Honestly, I need a friend to talk to, and for the life of me I can't think of anyone else who might understand."

Submit felt a warmth creep into her cheeks she couldn't control. All right, she would give him fifteen minutes. "If you'll wait," she conceded, "I'll be right back down."

He called to her, "Wear your hat."

"What?" She looked down from the landing.

"Your straw hat with the red ribbon." After a moment he added, "To protect you from the sun."

To protect her from the sun, indeed. She pointedly bypassed the hat upstairs in her room, muttering to herself. Whiskey at ten in the morning. Never mind the watches and rings. Dragging her to London to save him from hanging. Thanking her by lending William his flat. Then showing up repeatedly, as if nothing were wrong, calling her his friend. What exactly did he expect?

She was more irritated still when Graham Wessit wasn't in the eating common when she came back down. The innkeeper pointed through the entranceway to the other side of the building. "Went to check on his horse."

She could hear a horse stomping and snorting far off as she passed through an empty parlor. The parlor, an addition built of stone, led through to the carriage quarters, all built of brick. The old inn was a rambling congeries of styles and materials from over two centuries of rebuilding and repair. The carriage quarters took up more than half the building, their predominance coming from the days before trains charted the popular routes, when travelers stopped in fine, private carriages drawn by six or eight horses. Submit entered the tack room. It was filled with dried-out bridles, halters, stirrups, and cross-ties; it smelled of animals, old leather, old sweat, old straw. She ducked under a curtain of straps that hung over a low beam. Just as she did, Graham Wessit came in from the opposite direction, through a wide brick arch. She backed into the straps. They jangled and flapped.

Graham Wessit too was caught off guard. On the straw-strewn cobbles, his shoes gritted to a stop. After a moment, he threw an arm, a casually pointed finger in the direction of the carriage house and stable behind. "A rabbit," he said. "It got into the stall."

She stared at him. "So what is it," she asked finally, "that you wanted to talk about?"

He looked around. "Wouldn't you rather go outside?"

"No."

Frowning, he tapped his fingers for a moment on the only furnishing in the relatively bare room—a frayed saddle on a wood saddle rack. He considered her a moment, then capitulated, straddling the saddle rack and sitting on it. He brought one foot up to rest across the front of the saddle. Submit found herself staring at the sole of his boot, its dark, dirty-brown color contrasting sharply with the light cream of his pants. His trouser inseam pulled without making so much as a crease over his cocked hip. She looked up to his face.

He continued to study her. "Why," he asked as he crossed his arms over his chest, "are you so inhospitable? I don't deserve it." He squinted, then suggested, "If you're afraid I'll try and throw you to the ground, I assure you I'd hardly be so stupid." He made a wry smile. "At least, not twice."

Submit moved a bridle out of her way. Its solidness under her hand felt suddenly reassuring. She hung on to it. "Is this what you wanted to talk about? Throwing me to the ground?"

"No." He laughed in surprise—in almost self-rebuke. "No, with you I'm sure I won't get into trouble there."

She frowned, not entirely sure she was flattered by the remark. "So are you in trouble somewhere else?" She couldn't resist adding, "In need of another alibi?"

"No. And I didn't do anything last time. Not in London and not out in the field." He angled his head, as if trying to decide whether to take offense or not. "Look, I don't know what to say about all that. I didn't plan it. I didn't want you to have to come to London to defend me. I didn't want to expose you to the sort of prying that, by the way, I have known all my life. But you're perfectly safe now—"

"Am I?" She let her hands slide off the bridles and ties and put her fists on her waist. "Safely pinned here? So you can come calling whenever you like?"

"What?"

"If it weren't for you, I might be home right now—"

"What are you talking about?"

She took a step closer. "William. On top of everything else, you gave him your flat. How could you? He wants Motmarche!"

He blinked, a little startled, but answered calmly enough. "I should imagine he does."

She walked right up to him until her hoops pushed against the saddle rack. "It's my home."

"He was raised there." He leaned involuntarily back.

Submit let out a breath. "Are you telling me you think he should have it?"

He paused. "I suppose I am." He spoke much more evenly than she. "It's his father's house."

Submit could hear the sound of her own voice, emotional, irrationally upset. "It's *my* house, my home! I lived there for twelve years. Henry left it to me!"

"Henry did a lot of stupid things—one of which was, at the time of his death, to horribly slight his son. A son, I might add, who lived at Motmarche probably more years than you are old, who married and moved out to accommodate Henry and his new bride, and who in return was generally insulted or sloughed off." He looked at her sincerely. "I think it's abominable. There weren't even nominal compensations in the will. I don't blame William for trying to salvage his pride."

Submit couldn't speak for several long seconds. All she could finally get out was, "William—William is an idiot."

"Ah," he said with a nod. "And idiots shouldn't enjoy a father's love."

She turned away. Her heart was pumping madly in her chest. Her skin felt hot. She pushed her fingers back through the side of her hair as if a piece had come undone, but it was fine. For whatever reason, Graham Wessit had taken his cousin's side. She didn't need to talk to a man who listened seriously to what William Channing-Downes had to say.

She turned to leave, but something caught her skirts and pulled.

"Turn around," the man behind her said in the soft, unequivocal way that one might speak to a misguided child.

Her skirts were pulled back, all the way up against her legs. She looked down and around. The hem of her dress lay draped over the flexed ankle of Graham Wessit's boot, a foot off the ground. He'd put his foot under her dress and hooked it onto a hoop to hold her in place.

She gave her dress a jerk, but that snagged the fabric into something that caught more firmly.

"You're going to rip it," he said, bending over and down.

He unhooked the thin fabric from a small, sharp little spike—apparently Graham Wessit rode with a spur. As he rose back up, however, he kept hold of her dress. He settled forward to cross his arms and lean onto the head of the saddle, holding a fistful of black silk. He looked at her, at eye level now.

"William," he said, "*is* an idiot, of course." Submit gave a distrustful frown. "He is a silly, pompous, self-important

fool. And I know enough not to believe everything he says."
A little softer, he added, "I know, for instance, that you are
otherwise than he paints you." He sighed. "But I also know ·
he probably deserves better than Henry saw fit to give him."

Henry, their chief grievance with each other, materialized again.

"Henry knew I wouldn't neglect William," she coun-
tered. "He just didn't want William to have access to too
much all at once. You ought to give Henry more credit."

"I give Henry credit." He let go of her dress, brushing it
down. "Credit for riling William into a tantrum. Credit for
engineering my embarrassment—and yours—over the pictures. And credit for knowing everyone well enough to predict your homelessness right now." He shook his head. "Do
you honestly believe Henry didn't realize how furious the
will would make William?"

She could only frown down at the saddle rack, at Graham's bare, ringless fingers—neat, long, almost courtly in
repose—where they lay on the saddlebow's frayed edge.

"It was Henry's favorite game," he continued. "Playing
God. I even fancy he would like to have shown me his
pretty, young wife. If he hadn't been so damned worried I
might like her a bit too much—"

Submit's speechless confusion rose up in a kind of heat
behind her eyes. She stared at him from beneath a blush so
deep it seemed to come from her bones. He was inviting her
into rebellion against Henry. And against herself.

Graham Wessit swung a leg off the back of the rack, then
dusted off his pants. "William's mother, I understand, was
about sixteen when she gave birth. Henry would have been
about thirty. Which brings me to another little thing I've
been thinking about Henry. He had a rather embarrassing
affinity for young girls." He let his observation sink in before he went on to its inflammatory conclusion. "Which I
suspect didn't make him too comfortable with himself." He

laughed. "And which resulted in one shallow, literal-minded son, who, I know for a fact, made Henry pull his hair out. The thought of Henry producing a son like William, and knowing daily what he had produced, has always been one of the things that has endeared William to me most."

Submit found words. "You are a vindictive, irresponsible human being who makes unfounded accusations—"

"Are they?"

She turned and went briskly toward the door.

"Don't go—" she heard him say, but she pushed aside the dangling equestrian paraphernalia. Straps rattled and hit her shoulders. She shoved angrily at them, making them slither and clamor and drop into her face. Abruptly, she felt a drag on her dress again. She turned to upbraid him soundly this time.

He was down on the floor on one knee, untangling her dress from a heavy tack hook that had been left on the ground.

"Don't go," he repeated. "None of this—it isn't what I meant to say at all." He got up, dusting his knee, not looking at her. "Not that it matters much now, but what I wanted to tell you was—" There seemed to be real distress in his voice. "What I wanted to say was, well, it sounds rather stupid now—" He paused, throwing her a strangely wretched look. "It died," he announced suddenly.

"Died?" She frowned up at his inexplicably pained expression. "What are you talking about?"

"The littler one. At the hospital. I went last night to see how he was." He grimaced a kind of puzzled, unsorted expression of distraction. "His nose was running. His breathing sounded sloggy, like shoes walking in mud. He had a little face, all wrinkles, like some wizened old man, with a tiny little mouth that he didn't dare close—he couldn't eat and breathe at the same time." Graham drew a deep breath.

"Then, right as I was watching, he suddenly relaxed. At first I felt such relief, like watching someone put down a ridiculously heavy load. Then I realized what his lack of struggle meant. I started yelling for the doctors, calling for help—" He broke off.

The twin babies. She was amazed to realize he had visited the babies at the hospital.

He drew another breath, letting it out quietly as he smoothed his vest and buttoned the middle button of his coat. "That's all. I just wanted to tell someone—someone else who might mind. Well." He looked around for several seconds. "I think I left my hat inside."

Submit, with all the discomposure of reversed, contradictory feelings, watched the back of him disappear into the stone parlor.

In the common room, she found him putting his tangle of watches into the pocket of his coat. She didn't know what else to say except, "I'm sorry."

He looked at her. "It's not exactly bad news, is it? At least, I think that's what I'm supposed to feel: One less little bastard to impose on my charity." He pocketed the rings as well, then added as if she still might not believe it, "They really aren't mine."

"I know." She didn't doubt him; his simple statement had the weight of pure fact. That was the strangest thing about him. He was honest. From the first moment with the horrid pictures to his last word on Henry, he let her know what he thought.

"And the other one?" she asked.

"He's fine." He looked at her with an ambivalent frown. "I can take him home next week, they think."

She could hardly believe what she heard. "You're taking him home?"

"I suppose I am. When the other one died, I just went over to the district court and signed the papers. It felt right."

"Why? Why in the world would you take him home?"

He made another huge sigh. "Well, for one, I'm sick to death of going to court, and court seems to be the only way I can legally be rid of him." Then he dismissed this explanation with a shrug. "Who knows why I'm doing it? God knows I don't."

For almost a full minute, they stood staring at each other, then Submit lowered her eyes from the gaze of a man who did things without knowing why.

He murmured finally, "You remind me so much of Henry." He paused as if debating this change of topic, then continued. "Do you know how many houses I lived in between the ages of six and eleven? Nine. Nobody knew what to do with me when my parents died. I lived with my nanny at her sister's for a while, then moved in with my estate agent's family on the perimeter of my own property. I could see the house. I lived with a neighbor, a friend's parents, a governess the court appointed temporarily who stripped the house of its silver, then the sister of my mother's aunt. I can't remember the rest." Again he left a pause. "And, lately, I can't forget the last person I lived with as a child." He laughed. "Henry was by far the worst—I got along better with the governess who stole silver." He picked up his hat casually, as if to make light of what he said next. "So how much bother can one sickly little baby be? I'll stick him upstairs in the old nursery and hire a gaggle of attendants. I'll hardly see him. It's much cheaper than my arrangement with his mother, and he might be the better for it."

Well, Submit thought. What a confusing and circuitous brand of compassion he possessed, and for a baby who wasn't his, whose mother had sued him, clipped him for a good bit of money, then jumped out a window. She opened her mouth, thinking she could find words that would sort all this out and make logical sense.

Then he summed it up better than any logic could have. "What an unspeakable mess life can be," he said.

On his way to the door, he ran his hand along the flat of the counter, his finger up the curve of a vase. He ran his hands up and down the leather spines of the books on a shelf by the counter. Then he set his top hat on his head, quite naturally at an angle that dipped down over one brow, at what could have been called a rakish slant.

"Well, I'm sorry," he said, "for being such a bother." He made a faint laugh. "All the way around." At the door, he asked, "May I visit you Friday? The end of this week?"

"No—"

He went utterly still. Beneath the broad felt brim, his eyes went flat.

"I have to be in court," she explained.

His shoulders relaxed. "Lord, I thought you were telling me not to come back."

"No." Submit frowned. "Come next week. I mean, if you can. I'll be here most days after ten. I walk to the village in the morning." She found herself smiling at him, a little sheepishly. "I buy myself a sweet bun."

He stopped by briefly on Monday evening and again in the afternoon of the Thursday after that. Then on the Tuesday following, he showed up at eight in the morning with a dozen sweet buns, six oranges, and a bottle of champagne—all of which he described as his version of breakfast.

He had spent the weekend in London hiring a wet nurse and making arrangements for his surviving little ward. He was "on a dash" to Netham and could only stay an hour.

He stayed two.

"Champagne for breakfast?" She remembered the whiskey from the week or so before. The earl of Netham's reputation included, she knew, occasional drunkenness.

He was about to pollute the juice from the oranges with

the wine. She put her hand over her glass. They were sitting out on the stone-floored terrace. The sun was shining. Birds twittered overhead from a nest of swallows somewhere in the eave of the roof behind them.

"To summer." He held up his glass. She toasted with her orange juice. It tasted acrid and sour after the sweet roll. She thought, for some reason, of the clever, ambitious boys of Cambridge celebrating May Week, the last time she'd known champagne to flow where it possibly should not. She realized that though Graham Wessit may not have been the scholarly model of a Cambridge student, he had probably fit in rather well with his gregarious charm and outlandish exploits.

"Were you a good student at Cambridge?" she asked.

He poured champagne into his own juice and shrugged.

"Which college did you attend?"

He slid his eyes toward her sarcastically. "Which else?"

"Really? St. John's?" Submit put her glass down. Henry's revered institution, along with King's and Trinity, was one of the three biggest, richest of the twenty-six colleges that made up the University of Cambridge. These were well-off, landed schools that didn't favor old men by taking in their wards and sons. "What did you read?"

He made a facetious smile and took a long draft of champagne direct from the bottle, apparently dispensing with his orange juice entirely. "L.M.B.C."

Lady Margaret's Boat Club. It was an athletic club, the only boat club to lambaste the Other University regularly. Yes, she could well see the natty Netham with his champagne and scarlet blazer, racing on water, carrying on on land.

"What did you *really* read?"

"I told you before, humility."

"You're evading." She teased him with a sidelong smile. "I won't think less of you for having a serious scholarly interest." She realized she wanted him to have a hidden intellectual side. The actor, the exquisite, she had weeks ago discovered, was really quite bright, though no one seemed to notice. And no one, not even he, seemed to care. His intelligence was not the first trait he chose to bring forward. Still, he'd been raised by Henry. He almost had to have a predilection, she thought, for a science or modern languages or the classics.

He settled back into his chair, leaning on its arm, setting his jaw into his hand, one pensive finger up the side of his cheek. There was a trace of the actor in this; the handsome man who could strike a pose for effect. Despite herself, she was charmed.

"All right," he said at length. "Don't laugh." She waited. He smiled. "Theology."

They both laughed. "Theology! Not really."

"Really."

"As in wearing a white collar?"

His answer was to raise his glass and toast himself with a little poem:

> "The Reverend Pimlico Poole was a saint
> Who averted from sinners their doom,
> By confessing the ladies until they felt faint,
> All alone in a little, dark room."

Submit laughed, despite the flush that rose in her face. The earl of Netham was too unabashedly bawdy; she enjoyed it too much. And his frank manner did something else. It encouraged her tongue to say what she should hardly have thought: "You would have certainly brought the ladies into the confessional, one way or another."

They laughed, enjoying together the blasphemous notion for a moment. Then he said, "You have the nicest smile."

Involuntarily, her hand went to her mouth. "My teeth are crooked." She didn't know where to look.

"Yes, I think that's one of the things I like." He went on, as if there were no reason for discomfort, "When I was seventeen, I was very serious about serving the Church." He flashed a perfect, very unclerical smile. "I believed fervently in God, in people, and in the high theater of the Latin mass."

"Not to mention actresses," she offered cautiously, "and art."

He laughed at that. "Oh, I never thought to be a celibate monk or even a preaching Anglican, but rather a discreet single cleric until a wife came along. I fancied becoming a canon or prebendary attached to a grand cathedral somewhere that would stand as huge witness to my good, Godly intent." He began to play with a fork they had used to spear buns, rolling the instrument on end by its tines. "I wasn't completely insincere, I suppose. But I suspect now that my chief calling was to give old atheistic Henry seizures. Anyway, at the time it seemed right. I was being Good. I knew clerics had to be human, after all, so I didn't ask too much of myself." He glanced at her, as if trying to see how much of this she believed, how much he might risk by saying more. He put his finger in the sticky sugar on his plate then put the finger into his mouth. "Youthful delusions." He laughed. "My scholarship, now that you ask, was impeccable; my spiritual life, however, was a mess—and that, of course, is the substance of the Church. It doesn't take grand scholarship to have a pure soul. Or vice versa." He paused. "What did you read?"

"Pardon?"

"At Cambridge. What did you study?"

She was taken aback. "Why, nothing. I was just a distinguished lecturer's wife."

He seemed intent on watching her, as she immersed herself in the dissection of the remains of a pastry on her plate. "You loved it, didn't you? The academic world. You would have liked to have been part of it."

"I *was* part of it." But she knew what he meant. She would have liked to have attended lectures, read in the library, eaten in the dining halls, been privy to the whole. "There were evening discussions and afternoon guests. Henry's house was a very stimulating environment."

"Yes. And there you were, sixteen, seventeen, just the age a lot of boys come up to Cambridge. And you were bright—brighter than most of them, am I right?" He gave her no chance to answer. "And married to a man older than most of their grandfathers. Didn't you just once want to go with them, read their books—"

"I did read their books. Henry brought them to me."

"I'm surprised one of the boys didn't bring them to you, once they discovered that was what you wanted."

She looked down. "This is mean. Why are you doing it?"

"To try and get you to see—"

"I was *happy* with Henry. He gave me more than any callow young man could have given."

He laughed and stood up. "Don't bet on it." He took the bottle by the neck. At the break in the stone wall, he looked back. "Would you like to go for a walk?"

She shook her head no.

As she watched him do her own circuit to the poplars, she wondered about his motives for telling her these things, his motives for coming here at all. She looked toward the handsome, athletic, reckless, fearless, shameless man walking along the greensward, drinking champagne from the bottle at ten in the morning—so much the antithesis of Henry, the embodiment of all Henry wasn't and could never be.

My God, she thought, there must have been days when Graham Wessit's merely drawing breath was enough to make Henry weep.

* * *

Graham became a regular visitor that July. Sometimes they planned his next visit, sometimes he showed up without warning. In either case, he always talked a great deal, as if he were laying his life out for her inspection. She tried to speak to this, as if she could comment from an objective distance. The inn out in the middle of nowhere became a strangely conducive place for such talks.

Submit was less comfortable when the omniscient inquiry pried into her life. She tried to keep Graham's curiosity at bay, but he had a way of stopping, leaving long, interested silences that made her want to fill them in with honest, meaningful words. By the end of July, she'd told him of her father, her schooling, her marriage; she'd discussed the death of her mother. The inn at Morrow Fields seemed to be a private world where one could share such things.

— *Chapter 22* —

Evil villain that he was, the rakehell pursued the young woman into the back stable.

"No!" she told him once, twice, thrice, as he tossed her backward into the straw.

Her skirts flew up, offering a glimpse of white cambric drawers, plump calf, and fine, dainty ankle. It was not until he was trying to lift her linen petticoats trimmed with French broadlace, however, that she rallied the courage to say what needed to be said:

"I will not submit to any man's unbounded lechery, except for the procreation of legitimate issue."

Graham threw the rolled magazine across the room. The force of its flight made the crystal pieces in the chandelier sing. "What absolute twaddle!"

The more unwholesome passages of *The Rake of Ronmoor* read like a combination of church dicta and ladies' garment advertisements. For this, Pease charged an extravagant two shillings a magazine—twenty times the cost of a usual weekly and twice what an episode of the good Mr. Dickens brought. If people wanted a vaguely naughty little story feathered with celebrity innuendo, the publisher was making them pay.

And pay they did. Mr. Pease got his price, for hardly more than titillation, allusion, and social gossip, supposedly made palatable by the moralistic outrage as each misconduct was delineated in scrupulous detail. The numbered episodes of *The Rake of Ronmoor* had become the essence of Pease's *Porridge*. The magazine contained a few other bits of fiction, a few poems, some sheet music, and some hand-colored plates of men's and women's fashion. But the majority of the little publication's pages were devoted to serializing Graham, his past, and what people apparently imagined to be his present. In the loose fictional guise of Wesley Grey, Graham's history conspired with the current taste for a romantic villain people loved to hate once a week.

Graham had hoped that one good outcome of the death of Arabella Stratford would be that *The Rake* would falter, then stop. When it didn't, Graham reasoned at first that publication might lag a bit behind the actual writing of the things; there would be printing schedules and distribution. When still they continued after two weeks, however, he began to worry the culprit was elsewhere than in the grave. In any event, the implications of the newest numbers, fourteen and fifteen, were positively frightening: The author, M. Du-Jauc, knew Netham well enough to walk its rooms, shoo its geese, fish its ponds. Graham was suspicious that his tormentor was, or at least had been in one summer or another, part of his hand-selected summer crowd.

"Rosalyn, have you any idea who is doing this?"

Rosalyn smiled, putting the back of her hand to her mouth, possibly to suppress a giggle. "No, dear. Not a clue." They were in the upstairs parlor that connected to Graham's rooms. Rosalyn picked up the thrown book and began leafing through the pages.

Graham paced. "Tilney. It's Tilney, and you know it."

"Hm?" She wasn't listening. Absently, after a little delay, she answered, "No, honestly. I know nothing of the kind."

Graham looked at her speculatively. She had an ear for gossip, could know much more about him than he himself might have told. Yet the rhythm of the pen was English. Despite Rosalyn's ability to use phrases like "eh, what a fancy" and "by Jove," he couldn't imagine her carrying it off for pages and pages. And she spoke no French at all, a must for

The Rake and anything else one wanted to sound a little risqué.

It might be Tilney, of course. But as much as Peter loved to torment Graham, he seemed still essentially too meek and cowardly to attack with such straightforward gall. Graham even considered Henry briefly, then had to laugh at the very thought of the stuffy old pundit jotting off anything so frothy. More to the point: Henry, like the mother of the twins, was dead, which left Graham with only about two or three dozen more friends to rule out. William couldn't write a straight sentence. Tate was too busy by half. Graham thought of Submit—less because she was a very good candidate than because she stayed in his mind lately like a huge mystery herself. The more he knew about her, the more he wanted to find out. Whenever he thought of the serial and its carping tone, he thought of her and her quiet mitigating attitude of censure. She held almost the opposite view—the antidote to the fiction's interpretation of him. Besides, knowing as little as she had of his history, she was of course out of the question. Who, then? Who?

"Look at this, Graham." Rosalyn turned the book sideways and held it over her head to offer him a view. It was a drawing.

"Jesus Christ," he breathed out. It was a wood engraving done for the purpose of illustrating the story. Though the artist's name was different, Graham knew well the imitated style. The august Academician Alfred Pandetti was going to be less than pleased to be mimicked in subject matter as trivial as this. Graham frowned for a moment, thinking the new attack narrowed the field of prospective authors. It was someone who knew about the pictures, knew who the artist was. Then he realized that anyone who was associated with Cambridge at the time that he and Alfred were there might know.

Thus, whoever the person was, he or she was over thirty-five. No, *he*. A man, a man from Cambridge, because the details had been kept from the gentler sex. A Cambridge man, over thirty-five, who had been to Netham enough to know it inside and out.

"I find it offensive," he told Rosalyn, taking the book away. "It uses mistakes I made a long time ago that are best forgotten—"

She laughed and got up. "Mistakes that are funny. And sometimes very exciting. Don't take yourself so seriously, Graham." She turned around, leaning a knee into the seat of the sofa, facing him over its back.

"The mistakes were serious. And this—" He held the thing in his hand, bending it. "I hate the tone, all the shame and temptation of it. Every blessed misenterprise pronounced and moralized upon, like some middle-class—" The mores of the episodes, if one took them seriously, were very middle-class. He thought about this. A middle-class mind—or else a very prim one, much like the current royal manners—was writing these. This only left him more lost. "Rosalyn, how can you possibly not mind these?"

She laughed and leaned toward him. "I can hardly wait for it all to bend around to me. I am dying to see myself in print."

He sighed in exasperation. "While I'm hoping you're kept out of it. One more damned mistake—"

They both caught what he'd said at the same time. He looked at her abruptly—just in time to catch a pillow in the face. She'd thrown it at him as she'd backed off the sofa.

"Bloody hell," she murmured. Refusing to look at him, she straightened her dress.

Anger gave inside Graham. She knew it was an accident; he hadn't *meant* to say such a thing. He threw the pillow back hard, hitting her in the shoulder. She looked around sharply. "Bloody hell," she said more emphatically.

Graham narrowed his eyes. "Where do you hear such words?"

"None of your business."

He should have let it go, but at this point he wanted some conclusion reached, some sort of satisfaction. He grabbed her arm when she tried to turn and leave.

She looked him in the face, resisting just enough that he had to use both hands. When he had her by her shoulders, something softened in her, complying with his force. She went from an angry woman to one who was coquettish and cute, a child who wouldn't answer. Her eyes became warm, doeish, inviting more roughness, more dominion. He realized she liked it, his mastering her like—like a bullying rake.

Graham let go. He ran one hand back through his hair, then put both hands into the pockets at the bottom of his vest.

Rosalyn liked this stance, too. She laughed, running her hands up her arms with a shiver, her eyes up and down his length. "Tilney," she said in a throaty voice. "Tilney loves to tell me dirty words." She was tormenting him. "I dare not even utter the worst."

Graham turned away from her, not certain where to hide. "And you let him?"

"What? Say dirty words?"

"Say dirty words to *you*."

She laughed. "How can I stop him? It isn't rape, you know, Gray."

"You could tell him off, send him away."

She shrugged. "Why? He's a duke's son. I like him. So what if he swears like a lord. One day he'll be one."

"Peter has an older brother."

"Who is aged and ill."

He shook his head at this. "You don't put up with it from me."

"That's different. You don't need to say dirty words to me: I sleep with you."

He frowned at the specious wisdom. Rosalyn wouldn't put up with the butler swearing at her, and *he* didn't sleep with her. Or at least Graham didn't think he did.

"Do you sleep with other men?" he asked.

"Would it bother you if I did?"

"Yes."

Surprisingly, there was a long, guilty pause. Graham turned around to see her face grown serious, blushing slightly. The little tramp, he thought. His fury rose; the cad having been outcadded. Then she said softly, "Only with Gerald, Gray. He's my husband." Softer still, she confessed, "I can't seem to figure out how to tell him no."

Graham made a grim snort. "You could ask him if he'd like to whisper dirty words."

She laughed, becoming flippant again when he wanted her to behave. As she turned, she lifted her shoulders to look over one of them at him. It was one of her more appealing and inviting poses. "That's the worst of it." She spoke in her deep, flirty voice. "I like Peter to tell me dirty words. He tortures himself with them, with the situation. And it thrills me."

It didn't thrill Graham. He said, stone-faced, "The situation could change."

Rosalyn's look over her shoulder grew mean. "Then I could sleep with Tilney. He's everything you are. Except possibly *he's* in love with me."

"*Gerald's* in love with you," he corrected her.

She thought about it, then shrugged. "Maybe that's why I sleep with him." She paused. "Are you in love with me, Graham?"

He answered the question honestly. "I don't know."

* * *

Gerald Schild showed up at Netham several times more, with the same lack of warning or invitation—traveling ostensibly on his defunct marriage license. The other guests treated these larger exits and entrances of his with the same relative indifference as his smaller ones at breakfast or dinner. He blew into a room like a warm, uncomfortable air. People squirmed in their seats, got up to go for a drink, for a walk, never quite certain why, unaware of anything but a sudden change of climate.

As to the lover's triangle, in which he figured a drafty, southerly vertex, he had no sense of how the whole thing should be acted out. He cast himself in no part—not the outraged husband, not the shrugging sophisticate, not even the wretched cuckold. And this threw the other players off as well. Rosalyn would be flustered—caught between differing quartos of her own script, making dutiful noises and pecks on her husband's cheek while looking to Graham for direction. With Graham pulled back into the wings: A coward without some agreement on text, he had nothing to offer.

Schild didn't stay long; he didn't come often. But the fact that he came at all seemed the hugest breach of both protocol and good judgment. He barely spoke to anyone but his wife. And with her he was always too publicly intimate, no matter how formally he began. In the simplest greeting— "How are you?"—he sounded as if he asked a legitimate question. In "Is life treating you well?" *life* immediately read as "him, that Englishman," the category itself implying the distinction of another species—cold-blooded, alien, as if she had somehow taken up, rather appallingly, with a beaded lizard.

There was no sympathy for the man or for the inept, mostly unspoken speeches that brooded behind his eyes. He was generally shunned, this awkward foreigner from a crude country who could not hold a wife and yet could not hold himself from her, despite the fact that he had to scale the obstacles of her lover and all his titled, condescending friends to be near her.

For Graham, there was so much to be pitied and loathed in Gerald Schild, it was overwhelming. There was also something strangely heroic to him, though Graham was reluctant to admit or analyze what that might be. But it had something to do with his capacity to bare—and bear, both senses—his unblenching misery.

Graham remembered the handshake of that first morning, the slight horror of taking Schild's offered hand. It was small, fleshy—Graham thought of Rosalyn— a paw. Both Schild's hands had small mutilations, which fixed him firmly in the middle class. The right had a gnarled thumb. It was missing the tip and had only a fraction of the remaining nail. (An accident of trade. "He worked in the mills when he was young," Rosalyn explained.) The left hand, which so frequently petted the thinning spot of hair at the back of Schild's head, was marred by a fat, heavy band. A wedding ring. There was not another male guest in the house who wore one, the custom being unaristocratic, if not un-English altogether: A gentleman did not need to be reminded that he was married.

One of Schild's more memorable blunders was when he was in his cups late one night after dinner. He raised a fourth glass of gin and, from across a room, made a toast to his wife playing cards. He sat, one arm raised, one leg draped over the arm of a chair. Perhaps Rosalyn had a soft spot for drunks, for in this instance she seemed strangely affected by his inebriated gallantry. He spoke the toast aloud:

"It is no chaste love I bear my wife," he said. Chaste love. Graham had to look away. "It is jealous and adulterated." He added, "There are times when I would give it up. If I could."

Rosalyn blanched. The room grew silent. Then the lovely Mrs. Schild left for parts of the house unknown. Graham didn't find her till hours later. The event was embarrassing, but that didn't explain the way it shook her. She seemed to suffer as from a revelation, as if her husband's drunken, miserable love were somehow sobering. As if she were looking love in the face for the first time, caught unaware as she was by seeing it in all its intensity and flower in the most unlikely place, the ruddy, drunken face of her balding husband.

Chapter 23

This time, Graham was told accurately where she would be and what she'd be doing: at a clothesline in the sun, hanging her wash.

Behind the kitchen, some yards to the right and beyond the terrace wall, a line had been strung between roof corner and tree to accommodate the drying of laundry. Most of the articles on the line were obviously from the inn—table and bed linens, kitchen rags. But a small section seemed to have been given over to the use of the inn's solitary guest.

As he came out onto the terrace, Graham spotted her immediately. She was solid against the white laundry. He stopped just under the terrace's overhang. The day suddenly reminded him of the day he had followed her out into the field. The sun was bright. The nap of the grass separated and blew in the breeze, making a light, continuously shifting pattern as wide as the field itself. There was nothing anywhere, just the occasional and distant trees, the day, and this woman hanging her clothes. The only shade was the black waving patterns over her back as she bent. He watched her rise through these shadows as she stood, watched the clothes wrap around her and hit her in the face. Graham too felt wrapped—rapt. He was caught up instantly in the private watching of her, in the guilty pleasure of scrutiny without observation. He stood transfixed.

She was much less elegantly turned out today. Her dress was dark cotton, too faded to be called black. It was open at the throat. The small buttons up the wrists and forearm were undone, presumably for coolness or mobility or both. Her sleeves hung in flaps at her elbows. And another anomaly: no hoops. Her copious skirts had been pulled up and back into two wads and tied in a knot over her derriere, an improvised solution to keep the unsupported fabric out of her way. What a sight.

Her back was to him, the sun in her eyes—if she had stood the other way, the breeze would have had her perpetually tangled in neighboring sheets. He watched her as she raised a hand to shield her face, looking up with a piece of laundry. Then she would avert her head and pin blind to the clothesline. Back to the ground, bending in half; a rounded swaddle of dark cotton, the bowed ears of her knotted skirts dominating the air for a moment, raised over thin, stockingless ankles. She bent and stretched, pins between her teeth, her hands shielding, smoothing, shaking, organizing, stringing up clothes. A blouson. A chemise. An untold mangle of more wet clothes rested at her feet in a small basket. He came slowly around the wall, but she didn't notice him, so absorbed was she in her quotidian acrobatics. She made regular, rhythmic progress, nudging the basket with a foot or dragging it along, even as she retrieved a pin or a piece of clothing. She had a wonderful coordination, a loose-hipped limberness that allowed a foot to coax and an arm to reach without her having to watch either very closely. The ritual had for Graham all the perfect, unorchestrated balance of a bird with its jointed tail—life on a narrow limb, always a fractional adjustment available to accommodate wind, position, and view to the current task.

After a time, Graham began to feel awkward. He had been spying too long. He moved forward with no better introduction than to hand her a piece of laundry. She jumped—the startled bird—then laughed, seemingly delighted to have company and essentially unsurprised.

Yes, she was fine, she told him. Having to do a bit of her own work, but not minding it; having, after all, witnessed when she was very young the sight of her mother working. Before her father's abattoir, when it was just a butcher shop in London, her mother had done all the domestic work herself. It was only later that the troupe of servants arrived. Her father thought he was giving her mother a great gift— freedom from hard work. But her mother grew quiet and thin within the first year of this generosity. She died shortly after that, as if her purpose for living had somehow been undermined.

"I'm sorry," he said. But Submit waved it off.

And here they were again, talking of private things as easily as most people discussed the weather. Graham loved the close feeling of talking to her, made even nicer by the physical closeness he was presently allowed—the absence of hoops let him get right up next to her as he handed over a pair of wet stockings. He could smell the soap on her hands and something else, something that smelled of herbs and grass, and lilies perhaps. The soft, feminine smell of a woman's morning toilet. The idea of her owning fragrant soaps or perfumes, of her wanting to attract, unsettled him a little. He couldn't align this with another notion of her, of the shy, elusive woman quick to point out her slightly over-lapped teeth. He didn't know how to take these contradic-tory indications of vanity. How did a man respond to a woman who knew she wasn't beautiful yet who knew also, on some level, that perfume wasn't wasted? It was as if the prim woman in black understood—and conspired with— her own enigmatic carnal appeal.

He continued to hand her pieces of wet laundry, careful not to touch her. The memory of the physical rebuff the day in the field was suddenly keen again. Of course, that was be-fore they knew each other as they did now. . . .

"It's beautiful weather," she said. "I've never seen such a summer as this."

He agreed.

"Look up there. In the eaves over my room." He looked where she pointed, not at the eaves but at the window of her room. It would be up the stairs inside, then all the way to the back. "Swallows, I thought—their tails are split—but now I'm not sure. I'm terrible with species."

He smiled. "Other people's categories simply do not interest you, do they?" When she looked at him, a little puzzled, he answered, "A swift. The bird up there is a swift, which is unusual. They generally travel in great screaming packs."

The bird took off. They watched it fly out of sight. No need to make further conversation. Then he did something unlikely. He threw his coat over the line, rolled back his sleeves, and pinned up a pillow casing himself. Watching, she laughed.

"How very"—she couldn't find the word for a moment, then settled on—"*common* of you." It was a gibe, but also a compliment. He could take being called common by her and knew there were good things to being labeled so.

"Once," he said, "after the pictures, the pillory, the whole thing, after I was home on Henry's hands, I couldn't sleep one night. Henry was up, in the front portico, seeing a friend out. We were at war by then, Henry and I. Horrible. Both suppurating wounded for having torn into each other too many times. I'm not sure if I got up to fire off more cannon or to effect some midnight truce. But I could hear the friend leaving and wanted simply to face Henry again. When I got near the door, I heard them talking. Henry said, 'I can't help feeling there is no hope. He won't come into line.' He sighed a huge sigh then added, 'To do something so vulgar, so common. I shall never be able to get over it. I am so ashamed of him.'"

Graham paused, caught suddenly by the oddity of his telling her yet more, dwelling on his old problems, while he tried to minimize the accidental mention of a subject—a person—never too far from their conversational reach: and never within their agreement. "What I did was not very genteel, of course. But . . ." He let the thought trail off. There was nowhere to go with it. The memory wasn't flattering; not for Henry, even less for himself. Its only significance was that it marked the final realization that the approval and affection he had always imagined he could win were not forthcoming: destinations on Henry's map he would never reach.

Submit held a clothes peg over the folded edge of a shift, then wedged it down. "Under the circumstances," she said, "one would expect him to feel let down. People say things."

"That wasn't it. He made a third person party to his worst feelings toward me. My dirty linen." He smiled at the parallel, her clean wash in the sun, then looked at the ground.

"Yes," she agreed finally, "it wasn't very good of him." But her voice withheld judgment. For all concerned.

"You really must come to Netham," he found himself saying. "You would like it. If only for a holiday."

This won him only a funny smile, as if her taking a holiday at Netham were the silliest notion she had ever heard. But she thanked him. And bowed out: "I am closer to London here."

There was nothing more to say. They were at the end of an empty laundry basket, the conversation.

He carried her things in for her, his arm brushing against her breast for one tantalizing moment as he reached ahead to open the door. They came into the common room, the strange gaping dining hall of the posting house, full of its ready, empty tables. Graham set the basket down on one of these, then looked up to find Submit staring at him. She was frowning slightly as she did up the buttons at her neckline, where they ran from her collarbone by quarter inches up the full length of her throat. Graham began unrolling his own sleeves, thinking he might offer to help with the buttons as he had helped with the wash. He could imagine her raising her chin, allowing him access, while he worked at the slow, meticulous task of the tiny fastens.

He titillated himself with the thought as he watched her own fingers do the job. She patted the collar in place, then began at the run of buttons down her left arm. The two of them stood there, buttoning, unrolling, putting aright, quietly fixing their clothes as in the strange transitional silence of postcoitus.

"Well, thank you again," she said. Her coordination wasn't as good with her left hand. At her right sleeve, she had hold of a button, then lost the edge of the cuff. She had to start over, bringing the two pieces together awkwardly with the one hand.

"Here, may I?"

She contemplated his offer. Then, drawing a slow, even breath, she extended her arm.

He gripped the back of it firmly, beginning at the buttons with his other hand. He could feel a tension in her, a kind of reluctant willingness at her elbow and in her wrist. Under the tips of his fingers, the inside of her forearm felt cool, as smooth as the skin of a peach. He stared down, presumably to watch what he was doing. But in fact he was almost blinded by the simple enterprise. He could feel her pulse beating through her arm, beneath his hand. His own heart began to thud. He wanted to bring her arm up around his neck, bend his nose to it, feel the skin against his mouth, breathe in its smell, kiss it, lick it, bite it—

The sleeve flapped loose as he slid his hand up her arm, inside her sleeve to the bend of her elbow. He fit his hand flush into this bend—it was damp. He pulled her toward him. His mouth came against hers just in time for her lips, warm and dry, to brush his as she turned her face away.

"No."

He was left with her cheek, the edge of her hairline.

Against his mouth, she was velvety, covered in pale, fine hair, a peachlike down. She pushed him back.

"Why 'no'?" he asked.

She took his hand out of her sleeve and began to fumble at the buttons herself, leaning back against a table. She threw him a nervous half-smile. "That is strictly the response of a man who has not accepted 'no.' "

"Why?" he repeated.

"I don't owe you explanations." The rebuke was quiet, final.

He had to work at making himself smile. "I think, after hanging laundry together all morning, you do."

"You wouldn't like it."

"I don't much like not being allowed to kiss you."

She sent up a plea, a serious glance, but made not the first offer to explain. She was having no better luck with the sleeve on the second try. He took hold of her wrist. She tried to jerk it back.

"Be still. I'm only going to do the buttons."

In the most businesslike fashion he could, he pulled a chair around and put his foot on it. He laid her elbow on his knee. She balked when he stretched her arm out, laying it up his thigh, then warily allowed him to begin the tight, cinching motion of pressing buttons into loops.

A full minute later, he was only halfway done. They stood among the tables in this awkward, protracted silence; fastening, fastening. There were twenty-three buttons down her arm; he'd counted them twice. Then Graham saw, in his peripheral sight, an odd, unexplained motion. Submit bent her head slightly, bringing the back of her other hand to her mouth. He paused, reached up and took the hand away. And there it was: a faint smile. She tried to turn her head so he couldn't see, but there was nowhere to hide. He held both her arms, with only the mildest resistance. For several seconds, she tried to look at him but couldn't meet his eye. She fought her own odd, smiling expression as it broke over her face. Then shyly, self-consciously—beautifully, seductively—embarrassed, she bowed her head.

Graham was completely at sea. The bent posture, along with the feminine smiling and hiding, put such a contradiction to what had gone before that his mouth went dry. It was as if she were saying to pay no mind to any protests and . . .

As a way of undercutting it, she quickly owned up to her apparent ambivalence. "No matter what you're reading from me in one way, never think I don't have a strong sense of what is right. For me." She withdrew her arms. "I like you." She raised a brow, putting a demur—a disjunctive *but*—into her smile. "I won't tangle with you. Not in that way." In a softer tone, she added, "Still, thank you. You've no idea what self-justification you've just given me. To be able to tell myself the choice really did exist, not just sour grapes."

"That doesn't leave much for me, does it?"

"Don't be offended. No one is completely irresistible."

That subdued him. And incensed him.

"Don't," she said again, meaning he mustn't be angry.

"It's not you caught with your pants down."

"For pity's sake—"

"I'll get my hat."

He started to move past her, but she was closer to the hat. It hung at a jaunty angle on top of the newel post at the base of the stairs.

Submit wove her way between tables, straight to it, lifting it free. It seemed a bad joke to her suddenly, the familiarity of her knowing immediately where he would put his hat: on her stair post. Then she picked up his gloves from the crevice between post and banister. Without waiting, she walked toward the stone parlor beyond the entryway, toward the stables.

They went through the parlor. He held the door, his expression a rigid mask of indignation. She tried to ignore his anger; there was nothing she could do about it. Meanwhile, as she stepped down into the tack room, she became aware of the weight of her skirts, of the knot where it was tied in back. The knotted fabric bobbed over her buttocks, sliding and shifting no matter how straight she carried herself. Graham reached to hold back the clutter of straps, and Submit acutely regretted her lack of hoops. They usually kept him, kept anyone, at more of a distance. Now, at every doorway, at every pause in their progression, he was close enough that his legs brushed up against the bulkily tied skirts.

At the archway to the stables, he wouldn't take his hat. He went down the last three steps in a pique.

Then, right there before her, he suddenly turned and looked up. "Why? You damn well want to—"

She blinked. "I want to do a lot of things," she replied, "but I'm not willing to pay the price." She stepped down the last step, again offering his hat.

This time he took it as he said, "All right. I understand not liking others' disapproval—"

"It's not that. *I* wouldn't approve."

"If you want to do something, you simply give yourself permission."

"Like dirty pictures?"

He was taken aback. "Exactly like dirty pictures."

"My dear earl." She gave him a look of pure, indulgent forbearance. "I might like to live off cake, but I don't. It's not good for me. I wouldn't have done the pictures, no matter how much the idea appealed to me: They made you feel terrible."

"They made me feel wonderful, you idiot. I bloody *loved* doing them." His horse, tied to a ring on the wall, shied at the sound of his raised voice.

"Then hated yourself for them later on."

"I didn't—" She looked at him levelly. "All right," he said, "I did regret them a little. But only because—" His face drew into a frown that drew into deeper furrows, almost a grimace of pain. "Because," he said soberly, "Henry hated me for them. They became to him the final proof that everything I ever did was wrong."

"Oh, dear." Some of Submit's irritation abated, as she realized, whether Graham did or not, that he was speaking of how important Henry had been to him. In a much gentler voice, she put this into words: "You wanted Henry's respect."

"Well, yes." He gave her a funny look. "Just a little would have been nice."

"Surely Henry gave it to you for other things."

"No, madam, he didn't." He turned away, going over to untie the horse.

"He came to you when you were sick."

"That's not the same thing as respect."

"It's not the same thing as approval. But it was a way of acknowledging that he cared: I think Henry was sorry he couldn't approve of you."

He turned his back completely, adjusting the stirrup. "Bloody big of him." He put his foot in the tread, about to swing up.

"Graham—" It made her warm to hear his given name aloud out her own mouth, but she suddenly needed it, wanted it.

From his awkward position, he looked around.

"I thought about what you said the other day." She genuinely wanted to offer him something. "You were at least partially right. Henry hated anything that reminded him of his own follies. He liked to believe he was perfect. It annoyed him no end when he remembered he had fathered a dull-witted bastard. Or—" She hesitated, then said, "That he had a strong attraction for a young girl he was afraid he wasn't perfect enough—handsome enough, young enough—to keep. Henry hated his own passion. It frightened him."

For a moment, Graham just stared at her, holding the reins, one hand on the saddle's pommel, his knee in the air. Then he slowly turned around again, putting his foot back on the ground. He steadied the horse, patting it.

"Why does it frighten you?" he asked.

"Why does what frighten me?"

"Passion." The horse sidestepped nervously.

She laughed. "It doesn't," she said finally. "I've shared passion, I told you, with Henry."

"With a man who was afraid of it?"

Submit blinked, frowned, then let out a breath. "You must get it through your head, Graham"—she used the name now like a prim, lecturing nanny—"that I loved my husband and that I—I made his bed mine quite happily. Don't confuse that with the fact that I don't want to play flirting, kissing games with you. I'm not available to any man who happens to trouble himself to ride out and ask."

"Have other men asked?"

A burst of laughter escaped, disbelief. "Yes," she said. With a show of scholarly patience, "Other men have asked."

"And?"

"I've said no, just as I'm saying to you."

"You have never even *kissed* another man?"

She narrowed her eyes. "This is really none of your business."

"Then you have."

"No, I have not."

And this answer, quite surprisingly, seemed to provoke him more than if she had.

"Do you mean to tell me"—he leaned toward her with a kind of furious wonder—"you have never even kissed another man, no one but that nasty old curmudge—"

"Lord Netham." She held her ground, facing him nose to

nose. "Irrespective of my dealing with that nasty old curmudgeon, the answer is no."

He spoke directly into her face. "Lady Motmarche, I'm not a complete idiot: Irrespective of that nasty old curmudgeon, that smile a minute ago told me you wanted it kissed right off your face, wanted me to kiss you till your knees buckled and your drawers dropped around your ankles." He turned and threw the reins again over the horse.

Anger let loose in Submit, rich and hot. It flooded her veins. "That's a lie. A crudely put, self-deceiving lie."

He looked over his shoulder as he put his foot in the stirrup again. "I can get cruder—"

"Yes, I've seen what you consider art—"

"And I can be a lot more honest: You are a self-righteous, arrogant prude who only knows how to fuck a man with her mind. No wonder you and Henry got on so well."

He leaped onto his horse before she could speak. The horse wheeled around with surprising spirit. Dust churned. Bits of hay and dry grass flew. Submit backed up.

But she didn't back down. "Lord Netham," she called.

He brought the animal around, prancing in side steps. The horse whinnied and snorted at its short rein.

With perfect, quiet, malicious intent, Submit homed in on a little truth she was sure Graham Wessit would prefer not to see: "Would you be trying to seduce me if Henry were alive?"

He stared down, holding the animal in place. "Possibly," Graham answered.

"What if he were standing here right now? Would you want to—what was that word you used? I've never heard it, but I take it it's crude. Would you want to"—she marched bravely, cogently into this new word—"fuck me if Henry were standing here right now?"

Graham drew in a breath through his nostrils and scowled. "Definitely."

"Which is my point. You don't want to make love to me—as Henry did so very nicely, I might mention. You want to cuckold Henry Channing-Downes." Submit thought she had tied all this up for him rather neatly.

But he laughed. "You're bloody right, I would like to have cuckolded Henry. But Henry, my dear, is dead—"

"Not in your mind, he's not."

"No, it's in your mind he's alive. You're still trying to be faithful to a nasty son of a bitch who's six feet under the ground. And you can be for all I care—" The horse suddenly reared. Without a moment's hesitation, Graham leaned up on its neck, bringing it crashing to the ground. He spun the animal around, putting it right where he wanted it again, facing her. "The two of you are perfect for each other," he said. "A childish necromantic married to dead man who used children. Congratulations, you have found what I've been looking for all my adult life: a perfect match."

— Chapter 24 —

Back, back, wild throbbing heart! . . . back, back
hot blood! painting tales that should
never be told on the blushing cheek.

Mrs. Stephen's Illustrated New Monthly

"Nellie's Illusions," page 35

Philadelphia, July 1856

Netham, 27 August
My dear Cousin,

I beg your forgiveness for my reprehensible conduct last week. I was furious, of course, but I was infinitely more regretful than furious by the time I got home. I could barely credit what I had said to you. I humbly apologize. I blame the sun, my generally intemperate nature, and my long-standing inclination to challenge even the most angelic patience. I add, for the sake of soliciting your mercy, the idea that our last meeting might have represented a kind of final snap of relief for me over what has been, thus far, a truly difficult spring and summer. As for the words I chose to use in expressing my incredibly obnoxious thoughts, I hope you will forgive a man who, though born and bred into the life of a gentleman, spent an unfortunate number of impressionable months on the streets about Leicester Square. The theater district is no place to learn civil conduct. Not that that particular lesson has ever come very easily to me. I heartily promise, if you will be so kind as to excuse my outrageous behavior, I shall forever after remain a gentleman in your presence.

I hope you will demonstrate your forgiveness by allowing me to visit you next week. I will be in London on Tuesday to take the surviving twin home. Please say I can stop by on my way into the city.

Enclosed is a small token of my sincere regrets. They are for your wonderful straw hat.

Sincerely,
Graham

Morrow Fields, 28 August
My dearest Cousin,

The ribbons are lovely, though completely unnecessary. It is the easiest thing for me to forgive you. I too said things of which I am not very proud. The truth is, it was not the sun or anything else. We were both the victims of a kind of false intimacy bred of circumstances which, now that I reflect, are somewhat familiar to me: You were needing a little understanding. I should have known better. At St. John's, it used to happen with some regularity. Henry would yell at some poor disciple or other. The poor lad would come to me. I would listen, help him reinterpret. He would be angry that Henry hadn't said things my way to begin with, then terribly, terribly grateful that I had. I used to—if I may be so candid—turn away sexual offers on the average of two or three students a year. What was so difficult was that I was so close to their ages. These young men never understood, but Henry, when I would confide, did. He used to laugh about it, a little nervously, I might add. He always teased me that there would one day be one I simply wouldn't want to tell him about. But there never was.

Please don't think I am drawing broad parallels between you and callow university men. You are certainly much more worldly and mature, which is why I was so much more flattered— and, I think, so much more shortsighted than irritated over what I had encouraged.

With regard to your proposed visit, I have given the idea

careful consideration and find—no matter how much I might wish it otherwise—your traveling here again is simply inadvisable. I ask you instead to please refrain from coming to Morrow Fields, where I seek only solace and peace. I think perhaps we have said all that really needs to be said between us. Believe it or not, I am glad to have had your somewhat unorthodox observations and opinions of Henry. These have helped me to define more clearly and more realistically my own conclusions, be they so very different from your own.

Please believe I harbor no grudge and will cheerfully greet you, should we meet by chance.

Your respectful cousin,
Submit

Netham, 29 August
Dearest Cousin,

If you will not allow me to visit you, please reconsider coming to Netham. There are forty-seven people here at present—a host of chaperones. You would be a welcome addition. Rosalyn asks after you and would love to see you again.

Affectionately,
Graham

Morrow Fields, 30 August
Dear Cousin,

My thanks for your kind invitation. I regret that I shall not be able to come to Netham this summer. Thank you for thinking of me.

Yours truly,
Submit Channing-Downes

Correspondence plagued the month of August, it seemed. Submit received a letter from Tate, detailing in writing some of the difficulties he was encountering with William's lawsuit. The worst seemed to be that the other side had found a case of precedence. A bastard son a dozen years ago had been given the status of a younger son during his father's lifetime. Then the older son died with the father in a train accident. *Voilà.* There was at least one country baron in Kent who came of illegitimate birth. Of course, this was a very long way from refuting a perfectly good will that laid things out in a very different manner.

Submit also received a letter from William decrying much the same point, but in broader, more threatening terms. Then there were the letters from Graham Wessit, at first consoling and flattering, then irritatingly persistent.

His first letter had eased something. The thought of Graham thinking of her with nothing but contempt had left Submit feeling surprisingly discontented. Despite their rough parting, he remained in her mind. Over the course of the last weeks he had become an astute companion with whom she talked about a number of things, if not always calmly, at least meaningfully. His letter of apology brought a kind of relief, a reprieve. She could envision his liking her still, even admiring her. How strange that she should want this, she thought; but she admitted to herself she did. Just as she admitted to herself that it was only courting disaster to allow him to think they could be friends. They disagreed on too much. He was a paradox. Genuinely a gentleman one moment, then shockingly crude the next. She couldn't sort him out. Better she didn't try, she thought; better they cease their struggle for a friendship that was in fact impossible.

The most interesting correspondence came at the end of

the first week in September. It was from a stranger, a man she had never heard of, let alone met.

Submit turned the brown business envelope over several times, puzzling over it. It had arrived with a large grey box. When she opened the envelope, a letter unfolded, and a slip of paper dropped out. It was a bank draft for twenty-eight pounds, in her name. She let out a little gasp of pure delight. It was enough money to pay her room and board at the inn for a dozen weeks. She bent her attention to the letter with avid interest.

Madam,

My sincerest sympathies with regard to the death of your husband, the Marquess of Motmarche. I lament with you his passing, especially as he was in the process of writing a most impressive work. Enclosed you will find the balance owed for that which he completed; we are now current to date.

I now write to further suggest, if I may be so bold, that perhaps I could do you a good turn in your time of quiet mourning and that perhaps you could do me one as well. I have included here with this letter a box of notes and papers that your husband sent to me when he realized the sad state of his health. They represent what would have been the end of the book he was working on. It seems possible that a gentlewoman with the time, breeding, and long exposure to the articulate style of your good, departed husband might be able to make sense of these bits of paper to the point of finishing the work yourself. Of course, I would be pleased to compensate you for your efforts, as befits the dedication of a wife who takes it upon herself to finish what was so important to her husband and the obligation he made before his death.

I present my condolences and compliments to Your Lady-

ship, *the Marchioness of Motmarche, and in submitting my request await your further instructions.*

> *I have the honor to remain, madam,*
> *Your most obedient servant,*
> *William Task Pease, publisher*
> *Porridge Magazine*

The box was full of notes in several shades of ink, on all different sizes and scraps of paper, some faded with age, some new. Some of it looked like the remnants of a diary. The contents of the box were a wild confusion, much more disorganized than Henry usually was. As she laid out all the slips of paper, in their very familiar hand, she felt a tremor run through her. There was almost a kind of fervor to the quantity, the bulk and disorder, the scribbles that ran to the end of a page then up the margin and around. When had Henry done all this? And under what sort of mad inspiration?

Tucked at the side of the box, in a tied, neat bundle, were a stack of magazines. Again the name, Pease's *Porridge.* A note, in the same handwriting as the letter, was attached to these: "You will find the first dozen episodes your husband did, here entitled *The Rake of Ronmoor.*"

It took all the rest of that day to glance through the printed episodes. The source of Henry's inspiration became obvious: joy. The story—it was a little fiction!—was wonderful. It was fun, exciting, silly in a way Submit had never dreamed Henry's imagination could run.

No one would have thought it possible! one recent number read. *In public, Ronmoor danced the young girl out, in full view of her mother and a hundred other guests. The girl seemed in a dream, under a spell, as she most surely was. Ron-*

moor that night was the devil himself. He swirled her round the room, past dukes and viscounts and admirals, never letting a more appropriate partner claim even a dance.

By the end of the evening, people's whispers had grown bold. The girl herself looked as though she might faint. Yet never did she take her eyes off the face of the notorious young scoundrel. Her expression was blissful, the look of a kind angel who saw a sinner to save.

Then, in the middle of the dance floor, the sinner had the audacity to press his vile lips onto the angel's as-yet-unkissed mouth! The music stopped. The girl's mother stood up from her chair. Surely, this will tell the tale, the reader must think! The young innocent will awaken with that kiss, as the dazed Sleeping Beauty, and see she is dealing with no prince!

But nay! Right does not always win! The mother threw the knave out. And the daughter rushed upstairs in tears. Of embarrassment, people whispered that night. But of passion, it was said later. For the little angel had developed a deadly appetite for the likes of the Rake of Ronmoor.

That evening, when she met him in the garden, she said nothing again, when his audacity led him to lift the delicate eyelet of her cambric petticoat and touch his hand up the smoothness of one pink silk stocking. . . .

"Henry! My word!" Submit said aloud. But she kept reading. This was very cheeky stuff.

. . . up the smoothness of one pink silk stocking to the garter that came from Brussels, with its copious layers of fine, feminine, sweet Belgium lace.

Three discreet asterisks were left. Then a single sentence: The cad wore her garter on his sleeve as he rode home!

Submit felt herself grow warm. Lo and behold! Henry's magazine fiction was not only playful and inventive, it was vaguely naughty as well! Though he had some of it a bit wrong, she thought. What was all this Belgium lace and silk stocking business? Followed by a little sermon after that?

Submit frowned. When a woman's virtue was in the balance, she supposed, an author had to make the moral point. Dickens did. So did Thackeray and Lever. So did they all. But Submit knew how the young woman *felt*. That was what she could add, if she were to write these. . . .

She was contemplating doing what this Mr. Pease asked. And, partly, it was Graham Wessit goading her on. She *had* passion. And she was *not* wedded to Henry's memory. She could riffle through Henry's notes and strike out from them on her own. Submit even considered, looking at all the notes and the published pages, that she might have been mistaken about Henry himself. He had certainly left behind a body of prose which was fearlessly passionate in its way. The more she looked and spread things out, the more Submit could feel a new kind of excitement welling up. There was something here—things that drew her in, things she would do differently, things she had never dreamed of doing in her life—to which Henry, in the largest way, had given his secret imprimatur. The idea of exploring what was here began to fill her with heart-pounding, trembling delight.

It took another hectic day and a half to get the gist of the notes. The notes themselves were less wonderful, stopping and starting through a jumble of half-written scenes and phrases of description. Some of it couldn't even be followed, the writing was so offhand and quick. Henry's notes heralded a lot of work, if she were to stick to Henry's plan. They were also a bit overdone. Henry seemed to be hammering a point home. Submit picked up a pen.

The very first scene was incredible fun. It was play! Great play! She discovered she loved moving the wonderful blackguard around. Clever, clever Henry! She could make fictional creatures do all the things she might like but never have the courage—or stupidity—to try. She could lambaste the rake for his cheek, reward him, rebuke him, lay him out flat, then draw him up, back to life again, like a puppet on a string. Only it was much more fun than a puppet: The only limiting aspect was the thread of her own imagination.

By the end of the week, she had sent the first episode off—and received a prompt payment with a sincere, effusive letter of thanks in the mail. Henry's trust account for her, she called it, as she tucked the second draft into her pocket. Hang William. Hang them all. Her future was secure. She could even begin to pay a little to Arnold Tate.

Submit wrote her way into the next week, staying up much too late, sometimes forgetting to eat. But she had found something to do, something that set her on some course at last, and it felt positively grand. She even found herself using some of her observations of one of the more interesting men she knew, Graham Wessit. She disguised these details, of course; she wouldn't want to offend. Then again, he probably would never read such a thing. Still, Graham Wessit did somehow remind her a little of the fictional rake. . . .

— Chapter 25 —

Getting Submit to Netham turned out to be not nearly so difficult as Graham had imagined: Tate brought her.

At the beginning of September, Graham was in London, tying up the last of the loose ends regarding the legal status of his new little ward. While there, he went by Tate's chambers to make sure there was nothing the counselor might add, nothing that Graham's solicitors might have overlooked. He and Tate had ended up talking about what seemed to be a magnet topic of interest for them both, the "unhealthy and reclusive aloofness" of the lovely Widow Channing-Downes. Graham had mentioned in passing that he had invited Submit to visit his summer estate.

He could only speculate as to how this notion took root in Tate's mind, matured, then yielded fruit. But Submit arrived at Netham a week later, escorted by the barrister, Graham suspected, quite possibly for the unaltruistic motive of wanting a place to take her that would be removed from circles that included *Mrs.* Tate.

Graham knew the attorney to be taking a great deal of personal interest in the young widow. Besides Tate's preoccupation with her "remoteness," Graham suspected he was handling her court proceedings as a "favor to her husband," that is to say, for little or no material compensation. Graham knew Tate had taken her to dinner once in London then sent his own doctor to the inn the next day, because the widow had developed a chill and sneezed. (Ah, the tight circles of London. Tate's doctor was also Graham's own, taking care of the remaining little twin, who had developed diarrhea. The doctor was staying at Netham Hall for the weekend.) It seemed that Arnold Tate was in full magnetic attraction to the widow's latent charms.

And he must have been feeling the pull rather strongly, for he descended his little carriage that morning with a look of marked imbalance—the discomposure of a person whose feet, now sliding uncertainly, had been planted wholly in his own self-righteousness. Arnold Tate, it occurred to Graham, was coming to know that sin had less to do with moral pitfalls than clay feet, and he seemed shaken by the knowledge. For, as he squinted against the sunlight, offering his hand toward the open carriage door, his eyes rose disconcertedly up the high chimneys of Netham Hall. Then a white hand settled into his, and the widow appeared. Stepping down beside him, she looked serene, the picture of unassailable peace—a madonna. Perhaps that was part of Tate's problem. Next to Submit, anyone looked a sinner.

Whether or not Submit liked Tate's attention, she seemed to put up with it with a stoic patience that Graham suspected came from a history of obliging mentoring old men. She allowed him to think she would be put wherever he guided her. And that September afternoon, he guided her by the elbow up the steps of Netham Hall.

By coincidence, Gerald Schild was leaving at the same time. Graham, as he had come to be in the habit of doing, was seeing that he did. (Only by hiding Rosalyn and presenting the bold face of Graham alone could Schild ever be brought to leave.) The four of them, Tate, Submit, Graham, and Schild, all stopped outside the front door, as if surprised by the strangeness of fate in providing such accidental groupings.

An almost irresistible temptation called to Graham as he made introductions: *This is my lawyer for a false paternity suit. This is my mistress's husband. And here, my dead guardian's wife, a woman for whom I would give both testes in toto for the pleasure of sleeping with for just one night.*

After more decent amenities, Tate shook the American's offered hand, while further mumblings conveyed that introductions between Submit and Schild were unnecessary. They had met before in London, at Schild's own house. Graham knew a horrible jealous pang of a moment before he realized that, of course, Rosalyn's house in London was also Gerald's, and that he had met the widow there on one of his brief, shadowy visits to his wife. The two of them nodded at this connection.

Still, there was something less easily dismissed that passed between Gerald Schild and Submit, Graham thought. Even before they had attached faces and names to place and reason for familiarity, there was a recognition: two privateers hailing each other in passing. They were both outsiders to everything on the inside of this house. They each knew it and acknowledged it in the other, making the nod and the connection into something more. Then Submit was ascending the front stairs on Tate's arm (Tate, the flagship now leading his pinnace to foreign harbor).

"An interesting woman," Schild said as they disappeared inside.

He spoke this not as an observation but as a suggestion. Perhaps he noted Graham's overlong stares at the widow. Then Schild walked down the steps and heaved himself into his carriage. Once inside, he looked at Graham. "An interesting woman," he repeated.

The message was clear, and anything but heroic—a crass invitation to heal his own sorrow at the expense of his wife's. He might as well have said, "Please take up with her. If I could be of any help—"

Of course, he could have been. Graham was left wanting to call a shot back, wishing for the man he had fervently wanted out of his house a moment ago now to reconsider, to stay and help deceive the deceiving wife.

Schild leaned out his window and added, "But then, no one loves where interest might logically guide them." He paused for a moment more. "If you only knew how I love her—" he finally said. Then he pulled back into the carriage and, with a lurch, it rolled down the drive.

Graham was glad he was gone. There was something exceedingly foolish about a balding, middle-aged man who spoke so earnestly of love. Graham understood the word only in the context of the wise and worldly: cynicism. Worse still, the "love" Schild spoke of was blandly, unromantically his wife, the object of unconjugal obsession, a woman who did not return even a fraction of the feeling, but gave it blatantly, prodigally elsewhere, where he himself could not understand or tread, except as the gauchest foreigner.

It was this, Graham realized, that gave Gerald Schild his poignant, ambiguous nobility. For Schild knew his circumstance and bore up under it. He was a fool without the delusions that might have saved him from seeing himself as such. A self-informed fool; it was atrocious. And the man kept going anyway, speaking his feelings with the most inadequate, unoriginal of words, knowing this was all he had—the blurred and smudged reflection of something powerful, ennobling. Heroic. All this in the name of love.

Of one thing Graham was sure as he watched Gerald Schild's carriage disappear that day. It became all at once so clear, so evident, he could hardly believe he had entertained notions of anything else: He himself did not love Rosalyn. Not romantically. Not even a little.

Graham Wessit's country house was a harmonious construction of reddish stone with patterns of yellow-red brick up the corners, around the windows and doors. The building was centered about a large, rotunda-sized tower, whose crenelations overlooked all other points of the houses' roofs. This towerlike structure was set symmetrically into the center of the architecture, dividing the left half (rising to three stories plus an attic of windows and chimneys) from the right (a story lower, scattered with taller outlets for fireplace smoke). It could have had the feel of a hodgepodge, not an uncommon English problem with old buildings built in pieces through centuries of differing tastes. But it did not. The arches of the high, paned east windows, the central tower's vertical succession of round windows, a low line of square, westerly windows, as well as the fanlights and sidelights of the double doors were painted in a unifying, crisp white. All this was nestled in trees and decorated with climbers and flower beds. It was a lovely house.

As she and Arnold had driven up, Submit had been surprised by the size of the house. It was smaller than she had expected. Motmarche by comparison was a city unto itself. And the estate was more quiet. At first, no one seemed to be about. The side croquet lawn was vacant. There was the usual sort of rural buildings beyond that, a poultry, what looked like dovecotes. On the other side of the house there was a small orchard. Twisting, grey-trunked apple trees ran in neat rows within ten feet of the building itself. She and Arnold had stepped out of the carriage into the driveway of a peaceful little manor house.

Then the front door had opened onto the awkward, somewhat embarrassing reunion on the front steps. Graham had seemed taken aback to see her, but not unpleasantly so. Submit had felt a rush of guilt at turning up on his doorstep after so curt a refusal only two weeks before. But Graham had seemed gracious, just as Arnold had assured her he would be. Then Submit had felt her embarrassment turn into something else: warm pleasure at seeing someone— a friend, she could not deny—to whom she had spoken of feelings, Henry, life, everything, anything that might come up; her confidant from Morrow Fields. Despite the prickly memories of their disagreements and some of their more-than-simply-pointed remarks, she found herself liking that she had come face to face with Graham Wessit again, liking it surprisingly much. She entered his house with unpredicted ease. The most puzzling thing, on reflection, was that her host and Gerald Schild appeared to be on very cordial terms.

Inside, she and Arnold waited for a housekeeper whom Graham had mentioned but who didn't materialize. Arnold pulled the bell cord again. He stood at the side of the room, more or less at a loss. Submit wandered. The house itself felt almost familiar, welcoming, as if she had been to Netham Hall before. It reminded her very much of the disorganized, unself-conscious man who had come to visit her at the inn.

A little entry passage gave onto a reception room, which, like the rotunda that housed it, was round. It was informal, a room people lived in. A scallop of bay windows along the back of it lit the room with unexpectedly vivid and gentle light. Wallpaper of willows and roses met dark wainscoting. A dark wood table, pushed against this, had garden roses sitting on it overflowing from a huge bowl. The room was a contrast of rich color and dark wood. There were bookcases lined with bright and dark spines, oak flooring peeking out from under a worn Persian rug, and a chest in the corner beside a chintz-covered sofa and chair. Neither the patterns nor the colors on the sofa and chairs and wallpaper quite matched, though mysteriously they harmonized. An ancient boot remover with an abandoned pair of muddy boots stood beside a brass umbrella stand full of walking sticks, not umbrellas. An insouciant, speckled setter looked them over, then went back to sleep in a basket under the stairs. He could have been out of an eighteenth-century painting—an English setter in an English gentleman's parlor. There were real Gainsboroughs on the wall. The staircase over the dog rose dramatically, circumvolving half the room on its way to the next floor. It led the eye up to a high ceiling, perhaps forty feet in the air. The room had all the charm of old aristocracy held together with the careless aplomb of a country gentleman, a provincial lack of fuss.

Submit frowned. The staircase, the dog, *something* made a sense of familiarity creep over her again, but not in so pleasant a way. She felt an odd kind of preknowledge of this house. She opened a drawer in a small morning desk and knew before she saw that it was filled with a collection of pens and loose change. Pennies, shillings, and gold nibs winked up at her. Submit couldn't understand how she knew. Her heart gave an erratic beat. The pleasant, pretty room began to feel a little eerie. Though of course, she tried to explain to herself, the desk drawer was the logical place to keep these things—

"Going through my drawers?" Graham Wessit walked quickly into the room, full of energy, all smiles.

"I wasn't—"

"I hope you were." His smile became personal, warm. "I would love to be a matter of riveting curiosity to you."

Submit closed the drawer, frowning.

He took her shawl and her hat, as well as Arnold's. "How very nice to see you again." He threw Arnold a glance. "Both of you." He tossed their things on a chair. "Would you like to go upstairs and freshen up?"

"No," Submit answered a little awkwardly. "We're fine."

"How long can you stay?'

Arnold interjected, "Just the weekend. If you don't mind."

"No, no, I'm delighted. Stay longer if you like. Come with me; I'll take you outside. Everyone is in the back."

They went out into a garden, a florid display of color. Opening buds bloomed beside full-blown flowers, along with drooping, unclipped roses with half their petals blown off. Graham said to Submit, "I didn't expect to see you at all the rest of the summer, after your last rather abrupt note."

She was caught off guard by his seemingly sincere pleasure that she'd come. Her last letter, despite the circumstances and high feelings that had engendered it, seemed all at once rude. "I—I thought better of it, I suppose."

"I'm terribly glad you did." He smiled a wide, ingenuous smile. Submit felt herself being wooed by the infamous Netham charm.

Arnold came up beside them as they walked. "It was at my insistence she came," he said. They walked three abreast, Submit in the middle. "I thought, after talking to you in London, it was best if someone browbeat her into coming out to the country for a few days. For her own good."

"Ah." Graham left a pause, then asked, "And how is Mrs. Tate?"

Arnold made a misstep over a loose stone in the path. "Fine."

"The children? Your oldest is at Oxford now, isn't he?"

Arnold's face grew dour. "Yes." He stared at his own feet tramping along the path.

"And you, my dear cousin?" Graham asked Submit. *My dear cousin.* It was the form of address he had found in the letters. It put him somehow uncomfortably near, a figurative equivalent to finding herself without three feet of hoops.

"I am doing well—"

"She's not," Arnold broke in. "She's working too hard, seeing nary a soul, getting thinner and paler by the day—"

"I disagree." Graham smiled at her as she passed under his arm—he held back a particularly brambly cane that bounced loose across the path. He came up beside her again just as the path turned and narrowed. Arnold was left to walk a few feet behind.

In the distance, Submit could see more dovecotes, a little pond covered in water lilies, and a funny little building, a follylike gazebo by a lake. White fences and horses ran along one side. A small, select society, the women spread out in bright dresses, the gentlemen in more somber tones, was sitting inside the folly, at a long picnic table. The tablecloth, red and yellow and orange and green, stood out as brightly as the people's clothes.

"What are you working on?" Graham asked.

"Pardon?"

Graham smiled at her. "What is it that Arnold thinks you are working on too hard?"

"Oh." Submit bent her head. From within the dovecotes, as the threesome passed, came the soft clamor of busy, purring trills, followed by a swell of laughter from the folly.

She had told no one the details of the wonderful and lucrative new project that was taking up so much of her time. Partly out of a kind of possessiveness, to have it completely for her own. She was finding out something very new about Henry. He liked adventure, foolish, physical, outlandish adventure. At least he admired it in a kind of backhanded way in print. So did she. And partly she had kept quiet because there was no one to tell. Even Arnold would very likely not approve of the marquess's wife indulging in frivolous fictional escapades. Yet Submit realized, as she walked beside Graham, that she could tell him, that she would even like to.

For the moment, she held to the generalization she had already given Arnold. She shrugged. "Some of Henry's old notes, some articles he'd half done. If I finish them, the publisher has promised to pay me the sum he and Henry agreed upon."

"Aha." Graham nodded politely. "That should keep you busy then."

They walked across the grass, Arnold remaining unnaturally quiet, resigned to his place a few steps behind. The folly ahead materialized fully over a bramble of grey willow and bryony. Submit paused, unwillingly impressed. It was one of those incredibly contrived vistas that nonetheless was simply beautiful. Someone had picked just the right rise of land, the perfect angle on the lake, then erected stone by stone a fantasy of classical form. It was a miniature, whimsical reconstruction of ancient Rome in decline. The crumbling walls seemed to be held together by little more than ivy. Engrossed, conversational voices came from between leaning Doric columns. From under a sloping entablature, hoots of laughter followed. These were the sounds of a careless social gathering whose members were inured to beauty and complacent toward their own security.

Submit entered with Graham and Arnold through a doorway with no door. Inside, the building showed its strength. The decay and crumble were an illusion, supported by cantilevers and beams barely discernible through vegetation and architectural disguise. As they entered, several people turned.

"Graham! There you are!" A heavy woman with a cumbersome body, a chest that could have graced the cutwater of a battleship, got up from the table. The table was long, running the diameter of the circular folly. It was set with flowers, wine, silver, and leftover food, all on a bright, striped tablecloth; a gay, bucolic disregard for formality. "We've been wondering where you got off to," the woman said to Graham, but her eyes settled on Submit.

In fact, a number of faces turned to Submit, as if they were trying to fathom her connection to the earl.

Graham established it for them. "My cousin, Lady Motmarche. And Arnold Tate, a barrister at the Queen's Bench." People peeked around Graham and Submit. "Lady Stone," Graham introduced the heavyset woman, then nodded toward a man seated at the table. "Sir Gilbert's wife." Several gentlemen stood.

Graham made more introductions, names that passed in a blur. Lord and Lady This. Sir Something and Lady That. Until he came to a guest Submit had simply not expected to see. "Of course, you know William Channing-Downes."

William was seated—he didn't bother to stand—at the far end, smiling his knowing, superior smile from behind a lady with a large fan. He leaned forward, tipped his hand, as if he were wearing a hat.

Submit's heart began to thump against the wall of her chest. She couldn't help but throw her host a look. William was so very comfortable at Graham's table.

"Why, Graham, she's lovely," the chesty matron declared. She took Submit's hand, leading her to the table. Submit was uncomfortable hearing the word "lovely" applied to herself. It simply wasn't true. But the woman went on. "To keep such a pretty cousin all to yourself, Graham." The woman glanced at Submit's dress. "And a widow, too. You simply must get to know everyone."

Graham turned Submit over to the woman and sat by an empty chair at William's end. There were more introductions. There had to be fifty people in the outdoor house. Half a dozen Submit knew from Mrs. Schild's. Oddly, Submit noted, Mrs. Schild herself was not about. She found herself looking at the empty chair beside Graham, not certain if he meant for her to take it or if the American woman were about to arrive.

Ultimately, people moved down, placing Submit in the chair next to the vacant one, leaving a telling space between herself and her host. Arnold was placed at the far other end. Submit looked to him longingly, but he wouldn't meet her gaze.

"Well," a chicken-beaked man beside her said, as he pushed a glass of wine into her hands, "we were just discussing the likelihood of truth in what that supposed scientist gave to the world last month, the claim that we all came from monkeys." Several people laughed heartily.

"Darwin?" Submit asked.

"You know of him? Good!"

"What do you think?"

One slightly inebriated young man in the middle of the table gave his opinion by making a few monkey sounds. *Chee, chee, chee.*

"I think the theory of natural selection is valid."

"Geoffrey," the man called to another over a woman's head, "you have another on your side." The table broke into more heated debate.

Submit glanced at Graham. He was looking at her, not taking part. Such a look. Wonder, pleasure, curiosity. Too much interest for her to be comfortable. She looked away.

The man beside her patted her hand. "It's always nice," he said, "to see a widow getting out and about. Nothing so dismal as a member of the gentler sex collapsed in a houseful of black-draped gloom."

Submit felt black-draped gloom descend before her eyes. She had as much in common with these people as she did with a jungle of simians. They laughed too loudly, made light of serious topics, and several of the men—it seemed a popular affectation—wore reams of watch chains and bushels of rings. They could in no way compete with the women, however. Midmorning found them all dressed out in eyelet and feathers and fans.

These women, from time to time, gave her cool glances. Sometimes not so cool. One attractive brunette threw several heated little glances between Submit and her host. A young girl with a pointy chin and a pouty mouth gave her an overall puzzled look, then glanced away. It was a gesture of relief and dismissal.

The introductory warmth lasted about sixty seconds.

Submit reached for an orange, the only thing in the little folly that seemed even remotely friendly besides Arnold, who was too far away, and Graham, who was too close.

After a few minutes' discussion of Darwin and the paper he'd read to the Linnaean Society, William leaned toward Graham and speared a cold piece of roast pheasant with a fork. He talked across three other people to ask, "Do you believe species can transmute, Gray?"

Graham looked up. "Everything changes. Why not? I suppose."

"But why monkeys? Why not"—William paused and glanced toward Submit—"spiders, for instance?"

A man at William's left laughed.

William went on. "Do you remember, Gray, those little jars Henry used to have?"

"Jars?"

"In his study on the shelf. Every manner of thing."

Graham was staring off, hardly paying attention. "Yes, vaguely."

"In one of the jars was an American spider. A tiny little thing." He shifted his glance pointedly toward Submit. "A black widow." He added, "Do you remember the jar, Submit?" William smiled at her.

She only nodded as she sectioned the orange.

But other people had begun to understand his game. The lady with the fan grew silent. The man beside Submit turned in fascination, his ready attention waiting for someone's discomfort—or better yet, an argument, a fight. Down the table, voices laughed, counterpointing the ugly little quiet that had settled between William and Submit.

"Deadly," William continued. "Tiny, delicate, yet it can kill you with one bite. Or certainly make you very sick." He added gruesomely, "Though a bite would kill a child." He turned fully to face Submit. "Is the jar still there on the shelf?"

She looked up at him, wondering when someone would stop him. "So far as I know."

"They mate," William said. He gestured with his knife. "Then they eat the male. That's where they get their name. A regular femme fatale, don't you think?"

"I think," Graham interrupted by stealing a piece of pheasant off William's plate, "that you, like a great many people, are a little shortsighted when it comes to nature. The spider in the jar is *dead*. Whatever small poison she had was apparently inadequate in the overall scheme of things."

"Small poison," William repeated, glaring at him. "Not so small, if it's you writhing from the bite. Or," he added, "dead or dying in her web—"

Graham laughed. "Have some wine, William. It'll ease the buzzing in your head."

Submit glanced at her rescuer. If one could call it a rescue to be labeled inadequate and compared to a dead spider in a jar. Graham had sat back into a kind of characteristic pose, his arm on the chair, his jaw balanced in three fingers and the heel of his palm. He was looking right at her with an interested stare. She minded this interest all at once, as if she were some specimen, some new species to watch. And she minded all over again that Graham didn't take her side more strongly against William in other things, that he gave him a place to live in London, invited him to his table, then laughed when he attacked her over lunch.

Rosalyn Schild was the one to break this up. She came through the doorless entryway, breathless, at somewhat more than a graceful walk. "Graham," she said, "I think Charles has put Claire's eye out."

Graham stood. "Excuse me." He was out the door like a shot.

Rosalyn didn't follow but greeted everyone warmly. When she sat down beside Submit, however, she did a quick double take, then recovered with applaudable sangfroid.

"Why, Submit, how nice to see you." The gregarious woman rolled her eyes and leaned closer, as if she and Submit were old, confiding friends. "His children," she whispered. Her eyes made another theatrical swing toward the ceiling. "Horrid, horrid, horrid," she pronounced.

Submit saw Graham only briefly again that day, just before she retired.

He stopped her on the stairs. She was going up as he was coming down. "I'm so very glad you came," he said. "I'd love for you to stay longer than just the weekend."

"I don't think so." To change the subject, she asked, "Is your daughter all right?"

He shrugged. "The doctor put a patch on her eye. We have to wait."

"It's very bad then?"

"*She's* very bad. She and Charles both. They were fighting. Every time they do something like this, I want to banish them to a boarding school, a foreign country, as far away as I can put them from me."

Submit would have imagined such, that he would be admittedly not very fond of children. "You don't like them very much?"

He laughed. "I adore them. You obviously haven't been around children much. They're all like that. Monsters. Till they get old enough to hide what they really feel and want and think."

She smiled a little at his cynicism. "How old are they?"

"Thirteen."

She waited for another age, for numbers to fall into an order. Her anticipation must have shown.

"And thirteen," he added. "They're twins."

She couldn't keep the unpleasantness of this surprise from showing on her face. With distaste, the whole business at Scotland Yard came to mind, the poor girl with the twins.

"Well, I'm not responsible for every pair, you know," he said. "Just one set."

When she looked, she found him smiling, privately laughing at her reaction. She smiled, too. "No, of course not. But it's an ugly coincidence."

"It's no coincidence, I'm sure. The girl found herself with twins. It's common knowledge I'd fathered twins once. Most everyone knows I have. I was sure you did, too."

"No." She shook her head. Sincerely, she told him, "There are the hugest gaps in what I know about you."

He made one of his wide, fabulous smiles: white teeth, inch-long dimples down his cheeks, the dark, down-slanted eyes crinkled at the edges in friendly, warm regard. "Stay and find out."

That night, Submit was looking through a handful of Henry's notes she had brought. Pease expected the next episode by the following Wednesday.

Everything was always rushed with him. He was running a bare episode ahead and wanted her to give him more as quickly as she could, presumably to allow for her loss of interest, her loss of faculty, or her demise. Pease wanted the finished book in his hand. Submit obliged, but wished she had more time and leisure to go through everything more carefully.

She read the words, "Ronmoor had inherited a folly. A real, literal, architectural folly on a lake. . . ."

She stared out into space for a moment, realizing suddenly why she had known the room downstairs vaguely and the little desk with its drawer particularly well. Ronmoor had given an upstairs maid money from that desk drawer—in Henry's notes—last week. She began to leaf through Henry's pages.

"A tall, charming man with a predisposition for easy women, fast horses, and trouble . . ."

"... in the center of a cliquish little group of the more extravagant and outrageous of London upper-class society..."

"Rather surprisingly, Ronmoor had legitimate issue, whose birth was, like everything else in Ronmoor's life, twice as difficult, twice as much as needed—the children were twins."

Lord God, Submit thought.

"Ronmoor sat his arm on the chair, setting his face into his palm, three fingers up his cheek, his little finger fitting into the deep groove of his well-defined chin. . . ."

It was Graham Wessit. The fictional man she was moving around on paper was nothing but a loose fictional—haranguing—reflection of the man entertaining friends downstairs. Graham Wessit was the Rake of Ronmoor!

Chapter 26

There was a rapping at Submit's door. From the hall, a voice called urgently, quietly, "Wake up! You have to see this!"

She rolled to her elbow. It was still dark. She was in a valley of down pillows, in a thick fog of sleep.

The muffled voice called again. "Come on! Wake up! We have to hurry!"

She pushed a pillow aside, climbed over another. Slowly, she made her way up from the groggy stupor that comes of brief, heavy sleep. She had lain awake for hours before finally drifting off. "I'm coming."

Her braid fell heavily onto her back as she flipped it out from where she'd trapped it in her dressing gown. The floor was cold under her bare feet. The mantel clock, as she passed, read four fifty-three. She cracked open her apartment door.

Graham Wessit was on the other side, fully dressed, in the same clothes she had seen him in last night. His neckcloth was undone and so were the top buttons of his shirt. His face, even in the demidark, was flushed.

"You've been drinking," she said.

"Only all night. Come on—" He reached for her hand.

"Where is Mrs. Schild?"

"Asleep. Will you hurry? Put something on. You'll miss it."

"What?"

"Just hurry up."

Three minutes later, he was pulling her along at a half-run with about a dozen other people, through the brambles, then across the grass of his back garden to the lake. There, a dozen people manned half a dozen boats, little rowboats by a dock. Everyone was slightly inebriated and laughing. Submit meant to be irritated at the insanity she still didn't understand. But the grass was cold on her dampening shoes. The morning air was crisp. And Graham Wessit's hand was warm.

He lowered her, grabbing her under her arms, into a rowboat. It wobbled under her feet. She fell immediately to a crouch.

"You're no sailor," he said and laughed as he climbed in.

A minute later, all six little boats were cruising out silently into the middle of the lake.

Graham lifted one oar of their boat, dipping the other deeper into the water. He let the submerged oar and their momentum—he'd rowed like the devil—turn them around. "There," he said with an air of great satisfaction.

It was the sun, rising over the silhouette of his house, casting a pink-gold haze over his wild, uncut garden.

"Oh, my." It was spectacular.

Someone in another boat cheered. Graham passed her a bottle of champagne—no glass, just the bottle.

She laughed. "Where did this come from?"

"Had it in my other hand all along." He looked down at his arm. "Spilled half of it all over my cuff." His face had one of those magnificent expressions he could make, smiling and frowning at once: a man in love with fun who was not so unself-conscious as to miss, or not mind, what an idiot this could make of him at times. It was strange, but she really had begun to appreciate this peculiar-sad awareness of his—the way he just rolled right over it anyway when fun was at hand.

She took the bottle. When she hesitated, he motioned with a twist of his wrist, showing her to tip it up. A man's voice, about twenty feet off, had begun to sing "Rule, Britannia," a good seagoing song. Submit put the bottle to her lips. When she tilted it, nothing came and nothing came, then a whole slosh of it poured into her mouth, up her nose, and down her cheeks.

The boat rocked, and an oar clattered as Graham leaned to mop her up, putting a neat folded handkerchief at her chin. The handkerchief smelled of fresh starch and sweet bay. She drew back. Without seeming to notice, he shifted further forward an inch. His arm braced itself on the gunwale right by her waist. The boat leaned into the water at a slightly precarious angle. The lake lapped against its sides.

Beyond them, across the lake, the man singing of Britannia was truly getting into the spirit. He sang out the last stanza, "And manly heart to guard the fair." He began on the refrain. "Rule, Britannia. Britannia rules the waves. . . ."

Counterpoint to this silliness, Submit's heart began to jolt in her chest. Graham's handkerchief blotted her chin, her cheek. He took it back for a second, looking for a dry spot as he folded it. His fingers were dark against the white linen; long, graceful, perfectly rounded at a clean, short nail. They were hands that didn't do much, except maybe wipe up champagne. Submit could feel the coldness of her spill running down her neck. He seemed about to dab this up too when he stopped. They stared at each other in the rising light of dawn, his weight on one knee between her legs. There was no crinoline, nothing again to hold him back. Submit's heart felt as if it were going to pound right up her throat. Then he seemed suddenly to realize she had backed up, all but ready to arch out into the water away from him. He took the bottle from her hand. In something of a huff, he sat back.

"Lord, you spook easily," he said, "like some virgin housemaid with the bloody lord of the manor she's afraid to offend." He stretched out, with an exaggerated obligingness, his elbows back on the transom as far away from her as he could get. He planted his feet under the rowing thwart, his legs sprawled open.

Her next remark just came out. "As in the serial?" Ronmoor, these days, was chasing a housemaid who didn't run very fast—she had a limp.

Submit was suddenly keen to hear how he would respond. She wanted to hear that none of it was true, that all the insane adventures weren't really his. Or perhaps that he didn't mind—what a good joke it all was.

Or better still, she wanted to hear him say he didn't know what in the world she was talking about.

"Jesus Christ," he whispered, then took a long drink from the bottle. "Who would have thought that bloody thing would have such a broad readership."

"It *is* you?" When he only took another draught from the champagne bottle, she asked again, "All those awful, exaggerated things? They are true?"

"In a less exaggerated form."

She bowed her head. "How terrible. And how very, very mean." A sharp, undiluted anger at Henry rose up. He had laid out in print a real man's debacles and peccadilloes, laid them out in infinite, ludicrous, embarrassing detail. Henry had made a pillory of print—then handed her the key. All at once, sitting there in the rocking boat, she wanted to cry. Shame and regret overwhelmed her for a second. Lord, how she needed this money—and how she had enjoyed the writing when it had seemed innocent. And, Lord, how she was going to hate giving it up.

"Yes," he snorted, "someone is having a lot of fun."

"Hey, Netham!" A young man in a far boat was standing, waving for his attention. "Fifty pounds says I can beat you in."

Graham yelled back, laughing as if everything were fine. "You're fifty feet closer to shore!"

"Give you a thirty-second lead," the man called.

"Thirty big seconds?" He laughed, suddenly getting up. "All right. Fifty pounds says you're on." He began stripping off clothes. His coat and vest went. He worked his shoes off as he began undoing his trousers.

Several ladies squealed. Submit backed into the corner of the prow, not quite able to believe. . . .

"Egad, man, your boat!" the other man called. "I meant rowing in!"

"You said you'd beat *me*. Now either jump in the water or start rowing. I'm a bloody fish once I start."

"I can't swim!"

Graham laughed heartily, his shirttails flapping in the lake's gentle breeze. "And someone here needs to tow Lady Motmarche in." He nodded toward Submit, then the shirt came off. Down to his undervest and drawers, he dove in.

He was on the shore before the other man even had his boat turned around. Submit watched as he rose up and walked out of the lake, framed by the columns of his Roman folly. Like a god, Neptune, in the morning sun. He was backlit, a silhouette. In this hazy nimbus, he ran his hands through his hair, shook water out. His underclothes clung. She watched him walk up into the folly and out, into the brambles of his garden. His shoulders were wide, his back broad and muscular, his buttocks strong. His long, sinewy legs moved with a graceful, purposeful stride. Modesty said she should look away. She stared. He was the most beautiful, most perfectly proportioned man she had ever laid eyes on.

An awkward young fellow with a heavy public-school vocabulary (*egad, jolly good, by Jove*) rowed up. There was a young woman already in his boat. He was diffident, polite, respectful almost to the point of reverence, as he tied Submit's boat up. He began to row, Submit trailing along behind. It was slow progress after the near race to get out into the middle of the lake. Theirs were the last boats coming in. As they glided along, Submit sloughed off her damp shoes onto the wooden bottom. She let her bare feet slide under

Graham's abandoned clothes. His vest was satin, blue satin
with a black velvet reverse. It was incredibly smooth and cool
against her instep and along her arch. By the time they ap-
proached shore, her toes had felt their way along the pleats
of his shirt; her ankles were loosely tangled in the braces of
his trousers and in a skein of watch chains that lay hidden on
the bottom of the boat.

The Lady Claire Wessit was thirteen, pushing with all her
might at twenty-five. She played precociously and adeptly
at being older, and Graham allowed it. She wore a bit of
color on her cheeks and mouth, did her hair up on her
head, wore low décolletages over her small bosom, and
wore her mother's dangling pearls, all with the practice of
one who had dressed up, pretended, for many years. Her
childish imitation of adulthood did occasionally capture a
refined, uncharacteristically mature style. The effect was
portentous of the great beauty she would one day become;
then the next moment, in one nauseatingly apt word, it was
cute in the way little girls can make horrible, bumbling asses
of themselves. When Graham looked at her, he always felt at
once both a magnificent success and utter failure as a father.
She was lovely, full of grace, feminine down to every aspect
of that word's ineffable charm. She was also fainthearted
and headlong by turns, never at the right moment, and
prone to tears, tirades, and conniving. So far as Graham
could remember, she was nothing like her mother. And not
very much like her father—primarily, Graham thought,
from lack of exposure. He saw her only irregularly, on holi-
days and such. The looks and much of the temperament,
God help her, were his, but she handled them with a completely different tack. Graham considered himself particularly ill-suited to deal with her and generally shrank from
confrontation whenever she gave him the opportunity.

Charles was another matter. Though twins, they hardly

looked related at all. Charles was gracelessly accommodating an ever-increasing height. His body had taken on, with a sudden vengeful will of its own, the idea to mature at a pace he could neither intellectually nor emotionally match. He stood only slightly shorter than Graham, with all the wrong proportions. He had a thin, boyish slouch. He was sullen, brutish, and dealt Claire possibly the only thing that saved her: occasional blows of undeserved meanness that stunned her, at least for moments, into puzzled humility. The two were close despite this, with a genuine affection for one another. They bickered. Charles sulked. Claire was kind to him, cheering him on occasion as no one else could do— and as she did for no one else. Charles kicked her for her trouble, insulted her, tormented her, then wanted her to talk to, gave her "lends" from his allowance that he neither saw returned nor asked for back. They each loved to be the center of attention, orchestrated the other's downfall for the purpose of looking good by comparison, and were happy if the other didn't show at all. Then, an hour after, one was asking for the other, *When will Claire, Will Charles come— not that I care, mind you, the fart ass.* They could also be extremely foulmouthed, though here they walked a delicate line with their father and knew it.

They didn't invite his temper, but Graham did lose it on occasion, for which he always felt the worse. They could become so frightened, so cowed. They didn't see him often enough to know he was hardly worth being afraid of. Graham knew he intimidated his children, but he was loath to give this up, since it seemed to be the one weapon he had over them. Claire in particular dissolved into a snotty, childish mess should he firmly voice his opposition to her. So for the most part, he didn't—thus his actions devastated all the more when he did.

Graham considered his relationship with his offspring certainly less than ideal. Fatherhood was a disappointment, a proposition on which he had, by now, all but given up. He performed the role mostly by long-distance fiat and delegation. And he dealt from a position of strength—long experience at moving subservient adults to his will—with tutors, governesses, and headmasters. He was the bane of several school committees, which he thought (an hypocrisy he was not about to let them understand) were not living up to the responsibilities of their task, i.e., to educate and train his offspring. Like many parents, he never let his hypocrisy get in the way of his children obtaining somewhere else what he himself could not give. The odd thing was that he loved them so much—and was so frustrated at the poverty of that one single emotion with no other skills or abilities attached to it—that he willingly gave them up to the nurture of others. This brought to Graham's mind the other remaining little twin, not doing terribly well in the nursery upstairs.

Graham had brought his new ward to Netham at the end of August. He had reopened the nursery on the uppermost floor, hired a nanny and wet nurse, then abandoned the situation in hope of hearing no more than a whimper now and then from the little fellow's life. On a whim, Graham had named him Harold Henry, to be called Harry; Harry Stratford sounded like a good, sturdy name. But Harry wasn't a sturdy creature, and "Harry" was too close to "Henry"; he almost always referred to him by the wrong name. Harry-Henry went from runny nose to runny nose; he had never breathed a clear day in his life. Presently, he had diarrhea. He cried incessantly, long into the night. The nanny said he wouldn't live the summer and that the nurse's milk was poisoning his blood. The wet nurse, a heavy woman one didn't cross lightly, said he'd be fine if she could take him to her bed and nurse him around the clock.

Graham had no idea who was right. He brought in his

doctor for the sick infant and let the three of them work it out.

"Father?"

Graham was glad he had a doctor on hand when he looked at his daughter, Claire. She made a grimace as the doctor removed an eye patch from her right eye.

"Who is that awful, bleak woman?" She wasn't in so much pain that she couldn't turn the grimace into a moue of disdain. "The one who came yesterday with the bald, pudgy barrister?" Claire was not tolerant of any irregularity from beauty; she adored Rosalyn Schild.

Graham gave her a wry look. "Her name is Lady Motmarche, and just for the record, you have very indiscriminate taste. The lady is a lovely, intelligent marchioness who will undoubtedly come into at least part of a fortune that will probably make her the richest woman in England, save the queen."

"Is that why you like her?"

"No."

"I think she's dour and plain."

Graham set the coffee cup he'd brought in with him onto his daughter's breakfast tray. "She's lost her husband. And her home. You might be dour too in such circumstances."

Claire laughed at the thought. "But never plain."

"No." He smiled at her over the head of the doctor. Her eye itself was bright red. The skin around it was black and blue and yellow—she'd been hit with a croquet ball. But the eye, without its patch, shifted to look at him. "No," he reassured her again, "you'll never be plain."

The eye, with its dark, rather stunningly large partner, stared up as Claire spoke in a rush. "I love Mrs. Schild. I want you to marry her. She says you might. Will you? I'd love to have her around all the time. I want to be just like her—"

His expression must have given him away. As the doctor

turned to get something from the table beside the bed, Claire quickly became a bumbling, apologetic little creature, playing with her bedcovers.

"Well," she continued, "not completely like her." Then she threw him the most unlikely glance, a tilted chin. Her watery eyes—her injured one in particular had begun to run—held for a moment an unprecedented willingness to confront him. "Why can't I be like her?" she pouted back at her covers. "Why do you like it just fine for *her* to behave like a courtesan, yet I can't admire such a free life?"

Graham turned away from the bed, looking over the doctor's shoulder. "I won't even dignify such a question with an answer."

"Because she behaves like a courtesan with *you*," she accused.

He was forced to turn back to her at that remark. He sat on the arm of a chair and looked at his daughter. "Absolutely," Graham said. "So don't you dare get involved with anyone like me."

She made a face. The poor, puffy black eye did not quite work with her antics. She winced. "I'll never find anyone so fine as you," she said with childish sincerity. "I think Mrs. Schild is lucky."

He didn't know what else to say. "Thank you." He paused, then said, "I think Mrs. Schild is lucky, too—she has a husband who loves her very much."

"You don't love her?" The doctor was putting some sort of goo on the eye. She kept flinching, getting it all over her cheek.

He didn't answer the question but said after a moment, "See that you're polite to Lady Motmarche." He got up again, thinking their little conversation done.

"Graham—"

And this really brought him up short. He turned, frowning deeply at this new facet to Claire's experimentation in the forbidden gardens of grown-up life. "I'd prefer 'Father,' if you don't mind."

Her chin lifted away from the doctor's hand. "And if I do?"

"Then you can have your supper in your room till you change your tone with me." He turned his back again.

"My eye hurts," she complained, trying to lure him back.

"Dr. Grable can put another patch on it."

"It makes me look ugly."

From the door, he told her, "It makes you look injured, which you are."

But she didn't want to be rational. As he left, she called rather loudly, "I don't like that stupid widow. I think she's boring. So does everyone else."

The words trailed after him down the hall.

William caught him before he could escape for a nap, his cousin getting finally to the point of his visit. William came periodically to hit anyone up for money he might have missed the last time around. People groaned when they saw him coming. Today he wanted a great deal more than usual. Graham wrote him a draft on his bank—it seemed worth it just to have him leave and thus leave poor Submit alone.

Unfortunately, William was thanking Graham effusively at the door of his study when Submit walked up.

"Graham," William was saying, as he ogled the bank draft, "you have no idea how much this helps. I will be forever in your debt—Why, Lady Motmarche, we were only just speaking of you." He smirked. "Indirectly."

She looked from William to Graham. It would have been hard to convince her, Graham thought, that he hadn't been speaking of her. He had been thinking of her as he had contemplated, then written and signed, the draft. The awful, insidious pleasure of giving William the money was that it guaranteed a longer lawsuit. Graham would have supported

William anyway perhaps, but it was an added attractiveness that he was, by helping William, incapacitating Submit, tethering her economically either here or to the inn, never too far away. Whenever he had looked at her over the last twenty-four hours, in his house, in his garden, in his boat on the lake, he'd felt a kind of elation—and a kind of terror that this bliss would end. It seemed hardly more than whim that had brought her here, making it seem equally plausible that she might suddenly, whimsically reverse all his pleasure and leave.

"Motmarche," William was going on. Submit's eyes had fallen on the draft in his hand. He made no effort to hide the zeros; there were three of them—his thumb over even one would have been nice. "Beautiful, beautiful Motmarche," he said as he slowly began to fan the draft, as if drying the ink. "You have a lovely home, Graham, don't misunderstand me, but Motmarche. . . . It's a palace, a land of its own."

"Yes." Graham looked down. "It was incredible."

"*Is*," William corrected.

"Yes, it is incredible," Submit spoke finally. She was eyeing him with a perfectly focused and condemning regard.

"Well, thank you so very, very much." William lifted his hat. "I must be off."

She waited till he was out of earshot before she said in a low voice, "You gave him a thousand pounds. Do you know what that means to me?"

Graham frowned uncomfortably. "I've never made a secret to you of how I feel about William and Henry's will."

"Have you been giving him that kind of money all along?" He had no idea if she would believe him. "No."

"Why now?"

"He asked."

"Lord." She turned, actually pushing him in the chest as she wheeled around. When she glanced back at him, emotion sparked off her eyes. "This is unconscionable, do you know that? You deserve that stupid serial. You *are* a blackguard."

She disappeared up the stairs with a familiar sound: the churn of yards and yards of taffeta moving along at a crisp, angry step.

"The Black Widow," William said again as he was getting into his coach. Graham had walked him out.

"Leave her alone, William."

He smiled from the seat of his open landau coach. He had a driver in full livery—Henry's livery. The vehicle was new. William was not suffering much through his lawsuit against the widow, though Graham shuddered to think of the debts that had to be mounting up.

Graham stepped forward to close the door, then hung on, speaking over it. "If you come again, don't humiliate her, don't torment her, don't say one miserable thing, do you understand? If you do, I'll never give you another halfpenny."

William looked a little alarmed. "I thought you understood, Gray. She's awful—"

"She's very nice," he contradicted.

"Then why are you helping me?"

He shrugged. "Habit, I suppose. It's always seemed so pathetic that you can't help yourself."

William pulled his jaw forward into a jowly frown. "I can help myself, if you'll let me. I could crush that silly girl who thinks she's getting my father's house and money."

"Leave her alone."

"She's been nothing but a—"

"She's not done a thing intentionally to you."

"She took my land! And my father's love!"

"Damn it," Graham said a little impatiently, "you can't sue for a larger portion of your father's love. You're going to be in litigation forever with this attitude. It's going to gain you little but debt, and I'm sick to death of bailing you out."

Abruptly, William's face changed. His expression became stricken—humble remorse so perfectly contrived that Graham half believed his cousin felt a fraction of it. "Don't think I don't appreciate what you do," William said. He leaned forward, putting his elbows on his legs as he looked between them. "Do you remember when we were younger," he said to the carriage floor, "the time you told Henry *you* took the money meant for the milkman?"

Graham nodded, wondering where he thought this was going to get him.

"God, I was so grateful. Rugger was going to kill me if I didn't pay up. Then Henry—you took such a whipping for it. I was sure you were going to tell: I would have. Every time I saw you flinch, over the next few days, I felt horrible." He put a pause here, then said with facile, somewhat belated sympathy, "It must have been damned awful." He looked at Graham, as if expecting some sort of comradelike corroboration. When he didn't get it, he went on. "I also felt I had a friend. I thought—still do—you were the most loyal, courageous ally a man could have." He waited till Graham looked at him, playing it very broadly now; sincere. "Thank you for the bank draft, Graham." He made a faint snort. "Henry would hate you for it."

There was a funny little moment. Perhaps it was the snort that made it so, accompanied by a sideways, crooked smile. These were the only honest expressions of pleasure that William possessed.

Graham tapped the top of the carriage door once as he stepped back. "You're right. He would." Henry didn't believe in anyone getting anything without just merit: Henry didn't believe in compassion. Nor could he have believed for even a moment that a resentful, rebellious young man might take a beating strictly for the satisfaction of undermining a pedant's pitiless ethical code. Now, as then, Graham found a kind of blissful power in granting William a reprieve, while at the same time turning Henry's version of life's order and consequences upside down. He felt a smile pulling at his mouth. "It's what makes helping you so appealing, I'm sure: Henry wouldn't like it at all."

"And she's his envoy."

"Pardon?"

"Submit. She's his representative on earth. His votaress." William was absolutely serious. "Mephisto's wife."

"You have completely lost your mind, do you know that? You see devils in the skirts of a woman who is frightened and alone."

"I see a Black Widow. And if you're smart, Gray, you'll bear in mind what I say: She's poisonous, and she bites."

When Graham saw her again, it was from his bay window. She was out in the back garden peeling an apple with a little knife. Looking at her, he thought, *My God, she does look deadly determined sometimes, lethal.* But it was not in the way that William suggested. Submit Channing-Downes's lethal streak had a kind of objectivity, the same sort that characterized the necessity of nature, no matter how brutal the act. Something in her seemed to feel it vital that she go back to Motmarche. Graham had felt, in that moment when her eyes had glistened with tears, her tenacity, her determination to have what she needed. Like the spider. Submit survived in the way all relatively defenseless creatures did, Graham thought, her most wholesome, self-preserving traits misconstrued, maligned, and blown out of proportion.

Others besides William had trouble defining her or giving her a category. It would take Graham the rest of September, however, to understand that Submit was not universally liked. He knew already that Claire was no fan. Neither was Charles. That weekend, Tilney began referring to her as the Little Motmarche. He called her "wooden" and said she gave him the chills. Her detractors began to make up a kind of club in Graham's mind; the young, the literal, and the inane. She was becoming a kind of dividing line among his friends. Those few who had the discernment to like her—even Tate—grew in Graham's eyes.

Graham watched her bite into the apple, her wet, mobile lips, her little white teeth crooked enough to make him push his tongue against the backs of his own, trying to imagine what her teeth would feel like. He was attracted to her. Perhaps *because* she was so difficult to classify. Watching her, he couldn't decide what sort of female he was staring at—the arachnid, with its single fatal sting of sexuality, or the eternally attractive Eve.

"Submit?" Arnold Tate caught her attention. She was sitting on a bench in the back garden by the apple orchard. "I'd like to talk to you a moment."

She didn't feel much like talking, but she moved over and made room as she put the last bite of an apple into her mouth.

"I'm leaving," Arnold said as he sat. He put his palms on his thighs and absently rubbed. "As soon as I can get my things together—and you yours, if you'd like. I'm sorry, but I can't stay the whole weekend."

She looked at him. "Has something happened?"

"No. Not exactly." He was playing with his watch fob. "Well, in a manner of speaking." He took a long, despondent breath. "What has happened is, well, Netham is right. Lawrence Carmichael jumped to a rather ugly conclusion about—about you and me last night. I have no business escorting a young woman to a country house for the weekend."

"Arnold, don't be silly. There is nothing—"

"Hush. I have a wife, with whom I don't get along very well, I'm afraid, and two children I hardly see, but I have responsibilities to them, to myself. I shouldn't be here."

"You shouldn't let others paint a picture for you that you don't like, one that isn't true. Nothing could be more innocent than you and I."

"Of course you're right." But he scowled at his shoes for a moment before he looked up. "I'll see you in London next week, for the hearing on dower rights." He paused, then asked, "Would you like to travel back to the inn with me? Or would you prefer to try to find your own way?"

Submit thought about that. "I'm not ready to leave," she found herself saying. After a moment's consideration, she continued, "When I'm ready, I can get someone to take me to the train, I think. I've gotten myself to Morrow Fields once or twice from the other direction, from London." She looked at Arnold. "No, don't worry about me. Do as you like."

"But I do worry." His face furrowed. "People are talking about more than just you and me. They don't know what to make of you." More quietly, he added, "I heard about the dawn ride in the boat—"

Submit was miffed that he should mention the ride. "In clear view of a dozen people. Again, nothing improper."

"What were you doing up at dawn with him?"

"He came and got me up."

"Why?"

More irritated, she replied, "How should I know?"

He hesitated before saying, "Submit. Netham has a tendency to—to reinvent things, to make dalliance, whimsy into something momentarily respectable." He paused. "How do you feel about him?"

"We are friends." Then even Submit frowned at this definition of her and Graham's relationship. "Or something like that. We find each other . . . interesting, that's all."

Without warning, Arnold took her hand and brought it

to his mouth. He kissed the backs of her fingers. "Be careful," he said.

He left her outside to watch the sun rise over the trees, high into the sky, over Graham Wessit's edible landscaping, his apple orchard.

— *Chapter 27* —

Extreme remedies are very appropriate
for extreme diseases.
HIPPOCRATES
Aphorisms, Section I, 6

Submit had decided to "write him." That was the way she phrased it to herself—*By God, I'll write him*—the way someone might think, *By God, I'll shoot him right between the eyes.*

By the time Arnold left that afternoon, Netham Hall had grown very quiet. Most everyone had retired to rest before dinner. Graham and those who had been up all night had gone to bed earlier and not been seen since. On her own, Submit began to explore the house.

She touched furniture and doors, knowing she was going to make this room, that couch, that Chinese vase into a paper backdrop. Her tour had an odd, almost dizzying effect. A room would suggest ideas or suddenly pop out, amazingly familiar from already having been visualized within the loops and jags of Henry's close scrawl. There was something circular here, a fiction come to life, while real objects suggested ways to build more fictional plausibility. In her room upstairs, Submit had further notes on the seduction of the upper housemaid—a housemaid Graham had, only four years ago, brought to London to the horror of everyone. He had sent debutantes home early so he could carouse with a heavyset girl with a thick country accent, a girl in service. In service, indeed.

All the servants knew. Eventually, Henry and anyone else who cared to know were acquainted with the situation:

Though Graham and his housemaid did not exactly laugh and shriek and chase each other about the bed, she stomped—she had a pronounced limp. Anyone who happened to be in the vestibule below knew when she was upstairs in the master's room, when she got in and when she got out of bed. Henry's notes even hinted that she was a bit slow-witted, and she was certainly uneducated. She couldn't even write her own name. How any man could take advantage of such a creature, Submit didn't know, but she intended to make a rollicking lesson of it that would last several more episodes.

Anger, rampant curiosity, and a confusion of compelling emotions made her want to lay Graham Wessit's life back to the bone. She discovered as she went through his house, she didn't just want to be able to visualize a room, a corner; she wanted the house to somehow give evidence of the man, to give secrets he hadn't shared.

In the dining room, she picked up teacups from a shelf and turned them over. Chinese porcelain, forty years old. The same with the silver in a chest. Traditionally fine, old; something that had little to do with Graham, more to do with Netham. There was a sideboard laid out with brandy, port, a humidor full of dark cigars. These didn't interest her. She didn't know exactly what she wanted, but she knew these weren't what she was after.

There were several more rooms like this, kept more by the servants than the owner; impersonal rooms as in a dozen other English homes. Parlors, halls, a recital room. A game room was slightly more interesting—nothing like it had ever existed at Motmarche. But the game room was ultimately less remarkable than it promised. It was what it seemed, with card tables at one end, a billiard table (with a roulette wheel currently set up on it) at the other. The room's drawers and cupboards held only roulette tiles, neatly boxed decks of cards, score sheets, and pens. A few old games on discarded pages had been shoved into one drawer, an offhand written record. Graham's name was on all of them; he usually won.

Then at last in a small conservatory Submit caught a breath of something individual, eccentric, though for a time she couldn't put her finger to what. The earl's conservatory was the usual sort of addition that over the last three or four decades any Englishman, with any pretension to taste and sensibility, put into an outside wall of his house. It was a room made up of windows and light, giving onto a good view of nature outside, filled with it inside. This conservatory was green with plants and heaped with flowers culled unquestionably for their scent. There were white jasmine, gardenias, and something rare—large, fragrant orchids. Submit found herself staring down the throats of half a dozen large, white cattleyas in full bloom. For a moment their snowy sepals and petals held her attention, white ruffled lips narrowing and blushing pinker and deeper into each flower to a dark throat the fuchsia color of crushed raspberries, the whole giving off a sweet, delicate perfume. The sight and smell of these lush flowers were disturbing, as if each had taken pungent, three-dimensional life from the top of a black-lacquered box.

From here, she seemed to enter a preserve, a personal area. It began with a cloakroom full of not only the expected winter overcoats and hunting jackets, but also a rack of freshly pressed shirts, all Graham's. A bust of Aristotle stood, presumably stored, in the corner of the cloakroom. The stone head wore a whimsical stack of real hats: a bowler, two straws, a furry hunting cap, topped off with a silk top hat. This was off a library that was very male, filled with dark wood and leather.

The library held the expected walls of dark books, a large heavy desk, a stuffed chair, a lamp. A gentleman's couch sat by a window, for snoozing or reading. But the half-wall behind the desk was given over to an assortment of loosely bound playbooks, and a glass case at the back of the room contained a particularly fine collection of early Shakespeare quartos. Playbills (none with Graham's name on them) and opera programs decorated a space over some shelves, as did photographs. She looked at pictures of a theater under renovation. It was the opera house in Covent Garden, currently only half rejuvenated, though operas continued to play there.

More photographs lay in a pile. She flipped through them, looking at scenes from London last June, the group in Rosalyn Schild's front parlor, various people in front of Rosalyn's London house. Then, quite surprisingly, she saw a picture of herself. Submit stared at the photograph. Graham had a picture of her watching from the back terrace. She had thought he had been photographing the group in the foreground; but she remembered his taking off his coat, the sight of the bright red vest, his head ducking under the camera cloth. He had focused on her. Disquieted, she set the bundle of photos down.

On the desk was an appointment book, its entries jotted in a neat, elongated hand. The pages were thick with obligations, social commitments. Rosalyn at two; the Carmichaels for dinner on the fourth of last April. Tate on June twelfth. On July third, dinner with Alfred, Minny, Lloyd, and Elizabeth. Submit opened a desk drawer. There she found clips, papers, and the plans to the opera house, a drawing of how the finished façade was supposed to look. He was still involved with theater somehow. Another drawer contained a liniment for sore muscles and a miscellany of old equestrian rosettes; they were prizes for jumping, all the earl of Netham's, though the most recent was eight years ago. In another drawer was a ledger; Graham Wessit did his own books, it seemed—it was written in the same hand as the calendar. Neat, balanced columns showed Netham, through stock investments, to be running in the black. How surprising. This was nothing in the way of a surprise, however, compared to what the next drawer contained.

In a small side drawer was a little parcel wrapped up in brown bookstore wrap, like a book the earl had yet to open and put on the shelf. Submit fiddled with the string, trying to see if it would untie in a manner that could easily be fixed back. The string gave. The paper unfolded neatly, but inside was not a book at all. Instead, she found a discreetly disguised half-dozen smaller packages, at first puzzling, then so alarming that Submit dropped them. They scattered all over the floor with a racket, as if she had walked under a tree suddenly shaken of raindrops—*pat, pat, pat.*

"Well," she murmured, "I wanted something personal."

She stared for a moment at the little parcels lying innocently in the light from the window on the carpet. The scrolly print on each could be easily read, right-side up, sideways, upside down: Freeman's Safety Sheaths for the Prevention of Conception. She stooped down and began picking the things up, dropping them delicately into her skirt. Her hands shook slightly. She could feel the device inside, light as air, like a piece of paper or skin. What did it look like? No wonder the immoral creature was so sure he wasn't the father of the new twins—

She got a moment's warning. A noise, a yap. Submit hardly had time to stand and dump the packets into their wrapper. As she was knotting the string again, she had a witness—the earl's English setter bounded into the room. Like a clumsy tocsin sounding the alarm, his tail whacked the legs of tables, the backs of chairs, her dress. "Easy, there," Submit murmured, trying to keep the dog's nose out of places it didn't belong. She had to push his head out of the way in order to close the drawer, her heart thudding all the while, matching the rap of the silly dog's tail.

She went out quickly, heading for the back of the house

and outside, walking through a part of the house she had
never seen. She got as far as the next room, a little vestibule
that gave onto the back garden. There, she was stopped by
Graham Wessit himself. The room was small, with a table in
the middle of it. He was sitting on the far edge of the table,
taking off a pair of muddy boots.

"I thought you were asleep," Submit blurted.

Graham looked over his shoulder with an expression of
pleasure and surprise. The dog circled them both. "No." He
took hold of the dog's neck and gave the animal a shove. It
went under the table and lay down.

It was a funny room. Messy. Muddy. Used. On the table
were a set of spurs, some wood boot stretchers, and a pair of
boots dulled by setting polish. A tin, rags, and brushes indicated servants used the room as well.

Graham turned around and looked at Submit. His
smile was hospitable. "Well, how nice. I was so sure you
would leave with Mr. Tate. I'm glad you didn't." He leaned
on the corner of the table and peeled off a wet sock. He
wiggled his toes. He threw the first then the second sock
into a sink. The room appeared to be a kind of back wet-
entrance. He offered by way of explanation, "I was out riding." Looking down at himself, he added, "Through the
mud, I'm afraid." He had dirt on an elbow and mud down
one hip.

"You look as though you crawled through it."

He laughed. "Blasted horse." He took off his coat. His
vest was spattered. "The one from the inn. Do you remember? Mean as the devil. Fast as the wind. I don't know
whether to sell it for glue or enter it at Ascot." At the sink, he
washed his hands, glancing over his shoulder. "How long
are you staying?"

"Another day."

"You should at least stay through next weekend. It's the
fall regatta. There'll be people, boating, nice weather with

picnics. It's really fun." He gave her a tormenting look as he grabbed a towel. "You understand the word 'fun'?"

She frowned at him, then was distracted. He reached the sole of his bare foot over to nudge and pet the rump of the dog.

"I'll be taking the train back tomorrow afternoon," she said.

"You'd be welcome to stay longer."

"Thank you, but I only brought a few things. And I have work to do."

"Ah, yes." His eyes rose past her, toward the direction from which she'd come. "Been walking through the house, have you?"

"I—ah, no—"

Without a moment's concern, he took this for yes. "It's a wonderful old house. Nothing so grand as Motmarche, of course, but with its own charm. Would you like a tour?"

"A tour?"

"Come on. I'll show you through." He came round the table and moved her by the elbow. "Sit here a moment while I change my shirt." He left her on the day couch in the library, walking barefoot into the cloakroom beyond. These rooms, with him in them, seemed very much his domain. Submit was left staring at the walls of playbills and the huge desk, its drawer of contraband.

He came back a moment later, wearing a fresh shirt, a fresh vest and carrying a pair of clean boots and half-stockings. He sat on the couch beside her, pulling the stockings on.

"Would you like some tea? I could have some sent ahead of us to the conservatory."

"What?" She looked down. "No, thank you."

Graham pushed his foot into a boot, stepping his heel into it, tap, tap, tap. He seemed so open, like a man who didn't have a thing to hide. How very awkward she felt. "Did you see the *Ronmoor* serial this week?"

He made a sound of displeasure. "*Pffs*, yes."

"What did you think?"

"That I'd like to throttle the chap who's doing them."

She let her eyes drift along the wall. "You must have an idea who."

"Not really." He tapped his heel into the other boot, then caught her eye. Another teasing look. "What about you? Could you write scathing fiction, Lady Motmarche?"

"Yes. Probably I could." She looked away.

"That's what I like about you," he said. She saw a leg stretch out. He'd leaned back. "You're so damned honest."

At this, she felt truly awkward, then alarmed. His hand touched her back. Lightly, he ran his finger down her spine. It sent chills and made her back arch. She looked around at him. He was slouched against the wall, one knee up, eyeing her. No more smile, no teasing, just staring at her with his large, dark, morose eyes.

"I like that you're here," he said. "I like that you're wandering through my house." Before she could protest, he continued, "Trying to figure me out. When I think of your being curious enough to stay, curious enough to touch things, open—"

She stood up. "I was lost."

"I know the sound of my own desk drawer closing."

She looked around at him.

"Which one were you in?" He laughed and answered his own question. "All of them."

He was playing with her. Honest, indeed. He knew she'd been prying and was intentionally punishing her a little for it.

"What do you want to know?" he asked.

She shook her head, irritated, outmaneuvered. It was a strange sort of punishment.

He began patiently. "I was born in 1820, right here in this

house. I don't remember much, except a constant shifting of nannies. My mother and father, when I saw them, seemed rather nice. When I heard they were dead in London, that seemed a little sad, but all right too. I didn't know them.

"Henry came on the scene somewhere after that. You know a lot in between. I married at twenty-five, had three children, one died. My wife died miscarrying our fourth. Let's see—"

"Oh, stop—" She turned her back.

"No. I'm trying to tell you. I'm completely at your disposal. You don't need to look around. Or read a bloody serial. I'll tell you, show you anything you like."

She looked at him. "Why?"

He gave the question more consideration than she expected. "Because, I suppose, I'd like a friend." He left a pause. "And you need one."

"No I don't."

"You do."

Submit wet her lips and looked at the carpet, at the Persian patterns of red, indigo, and ivory. "I'm not sure of our friendship," she said. "You shouldn't trust me so much."

"I see." There was another long pause. "If you aren't sure, then what were all those talks at Morrow Fields?"

She didn't know what to answer. She remembered the talks as events that had oddly thrilled her. His arrival had always meant wonder, pleasure, a peak of interest that far outreached anything else happening to her there. Even Arnold's visits, their discussions of the machinations of the courts that bore so directly on her future, were not so enthralling. Yet there had been a burr in every conversation. Their exchanges had often been trying, sometimes mean, once out-and-out bitter. Morrow Fields had been a funny world, an unnatural place where an impossible, overstimulating friendship had existed for a few weeks.

Something made her pursue what he offered. Curiosity.

Opportunism. The desire for accuracy, she thought perhaps, detail in the written text. She asked, "Why did you marry your wife? Were you in love?"

"No." He shrugged. "I was exhausted. And tired to death of fighting all that was expected of me. It was a brilliant match. It meant money and prestige—her mother was a duchess in her own right." He paused. "Even Henry couldn't disapprove."

Submit frowned as she thought for a moment. "She was the one in the serial a few weeks ago, wasn't she?" she asked. "The society daughter of the old duchess?"

He sniffed but ended by giving her another wan, self-mocking smile. "I would protest, except the reality was not much better than the caricature."

"What was the reality?"

Graham put his arm along the back of the couch. He crossed his legs and looked at her. He seemed to be further assessing her interest—assessing and finding it somehow all right.

"There's not much to tell. Elyse—that was her name— had a pedigree that easily outreached the notoriety of a few ink drawings. Being sheltered from the specifics, she was deeply in love with the notion of winning a scandalous man. The duchess, at first, did not approve. In the end, I more or less courted the mother. I played a part, the engaging, raffish role associated with me since my theater days. It was a kind of bridge on which I walked back across into acceptance."

He let this sink in before he went on. "Elyse and I were married. Henry was overjoyed. 'Finally a worthy achievement,' he said, though worthy of what, I was never sure. I had married a young girl I hardly knew. We were married just over two years when she died. Shall I go on?"

"No." Submit turned around completely to look out the window at the garden, the distant pond and folly, the lake under a darkened sky.

She didn't like this. She remembered other frank talks, when somehow things were more mutual, less imbued on her part with mixed emotions, ulterior intent.

Her own skirts moved gently behind her, a rustle, as her crinoline bowed, the structure of steel hoops quivering from side to side. He'd come up behind her. "I wanted to love her," he said quietly. "There were things I liked about her. Her utter lack of censure. Her timid, gentle gusto—she was slight, shy, but eager to please.

"I can't explain exactly," he continued. "It was just—she never looked me in the eye. We both knew, somewhere, that we were not equals. I was always on my guard not to step all over her."

He was quiet a moment. There was just the sound of his even breathing. Submit almost wished now that she could shut him up. He was saying too much, revealing himself in ways that seemed if not in poor taste at least in poor judgment.

This was too easy, Submit thought, so easy it felt unfair. But there it was: She realized some affinity made him confide. She could not only live in his house, gather all the physical details she wanted, she could also have his full cooperation, his verification on any fact or incident she wished.

After she left the room, Graham remained, looking out his library window. He considered it a somewhat puzzling but generally positive sign that Submit had begun to make references and ask questions about other women in his life. A woman interested in a man's past was usually struggling with something presently on her mind.

Rosalyn, by contrast, took a broad tack on such matters. She didn't care for details, but inquired ruthlessly after a list. She pressed for names, titles, titillations. Rosalyn liked to believe in a mythical multitude. She liked to think that her beloved was a prize. Fewer co-fornicators, or at least fewer contenders for this position, would reduce his value. It was like a list of invitation to a party. No matter how august the individuals, a few were just a gathering: It took a certain number to make it an affair. She grew positively sullen when he insisted he had been faithful to his wife.

Graham did not commend himself much on his marital fidelity, believing that he simply had not had enough time to rouse himself to a breach of faith. Besides, there were other kinds of infidelities. Elyse simply died before he could run through them all.

For the first time in a long time, that afternoon Graham's mind dwelled on his dead wife. Submit had accepted what he'd told her so easily. There was that temptation with Submit, to tell her everything. Hearing his own recountings voiced, watching Submit accord his views the respect one gave the truth—no contradictions, reinterpretations, no panicking remonstrance—made him want to go on, made him willing to review.

He hadn't told her the more harrowing parts. Childbirth had been hard on the delicate Elyse, the way bearing young can be hard on an overbred mare. She grew progressively more unhealthy with each gestation. Yet nothing seemed to keep her from pregnancy; one chance encounter, near unconscious in the night, would yield a child. Or two: Claire and Charles were born when he and Elyse had been married only nine months. A third child, Michael, who died when he was three, was born ten months after that.

My God, people said when she was pregnant with their fourth child in two years, *someone ought to put you out to pasture for a while, Netham*. Their union was considered fair game for such jokes, the consequence of a storybook match between a very marriageable young woman and a notorious young man. All of this was so sadly in conflict with the truth, however. Graham was so depressed, he hardly touched her. And Elyse was befuddled by the turnabout of her romantic illusions. She'd been married less than two years, had a husband who hardly looked her way and three children all under two years—and now she was pregnant again.

In miscarrying the fourth child, the mother miscarried also her own faint claim to life. She'd developed an unknown infection that brought on rapid deterioration, then death. All in less than two days, though she was given every attention: the best doctors, the best medicine, a husband's night's sleep. Graham couldn't help believing that Elyse was ignored to death. Her real life faded out like a ghost in whom no one believed.

Shortly after this, Graham discovered "Malthusianism," the creed of population control as expounded by Thomas Robert Malthus. This seemed like a very sane idea in light of the deadly consequence of unlimited pregnancy. For the next half dozen years, he practiced what the French called *la chamade*, the retreat. He became quite adept. Then he discovered that a very functional device, a sheath of lambskin, could be purchased at certain bookstores. The slightly odd outcome of this was that, as his sex life became less anxious and more satisfying, his library expanded, and he read more. He had a tendency to browse and select books while the bookseller discreetly wrapped his somewhat controversial purchase into a book-shaped little pack.

In the course of this portion of Graham's education in bookstores, he learned to ask for "French letters" in England, "English hats" in France. It amused him, even now, thinking of the distinction. Aside from the national slur each country intended, these images also unintentionally revealed each country's national character. No matter what they called it, the English envisioned the item neatly wrapped up, out of sight; the French envisioned it on, like a jaunty cap. There were other names besides "sheath." If a gentleman bought these conveniences at a more sordid establishment, he might have to use the dirty name, c——m; even the most salacious literature never wrote the word out. Graham wasn't certain how to spell it. *Condim? Condom? Condum?* But he knew how to say it, in several languages, in a dozen euphemisms, up and down the class system, on and off the Continent.

The next morning, Submit left bright and early. Graham was surprised. And disappointed. He had expected her to stay the day. But she said she would come back the next weekend. If she didn't come, he determined, he at least had an excuse to visit and inquire why.

And an excuse to continue to think, explain, revise. Graham had begun to remake himself slightly, not to mind some of his sillier, or meaner, attributes. He wanted to be more worthy, he realized, in his own eyes.

— Chapter 28 —

TO YOUNG AUTHORS AND INEXPERIENCED WRITERS

Now ready, for 12 Stamps, Post free,

HOW TO PRINT AND WHEN TO PUBLISH

[ADVICE TO AUTHORS]

Condensed information on all subjects connected with
PUBLISHING and bringing out a Book with most
advantage to its Author is the characteristic of this
useful little Pamphlet. SAUNDERS & OTLEY, PUBLISHERS,
CONDUIT STREET, HANOVER SQUARE

Advertisement from numbers 19/20 of *Little Dorrit*

by Charles Dickens, Issued June 1857

There were days at the inn when Submit felt herself leaning
into a kind of frenzy. She couldn't write enough. Writing
about Graham, his slouching charm, his polite immorality—
all his outrageous contradictions exaggerated into Satan
personified in the form of Ronmoor—proved such a release
she was sometimes compelled to go pages and pages beyond dinner and sleep.

Sometimes this left her feeling wonderful, exalted. She
could become so besotted with something that was happening in the serial that she couldn't go to sleep even after she'd
gone to bed. She knew it was exciting. She knew it had a
waiting, ready audience that was paying well for it. After a
quick trip to London, Submit had realized that her efforts
were worth a great deal more than Pease had originally let
on. In this light, she had stopped by his office and held him
up accordingly, insisting on a "fairer" fee, which, needless to
say, Mr. Pease didn't find fair at all. But Submit was beginning to hear a faint, implacable gripe in herself, one she

hated to hear in a woman since she had always felt it self-excusing and petty—the complaint of a conspiracy of men. Male courts were holding her inheritance in abeyance. A male heir was pressing the matter, abetted, she had begun to believe, by a male cousin. And Henry, dear, sweet, old Henry, a primogenitary male if ever there was one, had put her in this position. Even Arnold seemed in no hurry to gain her relief. She had taken Pease's money and made arrangements to begin interviewing for a maid. She had ordered a new dress. She had even sent Mr. Tate and her solicitors healthy fees for services rendered to date.

At other times, however, this whole venture, as it propelled her forward, felt vaguely unhealthy. She spent more time writing *Ronmoor* than she did speaking to real people. Sometimes, when she stood up to stretch or finally to eat, she would look around her and feel a flatness in the reality about her. The atmosphere of her room, of the inn itself seemed dilute, thin. As if life itself were hardly more than a sketch, only gaining meaning and authenticity when she could insert it into the mazelike inventions of her own mind. The idea of needing to go back to Netham was perhaps born in these vague moments. At the inn, her heart beat madly over written pages. At Netham, reality and unreality seemed to mix together into experiences she had never had. Her heart thumped in gardens and follies and little boats.

Occasionally, by the light of morning over a poached egg, Submit would wonder just how treacherous and self-justifying she was letting herself become. It was Graham after all who was making the serial popular, much more so than Henry's skills or her own. She wondered, for uncomfortable moments, if anything entitled her to use Graham, his past, his public persona, in a way that he found painful and loathed. Then she would spear her egg and run it onto her toast. If he could support William's suit, he would blessed well support hers. None of this would have dragged out so long if he had just let well enough alone.

Submit wrote all day, all week, most nights. She ran through Henry's notes, then made notes of her own. Graham's hospitality became a kind of road map; his confidences, a kind of fodder. The narrator of *Ronmoor* ranged the rooms at Netham with authority while everything Graham had ever told her began to flow and mix with Henry's annotations; it all worked so well. Even Submit realized that Ronmoor was taking on new life, new vividness, under her pen.

She was only taken from the world of paper and words once in that week. It was with quite a start that she heard the innkeeper announce, "There is a gentleman downstairs to see you."

Thinking it could only be Graham, Submit was suddenly flustered, almost afraid to go down.

But it was not Graham. It was Gerald Schild.

"Your coat."

As she came to the base of the stairs, he held out her old black coat, the one she hadn't seen since the beginning of the summer.

"You left it at our London house last May. My manservant found it and brought it along with the rest of my things. I've been meaning to return it to you for months."

He paused, slid his fingers over the back of his head, combing, like an old habit he couldn't break, nonexistent hair. He was not an unattractive man, Submit thought. He had nice features, softened a little by middle age, a pleasant good looks that, like the hair at the top of his head, had thinned out over the years. It seemed a shame he always looked so burdened and spent.

Submit took the coat, thanking him for his trouble.

Then he asked, "Have you got a few minutes to talk?" She didn't really feel she had. But before she could say anything, he added, "My wife is leaving me, I think."

* * *

"I want to do a play. It would be such fun." Rosalyn had come out into the garden with a stack of possible productions. She sat down in the shade on the bench at the edge of the orchard, plopping a stack of possibilities—playbooks—onto her lap. "Why don't you look through these with me?" She began to look by herself.

"I'm not wild for the idea of a play," Graham said.

"Don't be stuffy. It wouldn't be anything elaborate. Just for fun. Let's see. There are several Shakespeares. A Webster. *The Devil's Law-Case.* Do you know that one? Gray, are you listening?"

He looked up from the cat he'd been wooing with a sausage he'd brought from breakfast. "Yes. It's bloody serious."

"I've never heard of it."

He quoted a passage. " 'Being heretofore drowned in security, You know not how to live, nor how to die: But I have an object that shall startle you, And make you know whither you are going.' "

"An object?"

"A shroud. Though in one production it was a severed hand."

"Ooh." She made a face. "For goodness' sake, I don't want anything gruesome." She returned her attention to the pile on her lap. "What about this one: *All's Well That Ends Well?*" She giggled. "You could play the unfaithful husband?"

He frowned. "Not a good choice, I think."

As he stood, her eyes rose up with him. "You're not going to do any of them, are you?"

"You've read the serial. You should know why I don't fancy parading around in a play."

"Maybe your interest in the theater was never for the stage."

Graham looked at her. She was accusing him of something, though he wasn't exactly sure of what.

She laid it out. "He says you have an actress."

"He?"

"Peter."

Tilney. Graham snorted, discounting the source.

She persisted. "Do you?"

"No."

"Why would he say something so insupportable?"

"I have friends in the theater, among them an actress I
used to see privately."

She digested this. "The actress was just one fling?"

"A rather long fling." Graham had had a tendency to fall
back in with Elizabeth over the years, on his way back and
forth between others, like a familiar pit in the road.

"How long?"

"I don't inquire or complain about Gerald, you know."
Why was he doing this? Why not just tell her a soothing lie
and let it go at that?

She took this as she was meant to. She stood up in a rush.

"For God's sake, you're not telling me you still see this—
this—who? Who is it?"

He looked at Rosalyn, beautiful, porcelain-skinned,
standing with her fists braced at the top of a mountain of
aquamarine silk. Why? he asked himself again. She stood
there in her colorful dress with her extraordinarily pretty
features, a cultivated little jewel set off by the garden of
wild, tangled weeds behind her—spurge and red poppies
and purple honesty with their satiny pods. Surely, if he did
not love this woman, what he felt for her was just as good,
less vulnerable, full of pleasurable possibilities.

"I still see her," he explained, "but I don't sleep with her,
which seems to be what you want me to believe about you
and Gerald."

"Who?" she insisted. "Does this actress live in London?"

"Sometimes. She also has a house near Weymouth. And a husband. And four children, now nearly grown. We are friends."

"But different. You have shared all your other 'friends' with me. You don't share her." A pause. "Take me to meet her."

Alarmed, he asked, "Why?"

"I don't know. She frightens me. Her existence frightens me." After a too long pause, she said, "She must be what I feel."

"I don't know what you mean."

"I mean, sometimes I sense a presence in you. Or perhaps it's an absence." She waved a hand in the distilling light of the morning sun. "Oh, I don't know. You're not entirely with me all the time."

She went past him, as if she would leave, then she turned to face him from under the shade of the overhang. He could no longer see the details of her face.

"Last night, for instance," she said. "You were all over me, like you haven't been in months." She drew a deep breath, a catch, then went on in an intimate, distressed whisper. "You put your weight on top of me and didn't take me for the longest time. You called me loving names, more than I'd ever heard before. You moved on me and touched me to the point of my wanting to scream. It was so frustrating and so glorious. And so very, very premeditated. It seemed to have so little to do with me.

"A fantasy, I told myself. I should be flattered. But there was an element of reality, wasn't there? How can I explain? As if I were standing in for someone real and unreachable?" She turned away. After a silence, she asked, "Do you wish you could sleep with her, Gray? Your actress? Do you love her?"

He shook his head immediately. "No."

But he ran a hand over his forehead into his scalp. He remembered last night well, had looked forward in fact, a little guiltily, to repeating it. "It *was* a fantasy, Rosalyn." He added honestly, "It had nothing to do with Elizabeth." Somewhat less honestly, he added, "No face, no name, not at all like her in fact."

Graham suddenly felt a keen letdown. Rosalyn was absolutely the best woman he was ever going to possess. He didn't understand why he should have fantasies of Submit. She wasn't as pretty. She'd made it absolutely clear how likely he was to ever get close to her. She was probably right—part of wanting her was wanting to shag Henry's wife. The sheer intensity of the fantasy itself should have alerted him: It couldn't be healthy for a mature man to be that absorbed, like an adolescent in the first throes of discovery, that hot. It seemed hardly the reaction of a man of experience, approaching forty years of age.

He touched Rosalyn's shoulder, took hold of her round, perfect arm through the lace and silk of her sleeve, as if he could recapture something and hold on.

"Perhaps it was you," he murmured. "If not you, who else?"

Rosalyn was apparently not convinced, but she didn't give up. That night, she came straight to his rooms. No sneaking in the dark, no subterfuge. She just waltzed right in behind him when the card games downstairs dispersed. They had, for seven months, put up at least a sham of sleeping in separate rooms.

"Have we given up even the veneer of discretion?" he asked.

She closed the door. When he didn't move, she came forward and began kissing his shirt studs as she unbuttoned his vest. She dropped his trouser braces, untucked his shirt. Graham stood perversely still; faintly resistant, faintly curious for what came next.

Perhaps she'd been inspired by a boxful of adventurous

pictures; she liked to go through his things. Or perhaps Tilney had finally gotten to the Latin words. In either event, shyly, then more forthrightly, then with full robust enthusiasm, Rosalyn bent to her new task. She leaned and undid the buttons of his trouser front, opening them, pushing up his shirt. As she bared his chest, his abdomen, she wet her lips. She kissed his ribs, then his belly, eventually covering his navel with her mouth to work her tongue into it. Almost objectively, Graham felt himself becoming aroused. He stared down at her pile of fair curls, brushing against his waist, then felt her cool, smooth hands slide into his trousers around his buttocks. She began to knead the muscles. He closed his eyes. Her tongue traced the swirl of hair down his belly, while her hands worked his trousers down. Worsted wool crumpled to an angle, caught only by his slightly spread-legged stance. His erection hit her under the chin. Graham grabbed hold of a chair back. She didn't even hesitate: He caught his breath, then all but lost his balance as he was literally swallowed up.

Graham held on to the chair, some remote part of himself watching in disbelief. He was being ravished. Rosalyn's yellow head bobbed at an even stroke, her lips and tongue sucking him in. He groaned, called out something under his breath, almost a curse. She stimulated him so persistently, it was faintly unpleasant—while being overpoweringly irresistible. He couldn't have drawn away if he'd tried.

Just where she'd learned this, he didn't know. It certainly hadn't been in her repertoire a week ago. Nonetheless, the lady certainly understood the principle. She rocked him to her slightly, pushed him away in rhythm, digging her fingers into the ridge of his tightened backside—every muscle in his body seemed to want to contract. He clamped hold of the chair back, took hold of her shoulder. Her mouth was drawing on him so hard he could feel the bite of her teeth. He pinched his eyes closed. His head dropped back. A groan came out of him, a sound he hardly recognized. He began to ejaculate.

It went on and on. By the end, he'd looked down, his eyes narrowly open. Rosalyn was on her knees, making a neat catch of things in a handkerchief she just happened to have on hand. Wipe, wipe, pat, pat. He didn't have the impression so much that she'd enjoyed it as she'd been called upon, like a fine surgeon, to perform a delicate feat she knew she did with supreme competence. A moment later, she was removing her clothes.

Graham knew perfectly well what Rosalyn was about, but after the first shock, he became a willing coconspirator in his own seduction. While Rosalyn demonstrated heretofore unknown natural talent, or else enormously more experience than he had ever realized.

It was the dawn of a new dimension to their relationship. He took her naked to the bed and went after her with all the sexual tact of a satyr. Rosalyn was taken aback for a moment here or there, but never for long. If there was something she didn't like, she didn't say. There was nary a complaint.

Afterward, in the sore and satiated moments of premorning, Graham thought perhaps he *had* found nirvana. What on earth could be better than undisputed, undiluted—undeluded—sex?

— Chapter 29 —

. . . the writings of British and American women are now diffused; and the result is a rapidly increasing estimation of the powers of the female mind, and the consequent employment of female talent in every department of mental and moral exertion now, going on to improve the world.

Godey's Lady's Book
"Editor's Table," page 179
Philadelphia, March 1842

That day at the inn, Gerald Schild stayed only slightly more than half an hour. There was little Submit could do for him. She listened politely until he seemed finished, then offered the only wisdom she knew. He took it in silence, his eyes downcast. It was not very palatable to him. She wasn't even certain he was capable of hearing it: If someone is not good for you, if she cares nothing for your feelings, she told him, you should get away from that person.

On Friday, after a week of fevered writing, two more episodes mailed off, Submit packed for Netham again. This time she packed all her notes, all her clothes. She didn't anticipate returning to the inn. She would stay at Netham until she had imbibed enough of Graham to fill out Henry's notes, to bring them into the present. She should have enough by the end of the summer. Then she could afford a nice flat in London until William's suit had run its course.

She caught the afternoon train and enjoyed a strangely wonderful trip. Watching the countryside travel by, Submit felt herself cutting free, clacking along over the rails toward a new life. She could write the serial indefinitely; as long as she did, her security was assured. London waited. And at the very end, like a beacon, shined Motmarche. Wonderful, regal old Motmarche felt closer than ever before. It somehow seemed possible that she would get there again. Everything seemed possible.

Waiting at Netham was a letter addressed to her, set against a candelabra on a table in the entry room.

London, August 15, 1858
Dear Submit,

In reading over Father's will again, a small matter came to my attention I had not noticed before. It seems Father left Graham some sort of box. He asked that you deliver the box to my cousin. I realize that my father listed this item as belonging to Graham, a mere return of borrowed property, but we are after all questioning Father's state of mind at the time of his writing the will. I am most concerned now to find this box which is unaccounted for, not so much as a hint as to its character or contents. I don't doubt it is just some little nothing. I would be shocked if Father left Graham anything of real value. But then, with Father, one could never be sure. . . .

You will understand my concern, I hope, over having any piece of property go astray at this point. Could you please write and enlighten me as to what has become of the item, should you know, of course? I would prefer to go through the faster informal channels to solve the little mystery. I do so hate dragging everything through court.

Yours sincerely,
William Channing-Downes

Submit stared at the writing, more puzzled than alarmed. She couldn't decide how much to worry that

William should be asking after the case. Yet the box felt like a loose string, one of the many of Henry's ambiguous leavings, that could come round to catch her up in an unexpected loop. What, she wondered, would the good queen's court think of a marquess's sanity, a marquess who bequeathed, like surreptitious treasure, a box of pornographic art?

The large disasters, Submit would recall later, do not come announced with either bright trumpets or the dark baying of hounds. The larger disasters of life are usually laid and stored and built of ordinary things, assembled over time by one's own device, so that one feels almost on friendly terms with all the little bits and pieces; the false convictions, the unresolved incongruities. One lives always, Henry used to say, with the components of one's own undoing. Yet seldom had Submit ever seen calamity assemble so quietly, so calmly into so ferocious a mess as it did in the next twenty-four hours.

Disaster for her, she would always think, was announced by the sound of doves in dovecotes and the distant, healthy screams of children playing down by the shore of the lake. Graham's butler escorted Submit as she stepped outside into the back garden. She had already washed up and left her things in a room upstairs. From the window of that room, she had seen there was something unusual going on outside. There were boats on the lake—schooners, sloops, and cutters, along with some sculling boats, even two leisure punts. The third weekend in September, she was told, was the date of the Netham Fall Regatta. She smiled. The May balls at Cambridge were always held in June; the Fourth of June at Eton was usually at the end of May; Cowes Week lasted nine days. English upper-class logic. Of course, a fall regatta would take place several days before fall arrived.

Beyond the back garden and all around the lake were well-dressed ladies and gentlemen, with children and dogs allowed to run through this melee under the direction of uniformed nannies. The butler guided Submit down to the lake with apologies. It was difficult to find her host in such a mass of humanity. There must have been two hundred people, almost half of whom, the butler mentioned in passing, would be spending the night. Others were staying in homes and lodgings in the area. The regatta would go on for two days.

"This spot is fine, Mr. Smathers." A widow was obligated to be more an observer than a participant in such an event. Graham's butler settled her down on a blanket in a terraced part of the garden. Mossy steps and plateaus of blue campanula, forget-me-nots, and veronica made a soft, cushioned seat overlooking the lake's dock and beach. She was set back from the swarm of picnickers, though close enough not to miss anything going on. The butler handed Submit a hamper from the kitchen, then left her there alone, exactly as she wanted to be. Alone, an observer of Netham in frolic, with a hamper full of cold chicken, asparagus, strawberries, and champagne. Beyond, the water glistened. A conflux of boats at one end of the lake rocked at anchor. A band somewhere played the strains of a distant varsovienne. The people—the ladies in hats and dresses as bright as flowers, the men in frock coats and top hats—sparkled as prettily as the water. Submit found herself amazed, in every sense, to be at the edge of this.

Someone by the dock was yelling, "On your mark, get set . . ."

Four eight-oar sculling boats were about to race. Young oarsmen tensed over the oars, a coxswain at the helm. She noticed one boat decked out in colors from Cambridge.

"Go!" Cheers went up.

Her heart went into her throat. As if in a race of his own, Graham Wessit was trotting up the steps and runs of lawn toward her. No frock coat. No top hat. He was in his shirtsleeves and a lavender-striped vest made of satin that shone in the sun. Bouncing and flapping against this was a bevy of glittering watch chains. He came forward, following his own broad shadow, then stood before her, between her and the bright sun. Submit lifted her hand to shade her eyes. He squatted, leaning an arm casually on a knee for balance, then eased up onto the blanket to sit beside her, presumably to change angles and spare her eyes.

He made one of his brilliant smiles, the sort that fanned lines out by his eyes, cut deep indentations into his cheeks. "I had to come over and tell you," he said, "that that is the ugliest dress I have ever seen. Where's your hat?"

"What?" She was so confused by his smiling rudeness, she almost laughed. "Which hat?" She had one on, a small black bonnet that fit to the back of her head.

"The straw one with the ribbons. It's perfect for today."

"It's upstairs."

"Go up and get it."

She laughed outright. "No."

"I'll send someone."

"No." She couldn't help but be amused. "And this is a very nice dress."

"I hate black."

"That's entirely too bad."

In two disdainful fingers, as if it were wet or muddy, he picked up the edge of her dress. "It's keeping you up here. Come down and sit with us."

Submit looked in the direction he vaguely indicated to see who "us" was. She saw nothing but mobs of people.

"When did you get here?" he asked. He leaned back onto a forearm and stretched his legs out, making himself quite at home.

"About forty-five minutes ago."

"You missed a single-man skiff race. I won." He made a shrug that was almost a bow, mock modesty. He beamed self-satisfaction.

"You are a child."

"I should hope so. I would hate to become as stuffy as you." He looked at her again, his eyes circling her face, her hair, her hat. "What you need is a wide straw brim. With—" He paused in a brief, more sober introspection. "With ribbons someone sent you."

Submit felt a curious wave of embarrassment, as if within his flirtatious manner there were something she should take seriously, something her pride would not let her explore.

His sleeves were wet, his trousers spattered. Despite herself, Submit smiled. She found herself glad to see him. She even rather liked the way he looked, or at least she was getting used to it. How could one look away from a long-legged, gold-chained, black-maned centaur, with a vest striped the color of phlox?

She looked out over the lawn, at all the people chatting and eating on the patchwork of picnic linens. There was not a soul, she thought, who could match Graham Wessit for eye appeal. Then she realized she was doing something else; her eye was trying to locate Mrs. Schild.

A round of cheering rose up from the far side of the lake, marking the end of the race. The band, on a pavilion across the water, had taken up the more sedate rhythm of a Prince Imperial. On a platform beside the pavilion, people were dancing in the middle of the afternoon. Graham spoke.

"Are you staying long?" He was watching her.

"Do you mind if I do?"

"Not at all. I left all my drawers and cupboards in my private apartments upstairs unlocked." He rested his chin in his hand. "Come up and have a look."

He reached into her hamper and pulled out the bottle of champagne. He had already had quite a bit, she realized.

Across the groups of seated picnickers, Submit suddenly caught sight of Rosalyn Schild—and the reason Graham was free to sit where he was. Rosalyn Schild was standing near the folly with her husband. Gerald Schild had not stayed away as Submit had advised. Submit glanced at Graham. He set down the wire from the champagne and popped the cork.

"When did Mr. Schild return?" she asked.

"This morning."

"A little awkward," she said, "for all concerned."

He poured and handed her a glass, raising his shoulders slightly, a shrug.

She ought to pursue his disinterest, Submit thought. She ought to push her way into details of Graham's currently entangled affair for the future pages of *Ronmoor*. But instead she found herself shifting forward. She huddled her knees, staring off at Mrs. Schild—who, she noticed, was now staring back.

"In a way, I wish I were more like her," Submit said. "She seems so carefree." Even under the worst of circumstances.

"I keep telling you to go up and get your hat."

She slid him a look that said, *As if this would make me into something else.*

But he wasn't being dense. He was being persistent. He looked down, breaking off a piece of lilac veronica, running a thumb along its furry stem. He played with it, ignoring his full glass of wine. Very seriously, he said, "I really do hate that dress."

"It's Henry. It reminds you of—"

"No, it's you. We never talk about you. We've gone endlessly into my dissatisfactions with Henry, with my life in general. But you give very little of yourself."

"Perhaps because I'm not so dissatisfied."

"And you wear that dress earnestly?"

She looked at him, eye to eye, so there could be no mistake. "Don't doubt it," she said.

He sighed deeply and leaned back, downing the champagne in one swallow. "There's something wrong," he told her. "When I see you here, so delicate and light"—he held up the little flower—"I can't help but think you belong in bright dresses and sunshine, at parties, with people—"

"No, I don't. I belong just as I am. Don't try and make me into you. Or Mrs. Schild." After a moment, Submit tried to soften what she'd said. She explained, "If I knew how, I would make hordes of friends. Have ladies in, gentlemen in, parties, favorites to confide in, a gay time. Like Mrs. Schild." Submit looked at Mrs. Schild across the way. She had turned her back on them. "She is lovely. I admire her so," Submit murmured, only just realizing it was true. She added, "I only wish she would stop leading that poor man along."

But the man beside Submit, apparently feeling poor and put-upon himself, gave a snort. Then someone from below called out.

"Netham! Moffet says we can take *Bloomin' Madness* upriver if you'll sit the tiller."

He got up, brushing off the damp bits of grass and weeds, picking off one tiny crushed flower from his knee. "Would you like to ride upriver on *Madness* for an hour or two?"

He meant the question to have its funny ulterior meaning, she thought. "No." She shook her head. "Thank you."

He lifted off her hat.

Submit grabbed with both hands behind her just in time to feel its ribbons pull through her fingers. She let out an exclamation of complaint.

But it did no good. He ran with the bonnet, trotting down the terraced land onto the beach and out onto the dock with it crumpled in his fist. Perhaps he meant to throw it up and out, into the lake. It would have been quickly out of sight, the straw soaking up water, its veils half submerged like some tenacious seaweed. It seemed unlikely he meant it to do as it did. Just before he stepped onto the deck of a ketch by the dock, he sailed the hat into the air. It caught on the topmast, spinning once precariously before its ribbons caught. The ribbons, blown by the wind, tangled themselves into the rigging of the sail. The hat's veils blew out. The ketch shoved off.

Graham Wessit knew about sailing, like he knew about rowing and swimming and riding, anything that took energy and coordination, it seemed. The others on the boat took his direction. He moved them to one side, ducking under the boom as it swung. The boat jibbed, turned in a graceful arch and tacked out. Then, clear of the other boats, the wind full in its sails, it cut out over the water, flying a flag of widow's veils.

The sun set slowly, not fully down till almost eight. By then, all the boats had pulled to anchor, sails lowered and furled, oars put to bed. Late evening calmed to the clank and knock of riggings and masts, the murmurs of quieter talk. Guests milled about, waiting for something, while gnats gathered in clouds over the lake. At about nine, as if on cue in the dark, everyone settled back down on their picnic cloths. Submit had already risen and walked back as far as the orchard when it started.

A shrill whistle heralded the first burst. The sky exploded in light, a sunburst of fireworks sending out streamers of glitter. Submit's breath caught in delight, as the streamers separated and fell to earth like so many millions of gold coins. This display was followed by another and another. Chrysanthemums of red and green and blue. Bright explosions erupting endlessly, dripping filaments of silver, ending in ear-splitting pops. Then spiraling, dragonlike arrays of light that sped across the lake. The air began to smell of smoke.

Submit drifted back down toward the group, watching from the bottom of the garden, her head tilted up. She followed the next rocket streak backward to earth, wanting to find the magician making this display. She saw Graham, playing with fire. She recognized his silhouette through a cloud of smoke on the dock. He was holding a cigar, puffing on it one moment, holding it down to a fuse the next. Rosalyn Schild and a few others were behind him. Gerald Schild was nowhere in sight.

Mrs. Schild was animated, gesticulating, talking to Graham's back. His attention seemed focused more on the fire and fuses. A spattering catherine wheel started to spin on the dock, then a sparkling green tourbillion ascended in corkscrews.

A skyrocket went up, splitting into six, seven, a dozen loud pops then a thirteenth, fourteenth eruption, with sprays of silver stars. The sky was incredibly lovely. On the dock, over the water, Graham and Rosalyn had become eerie shadows, moving through the smoke. Mrs. Schild was growing more fierce, a pantomime of displeasure. The others hung back. Submit could hear the woman's voice, not her words but her tone, traveling over the water, punctuated by pops and cracks in the sky. Graham seemed to feel the best policy was not to respond at all. He squatted, disappearing. Submit wondered if even Mrs. Schild could see him. A spark sizzled. Then sudden light shooting over their heads revealed another act of the melodramatic argument on the dock. Their two shadows wavered, vivid and flashing on drifting smoke. Graham glanced over his shoulder once and made a sharp gesture, an arc of burning cigar ash. He turned his back.

Rosalyn Schild charged him. He was squatting. Just as another round of crackling light went up, she landed a blow on his back. Calm as you please, he stood through the smoke. She had just begun poking him in the chest, when he picked her up and threw her into the lake. A strange splash echoed flatly in the night.

Graham lit another round of fireworks before he squatted, speaking to or perhaps just contemplating the woman who floundered by the dock. After a moment he rose and pitched his cigar, a tiny rocket of miniature sparks, out into the lake, then called something to someone on the shore as he kicked off his shoes. The last Submit saw of him, he was struggling out of his vest. Another splash echoed as he jumped in. Other shadows danced out into the smoke. More splashes. With squeals of delight, the party took en masse to the lake.

At the dovecotes, Submit looked back again, listening to the birds' evening cooing play over the general free-for-all beyond. As her eyes adjusted, moonlight revealed almost half the people around the lake had gone in, half remained on shore to watch (while two lovers on a picnic blanket nearby, Submit noticed, were doing neither).

She sighed. The cool smell of night blew over her. Goose-flesh ran down her arms. She had never seen, heard, imagined such a horrible, beautiful commotion as that insanity on the lake. As she walked up toward the house, she had to put her arms up over her breasts—the nipples stood on end. She could feel the cold of the water behind her, as if it lapped against her waist, her ribs, her face, as if she were sinking through it.

"What an imagination," she murmured.

Inside, she took herself and her imagination upstairs. Ronmoor, wonderful, awful Ronmoor, had a housemaid to seduce.

— Chapter 30 —

Socrates was suicidal.

Graffiti from the slabs of Stonehenge as translated by

Graham Wessit, the Earl of Netham

He pushed Peg against the desk, bending her backward over it, crushing his mouth to hers. . . .

Submit scratched the sentence out.

Ronmoor danced Peg toward the desk, making a jigging waltz of her ungainly backward stride. She faltered. He caught her around the waist. . . .

Submit put a huge *X* through the entire paragraph.

It felt wrong. Everything felt wrong tonight. He might steal hats and light fireworks and throw women into lakes, but she couldn't make Graham insist or extort. He didn't need to. Why would he want a plain, awkward girl?

Peg willingly gave herself.

That made quite a bit more sense, but seemed ultimately as bad. It was pure deception for an earl to encourage a housemaid's attachment. When he married, after all, he chose the daughter of a duchess. Submit was sure she could make Graham into a scoundrel with this. Yet try as she might, her imagination ran dry—or to the ridiculous.

He kissed her mouth, her cheeks, her eyes and eyelashes, showering her with words of passion, of love.

She threw down her pen and scooted back from the writing table. She wrapped her arms around herself at her bedroom window as she looked out into dark.

While Submit was upstairs, trying to make the fiction and reality of Graham Wessit meet in a way that put him beyond the pale and beyond her yearning, Graham was outside, pursuing a little continuity of his own.

He walked out into the dark, through the garden. He had been among the first to change his clothes. Everyone else was still inside. The house behind him was filled with light and voices, people still shrill from the excitement of an exhausting day, topped off with fireworks, then splashing around in a dark lake. The drier guests could be heard in the music recital room at the end of the north wing. Someone was playing the piano, a waltz. Graham had no desire to be part of any of it. He wondered where Submit had gone. She had been the nicest part of his day.

Rosalyn had been the lowest. The incident on the dock had thrilled everyone—Rosalyn had had her little play. She had asked Gerald for a divorce this afternoon, in the midst of a picnic. Graham hadn't reacted to Rosalyn's announcement with the appropriate joy. Their argument had proceeded from there. Graham was still angry. He would throw her in the lake again. Poor Schild had left— Rosalyn had sent him away, leaving Graham to wonder what he himself was doing in the middle of their marital strife. Several people had hinted at congratulations, as if he were about to begin a little marital strife of his own. He couldn't imagine it. Yet he hated the alternatives as much.

Another affair ended pointlessly was something Graham shuddered to contemplate. He was frightened at the prospect of having failed again. He wanted a mate. Love, after all, was fairly rare and hardly required. (Did he need, he

asked himself, what made Gerald Schild nothing but a sad
and miserable sight?) He was not eager to be alone, not eager to have to start with a new woman all over again. Perhaps Rosalyn was a kind of answer to his plight, with or
without love. As so many people told him, she was perfect.

In the dark, Graham began to think of the serial. Affair
after affair, all snide, all exaggerated, all true. And Margaret.
His upstairs housemaid. Lord, he had forgotten about her.
Which was a shame, because there seemed within Margaret
a clue. Something about himself he had forgotten, lost sight
of, something good. . . .

Margaret, or Peg as everyone else called her, was an upperhouse servant. Graham could never bring himself to call her
Peg. Margaret had a limp, and not everyone called her Peg
in all innocence.

It had been midsummer. He had come home with the
usual exhaustion from a season in London. He hadn't been
at Netham ten minutes when he noticed, on his bedroom
dresser, the smallest crystal vase. At first he wondered where
it had come from, whom it belonged to. Then he remembered it from one of his own cabinets downstairs. It was
part of the clutter on a low shelf behind glass. Never had it
held flowers until now. It looked different with all the color.
The flowers, in order to be small enough to balance the few
inches of vase, were semiweeds. Wild violets, Sweet Alison,
Welsh poppies, others, a bit of green. One would have to
walk a long way to make such a fine collection.

"Who did this?" he asked his man.

"I'll have them removed immediately, sir."

"No. Who did them?"

"The new girl, I expect, sir."

"Her name?"

"Peg, they call her."

"What does she do? Besides flowers?"

"A bit of everything, sir. At a clump. One leg bad, sir."

Peg. It seemed a grotesque joke, a malignant prescience on the part of her parents. One of her legs had simply grown more slowly than the other. Peg rolled along like a one-legged sailor.

The flowers seemed all the more a miracle—a long walk, at a slow, difficult pace, to find flowers for a rescued vase.

The first night home almost always brought good dreams. That night he dreamed of young girls gathering flowers up and down the Hampshire hills, a slight, attractive hesitation in their steps. Skirts blowing in the breeze. Black-faced sheep watching this bucolic scene, chewing grass in their soft pink mouths.

But Peg wasn't what dreams were made of. In the flesh, she was short and rounded, with a definite waist but abundant in flesh. Her fleshiness was part of her appeal, as was, paradoxically, her very uneven gait. There was something feminine about her, of the earth, fertile. The limp gave her an unstable moment. One wanted to protect her somehow, though not for the sake of pity. She was too capable and self-sufficient for that. Perhaps that was it: She worked like an animal, dawn till dusk. She did unaccountable things, like deliver a calf once all alone and have to apologize for it, since the men around her told her what a fool she'd been, what a chance she'd taken: "I called. But no'un 'ud come, sir. An' the mum was gettin' fits at me yellin', so what was I t' do?" The limp put a vulnerable pause in an otherwise strong, progressive stride. When she smiled or when she shied because of sudden self-consciousness from dirt or flour perceived on her otherwise neat clothes or face, one wanted to scoop her up into one's arms, carry her off. Graham was attracted to her long before he admitted it to himself so much as to touch her.

She came from a family that owned its own farm a bit farther south in the district. With six sisters and three broth-

ers, her leaving the family enterprise was not looked on un-
kindly by her parents. They had enough to work the land
and had worried, Graham suspected, that they were saddled
with an unmarriageable cripple. He knew their letters were
infrequent. He knew Peg sent money home regularly.

Any such fears, however, proved unfounded quickly
enough. Peg had a beau in Netham the second month she
was there. Jim owned the farm on the northwest periphery
of Graham's own land. He was a nice catch for her. They had
been having breakfast together ever since he had delivered
the milk one morning himself—his farm was almost exclu-
sively dairy, odd bits for himself, a vegetable garden to put
any in the district to shame. He was one of the more notable
successes of the area. The general picture of Peg's future
should have pleased her.

But, to the point, it seemed flawed. Graham never knew
the specifics of what bothered her. But the more serious
things seemed to get with Jim, the more moody and quiet
her presence got about the house.

The matter shouldn't have disturbed Graham's life more
than passing notice. In September, he should have gone to
London, but he was suddenly taken to bed. Something or
other (the doctor's diagnosis) had his nose running, his
throat itching, and a cough sounding like a death rattle in
his chest. He didn't actually feel that bad, but a week in bed
was a week less spent in the whirlwind of London. It didn't
sound so terrible. So Graham followed the doctor's advice,
and Margaret became more or less his self-appointed
nursemaid.

At first it seemed she had taken on the extra duties for
the benefit of having a polite, captive audience. She brought
him breakfast, changed his sheets, administered some vile
medicine, while she sketched vague outlines of her past and
her future. "I certainly feel a very forchunt girl, marryin' my
Jim," she said many mornings. But there was always some-

thing reluctant and forced in this performance. Then little remarks started leaking into her monologues. "A girl ain't always ready," she said one morning, "to finish off like the world thinks she ought."

Equating marriage to a "finish" was a notion that drew profound sympathy from Graham. "Are you thinking of not marrying him, Margaret?" he asked.

Her eyes came up wide from the bottom of the bed. She'd been tucking a sheet. "Oh, no, sir." She frowned, then said very convincingly, "I'll be marryin' Jim, I'm sure."

Graham sat in a chair near the head of the bed. Margaret came in and changed his sheets every day. ("The sickness sticks to 'em," she explained.) She paused and took her time now, every corner of the bed just so. She was a bit of a tyrant in her perfection, running even the master out of a sickbed for the sake of order.

She didn't speak for a time. She fussed and moved and smoothed the sheet, the blanket, the coverlet, making them as smooth as if an iron had been put to them. She came around and sat on her handiwork, a few feet from Graham. She stared out the window.

"I would like," she said after a moment, "to have done somethin' 'ceptional. Y' know what I mean?" She looked over her shoulder at him, and he suddenly realized that something, however temporarily, had dissolved: She saw herself as his equal.

This staggered him at first. Then it strangely relaxed him. She played servant the same way he played master, with an underlying fear that someone should discover how foolish he found it all. It was not anything they ever spoke of, but the dropped roles happened then and more often later.

"Yes," he answered, "I know what you mean."

She waited another space of time, then she turned more toward him. "Why do you call me 'Margaret,' not 'Peg' like the rest?"

He was brought up short. "Would you prefer the other?"

She thought, though less about the question it seemed than, shyly, if she should continue. "I like real well you call me Margaret. I told Jim he calls me Margaret, too. It's got"—she looked down into her dress—"more dig-inty, y' know?" Suddenly bright, she offered, "The housekeeper, Mrs. Fallows, been teaching me readin'. I learned 'dig-inty.' I like them words." She looked serious for a moment, then suddenly flushed and turned away.

She let her embarrassment fade into silence. She swung her uneven legs against the bedstead, bouncing her calves off the frame for a few light taps of perfect, even rhythm. "I love Jim," she said, as if asked. "Ain't none better." A pause. "I really do love Jim."

She saw to Graham till the end of the week, through his sickness. They had one or two more such short conversations. Graham was left puzzled by them, caught in an impossible abyss between classes. He liked her very much. He was attracted to her. Yet, for these very reasons, he didn't want to encourage any illusions about what the world, himself a part of it, saw as their inevitable relationship.

In a vague sort of way, Graham began to prepare for London. He figured he would get another week out of "convalescence." A few days before his actual departure, Margaret was helping clear out his upstairs sitting room, draping furniture while he was supervising the packing over a newspaper and cream tea.

"London, coo." She shook her head cheerfully.

"Have you ever been to London?" he inquired over the page.

She smiled. "Might someday." A sheet gave a sharp snap, then floated out, suspended, to settle over a sofa as gently as snow.

On impulse, he made a decision—one of the best, though it would be viewed by friends in London as one of the worst, he ever made. "Then come with the others"—the usual staff—"just for a while."

She stared at him.

He smiled. "It's something 'exceptional,' like you said you wanted. You could return in three months when I go to Bath. There would still be plenty of time to make a wedding for you and Jim."

It was another week before the "something exceptional" included sleeping in the master's bed. It was not love in any romantic sense of the word. But he found himself caring about her, and she in her odd way watched out for him. Now and then, she preferred her own company for a night, and said so. Frequently, he came in late and didn't disturb the sleeping body, already in his bed. Once he told her a lady might come home with him, a prediction that proved true—and also proved, for the sheer complications it brought by comparison, to be the last of his philandering among his own class for a long while. Margaret replied that she'd been needing a night to her own again anyway. They had a happy domestic affair. By day, she made the beds; by night, she added to their muss. The strange light and dark roles they played seemed to make her content. And the double life Graham led suited him perfectly. No one understood why he had such a "dull-witted country bumpkin" in his fashionable home, "such a graceless, loping woman." And the secrets of her voluptuous body and sweet temper were enough to arm him through any social mayhem when he was without her.

He really quite missed her when he moved to Bath and she back to Netham. He found a rather fine crystal punch bowl and cups, which he sent as a wedding gift. Then—a stroke of genius—much later he sent the little vase she had rescued from the parlor cabinet. For the punch bowl, he received a sincere and formal letter of thanks, dictated then signed by Margaret with her mark, a perfect *M*. He saw her one more time alone. She was by then a married woman, poised and confident, the wife of a successful farmer come to call on the local lord to thank him personally for such a " 'ceptional gift": the small vase with its Etruscan lines. Simple, but pure and beautiful at heart.

As an odd postscript, the same little vase had recently made its way back into Graham's possession. Jim had given over the lot of Margaret's things to the local church when she'd died (of unknown causes, in her sleep) just the previous year. The vase had been among these articles when the church had had its annual fair. Graham had purchased it for a third its value. He was rather touched to find it was among her "personal things." Her husband Jim did not remember where it had come from.

"Never took much notice of all them little knickknacks she kept. Though I saved one or two real nice things to, you know, sort of remind me. A bear someone give her made out a' real seashells. A real nice toy man what dances when you tap a stick."

People missed things. People didn't notice; people didn't care. People's own misperceptions made black into white, made grey into whatever they wanted it to be. Graham began to think it was all fiction. Life was much less fixed than people imagined it to be. Then the thought of Margaret brought him back. She was a fixed point, someone he felt he had known, though briefly, truly well.

Margaret wasn't just a housemaid. And he wasn't, Graham decided as he came up the terraced land into the apple orchard, just a rake. Not even if all the world pointed at him and said he was so. No one knew him as well as he knew himself. He had been tumbled a little by events. He had brought a lot of those events down upon himself. But he

was essentially lucky and happy and rich—in many more
ways than in just money or status. There might not be a soul
alive who cared or understood, but he knew—at least for a
few moments in late evening on a warm summer night—
and understood himself.

— Chapter 31 —

Everything that deceives may be said to enchant.

PLATO

The Republic

Book III, 413-C

Graham heard an unfamiliar noise. *Chk, chk, chk.* He jumped at the sound, rolled, then hit something. Too warm for a pillow. A hip beneath covers.

"Roz?" he whispered, jostling the firm pile of bedclothes.

"Mmm," came a sleepy acknowledgment.

The mountain of hips and comforters sank. The whole bed moved and creaked. A white arm stretched out from the covers. Then the room was thrown into abrupt darkness, as if heavy curtains had suddenly dropped at the window by the bed. In reality, dark, quick-traveling clouds crossed a three-quarter moon. For flickering instants, the bed was pitch black. Then the light started to break again, a livid ghost-imitation of dawn. Graham looked over Rosalyn's hip.

Outside, silver trees bent. White-tipped grass ruffled in waves. The lake reflected choppy shadows, boats anchored in liquid, rolling moonlight. Everything rocked and swayed, strangely lit by a cloudy-bright moon in a starless sky. Graham stared out the window, listening for a few seconds to the windows in his bedroom vibrate in the gusts of wind. No, this was not the noise that had awakened him.

A complete pass of clouds opened the room up again to a lurid brightness. Under the canopy of the bed, the air felt stagnant. A dampness clung to the tangle of bedding: the sour smell of animals, fornication, territorial rights, as if a cat had sprayed his sheets. An hour or so ago, Graham's skin had become uncomfortably cool. He had pulled these sheets over him. Now, perspiring, his skin was crawling to be free of them. He flung off his covers, then tried to remove Rosalyn's, pulling at them, pushing her.

"I thought you'd left, Roz. Go on. See yourself to your rooms."

"What?" she said groggily.

"Go." He shoved at a shoulder.

"Mm-m," she groaned. "Why?"

"I don't know. I just want to spread out. I can't sleep."

She grumped incoherently, then seemed to doze off again. He was about to shake her when he was distracted by the unidentifiable noise once more. Not a rattling, but a scritch-scratching, shooshing sound. Both gentle and explicitly crisp, like taffeta or organdy would rustle if one grasped a handful and shook it. He raised himself up on his elbows. It took a moment to realize it was a tree outside making the noise, an old oak up against the house at the far window. One of its leafy branches sporadically brushed and screeched on the glass.

He looked over at Rosalyn. Her face was a series of changing shadows, her hair a distinct spread of purple on the greyish sheets and pillows. With a prickly sensation, he realized a prehensile coil of hair was wrapped around his forearm. By rotating his hand, he held a shank of hair in his fist. For some reason, he wanted to give it a hard tug. Or—he wondered what she'd do—find scissors and cut it off.

He rearranged his covers until only a sheet was over him. He looked back at Rosalyn. She had retrieved one of her loose nightshifts. She was tucked into the voluminous folds of one that reminded him of a fully rigged sailing ship. Large-boned Rosalyn strung and tied into wide, flapping pieces of cloth. Furled and vacant in sleep now. His own nightshirt was nowhere to be found. He fidgeted some more, poking through the covers. Pulling himself all the way out of bed, he found his trousers and shirt on the floor.

As he stepped into his pants, he saw Rosalyn curl back into a ball of hips and rump. The leaves again shooshed, a strident voice for the resentment he felt looking at the woman still in his bed, more comfortable there than he had been. He sat down beside Rosalyn, nudging her with an elbow as he fastened the cuffs of his sleeves.

"Rosalyn, wake up. I want you to leave."

"God, Graham," she groaned and stretched. "What time is it?"

"I don't know. Late. No, early. Morning, I suppose." As she settled into stillness again, he shook her shoulder. "Rosalyn, wake up."

"Why, in heaven's name?"

"I want you to get out of here."

"No you don't." She put her face in the pillow. "You're still angry with me for this evening. But I'm better now." The pillow slightly muffled her laugh. "Honestly." She added, "It's just that she's such a tiny crow of a woman."

He was silent a moment. "Come on, it has nothing to do with that. I want you to go."

"Why?" She turned toward him.

"It's my bed. I can ask you to get out of it if I want to."

"They're all your beds in this house. Are you going to assign someone else this one?"

He sighed loudly, air coming from between compressed lips. "In the middle of the night? Don't start this again."

"You're starting it. Leave me alone." She rolled back.

"Rosalyn, I want you to go to your own bed."

In a vehement whisper, she said, "This is my bed, damn

you. And after this afternoon, I'm guarding it. No less than five people told me you went running over to that woman the moment she appeared. And lay with her. Up toward the orchard where no one could see very well—"

"It seems five people managed to see—"

"You visited her at that bloody inn. Everyone knows that. And for a while, after everyone came in, no one could find either one of you. Where were you? Are you rogering that little goat?"

"A minute ago, she was a crow."

"I just remembered the hair under her chin. An undernourished little goat who. . . ." She went on.

Graham smiled faintly at Rosalyn, always carefully observant of other women. He thought of the widow, of the fine golden-white down that ran along her neck, across her cheeks, then blinked in her thick-tufted lashes. He had a sudden curiosity for more golden hair. Was it on her arms? Across her belly? Lower? Would the mound between her legs be—as Rosalyn never meant to suggest, but had—pale fur, like the cream-colored, bony butt of a kid-goat? The golden fleece.

Angrier still, Rosalyn grabbed his arm. "Graham, damn you—"

He gave an exasperated sigh. "For your information, I have never so much as kissed Submit Channing-Downes."

She was silent. He turned back to the buttons on his sleeve. In speaking the name, he had somehow made the widow materialize almost tangibly between them. She hung in the conversationless space, her importance implied in a curious elliptical manner, as with the tiny black asterisks that marked an omission in a novel, indicating the good parts were being left out to keep it clean.

A convention Rosalyn was not about to observe. She was crisply awake, bearing down in a cogent whisper. "You *did* lie with her. I saw—"

He laughed. "I drank some of her champagne. We talked."

"I know about your kind of conversation. I remember our first talk, in a dismal little carriage."

"Different."

"Was it? You suggested we go there to talk, remember?"

"I was drunk."

"I was married."

"You still are," he said. "Besides, I didn't know."

"You didn't care."

"Not caring is the whole point of being drunk, Rosalyn. Come on, go to your own bed. No remonstrations so long after the fact."

"I remember you only cared about one thing in that damned carriage. You didn't speak three words. And all your huffing and panting—"

"Rosalyn. You don't need to be told how pretty you are. And I don't need to be reminded. I've huffed and panted for you regularly since then. But right now I'm thinking of sleep."

"I'm prettier by a gross than that milk-faced, stiff-backed crow."

"For Christ's sake, a crow again. Rosalyn—"

"And she's older than I am, I'm sure of it."

"Stop it. It is pure self-deception to call her old or ugly. But if it will help matters, I don't think, even if I did offer to 'talk' to her, that she would succumb. Least of all on the floor of a carriage."

She made a tight little sound of indignity. "You gave me precious little choice on that carriage floor."

"That seems like a pretty poor place to be making one—" Catching himself, he said, "This is not our best reminiscence. Why dwell on it? I simply want the privacy of my own bed. Get up—"

"And there was no yelling for your mouth. And your hands and body—God, you were hungry and frightening."

Her mood changed. Plausibly, this was one of *her* better reminiscences. A small laugh rolled from her dark pillow.

Graham got up from the bed. "I never had the impression that you were about to call for help."

"Don't be wounded."

"I'm anything but wounded. I don't like it when you get coy."

"I'm just playing with you and your lovely male ego." She *tsk*ed. "So sensitive."

He shook his head silently. "Have you seen my shoes?"

The bed swayed and creaked behind him. "This damn bed," she mumbled. "It makes me seasick."

"A tribute to you, I keep saying. Sprung like a carriage. My shoes, have you seen them?"

"It's not sprung like a damned carriage. It moves everywhere." She sighed. "Come back. I think you are just about irritated enough for me to want to love you." He turned, saw her arms reaching out to him from the bed. "Come take me, Gray. Like you did in the carriage. Throw me off balance on this stupid contraption and play drunk and unruly."

"If you don't like the bed . . ." He lost track. His shoes weren't anywhere on the floor. He tried to pick up what he'd been saying as he got down on his hands and knees. "And I won't take you. In fact, I want to send you back."

To your own bed, is what he'd meant. But as he was feeling under the bedstead, he realized she'd taken it more broadly. The conversation had become chopped off.

He peered up over the bed. The only trace that Rosalyn was alive was the rise and fall of breathing covers. For an instant, these became violet-hued in the drifting light from the window.

Her voice sounded empty and far away. "Well. I asked to be ravished, didn't I?" She paused, then in a tighter voice said, "You really need to work on when to sound sincere and when not to, Gray. Some anger in your voice would have helped immensely just now." She took another breath. "Oh, God." A moment later, she added, "It *is* her, isn't it?"

It was a relative certainty, from the little pauses and wavers, that she was crying. Still barefoot, Graham pulled himself up to sit on the bed. He seemed to have stumbled into an untimely and inappropriate discussion of their relationship. Silently, he vacillated as to which way to go, whether to try to call back his words or launch further into the troubled waters of disentanglement: He felt ankle-deep in mismanagement.

"You're taking me very seriously tonight," he observed.

"Well, you are, aren't you?"

"What? Serious?"

"Finished with me—" There was a weepy catch at the end.

"That's a nice thing to say." A pause. "No. I'm not entirely sure this is anything more than petty bickering. Why are you so sure?"

"I don't know." He could barely hear her. She was speaking, muffled, into the covers. "It's just a sense I have lately. As if I were talking to—sleeping with—a wall. Or a cloud of smoke. Everything I say or do seems to pass right through you. Like tonight on the dock."

"During the fireworks?"

Mimicking his innocent tone, she repeated, "Yes, 'during the fireworks.' When I asked for some answers about your little picnic up in the garden."

"Your questions were stupid."

"You could have ended the stupidity with just a word of denial, some reassurance."

"Why? You were so enjoying going on and on. For God's sake, Rosalyn, what could I say? You weren't rational. Fuming and crying over nothing."

"It wasn't over nothing—"

"It was. You had it in your mind to spin some excitement into an otherwise easy night, a prodigious quarrel meant mainly for an audience. It was premeditated melodrama. I simply refused to play the part assigned."

"Damn it, Graham—"

"And neither will I do so now, so don't raise your voice."

Very quietly, with each phrase punctuated by a little squeak and bounce of the bed, she said, "You stupid. Sodding. Son of a bitch."

Then inexplicably, she deteriorated. He had to wait some minutes to be able to talk over the hiccoughing and sobbing and sniffing.

The crying, the defenselessness of it, scattered his senses and left him feeling unfairly debilitated. "Rosalyn, I'm not prepared for this sort of discussion. We need to talk, but I haven't thought it out—"

"I have."

She moved violently, a cyclonic whirl of bedding. Something hit him. His shoe. He stared, amazed at the sudden appearance of the lost item.

"Where did this come from?"

The other one hit him, thumping on his collarbone.

Bewildered, he asked, "What? Are you sleeping with my shoes?"

"They were here on the chair. I put them in bed with me a moment ago."

"In bed with you?"

"Never mind. You can have them now," she answered in a taut, sharp whisper.

The exchange made no sense to him. He felt exposed suddenly, as the strange night brightness flushed the room again. Rosalyn was hunkered down in the covers, her figure so etiolated by light, shadow, and bedding that the woman had all but disappeared. Then, even that much of her vanished. The clouds moved, and the room, like a run of ink, seeped black.

A draft blew through. In his lap, Graham's shoes were still warm from their cozy stay beneath the covers.

Gratuitously, her disembodied voice offered, "I hate you."

"No you don't."

"No, I don't, but I'd like to." The smallest bit of light from the window showed she was again, for no discernible reason, composed. Something to do with the shoes, he thought. He fiddled with the top flap on one.

"So," she continued, "what will you do once I've made my final scene?"

"What do you mean?"

"I mean, will you go after what's-her-name, the crow?"

"I meant, what do you mean by 'final scene'?"

"Oh, I don't know. Just one last little melodrama." He heard a catch in her voice, a betraying throwback to her crying several moments before. "Won't you cooperate with me this once? I know I can't, for my life, pretend to be calm. Can you see me sweetly waiting for my carriage beside all my trunks? I'd be shaking and weeping if—" More softly, she said, "Please. Let's make one last, great, tumultuous scene—"

"Rosalyn, you can't be asking me to condone such a thing." He was looking for a weapon against this. "Why make things appear what they aren't? Why make things appear at all? When in reality—"

She cut him off with a snort. "Don't lecture me on reality. What most people think is true is reality enough for me."

"Well, I've become slightly less democratic." Graham cleared his throat. "For God's sake, if it only took group agreement to make something true, then you would be no more than a wicked adulteress and I some—some prodigal rake."

Her silence was deafening.

"Rosalyn," he reprimanded-pleaded.

There was a long pause. In the darkness, she seemed to forge—in the sense of shaping something by blows that was too hot to touch—a bravery. She came out with, "I *am* a wicked adulteress."

He breathed out his displeasure and disgust. "Well, I refuse to accept the implication of that for myself."

"You hold yourself in very high esteem."

"I'm the only self I've got." He stood to go. "Do you want some brandy?"

She wouldn't give up. "And the crow? I suppose you like her reality, her definition of you?"

"Not particularly. And you're wrong about her anyway. By several counts."

"Less than you think. You're taken with her unapproachability, Gray. One good go at her would drastically alter your perception."

He laughed and turned toward her, a little shocked. "I can't even imagine—"

"Not much, you can't." Then there was a sudden catch in her voice again. She went from angry to disconsolate in one swoop. Sobs clattered out in a catenation, as if something had broken loose deep in her chest. It was a surprising, complete breakdown. She scooted and sniffled. Graham found himself holding her hesitantly, one arm over her shoulder and around the curve of her back, her head on his chest.

They sat for a while. Then he leaped to a subject that had always been paradoxically safe. Had Gerald gone to London?

No, Kent.

What would she feel good about doing? Would she go to him or their house in London—he had just rented a new place in East Kensington. Or would she prefer to go all the way home to Philadelphia?

She didn't know.

Graham leaned forward, patting her foot, while slowly swelling with humble self-congratulations. It was over.

"No scenes. Neat, clean. I don't see why we can't both keep our dignity," he said.

"No open season on crows?"

He shook his head. "A crow. Jesus. I should tell her."

"Don't bother. I will. I'm thinking of taking her aside, giving her a few pointers."

"She'd think you were certifiable."

A throaty giggle erupted through her sniffles, somewhat affected but not unappealing. The raciness intrinsic to Rosalyn's laugh was one of her best features, Graham thought. "You've tried, haven't you?" she said. "And been flatly refused."

"No to both."

"Then you have some immediate plans. That's why you're in such a hurry to have me out."

"What has come to a blind alley with you is not going to suddenly open up with someone else."

She laughed. "Well, we can eliminate celibacy, I think. So if not that and not an all-out rogering, then—God, you're not thinking of marrying her, are you?"

"You are a lewd and incurable romantic."

"Is there some other way to make this fresh beginning you seem to want?"

He kissed her forehead, then pulled his arm and shoulder, now numb, out from behind her. He got up from the bed. "I think I must have already been making one, when I so perceptively chose to pin you to the floor of a carriage. You are one of the nicest women I have attacked in ages."

"You'll let me know," she said, "if you find out I'm *the* nicest? Or maybe you'd like to do a running comparison? Just to check in now and then and be sure of exactly what you've given up."

He tried to laugh this off. "Too easy."

"But you'll think about it?"

"That's very bad of you to put such temptation in my path. No. I won't leave things as muddy as that."

"I would take muddy, if that were the only choice I had. And I'm doing my best to make things difficult, not easy." In the softest whisper, she said, "Graham, I love you."

He frowned, blinked, didn't know what to say. "I'm going downstairs. Do you want some brandy?"

There was a long pause in the dark. "And I'm getting the divorce. No matter what. Gerald says he'll give it to me, if that's what I want."

"With me as co-respondent?"

"You're the obvious grounds."

Graham's frown deepened. "He can ask me for damages, you realize."

"Don't worry. It will be straightforward, no fuss." She quoted him from a moment ago. " 'Neat, clean.' "

He didn't know if he said the next for Gerald Schild or for himself. Or, as he pretended, for Rosalyn's own sake: "You're throwing away a good life, a good man."

"It's a boring life, when you've lived all the excitements that were planned for you. Your first ball. Beaux. Marriage. Children." She'd left three back in Philadelphia. "What am I supposed to do now? Some sort of endless charity work? Well, charity begins at home, Graham." Her voice had grown fervent. "I want my life to be rich again. I want to be having an affair with the most notorious man in London. Or marry him and be the most glamorous pair on and off the Continent. The countess of Ronmoor."

Graham felt his jaw clench, his face grow warm. In his vanity, he had imagined that, mixed with her fascination for notoriety, title, prestige, Englishness itself, she was still primarily motivated by a love for him. For him personally.

"I will help you gather your things together when I come back up," he said. "I really need a brandy."

The doorknob felt cool in his hand. As he opened the door wide, diffuse light from down the hallway came in. A draft—more welcome coolness—blew across him. Behind him, he heard Rosalyn take a sharp breath, as if struck literally by some force in the corridor, then he heard the telltale jerking of breath. She was crying again. "But I love you," she said.

"You love my shoes," he told her. "You may have them. They're yours."

Of one thing he was certain as he began along the walkway: The farther he got from the room, the more he hated the idea of going back as he'd said he would.

If she really loved him, he pleaded fervently, she would leave while he was downstairs.

As he came around the walkway toward the stairs, the slight illumination became more pronounced. Light was coming from under a door. One step past it, Graham stopped. He paused to verify. It was—by a coincidence that gave a pang over his inability to control such things—the room occupied tonight by Submit Channing-Downes. She was up at this hour. He could knock and ask, *Is everything all right? Why are you up?* Then again, perhaps she had fallen asleep with the light on. There was not a sound.

As he began down the stairs, he felt frustrated and baffled by women, but paradoxically filled with an optimism for Graham Wessit. He was shedding Rosalyn—if not in the kindest manner, at least he'd given a thought to kindness. And he had just now walked past any immediate involvement with the lunatic widow. All of this, it seemed to him, was evidence that he was not who he had been ten years ago, ten months ago, ten minutes ago. It was proof of what he'd been trying to explain to Rosalyn tonight: A man by his own actions determines who he is and what he'll become. He took the last steps on the balls of his feet, feeling himself separate from Rosalyn's, everyone's, anyone's, concepts of him. He was his own creation. And not only was the end product more promising, but the process of rethinking himself sat pleasantly on him. He was *real* walking down the stairs that instant, or his own figment, which at least was better than being someone else's.

Instead of going for the brandy in the library, he took a very private delight in changing his mind. He headed for the kitchen. He intended to find something to eat, something sweet. He remembered a tray of honey tarts at breakfast. He imagined himself all alone, sitting on the cook's worktable, licking honey off his fingers, his bare legs and feet swinging in the night air.

From the dining room, he saw the light. A servant, he thought. Someone was awake in the servants' hall downstairs. From the top of the stairwell, he could see a light was burning in the kitchen. Then, midway down, as he bent to look under the soffit, he nearly lost his balance. He had to put his hand out on the wall.

Submit Channing-Downes was sitting in profile at the kitchen worktable, an oil lamp lighting her face. She was writing, bent over papers and pen. Graham stared. Something about her was very different.

A breeze blew, though not as forcefully as half an hour ago. The wind had been relieved to an extent by a light rain falling outside. Oblivious to the weather, Submit sat with her back to an open window. Wisps of hair blew into her face. She kept pushing and holding her hair back with one hand as she wrote with the other, not seeming to notice the inconvenience of the fine spray of rain that must have been hitting her though the ladder-back of her chair.

Quietly, Graham descended another few stairs. He watched her concentration, the steady crown of her head, her hand capturing hair, the other moving fluently over the desk's surface. She sat back suddenly, paused, and put the tip of the pen in her mouth. Graham backed into the dark, against the far wall, just as Submit tossed her pen down and stood. She turned to face the open window. As she reached to close it, he realized what was so unusual about her tonight: Her nightshift was white—plain, gauzy, narrow. Her arms shimmered, sleeveless; the nightshift was such a plain little thing. Her hair was in a loose braid, coming out in bits, making a nimbus of fine, unruly, wild curls. The effect would have been unpretentiously pious and virginal, a saintly air, except for the dampness on her back. The shift clung across the valley of her spine. He could see the distinct movement and fleshy color of her shoulder blades as she latched the window then flexed her back in a leisurely stretch.

Graham held his breath. If he so much as cleared his throat, they would be in conversation. In damp, sleeveless, open-shirted, barefooted conversation.

She picked something up from the table—a dressing gown. It was dark purple, heavy. It looked like satin, the color of plums. She slipped her arms into it, lifted her braid out. Then she sat at the table again and began to write once more.

He ought to leave, Graham thought, but his feet carried him down another step, then another. Something about her absorbed expression, her bent, diminutive grace, her rapidly moving hand compelled curiosity. The last step creaked.

With a start, she looked up, covering what she was writing as if it were her naked body, as if what she wrote on the page were as private as pink-tipped breasts, white belly, and gold-fleeced pudenda.

"Who's that?" she said, her face white with shock and fright.

Graham came out of the dark. He smiled. "What are you doing?" he asked.

Chapter 32

He came forward, buttoning his shirt. The sight of him coming out of the dark made a lasting impression, as if Ronmoor had stepped out of the shadows, disheveled, half dressed. His skin was dark, his chest and belly plated with muscle, covered with a fine smattering of coffee-black hair. The hair, straight, smooth, soft-looking, ran into a deep channel down the muscles of his chest, converging into a neat, almost delicate line that ran straight toward his groin. Graham. Looking as though he'd come after the housemaid, down into the nether reaches, into her part of the house.

Submit felt her face grow cold, hot, cold again. She couldn't speak. She couldn't cover up fast enough the pages she'd been writing. Her hands simply weren't big enough. She turned the pages over, pulled her dressing gown around her, pressing her palm up her dressing gown to her throat. She shoved herself away from the table, the first movement of flight.

"Don't get up." Graham Wessit held out his hand.

Submit was so guilt-stricken, she couldn't decide if he were genuinely trying to allay her fear or playing with her, commanding her presence. She felt caught, like an animal in the dark immobilized by a sudden bright light. She stared at him from her chair.

"Take it easy." Graham laughed at her. "I'm sorry I frightened you—you really gave me a start. I was so surprised to find you down here." He glanced at the papers on the table. Conversationally, as if they were going to talk about these, he said, "Henry was a great one for letters. He wrote volumes and kept all the letters he received in a trunk." He reached his arms wide, demonstrating size. The top of his shirt gaped open. She got another glimpse of shadowy hair, the recesses and ridges of chest, the topography of an athletic man. He sat on the edge of the table, innocence personified, looking down. He asked, "Whom are you writing to?"

She slid the inverted pages toward her, laying her arms over them. "No one." She picked up the pen, turning it in her fingers. It amazed her to hear her own voice.

"What are you doing down here?" he asked.

God, she didn't even know. When she had come down an hour or so ago, she had thought she did. This was the housemaid's kitchen, the housemaid's world. Only there was no housemaid here. Just the regular underworkings of a house. A pantry. A buttery. A butler's cupboard. A servants' hall. Service bells along one wall. Plain, solid wood furniture. Neat, tidy, clean. And empty. Except now for the master of the house.

Submit's throat had gone tight. She couldn't meet his eyes. She was caught again in a strange corner of his house, this time in the middle of the night.

Graham watched her very nervous reaction to him. He would have liked to put his hands over the ones playing with the pen, but he didn't dare for fear the rattled woman would leap up and run.

He glanced again at the pages she guarded. "Henry's women," he said, "were frequently ugly and always letter-writers, trying to make up for their plainness with beautiful prose."

She glanced up quickly, a half-angry, half-wounded look on her face.

"Not you." Graham laughed, amazed. He was so surprised that she could imagine he found her ugly. "You are the contradiction, I meant. The contradiction to everything I know about Henry."

"Not very much of a contradiction, I'm afraid." Submit shook her head and tapped the pages. "It's poetry."

"Is it?" He reached.

She pulled the papers to her and sat back into the chair, finally meeting his eyes.

He smiled. "Well, you don't write fancy prose, at least."

Almost inaudibly, she agreed, "No."

"You are not, as I said, very typical of Henry's tastes."

Submit tilted her head in frank curiosity. "I can't believe you find me pretty."

"You are stunning."

"Not very many people would agree with you."

"Perhaps not that you are pretty, but anyone would agree that you are stunning."

For a moment, she puzzled over this.

He walked around her to a cupboard. After half a dozen doors were opened and banged shut, he brought forth an empty tray, empty but for one well-done little pie. He made a sound, his tongue against his teeth, in dismay. He set the pie on the worktable and went to the cold larder.

"Milk?" he asked over his shoulder.

"No, thank you." She already knew there was none.

"Good thing," he said as he came to the table. "We're an hour or two away from having any, again." He put the pie on a plate. "Would you like some?"

Submit quickly shook her head. "Oh, no—" She couldn't quite look away from the tart. It was crispy brown, shining with an overflow of syrupy filling.

Despite her answer, he found another plate and cut the sweet in half, depositing her portion in front of her. She stared at the offering. Another picnic. She wasn't sure what to make of it.

After a rather long search, Graham produced a single fork and a kitchen towel—he could find nothing in his own kitchen. "Here." He let her use the fork. They shared the towel as he used his fingers.

He watched her. After several bites, Submit looked up with a smile. "Thank you," she said. "It's delicious."

Graham took her in. Her thanks. Her smile he liked so well, warm and alive. The very appealing display of the many small teeth. He returned the smile wryly. "You're welcome. It's a little talent I have, knowing when 'no' means 'yes.' "

She didn't like this at all, suddenly frowning and returning to the tart. She took a fierce bite, then pushed the rest away. "Well, thank you very much." She yawned and pushed her chair back.

She stood. He stood, his reflexes making him a gentleman in bare feet. "I haven't finished mine." He gestured to his own half-eaten pie, as if some etiquette applied at four in the morning.

Submit was confused, marginally apologetic. She stood until she realized he would too unless she sat down. She plopped into the chair, setting her stack of pages on the table.

He sat down and took them.

She reacted immediately, reaching across the table. Her chair scraped. "No!"

He held the papers away from her.

She came around the table. "Give those to me!"

He stood up, easily holding them above the length of her arm.

As they jockeyed for position, Graham caught a glimpse of the first page, and for one brief, defensive moment, he imagined something impossible. A nasty little serial with him at its center. Not very plausible, he thought. There were a hundred, a thousand, people who knew more about him than she. Still, the way she defended the handful of pages, even risking brushing up against his back, reaching around his chest. She stopped suddenly, both of them aware of her breasts, unbound beneath the dressing gown, jostling against him. For a few seconds, the rise and fall of their breathing made a soft rhythm, bosom to solar plexus. Then Submit retreated, not only physically but into a superior tone.

"This is a rude game, Lord Netham. Those are private."

"Lord Netham," Graham repeated. He wanted to plunder her suddenly, knock her down. He had to fight the urge to do something masculine and dramatic, to set the papers aside and leap the chairs and table she was now putting between them as she wandered away to a corner of the room. Somewhat maliciously, he lowered the papers to eye level.

"Go ahead. If it's going to give you so much bloody pleasure—"

A Rosalynism, whether she'd meant it to be or not. He made a pull of his mouth and began to page through what were actually a collection of handwritten poems. Although the bully's pleasure was dulled now by her indifference.

When he set the collection down, she shoved it across the table at him. "No, read them. Every bloody one." She was adamant.

And had somehow turned the tables. There was a vulnerable bravado to her, a fear associated with the poetry that she threw at him. It was something he could understand. He picked them up again and sat with one hip on the worktable. Again he looked at the sheets of paper.

After a moment, he looked up. "The meter is off." He could have said worse. The first was a perfectly morbid little sonnet.

She was watching him, waiting for something, but not criticism.

"Do you write much poetry?" he asked.

"A little." Her head bent down and admitted, "A lot. I have boxes of it."

There was a long, awkward silence. He set down the pages. "I should have to read more, and my opinion matters very little, but it seems a little constrained." Quickly, he amended, "But interesting, nice."

She took this as criticism. "I know." She sighed. "They're all like that."

He offered the rather hollow consolation, "One does not become a poet overnight."

She shrugged and pushed her hands deep into the pockets of her dressing gown. "I suspect one does not *become* a poet. It is something one simply is or is not."

"The language is learned."

"If it were only language."

"I don't doubt you have the soul for it, if that's what you mean."

Submit gave him a rueful smile for his chivalry. "Henry loathed them."

She began to straighten her papers, gathering them up. She put them together, then dumped them into the garbage bin at the end of the table.

Impulsively, Graham tried to save them. But the bin was wet and faintly septic. The ink was running already with an unpleasant odor by the time he had lifted the first sheet.

"I wasn't suggesting—"

She cut him off abruptly. "It's no loss. I have tons of it. Much of it unwritten yet, I suspect."

He dropped the damp pages back into the bin and looked at her, a strange young woman huddling into a slightly faded dressing gown. She began to pick at the remains of her half of the honey tart.

"You mustn't mind me," he said.

He felt as if he had squashed something in her. Something nice, yet inchoate. It was nothing he could put his finger on so easily as her being a budding poet, which he felt perhaps she was not. But he sensed a struggle in her, not unlike a birth. A desperate effort at trying to draw breath as a separate being. It was an empathetic note, more intimate than anything they had yet shared. A common experience was at last forming. It lay between them. Vulnerable. Strange. Lonely. It involved Henry. Graham had already gone through this peculiar process, separating himself from a brilliant, enigmatic, highly opinionated man.

"Get rid of him," he said out loud. "He was just a vain old man."

She shivered and gave him a startled, peculiar look, as if he had touched too close, as if he had indeed read her mind.

She closed her eyes and bent her head. When she spoke, it was from an unexpected direction. "Did you know there were irregularities in the will?" she asked.

"No, but I suspected. What with all the difficulty."

"At the end, he was obsessed with time. Time and the idea that he was not leaving me enough.

"It was so absurd," she continued. "I had no idea he had taken a new will to Arnold. He wrote it himself, without a solicitor's help. So ridiculous. It was both overgenerous and uncharacteristically careless—even Henry should have known here was not something a layman should do himself. His estate is enormously complex." She paused. "I have tried so hard not to wonder about that." Submit pulled out her chair and settled into it, wrapping her arms about herself, looking down at a table leg. "Arnold says it was because he began to feel rushed, that time was running out, that it was not uncharacteristic of the end of a life. But I don't know." She shook her head. "Sometimes I think Henry put obscure sentences and double meanings into the will on purpose, then sent me to you with those miserable pictures. I worry he didn't intend to make things easy for me, but rather set me up to flounder like this, one of his Socratic lessons of discovery." Submit smiled wanly up at Graham. He was attentive, his face drawn into a look of concern. She made a feeble effort at trying to lighten what she was saying. "A variation of your own suspicions, which you should approve of."

She went on quickly before he could say anything. "I wish I could convey to you— At the end— Henry kept telling me he had to pack several more years into whatever time he had left. Even—" She halted, pressed her lips together. She wanted to tell Graham something, something about Henry, herself, without laying either of them open to quick judgment. She tried to pick up a new thread, a more presentable brightness. She made a slight smile. "Henry rose up in bed one day. 'I'm not finished!' he shouted. 'I'm not ready!' Then he leaned back and said he had made a deathbed discovery. It was not, he said, that he didn't believe in God, as he had professed for some forty years, but that he had simply become furious with Him. He wanted to snub God, give Him the most frigid cold shoulder, 'for having created anything as frustrating and unsatisfying as this.'

"I was his dutiful student, quoting his own lessons at him. 'God,' I said, 'is our own creation, born of fear of the unknown.' But he would not be pried from his new position of self-doubt.

" 'It was not I,' he said, 'who made the earth spin round the sun fifty-seven times before I ever met you. Nor I who now insists that I have had my ride and must get off.'

" 'Don't anthropomorphize,' I said. More from the gospel according to St. Henry. I wanted him to stop it, be himself again.

"But he only stared at me, his old scholarly stare, as if I had answered a conundrum thoughtfully but wrong. I was expected to come up with a better answer.

"When I got up from the bed, he grabbed my arm. His hand was so cold. It shocked me. He could hardly move it from arthritis. But he used this infirmity, like the strength he'd once had. He had a hundred ways to arrest me.

" 'Don't,' he said, 'believe everything I have ever said to you religiously. You must question everything. Even me, which has never been a problem for you, so long as I have been standing next to you in my full and rebarbative flesh. But be careful, Submit, when I am gone. We have loved each other in a peculiarly close and unorthodox manner. Don't build a shrine to that.' "

She couldn't go on for a moment. Then, "He died that night while I slept in a chair by his bed."

Submit glanced at Graham, expecting him to be showing signs of discomfort with all this. Or boredom. He didn't show either. Instead, he watched her directly, waiting, leaving silence for her to go on, if she wished.

She stared down at her hands, playing with the front of her dressing gown. "Until the week before, I had slept in the bed with him. I don't think he ever realized how ignoble my motives were in wanting to sleep there. It was as if I were guarding my life, not his, guarding him from taking everything I valued from me—the way I talked, thought, moved, felt. He had coached and coaxed and badgered me into being the person I wanted to be. Simplistically speaking, I knew that I had always played a kind of terribly grateful Galatea to his Pygmalion." She paused. "Then the awful shock, that week before, the sudden wetness in the sheets. His bladder let loose. I was so frightened. I had heard that in death everything, every muscle relaxed, and that was what I thought. When I touched him, felt him breathing, the relief was so great, I can't describe it. I was crying, kissing him, tears of gratitude, as he groaned and tried to push me away. He could barely talk for his defamed pride. The wet had awakened us both. He was mortified. Such carryings-on. I could have taken care of it quietly myself, but he would not cooperate, would not let me get at the practical management of taking his sheets. He wept like a child, beseeching me to leave him alone. I don't know, I suppose I was afraid he would take his life then and there if I did. We had a terrific row—with me helplessly having the upper hand, no matter how I might have liked to have given that over to him. He did not allow me beside him after that.

"Then that morning a week later. The incredible absence. It was so unmistakably different, I couldn't imagine lying next to—in—his warmth and thinking he was gone. The room was cold. I awoke, stiff, cramped in my chair. There was not a sound. The stillness was so complete.

"Oh, there were birds, the bustle of breakfast and beginnings downstairs. But that was what made it so remarkable. Henry used to speak of death as Nothing, a void: Well, it certainly is so for the living. Henry was simply not there. Like waking to find that in the night, quite naturally, without a trace of blood or pain, one's limbs had become disconnected from one's torso. I sat there for more than an hour, without the first notion of how I should ever be able to move again. The maid found us both. Henry. And me, not having budged from my chair, but knowing with a certainty I can't explain. . . ." She let her voice trail off.

She had nothing more to say.

Graham left the silence undisturbed.

Submit went back to her honey tart, eating it slowly. Graham sat across from her, watching her. The billowy hair—the loose braid hardly contained it. The loose-fitting nightclothes. She didn't seem to mind his staring, but ate, indifferent to anything but the sticky pie. She appeared to relish the sweet now, carefully cleaning a finger with her tongue like a cat. Eventually, he pushed his own half-eaten portion toward her, which, after a moment's hesitation, she took.

The kitchen remained quiet. An animal outside, rummaging in the dark, appeared to have discovered the trash heap from the day's meals. Inside, the honey tart was gone. Submit began to tidy her area on the worktable.

"Cook will get it," Graham said. Then, as if it were part of the same thought, he asked, "What do your friends call you?"

"Submit."

He rolled his eyes.

She laughed shyly. "You don't like it."

"I was hoping for a reprieve." That sounded horrid. "That is, I was hoping for a fond name."

"My father was fond of it." She was smiling, teasing him. He was left on the hook for a moment; then her eyes became direct. "Like my husband, my name was my father's choice. Proving, I suppose, that my father was not very astute in his choices, merely lucky." She smiled. "Still, it has been a protection for me in ways he never dreamed."

"I'm sure." There was an awkward moment while they both knew he was trying to get over the name. "Submit," he added. Then he made a face, a display of distaste and dissatisfaction with his own rendering of it.

She laughed again. "It puts the right sort of people off balance."

He didn't like this and said as much by a look.

She shrugged. "Henry used it from the first moment he knew me. Without a qualm."

"You were a child."

"It wouldn't have mattered. He was comfortable with the concept: What a situation called for he did without hesitation."

"How wise of him." Except his tone didn't much respect such wisdom.

Submit bristled into a little speech. "He was more than wise. Henry had the humanity that you—and your silences and innuendos—always accuse him of not having. He made dreadful mistakes. But those who live by committing themselves often do. Henry loved."

"I have always known that."

Submit didn't believe his sincerity for a moment, then the earnestness in his eyes became so frank, she had to turn away. "I don't mean to sound so presumptuous—"

"You don't. You only sound convinced. As you are entitled to"—only the slightest pause—"Submit." It was coming out more easily now. He released a laugh. "It is a nice name, a nice sound." He almost meant it. He repeated the name, listening to the particular sough and tap of the letters. "Submit." It was formed almost entirely at the front of the mouth—teeth and lips; one hardly needed voice. The sound of a wave breaking on the shore. He was caught repeating the name several times more.

Her eyes fixed on him, a kind of doubt invading her expression, an embarrassment that he would squander such attention on her name. She looked away.

"Some of the best things one has of oneself," she said, "are only flaws one has made to advantage. Don't examine me too closely."

There was a break. She snugged the wrap of her dressing gown about her and went toward the door.

"Submit?"

She stopped. He came up next to her. It was the first he was sure that things had changed between them. She lifted her face toward him, her eyes mildly challenging. He pressed closer, took her chin in his hand. As his mouth came near hers, she pulled away.

"No." Like the day at the inn.

He couldn't keep himself from the same response. "Why?"

"For pity's sake," she said. "Let's not do this again." After a pause, "Good night." She was going to leave.

For an instant, he was nonplussed. He dropped an arm

down to the door frame. His arm caught her against her ribs. He felt her halt, arch her body just enough to take the weight of her breasts from the top of his arm. She looked at him. And it was he who was caught, pinned to a page from the serial romance: *The cad barred her way with the object in mind of forcing himself upon her.* Graham couldn't quite see how to make this different—perhaps it wasn't different. In any event, it was the wrong move; he could see it in her face by the look she gave him.

She leaned back on the door frame, her hands tucked behind her. He made a wry face and dropped his arm. Her confined hands were categorically not a coyness, not a clearance for him to continue, but an explicit message: There would be no physical contact. They stood looking at each other a moment. Then that stupid, insulting, flattered, feminine smile came faintly into the corners of her mouth. She bent her head, trying to hide it once more.

Graham was quietly infuriated by her attitude, the old, revisited, hypocritical pose. "I'll get the lamp," he said.

He burned himself picking the lamp up by the base. There was a clatter of glass and metal as he caught it from falling over, tapping and touching its hot edges back into place with both hands. His hands stung. He muttered obscenities and put his fingers in his mouth. With a failing sense of control, he realized he was on the verge of an old assault. Henry. Her relationship to him. The pictures. The large sum of money this young woman was due to inherit from the old man's estate. William's words, and worse, all these he was about to utter out his own mouth. But when he turned, she was right as he'd left her, standing presumably on her mute concern for his burnt fingers.

"So why are you still here when I've just played it as written: Netham the rake?"

"You're being much harder on yourself than I'm being."

"And why is that?"

"I don't know why you're so hard on yourself."

"No. Why are you being easy on me? I don't usually inspire moral generosity. And I have the impression, in any case, you don't usually give it. 'A hard woman,' I've been told."

"By whom?"

"Not until you've been more specific as to why."

"Why what?"

"Why, if it's not just a maneuver to you"—he was irritated with himself for this schoolboy pressing of the matter—"can't I kiss you?"

Submit frowned quickly. "But it was maneuvering."

"And that's the reason."

"No."

He took an exasperated breath.

"Risk, I suppose. I'm not that brave."

"For a kiss?"

"Don't pretend."

"All right. I want you. All of it. The kissing, the panting, the sweating, the nakedness." He would floor her figuratively, if he couldn't otherwise. "I have wanted to climb on top of you, I think, from the first moment I saw you. How does that strike you for a direct lack of pretense?"

"Not very politely spoken."

Also not precisely as he had wished. She cast her eyes down, and there was unmistakably the traces of the smile again, that peculiarly feminine inconsistency. It grew and became—as large as a walnut—impossible to hide inside her mouth. As she tried to contain it, it came out in little puckers of self-consciousness. She put her hand up to her lips, as if she might catch it. Her head bent again, into her hand. A woman laughing. He found it insulting; he found it infinitely attractive.

"It's not funny," he complained.

"No. I'm sorry." She looked up, an attempt at contrition.

But then her hand came to her mouth again. "I can't help it. It so amazes me that you should—should want me in that way." She forced her hand down, her head up. The smile was openly feminine. "I wish it didn't please me so. Because I just can't. It wouldn't be any good."

"Thank you very much."

"You know how I mean it. For pity's sake, leave us both a way out."

"You've no right to a way out, not gracefully, dressed in your widowhood from your throat to your knuckles, to the limits of public behavior—when, in the dead of night, you laugh up your sleeve—"

"Don't be mean."

"Bluntly candid. Following your example."

"All right. Then we're even. I'm sorry." She was not put down, only vaguely put out, the righteous heroine to this villainous affront. She took the lamp by the handle. "It's my upbringing, I suppose. A tendency to butcher genteel scenes. With the giggles or bluntness." But her apology, her refound role were anything but blunt. He felt cut clean, neatly left at bay.

She had turned and quickly became only a glow in the dining room, a rhythm of light that paralleled the long, vacant table, an echo of diminishing steps. When he rounded the archway into the entrance hall himself, he saw her sidelit profile, her superior bearing ascending the stairs to the upper apartments.

"Submit," he called.

She turned, halfway up. It seemed conceivable now that she minded his possession of the name, his compulsive use of it. She made a brisk, inquiring pause. "Would you like this? If you are staying down, I can see the rest of the way."

She held out the light, offering to keep him at a literal arm's length. For a moment she reigned over the lamp, over the pose, like a worker of spells. Until Graham began up the stairs.

He took the lamp, blew it out in one motion, and set it out of the way on a step. In the dark, she was as still as a held breath. If she had remained so, perhaps he would have been stymied, too. As it was, he responded to a sound and put a hand on the banister, one hand above her, and one below. He had her trapped against the balustrade. The stairs made an easy adjustment for height. They were nearly face to face. He could hear her breathing, the nervous agitation of someone mildly frightened, out of her depth. He closed the distance, and she drew back. With a kind of ludicrous desperation to evade him, she began to arch out over the entrance room.

"It's a long fall," he told her.

For a moment, this seemed a possibility, that she would simply continue to lean until she toppled over the railing. Or, for a split second as she held her position at last, there was the angry little possibility that she would spit in his face.

But in the end, she only made a small complaining sound and said, "Don't."

He kissed her. It wasn't very exciting after all its imagined fever. She was rigid up her back. He could feel a huge resentment in her thighs, her hips, her small pelvis. She must surely be making, he thought, the carved impression of the handrail across her buttocks, so hard did she try to avoid his pressure. After some moments, she called it off, turning her head abruptly.

"You've had your—"

He lifted his fingers to the nape of her neck, put a thumb to her jaw. By this, he contrived to kiss her again. Then he pulled her from the banister, as reluctant as an ocean animal being taken onto land.

It was remarkable how solid she was, not a spirit but a

firm body. And best, like finding the little smile waiting for him, he was in her mouth. The tight lips opened on a warm place, a small area in possession of a tongue as real and shy as a bird's.

Neat, layered teeth. The pleasure of knowing their tightly fitted surfaces, the spot in front where they overlapped. Smooth, new surroundings, these distinctly humid with honey tarts and the stale taste of early morning. Still, it was the taste he wanted. Her hands at last came to rest on him. He could feel her fingers, like lace, at the back of his collar. They exhibited a hesitant curiosity for his hair.

Their kiss became more. Slower, latent, potent. His tongue reached into her mouth, the movement strong, inciting imprudence, involvement in what seemed a crazy whim of his to take this as far as he dare. As the kiss grew wetter, less temperate, Submit found herself following it, turning her face. It seemed almost natural, with such an intimate kiss, that his hand should slide along her back, under her arm, to move into full-palmed possession of a breast.

Natural, and incredibly arousing. Every vein in Submit's body seemed to dilate. Flushes of warmth ran through her, waves of it, from the ends of her toes and fingers to the backs of her eyes to the tips of her puckering breasts. She felt Graham loosening the tie at her waist, undoing her a step further from security. She let him, lifting her head back. He kissed his way up her throat.

Her dressing gown opened completely—he pushed it open with the backs of his hands, its trapped warmth emptying into his arms. Submit shivered, making a muffled sound, as the coolness of the night invaded her clothes. Then his fingers were riding her shift up, inches at a time, until he slid his hands under it to press his palms onto her bare thighs. Her nightgown gathered on the tops of his forearms as he slid his hands up the curve of her hips to her waist all the way up her ribs to the outside curve of breasts to her armpits. Naked. She heard Graham let out a sound, a noise or word, but she couldn't decipher it for the rasp and pace of her own breathing. He bent, opened his mouth over the tip of her breast, tasting, suckling a moment. Then he drew her fully against him into the crook of his legs.

He was caressing her, handling her with his hands, mouth, tongue, body, kissing her deeply while rubbing the wool of his trousers against the rise of her pubis—she could feel a hard erection, a solid reality that flooded images, sensations. Lakes . . . flowing into dark, warm inlets . . . into caverns filled with shadows, slippery places . . . gliding in on bubbles of pleasure . . . huge, leaning, sleek Doric columns . . .

She felt his fingers brushing against her abdomen, undoing the buttons of his trousers.

The weight of his penis dropped onto her belly, firm, shocking. Against her cool skin, he felt heavy and hot. What remained of Submit's composure yielded, explicit, definite, in that moment. She pulled in her breath. She wanted this man so fiercely, it made her legs weak. Graham's arm constricted about her waist. His palm lifted her by the buttocks. It wasn't a gentle caress, but a strong, possessive throe of longing—and the necessity of support. Submit was going to fold, she wanted to lie down with him so badly.

He freed his pants from his hips with the pitch of a fever, reaching over her buttocks, sliding his hands down the backs of her thighs. Opening. Parting. Lifting. And with a sureness that stunned, he was suddenly, swiftly, deeply inside.

"God my God in Heaven."

There were other invocations, vague magnificats. He braced her against the banister, groped once for balance, but his legs were buckling. With an awkward fall for the last inches, they were somehow on the ridges of stairs.

They managed to get sideways, perpendicular on the staircase so she was flat, but they lost entry. He backed off enough to gain position. Dim light, dawn, was coming from below now, reflecting the balusters across her like a cage. One of her hands opened then contracted on the ledge above her. Submit wet her lips, closed her eyes. She was lying on one stair, spread across three. As compliant as a concubine. The delicate shift lay rumpled above her flat belly, her buttocks resting on polished wood, her knees dropped—with Graham over her ragged, panting, backed off enough to cover her with his eyes, those dark, hot, piercingly beautiful eyes.

He stared at her. He had wanted exactly this, Graham realized: Submit's modesty and dignity annihilated. As if he could now reassemble her in some pattern that would be more intelligible to him. He looked at her slender, bare body, her raised shift, glowing white in the dark, her legs, open and inviting. It all seemed so incredibly, wickedly inapposite after the tightly buttoned black dresses. He wanted to hold this image, hold all of it—keep forever the sight, smell, sound, the taste, the feel of the moment—to him. But as he penetrated again, she arched suddenly, severely into him. And there was no holding anything. He aspirated a cry. Anguish. Pleasure. The small extortion of too much too soon. The spasms endured, repeated. Then it was just their echo in throbs.

Submit lay, unable to catch her breath, beyond speech, movement, thought.

Graham lay on top of her, one foot caught between the posts of the railing. By a wrist below and an elbow above, he was holding some of his weight off her. Just barely. It was a perfectly constrained—and tortured—position, but he couldn't immediately move. They were both in the limbo of exhausted breathing, the inanition of expended effort. He found himself looking down the stairs, edge coming on edge in rapid descent. They were steep, minatory from the angle of lying on them. Though dawn had begun to make them familiar, it was perhaps this familiarity that made him feel so strangely frightened, so inept: like a waking drunk who had just taken the length of them at a stumble and roll.

Chapter 33

Graham's first coherent words to her, "Are you all right?" acknowledged an ordeal, a survival. Though Submit felt less the victim of a flight of stairs than some larger disaster. A shipwreck, perhaps. A woman coming alive on some unknown shore. Her hair clung in damp wisps to her face. He pulled a piece from her mouth. She lay on her back, eyes closed, unable to move except to throw one listless arm over her face.

By the faint light and a draft on his backside, Graham began to know how compromised they were. He took in her plundered nightclothes, his own flapped shirt, bare flanks. He could feel the restriction of trousers not properly up or down. This sight, he realized, lay across a utilitarian passage, a stairway that would carry firewood, breakfast, and laundry in something less than half an hour.

Graham began to move awkwardly to his knees. He felt the first plummet of despair, irremedy, as if they had committed an error of unmendable consequence. But after a cursory look around, it occurred to him that there was not a reason—a witness—in the world that they should not get away with this; that, in fact, it was simply a matter of straightening clothes and resuming.

He tried to rouse Submit, but she was slow to recover herself. She slid up enough to sit against the wall, letting one arm go limp along the edge of an upper step. Slowly, she raised her other arm to put it behind her head. She leaned back into the crook of her own elbow. For a moment, they were face to face, calf to thigh, then Submit closed her eyes.

She tried not to see the fact before her. But she could feel him: Graham moving, brushing up against her calf as he pulled his trousers up over his bare backside. She could still feel the wet pulse, the welcoming, elated throes of her own body, wanting only that whatever he'd just done, he should please do it again. Having him there, adjusting himself into the front of his pants, brushing her belly lightly as he lowered her nightgown over her own supreme immodesty, made her want to cry. Her hands were warm. Every muscle in her body was relaxed. She uttered a deep sigh. She should have known better. The smell of burnt sulfur and niters clung to his skin, his hair. No moonlight swim could water it down. She opened her eyes to slits. And, God bless, she wished she hadn't. In the semidark, the angles and planes of his face were cast sharply. Graham was painfully handsome to her eyes. Her hands could still feel the fluid strength of his shoulders. His abdomen, her fingers remembered, moved by segments, individual tendinous divisions so distinct he could have served as an anatomy lesson; *linea transversae, linea semilunaris, linea alba.* . . . Graham was beautiful, as physically perfect as a statue, a god, though he was not Neptune tonight. More like Orcus, having taken Persephone and dragged her into the Underworld. For surely, Submit thought as she revived, she lay on the shore of Hades.

She had just made passionate love on a staircase with a man she had been horribly, sanctimoniously rebuking in print for just this sort of act. Submit groaned—no, she thought, this was no godly act. Just two messy, stupid human beings. She turned away from the actuality, bending her face into her own raised arm.

He murmured soft encouragements. "Someone will find us." "The girl will be up for the laundry." Submit responded with a hushed economy of syllables, none of them words.

He stood up, tucking in his shirt. She stirred, and he offered a hand. She pretended not to see it, moving on her own with the careful independence of someone deprived of a sense, as if she were blind or deaf or both. She put her hand flat, with slow precision, on the stair at her elbow, then raised herself up. Her clothing fell over her bare legs. She took one, two, three premeditated steps back to lean on the wall, then closed her eyes. She turned her cheek to press it against her shoulder. It seemed a milestone that she had made it to her feet.

Graham saw her remote, slightly wounded self-sufficiency and didn't know how to take it. He finished with the buttons of his trousers and stepped close again. When he took her waist, her palms came up instantly, firmly against his chest.

He studied the locked resistance, the averted face, her slow recovery.

"Has there been a rape?" he asked.

Her eyes flew up, surprised, preoccupied, then she looked away again. "No."

She eased herself from him. She wanted distance. She straightened herself, brushing down the length of her nightgown. Each movement was a jerk and tremble.

"What's wrong?"

"Nothing." She paused. "Everything."

"Look at me."

Submit did. And knew what he saw: guilt. She could feel it behind her eyes, hot and threatening to be wet. She looked down at the front of her dressing gown, hunting for the hooks. They seemed like little puzzles, foreign objects. Her fingers had no idea how they worked.

"No one is the wiser," he told her. He reached and did several of the hooks himself. "It is only what you and I make of it now. And I would like to make something more of it than a debacle on the stairs. I want to hold you, make love to you in bed properly—"

She pushed him away as she vehemently shook her head. "That's not possible." She wanted to break the mood. It felt so dishonest. "I must talk to you. In the light. I must talk to your face."

"As possible as the other. Let's talk upstairs." He laughed faintly. "If we can make it up the twenty steps and fifty feet to your room. God——" He let out a deep breath. "All I want to do is make love to you——"

She stopped him with a small, emphatic intake of breath. "No."

He waited for a space of silence, then asked, "You're not serious?"

She didn't answer.

It occurred to Graham that she might be earnestly contemplating this as a single episode. He tried to take her into his arms again, but her limber body found innumerable ways to shift from him. He expelled his frustration, a guttural confoundment. Empty hands. Then he touched her once more, taking the underside of her arm as he stabilized her on the stairs—she was not solidly on her feet—and even this was resented.

"Let me be."

"This is absurd."

"Please. I know how awful——"

"One doesn't take half-satisfaction on the spur of the moment, then toy with the idea of depriving oneself"—he dropped the impersonal pronoun—"of depriving you and me of more leisurely, more natural affection."

She fixed a watery look on him. "I'm not toying." She hung her head. "There are worse things I could do."

"The only thing worse than never would be once—and once poorly."

Her head moved back and forth in repeated denial he had any claim. "You think nothing could make you hate me more——"

"I don't hate you."

She looked up again, tears balanced, unblinking. "Listen to me—"

"As long as you don't talk nonsense."

She glared for an instant, then blinked, and a tear slid down her cheek. Her distress was unfathomable. She bowed her head into her hand, her fingers coming up over her mouth and nose and cheeks. Her shoulders shuddered.

"You have ruined me," she said. "You have put me where I can't win." Then she more or less leaned and slid down the wall, coming to rest in a pile on the steps.

Graham was silent. Her reaction, her every movement since reviving on the staircase, had been so much more extreme than his. It hinted at the edges of melodrama, of something somewhere of which he wanted no part. He didn't understand her difficulties; he couldn't seem to skirt them.

"If it is having been the faithful wife to one man for— what? Twelve years? If I have rushed you—" But what was rushing in on him was that he was somehow worse off than when he'd started—still longing for her, with her hinting at some hidden, insurmountable barrier he would never be able to scale.

She didn't answer. Graham was left standing above her, not knowing what to do with himself. He felt the predawn chill inordinately well. The draft coming up the stairs made him wish they both had on more clothes. He tucked his hands into opposite armpits, huddling in on himself, wondering where all this left him.

Below, in the entrance hall, a dim light was infiltrating the windows and draperies. A bird had set up an unpoetic repetition, a crisp *rirkk* coming from the woods across the orchard. Graham began to feel the disorientation of standing on a staircase. He knew he must move, only he hated to go without knowing Submit's direction.

"Will you pack your bags? The wounded heroine?"

She laughed, a sound as natural and disheartening as the bird outside.

"Submit—" The name again. He wished he could stop using it, or that she would start using his. "There is something desperately wrong here." When she said nothing, he continued. "When dark, quiet conversations lead to a consummation, be it ever so lacking in judgment. . . . And now, the two of us, to go our separate ways . . ." Which didn't adequately express it. "If I were the romantic I am supposed to be, I would know the right words. Or be less afraid of the wrong ones." He paused, for courage. "I would tell you that I can't bear to be without you, that I want to talk to you endlessly into every night. And that I *can't* keep from touching you, and you mustn't stop me; nothing else makes any sense."

Then he knew why he had used all the idiotic ifs and disclaimers, why he was trying to disown the statement before it was even out: It demonstrated their dichotomy. There were things each of them did not want to hear from the other. He did not want teary, apologetic explanations of why she was ruined for having lain with him. And she did not want to hear that he was in love with her.

The silence lay tightly between them, as solid and wedged as a lump in the throat.

Poorly, without conviction, he tried to break in on it from another approach. "It is not," he said, "as if taking a lover were such an enormous or terrible thing."

Then it was she who truly broke the silence, exposing his bald-faced lie: "I have a lover," she whispered.

He couldn't have heard right. And yet he knew instantly—

Everything stopped in him, as if his system had suddenly decided to pump his blood in the opposite direction. His stomach rolled over. He bent his head into his folded arms.

Tate, he thought. "Who?" he asked.

"Not who; what. Yves DuJauc. I *am* Yves DuJauc. I have slept with Ronmoor, day and night, for it seems like ages now. Henry, Graham. It is what Henry left me, without really meaning to. He wrote the early ones. I wrote the latter. He left me a box full of notes." There were five seconds where she wanted him to say something, a guidepost, an indication. When he gave none, she said, "Honestly, Graham, it was not until my first visit to Netham that I was sure the parody was intentional. But by then . . . well, it was what they were buying."

"They?"

"Audience. Pease. The people who honor the draft at the bank."

It hit him so suddenly, so sharply, that he said something equally sharp. "What a shame Henry left me the pornography. It's a small market, but so lucrative."

"That is an obnoxious and unfair—"

"Don't speak to me of fairness—"

"If you will only think for a moment—"

"Or of thinking, goddamn it—"

She tried to defend herself. "If it were simply venality—" She paused. "Have you no understanding?"

He knew she was waiting for a more definite reaction than sarcasm. Fury. Anguish. Forgiveness. Something. But he had nothing to offer. This information—that she and Henry were in collusion, had been betraying him in unison— seemed impossible to absorb.

"I wish I could explain," she continued, "the part I have loved about it. To have something of Henry's that William couldn't touch, a true legacy. It is mine. And it has been a practical necessity. I have supported myself by it." Her voice broke. She looked down. "God, what you have done to me," she said. "By your gentleness. By taking such genuinely innocent pleasure in my company. And then by making those other moments, those less-than-innocent moments also true. By being both: a cad and a gentleman."

"What you have done to yourself," he corrected.

She sounded weary. "Yes. Yes, of course you are right. But part of you is very much Ronmoor—a remarkably handsome man who relies flatly on that, almost as if he were afraid that nothing else about himself would ever measure up to the superlatives of his good looks."

Having summed him up neatly with that, she rose to her feet again.

"So," she said. She left a businesslike pause. He could imagine her differing over figures with Pease. "If I continue, I am a hypocrite. And if I stop, I am destitute. Or—I take it you would offer me an alternative—obliged." She lent the word an extra meaning.

The funny thing was, he would have taken that implied arrangement. Put her in his flat and fucked her silly. With or without the serial's stopping, there would have been satisfaction in that. He looked over his shoulder, at this dickering, word-struck female. "And would"—he looked for a better word, then chose irony instead—"obligation—is that what you'd call it?—be so terrible?"

"Yes. When I have just tasted, for the first time in my life, not being obligated to anyone. I want to be selfish. I *have* to be selfish right now." There was a frustrated pause. "Can't you see? I can't describe to you the sense of power—pure, halfpenny, economic power—I have over myself. The sense of freedom."

"Autonomy is more expensive than you think. And more lonely: I know."

She waited before she gave her pat, sophomoric answer. He hated her for what he saw as willful stupidity: "Well, I don't know," she said.

He didn't dare speak. He didn't dare move for fear he'd shove her down the stairs.

Seconds elapsed before he was finally able to say, "Then you must continue to sell me. To make commerce of my faults."

"You trade on them."

"They're mine."

She was not completely confident. "Perhaps I will find a way—a compromise."

He made a dry laugh. "Already compromise."

"You know what I mean. Temper it."

"No one will like that. Not what they're buying, as I recall."

She took a rebellious breath. "You are so sure I can't shift the attention, that I haven't the skill to create a fiction larger than yours?"

He lowered his head, his voice. "What I am not sure of," he said, "is that I have the skill to create a reality larger than it."

He glanced at her, but she was standing to the side, one step lower than he. All he could see was the top of her head, the dark shoulders of the dressing gown peeking through the hair coming out of her braid. Loose, her hair had no form. Not like Rosalyn's harmonious mass, but a thick multitude of wild, curling, independent hairs, each with a mind of its own. Light shone through and about this mass of hair, like a nimbus. Or a blur.

She had lost her clarity, her sharp resolution as an ideal.

He took the fact in with a kind of vacant acceptance, a refusal to put anything of himself anywhere. They might have stood there any length of time, each of them contemplating her fall from grace.

But on the periphery of his consciousness, he heard his name called from far off.

"Graham?"

He exchanged a look with Submit, but her expression

was only a mirror of his own modest embarrassment. The fog of murmured feelings and private disagreements was lifting.

"Graham?"

Again, the sound cut through the air, soft and crystallizing. It condensed identity, like cold water poured into his warm doldrums. His own name came to him like a familiar stranger.

Names, he thought. It was accurate, in a way, to call Yves DuJauc her lover. The pseudonym sang of Henry. Graham felt he was still competing with Henry, the seduction of his ideology. Independence, intelligence, reason over emotion. All this in the woman he loved. It was astounding. It was depressing.

"Graham."

They were no longer alone. Rosalyn stood at the head of the stairs.

Blearily unkempt, her hair a wild, artfully arranged tangle about her shoulders, she called out from the shelter of her semidarkness. "What's wrong? Are you coming back to bed?"

These mild words. Their strong meaning. They were spoken to Graham, but directed at Submit.

"Rosalyn, don't make a fool—" he began.

"Pardon?" As if she didn't understand. "I've been waiting for you." She was in her nightgown, the front ties undone to the waist. It revealed white flesh, pretty swells of breast, one perfect, round shoulder holding her modesty intact but askew. She looked ravished.

So did Submit. By the look on her face, his stance of moral indignity had been hollowed out, crumbling in the face of this seeming duplicity: Worthy of the convolutions of a DuJauc plot, he looked as guilty as Submit—trying to seduce one woman, while having another waiting in bed,

Graham wondered wearily if he didn't help write these things too much himself.

Submit started up the stairs.

Graham was paralyzed.

Rosalyn was talkative. "Graham, I have been waiting for so long. I had thought you were bringing the brandy. I have such a headache. And my back hurts. Would you please. . . ."

Graham felt an infantile urge to cry coupled with the monstrous urge to murder.

At the top of the stairs, Submit touched Rosalyn's shoulder. Rosalyn turned to her. For a moment, there was sympathy between them. They liked one another. How had he missed that? They seemed to tolerate each other on almost a friendly basis, when he had considered them—what? Rivals? Submit passed, leaving him with just Rosalyn's importunate voice.

"Are you coming?"

"Bugger off, Rosalyn."

"What?"

"You know damned well what's happening, so stop your spiteful acting."

Graham began up the stairs, two at a time.

At the sight of him, angry, on the move, Rosalyn shrieked and ran. It was the perfect, deranged scenario. Exit Ophelia. And an audience indeed began to gather.

As Graham rounded the banister, a door down the corridor opened. "What the blazes. . . ." John Carmichael in his nightcap peered out. Then another door opened, and another.

Graham had to dodge three, four, eight people, as he chased after the fleeing, screaming Rosalyn. He yelled at her. "I'm going to wring your bloody neck—"

At Rosalyn's doorway, however, another actress was in charge. Submit had taken Rosalyn into her care. Rosalyn was crying. Submit was sublime, encompassing, encompassed by her task of comfort. Rosalyn sobbed onto Submit's shoulder, as Submit patted and cooed. Then—it appeared so, at least—once they were sure he had seen them, they both disappeared into Rosalyn's room.

Complicity between the women invaded Graham's imagination. He felt unreasonably set up. Women had a right to competition, resignation, even friendship and compassion. But none of these should run concurrently, he thought.

Behind the closed door, anyone and everyone could hear Rosalyn. She lamented in wretched sobs that were loud and vocal, nothing like Submit's before. It was unabashed hysteria. He stood by the door as ten, eleven, a dozen more people came from their rooms. Graham removed himself to the railing, his back to the mess. He was staring into the entrance room below when he heard a soft click. The door behind him opened. It was Submit.

"Will someone get a doctor? Perhaps some laudanum." She looked past the others, straight at Graham. As if he were to blame for this, too.

He had reversed his stance, leaning, his arms braced on the balustrade. Someone shot off for the doctor, still somehow asleep down the hall. *Doctor, doctor!* Oh, the group fun of these minor excitements. People spoke in eager voices, already weaving their own versions of the event. Through this, Graham held Submit's eyes, preventing her in this odd way from closing the door. For a moment, it was as if the drop to the floor below were still in front of him. He couldn't surmount his fear.

"Submit, I love you." He said the only words that might continue to keep the door open. He said them loud enough for her, for anyone, to hear. "Stop with the damned serial. Marry me. I want out of all this. For God's sake, marry me, Submit."

It was not exactly the traditional offer of rescue, but it at least shut up a few people. The gathering crowd grew quiet, waiting for her answer. Only murmurs and Rosalyn, howling in the background, could be heard.

From around the edge of the door, Submit stared at him. Then without a word more, the door closed.

Chapter 34

Rosalyn asked Submit to stay with her, and so she did for most of the day. Partly, she remained with the poor woman because she had sympathy for her. Rosalyn, in trying to feign a nervous collapse, seemed to have gone too deeply into her role. She drifted in and out of medicated sleep, weeping and grieving and telling Submit more than she wanted to know. If she were honest with herself, however, there was another reason Submit stayed: Her own disrupted state of mind stood minimized by the grand and total breakdown of Rosalyn Schild.

Also, Submit realized, Rosalyn's room was the one place that Graham wouldn't go. Even after Rosalyn finally slept soundly, in early afternoon, Submit didn't leave. She picked at a tray of food brought to her from downstairs. After a time, she gave that up, standing to stretch. She stooped to pick up a crinoline that lay on the floor; she hung it in the wardrobe. For a few minutes more, she made a vague attempt to straighten the room. It was a mess. Bright, gay dresses lay in heaps, like deflated aerial balloons gone to ground. Jewelry lay scattered over the top of a chiffonier— Submit picked up one particularly glittering piece that lay on the floor. Spilled hairpins covered the surface of the vanity like abandoned armor, chain-link mail. The room looked as though Rosalyn Schild had been in a rage of indecision after her dip in the lake, creating a mess no lady's maid could, or perhaps would dare, clean up.

Submit gave up making order of the room. When the kitchen girl came to take the tray away, eyeing Submit with looks of suspicion and interest, Submit knew she could no longer gracefully stay. Not in this room. Not in this house. She had become part of what she was writing about. Those who would enjoy the story of a widow losing her head on a set of stairs would have all the details they wanted. Rosalyn was already murmuring incoherently in her sleep a fairly salacious reconstruction of what circumstances had led her to surmise.

In her own bedroom, Submit opened the trunk she had yet to unpack and got out a fresh dress. On the vanity in her room were a few toiletries, a brush. All she needed to do was pack these away, change her clothes, and ring to order up a ride to the train. Walking over to the vanity, she began undoing the last that remained of the previous night's braid. It was mostly pulled out already. What an untidy mess she'd become. Mechanically, she tore at the braid.

The sun shone through gauzy curtains at the windows. The room was bathed in the light of day. A fresh beginning, Submit thought and sighed. She sat on her bed, staring out.

Marry him, indeed. She did not want Graham Wessit. She wanted her life back. Her neat, organized, highly civilized life. A life of her own that she could control. Surely this was best for her. The most consistent thing about Graham Wessit was his attitude of open experiment. *Can you even imagine,* she asked herself, *plain, quiet, intellectual little you spending a lifetime on the arm of such a havoc-producing man?*

No.

But as she began to pack, tears began to roll down her face. They made Submit's nose run, her chest constrict until she had to lie down. And, once they had her down, the tears really let loose. She cried till there was nothing left in her, until her body was empty of anything but the desire for exhausted, dreamless sleep.

The next morning, Graham came in on Submit as she was having breakfast in the conservatory—a place, in view of the continuing regatta outside, she had thought would be free of people, especially him. He sat, ordering his own toast and tea.

He asked, in the most moderate of tones, for more details of how she could be writing the serial. When had she started? When had she realized it was him? How much of their private talks had she used? How much had come from the notes? He asked, it seemed, not for the information but for confirmation, the way someone wants the details of a fatal accident in order to better convince himself a loved one would never return. Submit answered stoically, surprisingly able to command her emotions. She told him plainly, and he accepted—the same way he accepted that she was packed and ready to leave.

After breakfast, he walked her outside. Submit thought she would get away safely now. He stood with her by her bags at the edge of the drive, waiting for the carriage that would take her to the train.

As Submit watched the carriage pull out distantly from its house, her eyes turned glassy. Her lips, of their own accord, pulled tight. She bit them, feeling her self-willed insentience breaking. She prayed for a moment he wouldn't notice, but then her friend from picnics and boat rides and talks in sunny fields turned her into his arms.

Graham took it upon himself to soothe her, though he felt it was a little unfair that he should be the one to have to comfort her because of him. He stroked her hair, saying nothing. She took this friendship, as after a long binge one gulps a last shot before one must sober up.

"Why is it"—she sounded to Graham unhealthily calm, taking every measure to assure a dry good-bye—"you destroy me?"

"No," he resisted quietly.

"You do." She paused. "I would have done very well without your being part of this summer, the serial, the pictures, everything."

"No."

"But yes." He felt her nod her head, rubbing her forehead on his coat where she leaned against him.

"I didn't set you up with all that," he whispered. "You're blaming the wrong man."

She hit him in the chest with her fist, a small, futile gesture of protest.

"You have taken him from me," she whispered. "I thought no one could do that. I feel as callow and stupid as I was at sixteen."

Again, "No." He stroked her thick, springy hair. "There is no one stronger."

The carriage stopped behind them. He walked her around while the driver loaded her bags into the luggage box in the rear. Graham opened the door and handed her in.

"Will I hear from you?" he asked.

First, she shook her head no. Then abruptly she nodded yes. Then her hand opened out and landed in her skirts. "Oh, I don't know." She looked away, a woman at loose ends.

"I still think you should stay. Less risk of a bad end." He made a wry smile. "They don't buy unhappy endings, you know."

She looked at him, defensive, possessive. "You can't take that, too—"

"I'm in it. The villain. Cum-hero, I hope."

"If you would only understand," she began. "I have loved it, treasured the quick pages I can scratch off in the night." This little speech fortified her somehow. She went on earnestly. "It is something the world has a use for that I can do. I might even be able to do it better in time. And I didn't do it—at least at first—to be mean." She took a breath. "But I want to keep on. To see where it leads. I *have* to. And I can't let you gentle me out of all the good that it does me by dredging up all the bad it may be doing you. You will simply have to accept that."

Graham leaned in and sat, one hip on the carriage floor, one leg dangling out. "All right." He took the hand that had settled into the dress and kissed it, first on the knuckles, then, opening it, on the palm. Her hand constricted, wanting to evade what was seen as a kind of treason. "All that aside, in spite of it . . . no, because of it"—she gave up her hand to him, letting him play with her fingers—"I still think I should take you to bed. Properly. Not for comfort or healing. And certainly not because the serial and the fact that you're writing it don't matter a great deal to me. But because the physical act has come into the middle of all this. Like an obstacle. We can't see around it. We, neither of us, know what is beyond it. You deny we've been on a mad run, heading straight toward it ever since we first met, until it is right before you. One should never hesitate, you know, Submit. That is the mess we now find ourselves in. One should always take a jump head-on. We stand a much better chance on the other side, rather than trying to regain our balance here."

"Graham." She took her hand back with a sigh. "Now you know why I can't stay."

"I don't."

"I couldn't withstand this for long."

"So don't withstand it." When she didn't say anything, he told her, "Take a deep breath and step out of the carriage."

"It's not that easy."

"It is. Just throw your weight forward—"

"Like leaping from the top of a bell tower?"

This caught him. She watched the blood rise to his face as he stood. Tightly, without looking at her, he said, "Fine."

She bowed her head. "I'm sorry."

"No, no. Henry would love this. Tricked, cornered, then punished."

She was startled. "I'm not punishing you."

"All right. Only for God's sake, Submit," he whispered

vehemently, "I don't know what I am supposed to do. I am obscenely jealous of a dead man, for whom I have an almost gushing gratitude: I sometimes think you've been bestowed on me, other times invoked like a curse. I am constantly aware of an intentionality on Henry's part, as if he were standing here laughing. You make me feel manipulated, teased, half-fulfilled, half-promised, baited, and caged. When are you going to let go of him, finally flout him? He meant for this to happen—"

"How ridiculous—"

"As sure as if he had written it into the pages of Pease's book." He was reaching for air now, hissing it out as he quietly spoke. "As sure as he wanted me locked in a pillory, bound on my knees—"

With equal conviction, she said, "It's all your imagination. Like all ghosts in the dark." Submit would tolerate none of it. "Henry wasn't your archenemy, Graham. He was a man, not a devil." She realized in that moment, "Nor was he a god."

Graham watched her wrap herself up in reserve with so much of her old, distancing objectivity, he could have shaken her.

"He intended this," he insisted.

She shrugged. Much more coolly now, she said, "Who knows what a dead man intended?"

When he only answered the question with a snort, she leaned forward slightly. "You can take responsibility for your own life," she told him. "It has nothing to do with Henry. Or me."

"It does. I love you," he said. But the more he insisted, pleaded, the more he began to feel like Gerald Schild. Hopeless. Foolish. An unwarranted cuckold to another man's game.

"I hope you do." Her voice was gentle, direct, the generous sound of a woman who kept her affections safely guarded. "For your own sake, I hope you do. Losing someone is not so bad, I've discovered. The real tragedy would be never to love anyone so much that you didn't mind the loss."

Graham had no word from her the next week. Nor the week following, nor the one after that. Silence loomed, indefinite. His only solace was that the episodes continued to appear in *Porridge*, as regular as clockwork. Ronmoor ran his course and faded out.

Then another book began to appear. Episode One. It began with an epigraph. *Being heretofore drowned in security, You know not how to live, nor how to die. . . .* And Graham watched with astonishment as he himself bent over a billiard table in the opening pages, about to be visited by an insane dead girl.

III

Motmarche

Taffeta phrases, silken terms precise,

Three-piled hyperboles, spruce affectation,

Figures pedantical; these summer-flies

Have blown me full of maggot ostentation.

WILLIAM SHAKESPEARE
Love's Labor's Lost
Act V, Scene ii, 406–413

Chapter 35

Wise men say that there are three sorts of persons who are wholly deprived of judgment—those who are ambitious of preferments in the courts of princes; those who ply poison to show their skill in curing it; and those who entrust their secrets to women.

PILPAY

Fables

Chapter 2, Fable 6, "The Two Travelers"

"William." Submit set her pen down as she rose from the table. "Come in. I'm so glad you could come."

She invited him into a sunny parlor that spilled with gentle light. "Thank you, Mills." She spoke to the short, slightly hunched man beside William. "Would you bring us some tea?" Turning to William, she said, "Come sit over here."

Submit directed William Channing-Downes to a small sofa and chair set into the curve of a large bay window. The view gave onto a lovely little provincial street. It was lined with trees, not streetlights. Beyond the street was a river that skirted the edge of a large, manicured grassy park. Submit considered the view the best part of the upper-story flat she rented in Cambridge off Jesus Green. She had a staff of exactly two, a retired porter whose duties she dignified by the title of butler and a girl from town who doubled as lady's maid and cook.

William looked around as he sat. Submit didn't mind. She gave him time. It was a nice, middle-class flat, perhaps even a trace more genteel than that. Though all William would notice, she didn't doubt, was that it did not speak of much wealth. Nonetheless, she was content here. Content, at least, so long as she kept her musings and recollections off Graham—a yet oddly painful subject that she tried to relegate to her fiction alone, where she might more safely sort him and herself out.

"Serial doing all right by you then?" he asked with a smirk.

"The new one is about to finish and never did bring as much money as the other. But, yes, I'm doing all right." She smiled. "As I understand you are. Congratulations, by the way."

Only the preceding Thursday, William had been granted a royal warrant that gave him the full honors of a younger son. The word "Lord" would appear before his name. The Lord and Lady William Channing-Downes would be announced, would go in to dinner with the younger sons and daughters of the marquesses of England, behind the earls.

He looked out the window. "Yes. Thank you." He said this with no enthusiasm, obviously not overjoyed. It was, of course, not quite what he had wanted. The privilege of younger sons did not pass down to offspring. It was a lifetime, not a hereditary, honor; but then William had no children as yet. He spoke what would be his chief objection: "It comes with no property, no land."

After a due moment, to acknowledge his disappointment, Submit said, "I have something to say that may help with that." His face turned. She had his vague, insouciant attention. She took a deep breath. "Of course, there are no promises with this, but, well, I want to get past our disagreement, William. I want to clean up the stray ends of my life as quickly as possible so I may start anew.

"If we can come to terms," she continued, "here and now, I'm willing to step aside, leave you a clear path to Motmarche."

He rose up straighter in his chair. His eyes narrowed.

"I want the right to take some things from the living quarters," Submit said. "A piece or two of the furniture I like, some things of Henry's. Then we divide up the other assets. I want mine in cash."

"Why?"

Submit blinked. "I'm planning to travel."

"No, why are you offering to help me now?"

She paused. "Let's just say I no longer feel I deserve Motmarche so very much more than you do." She offered a faint smile. "Humility," she said. "I feel a little less right-eous. And the absolute necessity of getting on with my life."

He answered only with a very unhumble shrug, as if to say: "Well, yes. Of course. Finally."

But he was not so cavalier as he pretended. When the tea arrived a moment later, she caught him glancing at her over the tray, taking the offered cup, stirring, sitting back with the cup, stirring some more. He didn't drink, but eyed her with suspicion.

"Motmarche is not yours to give," he ventured.

"Drop the lawsuit contesting the will. Living in it be-comes my dower right. I'll sign a rent agreement, yours for all your natural days for the rent of one pound sterling— that would make it yours, in fact."

His mouth pressed into a bitter, distrustful line. "You're doing this on purpose," he said.

"What on purpose?"

"The ruling came down just this morning. How did you find out so soon?"

"What ruling?"

"The will, along with Henry's posthumous wishes, was overturned this morning. Tate will no doubt get in touch with you today or tomorrow. I took the train right after the hearing; I was there."

Submit felt her blood shift, rush, before the actual fact

had penetrated every corner of her brain. "You're saying that Henry was found to be not of sound mind?"

"*Non compos mentis*, dear old Henry." William spoke with bemusement and a degree of ironic satisfaction. "The crowning blow being the box—what a dirty little box." He looked at her with arch surprise. "The box that my attorneys finally subpoenaed last week. The courts took one look at that, added it to a terribly young wife, an uxorious will, written in obsessive language, well—" He waved his hand. "There was little doubt where Henry's mind was when it came to you—"

Submit stood up. "Oh, William." She wanted to weep, throttle him, throw something, though less for either of their sakes than Henry's. "What have you done?"

William set the untouched tea down beside him as he stretched his arms out along the back of the sofa. "Hoisted myself, I think—if I can believe the sincerity of your offer—on my own petard."

Submit turned toward the window, staring out. He was hoisted indeed, for without the will or a title, William would get nothing at all. She herself would get only her dower share, a third of Henry's unentailed estates, which would not include the seat of a marquessdom.

For Motmarche, without the will providing for her living there, would revert to the crown, to be sold off by pieces. Or given to some distant kin or unrelated stranger for favors rendered—who would then probably run it to ground. It took a certain amount of sacrifice these days to keep such a vast property in good repair and operating in the black.

They sat in silence. When the butler came to get the tea, he gestured to William's untouched cup. "Your Lordship?"

William didn't answer. Submit turned.

The man had to repeat himself. "Your Lordship? Shall I take your cup?"

William looked up blankly, as if the man were talking to someone else.

"The cup, Your Lordship."

The form of address registered. William glanced at Submit, giving her a faint, half-crooked smile. As he handed the cup over, carefully so as not to spill a drop, he spoke with irony, but also with a measure of pleasure, despite himself: "Yes, His Lordship is finished with his cup."

Almost two hundred miles away, Graham remained at Netham with Rosalyn, the wounded, beautiful bird—the albatross who simply wouldn't go away. The doctors had recommended she not be "subjected to a move for a while."

These same doctors had given her weeks of crying and blank staring a new and chic name: neurasthenia. Even in illness, Rosalyn was at the forefront of fashion and trends. They fed her disease on laudanum and "quiet recourse." Something must have worked. By mid-October, she was more herself. She was a bit jumpy and had a tendency to sleep a great deal and to cry now and then for no reason she would share, but she had regained control. She remained at Netham. Graham had his own personal diagnosis of her symptoms—he lived in mortal fear that she was pregnant.

"No contraception is foolproof," he mentioned.

She only glared.

"Could you be, do you suppose?"

Her lips tightened.

Graham was at a loss.

Why was it, he wondered, that a man could make love to a woman and yet, with their clothes on and with his having certainly half-interest in the answer, this question became indelicate?

The matter was waved away with a peeved impatience he prayed was denial.

Life went on. The end of the month found Rosalyn still planted firmly in his house, for the very good reason that by now she had nowhere else to go. Gerald had indeed filed for divorce. Graham had been named co-respondent. He'd been dragooned into the courtroom and up onto the witness dock, where he once more got to go through the routine of incredibly personal questions. *Yes, I have had sexual relations with Mrs. Schild. Oh, tons and tons. We've done it from the rafters, the chandeliers, in the cellar, in the coal bin. We're regular wonders. . . .*

Though not lately. Graham hadn't so much as touched her since the fateful night. He'd even moved from his own rooms when she had wandered in, expecting, no doubt, some sort of a resumption. As far as Graham was concerned, there would never be a resumption. Among other reasons, Submit was gone, and he held this against Rosalyn; her fine timing for a nervous breakdown. The truth was, he wanted Submit and no one else, though she was so far from what seemed his lot as to be off the map of possibility. Graham's life took on the distinct prospect of a monastic existence, his home the prospect of a perfectly safe place for convalescing women.

So there they were, eight weeks and three days after the episode on the stairs, a very civilized and domestic-looking couple in his front drawing room. Rosalyn sat with a book and a cup of tea, strong with milk. He sat with a stack of ledger sheets and coffee with cinnamon—until she got up and with cold fingers unhooked one earpiece of his reading glasses (new since October—and by the drastic improvement they brought, a sure sign he had needed them much sooner). The glasses fell askew across his nose. He frowned at her, a cockeyed countenance, still a youngish man with inappropriate eyeglasses.

"I feel awful," she said.

"So they say." He repositioned the flexible wire and glass and went back to the tally sheets he was reading.

She left perhaps two minutes of silence. "She's a missed boat, you know."

He looked over the top of the eyeglasses.

"If you wanted a woman like that, you had to have made the decision twenty years ago." With a sad kind of contradicting spitefulness, she added, "I could make you happy, Graham. Let's go to London. The opera is opening with *I Puritani*—" Realizing that was hardly an appealing prospect, she spoke very softly, "You don't even know where she is."

This was absolutely true. She hadn't written. She wasn't at the posting house. She wasn't in London—Tate had volunteered that much in his stiff reply to Graham's letter. Graham had gone so far as to write to her family home in Yorkshire. An elder brother had answered curtly that he hadn't seen his sister in two years. Even Pease only heard from her by mail, the manuscripts having differing London postmarks, never being sent from the same post office twice. But all inquiries went unrewarded. Submit Channing-Downes had evaporated off the face of the earth.

Graham let the tally sheets fall onto the table beside him. He sat there, staring at the room over the tops of his glasses—a room he no longer loved, seeing Rosalyn, a woman he never had. She looked reduced through the lenses of the reading spectacles, a small, beautiful, frightened woman. Her lovely face was pale, her bright eyes both accusing and terrified. She couldn't give up wanting the fun of the moment, he thought, yet she seemed guilty and alarmed at all the hurt left in the wake of this philosophy.

He got up. "I'm going to London," he said. From the doorway, he added, "I'm going to get you a house and set up a modest income for you. Once I have things arranged, I'll come get you. Then we are going to part company. I will take care of you, if that is what is required, but I don't want to live with you, Rosalyn. I don't have to sacrifice my life for yours." He looked at her. "You *can't* make me happy. Only I can. Or at least I can pursue happiness a little more aggressively— an American ideal I think I must have learned from your American husband. If I'm going to be miserable, I might as well be miserable with my objective in clear sight. I'm going to find her. Now, if you want to do something else, you better decide right away. I'm leaving within the hour."

Missed boats. Unseen opportunities. Coincidences. For once, Graham caught one of these right. He had a small bag packed, his hat and coat in hand, and was standing in his own front hallway, when—by perhaps three minutes—he was found home. A special messenger from the Home Secretary was ushered in his front door. The man served him with a letter full of seals and ribbons. More legalities, Graham thought, and groaned.

When he slit the page open and read it, however, his hat slid from his hand. "My God." He fell into a chair. He read the letter, then read it again. "My God" was all he could say each time.

It took him half an hour, sitting in a chair in the hallway, to absorb the contents of that letter. Though the more he read it, the more it made sense. When he finally stood, tucking it into his breast pocket, he was filled with wonder. He didn't know what to think—if the letter was manna from heaven or the final blow that would make Submit want to kill him outright.

Graham arrived at Arnold Tate's offices at Inner Temple, thinking simply to hold the barrister against the wall until he explained where she'd gone. The man had to know.

Such force wasn't necessary, however. Tate willingly gave

up the information that could only wither Graham's spirits. Henry's will had been thrown out. Submit's dower was being converted to cash; that was how she wanted it. No land. What was still a fairly remarkable sum had already been transferred into her accounts. It was money which, had the English courts realized, might not have been made so readily available to her, since she was taking it out of the country.

"What?"

"Didn't you know? She is leaving for America."

"When?"

"Why, this week, I believe. Tomorrow or the next day."

"Where is she now?"

"Motmarche, of course. She has gone to pack. The court has recognized the house contains certain possessions of her private union with the marquess."

— *Chapter 36* —

The trees were always the first thing one saw. The road came through hedgerow, then straightened out. Trees sprung up, sweet chestnuts with their spreading crowns and their deep, spiraling fissures of bark. They stood in perfect lines, like sentries, straight, uniform, marking the way to Motmarche.

Nudging his horse, Graham entered the corridor of trees. Very distantly, he could see the gatehouse.

As he walked his horse along, he noticed that chestnuts lay in the roadbed, rolling about, crunching under the hooves of his horse, popping out of their spiny shells. He had never seen this before—the fruit ripening and left on the ground. He had lugged bags of these chestnuts up this road. He and William, with Henry overseeing now and then. The chestnuts were not to be entrusted to servants. For half of every year, they were the treat at eleven o'clock tea. They were the gift at Christmas for all the local scholars and farmers. Graham had forgotten about the chestnuts of Motmarche, nutty and aromatic when roasted. The taste of fall. Sweet, in syrupy jars by winter, available through spring.

At the gatehouse, he had to get down from his horse and let himself in; no one was there. Graham's heart began to thump. The place was deserted. He would be alone here with Submit. The thought began to beat through his brain.

On the other side of the gates, he urged his horse to a trot. As the trees flickered by, between them he glimpsed outer lands. There were woods, grasslands with black-faced sheep grazing, then came the family chapel, distantly nestled, with its twin spires. Behind the chapel was the dairy. Beside this was a poultry house so large it might have been taken for a small stable. The servants' quarters lay clustered together like the cottages of a village. There were orchards— four kinds of apples, an acre of French pears. There was a large, walled kitchen garden, its own small farm, and a distant pasture fenced off neatly for horses with the stable, a kingdom unto itself, beyond. Then, before him in the far distance, the house itself materialized.

Turrets and tiers rose up, like a slice of wedding cake, through the trees. Mullioned windows blinked in the sun. As Graham rode closer, Motmarche unfolded and unfolded and unfolded out of the woods that surrounded it, out of the lane of trees, born like a wunderkind to become an elegant, symmetrical castle on a rise of land. It was laid out in spectacular color, its turrets and domes a bright verdigris-blue against its marble white stones. It grew and grew, until Graham could see even the cressets at the far ends, bracketed into the thick walls. In times gone by, these metal baskets had been stuffed with ropes soaked in rosin or oil or pitch, to burn like beacons in the night. They had guided galloping horsemen across the fields, into the bowels of the Castle of Motmarche. Beneath the structure, the cavernous cellar, full of wine in Graham's youth, had once been a dungeon, a labyrinth pass-through that could swallow up a small army of warriors. Graham had never gone down there without hearing the echoes of hooves pounding in his imagination, at least fifty strong, the sound clamoring against the vaulted stone ceilings and walls.

Motmarche. At night, it could be lit up by its cressets and torches, becoming an incredible vision, its walls turned to sheets of fiery light. By day, as a man rode up to it, its balance and majesty impressed with their absolute authority to lay claim to the word *palace*: perfect, ornamented, bright. It stood before Graham, stone by stone, exactly as it had always been in his memory. The only surprise, as he tied his horse, was a vehicle he recognized down the bend in the drive. He could not quite believe it at first. It looked distinctly like one of Rosalyn's carriages.

Graham frowned, pondering the likelihood of her carriage being part of what he should see in Cambridgeshire—when two days ago he'd left her more than a hundred miles away. She couldn't afford to load her carriage onto the train. Was she careening, hell-bent, even as he had been arranging for a house for her in London? While he was talking to Tate? Had she known where Submit was all along? How much trouble could she cause? Graham hastened up the steps. He didn't care who stood between himself and Submit, he would have his say, plead his case—even though he hadn't quite been able to articulate to himself yet exactly what his case was.

The bell wasn't answered till the fourth pull. The servant who opened the door stepped back in startled surprise.

"Why, Master Graham."

Graham was for a moment equally nonplussed. He knew the man, though he couldn't remember a name.

The interior of the house had the same sort of feel, an astonished, welcoming familiarity not easy to label. The entryway, with its six-foot-thick walls, was wonderfully cool and dry. Niches along the wall held the exact same statuary as had stood in them twenty years before, including the broken "Phaedra in Repose," who had lost a marble finger when he had slung a cricket bat accidentally against it. As he was guided through, every room, every stairway, every hall called to him. He found himself surprised and pleased to find so much unchanged. It made him want to touch, to reexplore the most quotidian of corners. So much familiar association called to him to visit it properly, like an old acquaintance. In the main hall of the keep, at the very center of Motmarche, he stopped and looked around.

"Where are they?" he asked.

"The north terrace, sir."

"I know the way."

"Yes, of course, my lord."

On his own, Graham felt suddenly foolish. It felt odd, impossible, even silly that he had stayed away so long.

He came to the study full of books. Dark and ominous, with its Persian carpets and heavy woods and walls and walls of dark leather books, it was always the room that had felt most like Henry. Walking through it was like walking into the musty dense matter of another's soul. The terrace outside it, however, was the reverse. Crystal panes in the heavy oak doors looked out onto light. An old wych elm, older than time itself, more than three stories tall, sheltered a small patio like a green awning.

The terrace door opened noisily with a new squeak it had acquired. There were unfamiliar chairs of curved wrought iron, beautifully kept. A small table was set with confections and sherry. And beside this sat a young woman, her back partly to him, whom he almost didn't recognize. Small, petite, she wore a dress made of thin blue-striped taffeta, a white quilted underskirt, ribbons, lace, flounce. Her skirts spilled artfully onto the tiles of the patio floor, over the armrest of her chair. Her hair was pulled back into a net, a reticulation of gold threads that held her profuse hair in a neat billow, the style of the day. That was the word: a stylish woman. Tastefully decorated, demure, pristine. Like an idealized picture—young aristocratic woman, her position and accomplishments worn in the ease with which she sat. Gerald Schild was sitting opposite her, his legs comfortably stretched out and crossed: The carriage had transported the husband, not the wife.

On seeing Graham, Schild lifted his eyes. They were wary, withdrawn, revealing a man as hopelessly morose as ever. These eyes were reluctant to let Graham intrude, leaving the impression that if allowed, Schild would go on indefinitely as if Graham were not there at all. The man looked back to Submit.

"It's a domestic arrangement easily worked out," he said. "I shall write her a good reference and let her go. Perhaps you would prefer to hire one here, bring her across. It might make you feel more at home to deal with an Englishwoman."

"It doesn't matter, Gerald—"

Then she knew Graham's presence, even if Schild preferred not to acknowledge it. Submit turned her head.

There was an awful moment of recognition, not of each other, but of an outer context. They each saw themselves in roles never fully appreciated or experienced before: a delayed meeting between Henry's wife and Henry's ward. She was so perfectly composed, so at ease in this house. By some subtle shift, Graham was put in his place, his hat literally in his hand. He stared at its brim.

Submit didn't even flinch. Instead, as gracefully as you please, she rose. "Lord Netham." Her hand invited him to a chair. "Have you come to say good-bye?" She was politely, cheerfully, asking a lie.

Her civility, along with the unyielding self-possession in her face, seemed almost edged with defiance. Lord Netham, indeed. Graham sat. "No," he said. "I have come to ask you not to go."

Her eyes went down to her lovely manicured hands, then slid to Schild, as if asking sufferance. "Our boat leaves at four o'clock tomorrow afternoon," she said. "We shall not go until then."

Our. We. These small words weighed on Graham with the enormous information they conveyed. Blackly, looking from one to the other, he asked, "What *is* this?"

He must have looked as though he needed help, because she came to sit solicitously in the chair next to him, bending forward. "Cousin." She spoke very gently. "Mr. Schild has asked me to marry him. I'm leaving for America."

"How? It can't be true. There hasn't been time—"

"We started seeing each other right after he brought me a coat I had left at his house—"

"The black coat?" Graham asked. The black coat from months ago that he himself had found, then left, in London. His fury compounded.

"Why, yes." She was surprised. "Gerald brought me my coat. We began seeing each other right after that." She couched her face, not offering long explanations. "We are to be married aboard ship, on our way to America." Like a small concession, she added, "Perhaps you will visit one day."

Graham stood abruptly. "Oh, that would be fucking splendid. Schild." He turned on the man. "I want to speak to her alone."

"Not if you're going to speak like that—"

Graham took a step toward him. "Get out of here, you son of a bitch!"

"Now see here—"

"When did you take her the damned coat? Have we been trading women back and forth all summer—"

Schild stood. "I'm not leaving. If you have something decent to say—"

Submit interceded. "Gerald, he'll calm down if you go. And we still need to crate the carriages—there is so much more to do." She added, not rebelliously, but with a frightening, definitive competence, "You can't do anything about this." She could, her tone said.

Schild remained there, full of remonstrance. *For God's sake*, Graham thought to himself, *if I am here, you fool, then Rosalyn must be free. Why don't you go pester her?* The jealous question rose again. How long had the man been seeing Submit? Just who had been taking whose leftovers?

Reluctantly, Schild nodded. He kissed her quickly. On the mouth. He touched her arm. Both were the briefest of contacts, but nonetheless Graham wished fervently they hadn't happened: The man had kissed her before. How many times? He'd touched her before. In what way? How often? Graham turned his back, though not for their privacy but for his. His chest constricted so tightly he couldn't swallow.

As soon as Schild was gone, Graham turned on Submit, more violently than he'd meant to. "You let him kiss you, so easily, just like that?"

"I care for him, and I'm going to marry him." She spoke the words like a recipe or algorithm; her own little bland formula for happiness.

"And me?"

Her look hinted at more resentment for having to come across on this question. "You have always"—she paused, as if debating the wisdom of honesty—"thrilled me."

"You're damn right—"

"Like fireworks." She made a brisk, denigrating click of her tongue, so as he wouldn't misunderstand. "I can't live in the midst of your pyrotechnics, Graham."

"I'm more to you than that."

"Perhaps—"

"For certain. What sort of hysterical mess are you making—"

"I'm not the one behaving hysterically."

"Yes you are." He took a breath. "Yours is the worst sort of hysteria. Cold and controlled. When I asked if you were going to run away, I never dreamed you'd run as far as across an ocean to another continent."

She startled, frowned, then let out a little breath, before she said, "I'm not running. I'm starting anew."

He made a disgusted sound. "With a man who loves someone else—"

"Gerald loves me differently. Without all the unhealthy insanity of obsession and passion—"

"Jesus!" Graham threw up his hands.

He paced to the patio's edge, folding his arms, standing spread-legged; a slightly theatrical stance from having so little practice at rampaging in earnest. "You're running off, away from me. With a wounded man." Quoting Rosalyn without conscience, he said, "Who'll paw you like a bear. He has the temperament of a beaten dog——"

"Not with me, he doesn't. I'm good for hi——"

"The old, the sick, and the wounded, Submit." He looked over his shoulder. "What's wrong with loving a man who might give you a run for your money?"

She didn't answer. And finally she didn't look so damned calm. She had a hand pressed to her blue-striped breast, her fingers over the low neckline. He stared, then wet his lips. Perhaps the neckline wasn't so low, actually, for anyone else. But to see Submit's naked collarbone, her pale, freckled chest . . .

"Gerald is more than you're giving him credit for." She looked down, aware of his look. At the ground, she made an impatient face. "And with him, I feel balanced, safe. He's asked me to marry him. We have a commitment to each other."

"He broke his previous commitment."

"It was broken for him. Before the divorce."

"Or perhaps hasn't been broken at all, in that respect—despite a divorce."

"I will make what I can with what I am given."

"I can hardly believe this."

"Graham, you don't realize that Gerald—"

He interrupted. "No, I think I am the only one who thinks about Gerald, these days. In fact, I think about him quite a lot." After a pause, he said, "And it is the saddest thing I can imagine: to exchange one indifferent wife for another."

Submit let out a breath. "That's not your—"

"Do you like him?" Without waiting for an answer, he asked, "Do you even admire him a bit? Poor Gerald. He doesn't upset you—or thrill you, does he? He inspires only your sweet, comfortable indifference." He waited, then added harshly, "I think that is the most deadly reaction any human being can provoke."

She stared at him for a long moment. It was possible her lip trembled, but then she drew in a deep breath, before saying curtly, "I am content with the evenness of the course I have set for myself. Now if you'll excuse me." She indicated the door, turning briskly toward it.

He followed her.

At the door, he reached in front of her for the knob. He didn't touch her or even intend to. Yet the second she saw his arm, she turned—an abrupt churn of skirts that matched a ragged breath she drew in—and said, "I will scream, I promise." He saw her breasts heave once, twice.

It took him a few seconds to understand. He withdrew his arm, the same arm that had held her hostage against a staircase banister. "I was only opening the door for you."

There was an odd moment where, he could have sworn, a flash of disappointment crossed her face. Then it was quickly washed over by relief; she relaxed. Her skin flushed pink as she stared at him. She wet her lips, then pressed them together and swallowed. Her eyes dropped. She and Graham stood there, so near that their clothes touched, that his hat lost its brim in her skirts. He felt a vein in his neck begin to beat, the blood in his arms come alive. His groin stirred.

He stood frowning, baffled for several long seconds before it dawned on him. "You like this, don't you?" he murmured. "I'll bet you haven't had a good snapping fight in two months." He narrowed his eyes. "And you know how I feel. That I—" Emotion, yearning roiled up in him so powerfully, he realized he was going to say something sexual, something dirty.

He took a measured breath, inhaling slowly; exhaling. He did this twice. And still the words, the thoughts buzzed.

He wanted to penetrate this woman everywhere, with his penis and fingers and tongue, lick her naked body, without considering reservations or restraints. He wanted to express with all that was proper and all that was profane that he loved her beyond limits, beyond rationality.

He watched her close her eyes.

"Will you please go?" she said. Her voice was almost inaudible. "You're absolutely right. It's pure sickness that I should want—revel in—your upheaval." She turned her back on him, turning toward the wall like a child putting herself in the corner. "Go," she whispered. "Please just go."

Graham wondered what had become of all the pretty speeches he'd intended. "Submit—"

Vehemently, she said, "I am going with him. In one day's time. Why did you have to come? Go away. Just go."

He looked at her a moment longer, then, beaten, empty, frustrated, he turned and pushed his way through the door.

He might have finished there, kept up his brisk exit from room to room all the way out the front door—but for the sudden, reconstituting sight of Gerald Schild. He was sitting in the study behind Henry's desk.

Fury rose up instantly in Graham, like black bats taking flight from his chest. He bellowed, "Are you still here!" He half lunged over the desk. Schild sprawled backward, out of the chair. "Haven't you grasped that Rosalyn is waiting for you?" he shouted. "She is a thorough wreck. She is alone at Netham without the first idea what to do with herself. Waiting for something, for someone, for you!"

"Sh-she's not—"

"She is, if you'll make it so. You're packed, with two tickets for America. Go get her, for God's sake, and take her home."

The man's eyes lifted, helpless, full of apology and contrition. They spoke to a presence just beyond Graham's shoulder. "If—if she's really bad off—"

Graham heard Submit behind him utter the briefest of sighs. "Go on, Gerald. Check on her, at least. If it will make you feel better."

"Y-yes, I—I'll just see if she's all right—"

It was an ancient house, where every sound echoed off its hard floors, its stone walls, through the cool air and into its high domes. Gerald Schild's steps faded off audibly. *Click, click, click,* a turn into the next room, *click, click, click,* toward Netham and the beautiful, floundering—needy— Rosalyn Schild. The sound tapped a kind of certainty into Graham's brain: Whether Submit liked it or not, he had probably just disposed of Schild, as surely as if he'd shoved the man into the Atlantic himself, to sail out only on the small raft of wishful hope.

What Graham didn't know how to do now was dispose of his own emotion. He stood there, choking, his blood pumping, wanting this woman to understand something for which there seemed to be no words. That he loved her, loved her, loved her, loved her. That he would love her always, passionately, indecently beyond reason, and under any circumstance.

Submit stood by Henry's desk in stunned, silent disbelief while the far-too-handsome earl of Netham tapped his hat against the leg of his trousers.

"You have just done a mean and horrible thing," she told him. "Rosalyn doesn't love him."

Graham glanced at her, his dark eyes quick and intense. "So why do you have to save him?"

"I don't. I love him."

"No you don't. You love me."

Submit sniffed at that. "What an arrogant—"

"Arrogant but truthful. How many men have you screwed in a stairway?"

She blinked, once more having to leap to meanings. When he didn't take time to think, the man before her had an expansively coarse vocabulary. "None but you," she said with an uncomfortable laugh. "You're the only one who has ever wanted me to so badly."

"I doubt it."

Submit pulled her mouth into a tight line. It was a narrow look meant to halt this heart-pounding conversation where it was. She went to turn away.

"Damn it." He took her arm. "Any number of men would screw you in a second—"

"What a lovely thought. So beautifully expressed—"

"Listen to me! So would Schild—the poor man *likes* women who don't love him. But I'm the only one *you* want to touch you. You let me, damn it, because you are absolutely beside yourself with liking me—loving me—"

"Lusting after you—"

"Same thing."

"It's not!"

He laughed. "Yes it is. Trust me, I'm an expert on lusting. I love soft saddles and mean horses and bright, booming fireworks that end in a rain of sparkling ash. I would love to roll around on the floor with all of these, touching them with the most sensitive parts of my body. But the truth is, none of them are really as good for fucking as the woman I love. And you're it. I want to screw you till neither of us can stand straight, and the funny thing is, just my saying this I'll bet is making your knees weak and your head dizzy. And you're going to call it something else. Damn, mean, stupid woman—you won't let go of the fun of torturing me with this long enough to let it come." His voice broke. "God, come—" He let go of her. At least literally. He turned around from her, shaking, struggling for air.

Submit was transfixed.

And so flabbergasted, she couldn't move, couldn't think, couldn't speak. She had never heard such an insane, impassioned declaration. It offended her. It pleased her horribly.

It made her chest warm; it left her in hot confusion, without breath.

Then, as if her silence itself were censure, he said, "Right. I'm going." Graham pushed his way in front of her. She glimpsed the back of his coat, an arm, as he closed the study door behind himself, leaving her alone.

Submit heard his footfalls soften when they got to the carpet of the library, then fade down the gallery toward the entry room. A minute later, she heard the front door's familiar creak, then its quiet closure. As soft as the lid of a coffin coming down.

Submit's heart pounded for three, four, five long seconds. Then she picked up her skirts and threw open the study door.

"Graham!" she screamed.

She tore through the rooms, one after the other. Her shoes slid, her hands grabbed for balance at door frames. China in cabinets shimmied and clinked. Her legs wouldn't move fast enough. Her feet beat on the floor, her urgency jolting up her legs. She turned the corner, ran halfway down the long carpet of the entryway—and stopped cold.

He was standing there, his back leaning against the front door, his arms folded, his expression pensive, waiting. There was only a modest hint of triumph in his face.

Submit's face flushed. Anger. Outrage. Commotion rose up inside her. "Damn you!" she shrieked. "Damn you!" She clenched her fists, felt herself, let herself, shake with wrath. "You son of a bitch!"

He smiled that easy, creased, ridiculously handsome smile. "What a lovely thought," he said. "So beautifully expressed."

She could hardly believe it—chastised with her own words, on top of being duped by such an old, predictable trick. "You fraud!" she screamed. "You—you actor! You trickster!" None of these were really good enough. "You game-playing son of a bitch!"

Pure, blind fury swirled. In the midst of it, a funny feeling took hold. It started at her solar plexus, moved like a tickle. Her hands flushed suddenly warm, wet. It felt like something was releasing inside. And as it did, she found she couldn't quite fight back the smile that threatened to break through.

While the idiot man, maddeningly calm, took out his watch—he was wearing about eight of them—from a bright floral vest. "Go ahead," he said. "I'll give you ten seconds' head start."

"What?" She narrowed her eyes. Her breath wouldn't come right.

He said slowly, "Ten." Then, "Nine." He stopped a moment, tilted his head. "You know, Submit, you're smart as a whip and—William is right—pretty damn smug about it. But what you are a true novice at is pure, unadulterated fun." He glanced at his watch. "Eight."

"What?" she said again. She could barely get the word out.

"Seven."

Submit blinked, tried to slow her thudding heart with pressure, but it only beat like thunder against the heel of her hand.

"Six," he said. "What do you want, Submit? If you really want to fight it out, you'll stand a lot better chance if you take a running start. Five."

"Graham, don't be absurd." She swallowed a slightly giddy laugh.

"If I were you, I'd head for privacy. Because where I catch you, lady, is where it happens."

"Graham!"

"You'd better run."

She did.

It helped that he had to cover the length of the entryway. It helped that the staircase was close at hand. But by the first landing, he had one of her feet. She shrieked, "Behave yourself! Be civilized—"

She lost her shoe as they both went down. Hoops billowed. She couldn't even see but rather felt him grab her foot by the instep and arch. He ran his hand up her calf, to the back of her knee. His solid grasp made her dizzy, insanely furious. She kicked, fought, yet heard herself laughing. "This is"—she panted—"so stupid—"

It was. It was positively silly, though the fact didn't keep her from bashing him across the shoulder, then pulling a small jardiniere over on him. He made a sound, *oof*, as she scrambled through dirt and dried-out dieffenbachia, free of him again. Around the turn on the next landing, she pulled out every chair in the window bay, putting obstacles between them. He came anyway, cursing, laughing, shoving, vaulting them, not a man to be slowed down by dignity.

Behind her, up the next flight of stairs, she heard his clamoring footfalls. She felt a pull of her skirt, a hand over her arm, and he collided into her. He grabbed, tried to keep them both from falling, while Submit wrenched away—too hard. They went down. She went flying, sliding three feet on taffeta along the polished wood floors of the main bedroom wing lobby. She was stunned for a moment, as she lay on the floor sprawled, then she felt his fingers snake round an ankle. He pulled. On a shush of accommodating fabric, she slipped helplessly along the floor till she lay on her back beside him. He threw his leg over her.

"Don't." Submit tried to draw air into her lungs. Panting, she complained, "You didn't even give me ten seconds."

"Such a stickler."

He moved up to his knees, then lay his full weight on top of her, collapsing crinolines, gathers, ruffles, making a wobbly quiver of steel hoops as he made a valley for himself between silk-covered mountains.

Submit lay there, trying to catch her breath. She could feel their hearts, their bellies beating together. She could see Graham's dark face coming. He licked her lower lip briefly, wiping with his thumb the wet spot he'd left. She stared up, dumbfounded for a second as he massaged her lip. When he kissed her, he held her cheek, stroking her lip with his thumb even as he put his tongue deep in her mouth. She made a funny sound of befuddlement, resistance. She turned her face. "You—" Submit exhaled. "Not—not here— You can't—" His head followed hers around.

"Give in," he murmured. "You think too much, Submit. Stop thinking. Just feel."

He kissed her again, while adjusting his hips, till the outline of a firm erection fit flush against the rise of her mons. The instant satisfaction was indisputable, as if their bodies were the final pieces to a puzzle linking up at last. His hips moved with a gentle, rotating pressure that matched the action of his tongue. Submit groaned. What remained of her struggles became subdued, then shifted. Her arms went up. She clutched his neck. His hand molded up her ribs to cup her breast, his thumb rubbing its tip till the nipple pulled together into a hard, shriveled bit. The game rolled over on itself. Her stomach lifted, as if taking a bump too fast in a carriage going full pelt. She closed her eyes, and he kissed her with deeper, greedier, wallowing kisses, as she raised her knees and opened her legs to him—

"Madam." A voice rose from two floors below. "Is everything all right?"

They froze like guilty children, the heat between them trapped like a secret. Their breaths hissed.

"Madam?" It was the butler. His voice two flights below moved to the foot of the stairs.

"It's all right," Graham called. Which made him and Submit have to stifle laughter.

She chimed in, "Yes, I'm fine. Everything is fine."

"Come on," Graham whispered. He lifted her up and took her by the hand.

"My bedroom—" she began.

He threw her a strangely intimate look. "Yes. I know where your bedroom is in this house."

Graham pulled her up against him as he kicked the door closed, then backed her up against it. He kissed her insistently, but through her half-closed eyes over Graham's shoulder she caught a glimpse of Henry's wardrobe. It stood behind him, eight feet tall and six feet wide, a dark mass of almost black mahogany.

"Graham—" She turned her face to the side. His mouth followed. She turned the other direction. He found her neck. She flexed, bringing her shoulder to her cheek in an effort to make him stop. She whispered, "I think we should go some other place—"

He took hold of her jaw and backed off three inches, a distance from which he stared her directly in the face. "Yes, it's Henry's room," he told her. "And, no, I won't go anywhere else. It's Henry's house, Submit. It means nothing. It's walls and furniture. Now will you stop worrying whether everything is perfect? It's perfect enough."

"It's not that—"

He put two fingers over her mouth. "It is. You're frightened and you don't like to lose control, so your mind starts inventing excuses. Submit, listen to me. There are probably good reasons why we shouldn't be together. But the overriding fact is I love you, and you love me—you *need* me. I can keep your life from becoming hopelessly earthbound. And I need you, as sure as leaps in the air need gravity." He took a breath. "In the future, there will be times when I count on your guidance, times that call for a cool, rational head. There will be other times, though, when I expect you to trust me. We'll do things my way because I'm better at letting fly than you are." Very firmly, he said, "Now not another word, do you understand? I'm going to push you over the edge." He laughed. "Without mercy or compunction. I'm going to make love to you in ways that, if you stop long enough to think about it, will make you cringe. So turn your little mind off. It'll only get you in trouble."

If she could have found words to answer such a lecture, she didn't get a chance to. He kissed her open mouth and began to pull her toward the bed. With a foot and a knee, he knew how to manipulate the structure of her dress. He had no trouble getting under and into it, or unfastening crinolines and corsets and corset covers. Submit took his expertise in, as she fought her own odd moments of conditioned resistance. The adeptness with her clothes, she discovered, was not the sort of competence that made a man less attractive. As each hook gave, as his hands slipped closer and closer to the skin of her midriff, her breasts, her buttocks, the mild alarm of each invasion piqued a warm, expanding delight. A yearning deep in her belly began to squirm and become active. She caught a glimpse of Henry's four-poster, then felt Graham's hands, several fingers heavily encumbered with rings, move into the little recesses of open clothes. He touched her bare back, and every other awareness went blank.

His fingers ran up the hollow of her spine until her shoulder blades drew together involuntarily. The movement thrust her breasts out. She wet her lips as his hand took a breast. He lifted the small weight in his palm, then took her nipple between his thumb and the side of his hand, pinching and tugging in a movement vaguely akin to strong suckling. He bent his head.

"Gracious Lord," she whispered. She would never recover from this, she thought, the feel of Graham's mouth on her breast combined with the odd, particular pattern of Graham's touch, the feel of heavy gold warmed by smooth, inquisitive fingers grazing her belly and buttocks. She wanted to collapse from the joy of it. Then she felt his fingers go between her legs. She felt the delicate movement of his turning a ring with his thumb, and he used the edges of the facets against her.

"God in Heaven," she murmured. Her muscles contracted.

At the bed, he tried to lay her down gently, but she wanted suddenly nothing that left her nearly so passive. She refused to lie back but remained on her knees, pulling his face down to her. Her whole body strained toward him as she began kissing him and touching him. She was filled with wonder at the power in her: the power of letting herself want him, reach for him, be surrounded by him.

Graham twisted his head to take the kiss deeper. As he stood by the bed, he lifted her slightly to be hip to hip, searching, then finding that incomparable fit, male to female. They kissed with deep, thirsty ardor, arms, mouths, bodies. Submit couldn't believe he wanted her like this, that she could make him shake and shudder and pant for breath, that he couldn't control his response to her.

She let her hands roam his vest, a vest covered in a raised profusion of silk-embroidered flowers. She dipped her hands inside it. He was so tactile. His watch chains swung and tickled against her elbows as she ran her hands up the starchy pleats of his shirt, then inside his coat and over his shoulders. She pushed his coat off, with him helping and clinging at the mouth, sucking, slathering the dryness of lips and tongue and teeth with the longest, wettest of kisses.

She tried to pull him down on her, but instead his hands dug into her buttocks. He peeled off the last of her drawers. Like a madman, he was throwing off his own clothing. Watches scattered. Submit tried to help. She pulled at his vest and stripped his trouser braces down over his shoulders.

The bed sagged as they fell onto it. Submit closed her eyes, arched her back, and slid her hands under the shirt they had only managed to get partially unbuttoned. His chest was heaven. Warm, furred, fluid with muscle. His belly was paradise. She ran her hands down him, tracing the fine, smooth hair down the furrow of his abdomen to where it spread out and became coarse, a regular jungle. He groaned. He felt thick and resilient as she wrapped her hands around him. Hot, tumid, marvelous. Submit shivered, feeling sensations so strong they constricted her muscles till she coiled around him. She clasped him with her legs, shocked, entranced by the force of what was happening to her.

"Slow down." He laughed, then spoke in a hoarse whisper. "Not so fast," he said. "I want to savor this a little."

She didn't want to savor anything. Submit turned her head from side to side, fidgeting, twisting in denial.

He laughed again and pinned her back. She was like a spring that had to be stretched out. He laced his fingers into hers and forced her hands out by her shoulders, trapped her legs under his. He loomed over her, his face watching her. "Oh, God," he breathed, "I love you like this. I never thought I'd see it." He rocked and lifted his hips, nudging her between her open legs till awareness itself seemed to run into inky blotches.

"Graham," she murmured, "I'm going to pass out—"

"Shh." He laughed. "That's not what it's called." He bit her lips, her cheeks, her eyes. For a few more seconds, he left her hanging there, pinned out on the bed, near demented.

"Graham—" She felt herself straining, trying not to give way to something that was about to roll over her. It felt like holding back a boulder on the incline of a mountain.

"Give in to it," he whispered. "Let it take you."

Anticipation, a second ahead of reality, made the warmth start to flood. Blood rushed down her veins into her fingers and toes, to the center, the apex of her body. Slick, swollen, she began to convulse at the one and same moment she felt him enter her. And the world bent, refracted, then disappeared entirely into the central moment of Graham parting her, pushing her flesh aside . . .

into wanting, having, loving him . . . into a spill of sensation that held nothing back. . . .

Graham awoke before Submit to find himself lying quite peacefully in a place he'd only been partially aware of last night. What at dusk had seemed to him more Submit's room was, by morning light, the bedroom of Henry Channing-Downes. The room was not precisely the same as he remembered it. Yet there was a sameness to its colors and furniture and draperies, all permutations of past ones. There was almost no evidence that Submit had lived here at all. Her possessions were packed away in the boxes in the corridor, Graham presumed.

Graham looked over at Submit. She lay beside him, naked, one knee up, the other dropped, any pretense to decorum wiped out by exhaustion. She was soundly asleep, her thick hair all over the pillows. His eyes lingered on her. She was covered in fine hair, silver-gold, velvety. Beneath him, an hour ago, he had wiped sweat from her temple into her thick, curling hairline. Let down, her hair dominated the tiny bones of her face. If he wove a palm next to the scalp, it was warm, as humid as breath. If he combed his fingers through the heaped mass of hair, it became as cool and impersonal as a heavy armload of soft yarn. Looking at her pleased Graham not only sexually but aesthetically as well—and gave him also a surprising, sneaking contentment. She lay there, ravished and decimated in Henry's private bower.

He hadn't meant to lie to her last night, when he'd said it meant nothing that this was Henry's room. It was just that daylight always brought different perceptions. Graham couldn't help but love the images of the night before superimposed now on the fact that what they had done they had done on Henry's linen sheets, in the alcove of Henry's bed-drapes and canopies and bedposts. Whether for ego or a kind of exorcism, the sight of her there—so thoroughly loved—brought a solid satisfaction.

Graham kissed Submit lightly and got up.

Twenty years, he discovered, had seen Henry's dressing room converted into a huge bathroom with a large porcelain tub and no faucets—there was a dumbwaiter, presumably in place of plumbing. Graham sent this down. To his surprise, it came back up a few minutes later bearing a bucket of hot water. Meanwhile, he opened heavy, musty draperies to let in some light. Over a basin, set in the middle of dark wallpaper (green and brown pheasants taking flight), he discovered Henry's razor and brushes and soap, undisturbed. It occurred to Graham, by the way these were set out, that Henry had shaved his own face. Graham frowned, wondering when the change had come about. He could remember, growing up, a barber arriving every morning at eight. Like Graham, Henry appeared to have given the practice up, each man opting for the simplicity of serving himself. With the water, Graham began to shave in front of a large round mirror.

Graham paused, Henry's razor in his hand, Henry's soap all over his face. It suddenly struck him what it meant to be raised by Henry: that, for all his protests, his basis was Henry. He liked the same foods, the same music, the same plays—though Henry had never liked these quite so much as to want to leap onto the stage and be part of them. Graham knew he ran his house like Henry, kept his finances in the same sort of columns. He paid his servants on the same schedule, saw his tailor with the same regularity, though he bought considerably different items. They read the same books, though siding with different authors. And then there was the enigma of their strong attraction to the same woman. Wonderful, mysterious Submit. Like her vocabulary, he supposed, little syllables of Henry's life had worked their way into him until they were indistinguishable—inextirpable—from himself.

He caught himself staring at the face in the mirror. In that moment, it was the twisted, serious mouth of a man trying to shave his jawbone without taking off his ear. Though even relaxed, it was not the face of a happy man.

Henry had not been happy, Graham knew, at least not when Graham had known him best. Then later with Submit, Graham suspected, Henry wore his happiness like a torment, afraid of losing it—to a younger man, to the frustration of a diminishing life span. To a sense of having found happiness too late or of not deserving it. To the worry of stealing his happiness from Submit's storehouse. To the guilt over making a realist out of a romantic young girl.

Graham wanted to make Submit a romantic again. And he would like to be happy. All his life, it had been perhaps simply this: Not wanting to be different from Henry so much as wanting all he had in common with Henry to total a different sum—a happy existence.

He went into the bedroom, toweling off his face, and found Submit still asleep. Still utterly naked. He went over, thinking to cover her, then didn't. Instead, he lay down beside her. He would wake her, he thought, and make love to her again. But neither he nor Submit had slept much last night. He had no sooner brought her into the crook of his body than he drifted off.

It was hours later when Submit opened her eyes. She opened them slowly, to the sight of a moss green canopy overhead, to the weight of a man's leg over her, the sound of a man's even breathing. For a moment, her sleepy mind fell backward through time. When she turned, she expected to see Henry. But she saw instead a dark, naked man of superior proportion. The sight was unsettling.

Against the tangle of sheets, Graham's brown shoulders seemed out of place. His leg thrown so casually over hers looked foreign, as if she were a spy nested down cozily now with the enemy who'd conquered the camp. A sense of alarm grew. She looked around a room that was quintessentially Motmarche. It was made up of stone walls covered in tapestries, marble floors covered in carpets; Henry's taste first, only to become hers. Her eyes traveled over dark, heavy furniture, some of it as old as the name Motmarche itself. As she lay there trying to account for the previous night, she could bring back only wisps of the remembered euphoria—which promptly evaporated into a cloud of angst. The only clue to her feelings now seemed to be a sense of loss and guilt. Her unease was vague but more than an excuse, no matter how Graham might lecture; it was as solid as Henry's wardrobe standing in the corner. Submit lay back and stared up into the shadows. She could not avoid thinking, *What in the world have I done?*

She jumped when a voice beside her spoke.

"After such a wonderful honeymoon," Graham said, "perhaps we should consider getting married."

Submit groaned.

"Let's not announce banns or anything else. Let's go straight to London, get a special license, and have a magistrate do it."

She threw her arm over her face.

"No-o—" He pulled on her arm, trying to roll her to him.

When she wouldn't cooperate, he touched her hair and murmured, "What's wrong?"

She made a sweep of her raised arm. "Oh, Graham. This was all a huge mistake. Really—" She started to get up from the bed, but he wouldn't lift his leg.

"Good heavens." He laughed. "This is no mistake." He drew her snugly into him, her buttocks against his unaroused genitals. He felt so fragile and unprotected, so human. She let him put his arms around her.

"Look," she said. She made a feeble gesture to indicate where they lay. "It's Henry's bed."

"Mm, yes. I noticed that."

"It's awful. I have just made love—all night, in ways I am horrified even to consider—"

"It was *wonderful*," he contradicted and nudged her neck.

"Stop it. To a man who drove Henry positively wild. And I have done it in Henry's very own bed." Her lips began to quiver. Lord, she was going to cry. The prospect was humiliating.

Graham's tone grew more serious. He spoke gently in her ear. "Submit," he said, "don't pretend you can know Henry. Henry might, wherever he is now, be jumping for joy. Two people he loved very much are both terribly happy with each other." The idea cheered her a little, though not so much as it seemed to cheer Graham. He continued enthusiastically. "Whether he wanted to or not, Henry left you to me. And I want you. I want you to marry me."

She twisted partway around to look at him. He was smiling, relaxed, oddly wise, though it was hard to credit such a thing to a man so handsome. It occurred to her that Henry might not have exactly "left" her to him, but that Henry had left a myriad of ambiguities behind that simply couldn't be worked out. One thing wasn't the least bit ambiguous, however. With or without Henry's imprimatur, *she* approved of Graham Wessit. Indisputably. Very much.

"Say it," he told her.

"Say what?"

He only rolled his eyes, while lower against her hip what had seemed vulnerable and human a moment ago was nudging its way into a distinctly more manly presence. "You haven't said it. Tell me you love me." His expression took on a wicked glint. "Tell me you love me wildly, beyond control, that you simply can't fight it any longer." He said the last on the breath of a knowing laugh, no doubt at his own excessive demands—and perhaps at the excesses of his seemingly insatiable body.

Submit blinked, pressed her mouth. "I, ah—" She frowned. "I, um—" Why did he need her to say it? When she loved him and he knew it? He'd already said as much himself. "Oh, Graham," she *tsk*ed and gave up. "I can't right now. Don't be so insecure."

He rolled her shoulder and then her buttocks till he turned her to him. "I'm not being insecure. I'm torturing you. You can't say it. You can't let your feelings out, let them show. But I want you to."

She pressed her eyes closed again. Of course, she could let her feelings show. She took a breath, then muttered, "I, um, love you."

"Wildly," he corrected.

She opened her mouth—to protest—then a laugh escaped instead. "Um—" She felt her own smile pulling up at the corners of her mouth. "W-wildly." There. She'd done it.

"Beyond control. You simply can't fight it. Say it."

She thumped him once in the chest.

"I'm not letting you go till you tell me. Tell me what you feel."

This made another laugh erupt from her. Oh, she could say what she felt between them fairly accurately: a long, ever harder erection. She wiggled her eyebrows and smiled seductively, to say as much.

He smiled, but shook his head: not good enough.

"Oh, all right, I love you," she said quickly. It came out with ease, all but startling her, in fact. "Wildly. Beyond limit, beyond control or the first bit of common sense, quite beyond reason." What a surprise. It felt so wonderful to say it, she said it again. "I love you wildly." The truth, as she heard her own voice utter it, seemed to sing up into the canopy and spread out into the silence of the room. *She loved him.*

Wildly. It was true! Her heart sought his as passionately and relentlessly as her body reached for him as her mate. She couldn't resist adding, "So there, you arrogant, insane man. You have completely undone me. Are you satisfied?"

"Yes." He hugged her to him. "Enormously." He added in a murmur against her ear, "And, yes, I am quite proud of myself, since you asked." After a moment, "So are you going to be my wife?"

"Yes! Oh, yes. I want to marry you." She leaned back enough to find his mouth, then kissed him quickly, liking this new prerogative. "I want to marry you and leave Motmarche for good. It's never been the best thing for me perhaps—I think I have loved its old stones too much—"

"Oh, dear." Graham interrupted, pushing her back. "You'd better read something first then, if you're marrying me to leave it."

Over the edge of the bed, he found his coat, rummaging through its pockets. "Here." He handed her a paper with an embossed seal.

Submit unfolded it and read:

We have the honor of informing you, Your Lordship, that, upon the death of Henry Channing-Downes, the eleventh Marquess of Motmarche, and as the only son of Lucille Wessit née Lucille Channing-Downes, the only other grandchild to Archibald Channing-Downes, the ninth Marquess of Mot-marche, the tenth Marquess being already in demise and his only child, the eleventh Marquess, having no legitimate issue, you are the immediate and full heir to the title, privileges, and properties associated with the English Marquessate, the lands, castle, and moneys entailed in the name of Motmarche, your-self being its twelfth Marquess.

She looked up at him in disbelief. "How can this be?"

He shrugged. "It seems the title has come through my

mother, which I would never have dreamed. So far as I know, Motmarche has always gone through a male line. But then, I'm not familiar with the title too far back. And certain titles do pass down through the men and women of the family alike—we do, after all, have a woman on the throne."

Submit looked at the letter, with its signature of the Home Secretary. "You," she said in utter wonder. "You inherit Motmarche?"

He shrugged. "Henry must have known. Though I don't know how far back. Even as he took me for his ward, perhaps. Even," he teased her, "as he tried desperately to conceive a son." He was amused, not upset. "Surely"—he cocked a wry eyebrow—"as he sent his wife to straighten me out."

"That's not what he did."

"As I said, who knows? In any event, you are currently in bed, naked, with the marquess of Motmarche."

Submit was dismayed. "Oh, dear." She smiled slightly, feeling the beginning of untold delight. "You know what people are going to say? That I schemed to get the same marquessate twice."

"Which we both know you didn't."

"No, I didn't." She looked at him, her eyes widening, a huge smile coming. "I want to marry you. But, oh, Graham, it gives me goose bumps just thinking I don't have to give up Motmarche." Her smile became vocal, a deep, true laugh from her belly through her chest. Then this became wickedly teasing. "The real question is, Can you stand that I will enjoy marrying you a little because you are the marquess of Motmarche?"

"Absolutely." He rolled himself on top of her, then the smart aleck grinned. "The real question is, Can you stand that I always wanted to do depraved things to the marquess of Motmarche's wife?" Which made the new marquess of Motmarche laugh out loud—till her mouth on his stopped him.

Graham thought he was joking when he said he loved making love to her partly because she was Henry's wife. Submit suspected he was joking less than he knew. To a degree, she would always be Henry's wife—his rib—in ways that had nothing to do with sex or loving. She was Henry's creature, his creation, the product of cohabitation with a forceful and appealing personality. She didn't mind if Graham liked her for that. It was part of her.

Here was Graham's happy ending, she mused, the one he'd wanted so many weeks ago. Two people in love. The only problem she saw was that these two people were so different they might well drive each other crazy, if they didn't kill each other first. The only saving grace of such a match was that they were both probably mean and contrary enough to survive whatever the other threw at them. She wasn't sure their future looked very rosy.

In the interests of peace and happiness, she made a few private vows. She would not buy Graham a proper suit of conservative clothes. She would not put pressure on him to do so. She would not praise him effusively for running his finances at a profit nor tell him how nice he looked reading a book. She would not make him stop drinking champagne nor stop rowing in rowboats. She would not point out that a man who plays with explosives might one day blow up. She would try to enjoy Graham for himself without attempting to "fix" him. Poor, silly Henry hadn't been able to do this. But she could. Then Submit laughed at herself. No, she couldn't. Not perfectly. She would always be a little snobbish, a little smug, a little instructive. She understood suddenly why she was marrying someone so different from herself.

Graham, with his strong ability to maintain and voice his differences, was the bravest bid she could make to stay tolerant, open to life's diversity, and honest with herself.

— Author's Note —

For those interested in historical accuracy, I must mention a few stretches of fact I felt at liberty to take in the course of creating this fiction. The largest liberty in which I knowingly indulged is the fact that the pillory was abolished as a form of punishment in England in 1837. Thus, two years must be ignored to allow that young Graham actually served a sentence in such a contraption. The whole notion of being pilloried, however, seemed so central to Graham's problems and resentments, I blithely locked him in, hand and foot.

The cure for this, of course, would have been to set the book earlier, but from the beginning the ideas of this book were already straining at the other end of the time line. Discovery-inventions, such as photography and aniline dyestuffs, pulled at Graham's "flashy" character in his early stages of creation. Ideas, such as those of Marx and Darwin and Freud, tugged on Submit, pulling her firmly into the second half of the century. Rosalyn and Gerald of course needed the liberalized divorce laws of 1857. (My apologies for using the color magenta a year ahead of when it would actually be called so, but magenta simply seemed better than any other color for introducing Rosalyn as she made her way through the crowds.) The year 1858 was a compromise, a year intended to represent a fictional time frame in which nascent twentieth-century sensibilities, the likes of Submit's and Graham's, might truly have existed.

Thus, errors a few years in one direction or the other are hereby acknowledged, though with very little remorse. It was pure fun making up this world from the facts, the above-mentioned having been bent a little to suit. It is my sincerest wish that it should be pure entertainment in reading the end result.

Judy Cuevas
February 1990